Her dream had been too vivid to be only a dream.

So much of it was hazy now, but she remembered one thing: She sat upon a black throne, atop a mountain of—of what? Stones? Bodies? She didn't know. But she knew she had earned her seat with blood, the blood of her own body and the blood of those who stood in her way. The Wolf had given her this gift, but she had felt a promise in it—

It is yours—if you can take it.

By Riot Games

AMBESSA
CHOSEN OF THE WOLF

ARCANE
A LEAGUE OF LEGENDS™ NOVEL

C. L. CLARK

orbit

orbitbooks.net

™ and © 2025 by Riot Games, Inc.

ARCANE LEAGUE OF LEGENDS and all associated logos, characters, names and distinctive likenesses thereof are exclusive property of Riot Games, Inc. Used Under License.

Cover design by Greg Ghielmetti and Lauren Panepinto
Outside cover illustration by Kudos Productions
Inside cover illustration by Minji Kim courtesy of Riot Games
Cover copyright © 2025 by Hachette Book Group, Inc.
Endpaper design by Lauren Panepinto
Endpaper artwork courtesy of Riot Games
Map by Tim Paul
Interior artwork courtesy of Riot Games
Author photograph by Meg White

Orbit
Hachette Book Group
1290 Avenue of the Americas
New York, NY 10104
orbitbooks.net

First Edition: February 2025
Simultaneously published in Great Britain by Orbit

Orbit is an imprint of Hachette Book Group.
The Orbit name and logo are registered trademarks of Little, Brown Book Group Limited.

The publisher is not responsible for websites (or their content) that are not owned by the publisher.

The Hachette Speakers Bureau provides a wide range of authors for speaking events. To find out more, go to hachettespeakersbureau.com or email HachetteSpeakers@hbgusa.com.

Orbit books may be purchased in bulk for business, educational, or promotional use. For information, please contact your local bookseller or the Hachette Book Group Special Markets Department at special.markets@hbgusa.com.

Library of Congress Control Number: 2024951265

ISBNs: 9780316470056 (trade paperback), 9780316469951 (hardcover), 9780316470155 (ebook)

Printed in the United States of America

LSC-C

Printing 1, 2024

*To my mother, Rachel, and my stepmother, Cindy,
and all the other women who found me, claimed me,
and kept me steady on the path*

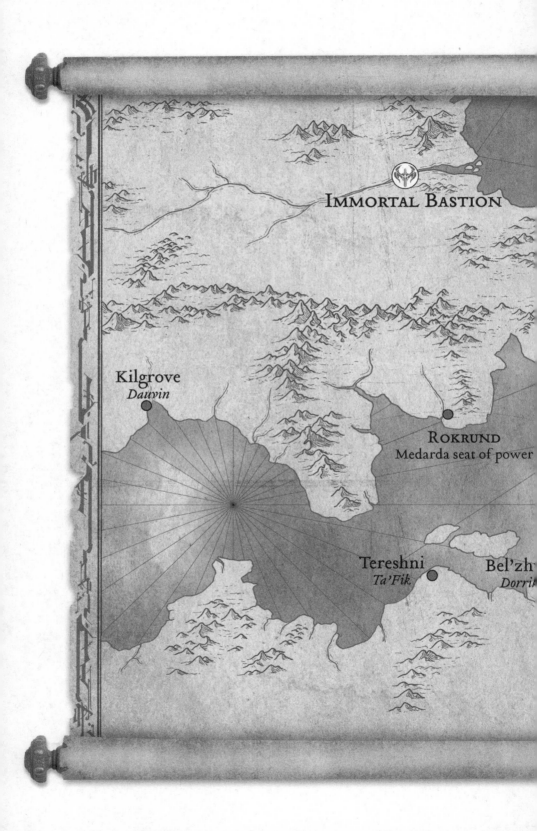

IMMORTAL BASTION

Kilgrove
Dauvin

ROKRUND
Medarda seat of power

Tereshni
Ta'Fik

Bel'zh
Dorri

Southeast Noxus

Basilich

Vindor
Amenesce

Fallgren
Jeon

Krexor
Lisabetya

Piltover

Kumangra

Trannit
Smik

Guardian's Sea

Map by Tim Paul

THE MEDARDA CODE

Medarda over all.

A clever tongue
is as valuable
as sharp steel.

A Medarda
strikes their
own path.

A Medarda
fights with
honor.

AMBESSA

Part I

Prologue

Ambessa Medarda flexed her fist around her katar. She sat heavily atop her mount as she watched the Raxii tribe's warriors clash against her grandfather Menelik's warbands on the rocky beach of the southern coast. The sound of weapons clashing and men and women dying was matched by the crash of the turbulent sea. She rested her hand upon the ungainly warmth that was her rounded belly. She had come home to Rokrund to fight a different kind of battle.

The Raxii were one of the old Noxii tribes who refused to join the Noxian empire at its founding. It was hard to say who had the strongest claim; Ambessa's family had ruled it for centuries. Though they dwelt in the mountains, the Raxii put their name to a claim as well, and clearly they had decided how to solve the dispute. So they would. As Noxians did. Rokrund was Ambessa's home. Her second child would not be born outside its walls, even if she had to fight through an entire army to make it so.

"Wolf's Reapers!" She raised her katar above her head, and the warband behind her roared their readiness. The Wolf's Reapers was her prized warband of the strongest warriors she'd seen fighting in arenas all across Noxus. The Raxii tribe would be too busy with Menelik's warbands in front of them to see the army that would ride down from the north and sweep them into the sea. "We have marched a long way, just to find our gates blocked. Come now, and open them!"

They rode down the rolling hills, the thunder of their mounts' hooves enough to drown out the ocean itself.

The first Raxii she met came at her with an axe in both hands, aiming high, to sweep her down from the saddle, but Ambessa's horse sidestepped the blow. Ambessa sliced through one of his arms, and he screamed, dropping the weapon. Blood sprayed, and he might have cried out again, but she was already gone.

Time slowed until Ambessa thought she had always been here, in this red mud, her breath heaving, her back aching. At some point, she was dragged from her horse, and she kicked herself free as the beast was killed. The weight of her belly was difficult to bear for long. Every step became a greater and greater struggle. Her right eye stung with blood from a cut on her face, but she couldn't reach it to wipe. She squeezed the eye tight and glanced around with her good eye.

As soon as she turned, she felt the rush of air behind her and ducked, falling to her knees to face her new opponent. A woman with a spear, muscled arms, teeth bared in fury. Ambessa had her own fury to contend with. She had not come all this way to watch her home fall into someone else's hands.

She pushed herself to her feet and leapt.

The woman was quicker than she looked and just as strong, parrying the thrust of Ambessa's katar and twisting away. She spun the haft of her spear, aiming for Ambessa's legs, but Ambessa had moved, arm cocked back ready to strike—

Pain pinned her arm down at her side. She looked around, but the blood in her eye still blinded her. If she were not a Medarda, Ambessa might have felt the first tickle of fear then.

Instead, she brought her katar up to deflect the spear woman's incoming blow, sidestepping until she could see her and the crossbowman whose bolt dug into her left shoulder. She couldn't raise that arm anymore. But he was reloading, and that meant she had time.

She ran to get inside the spear woman's guard, and this time, Ambessa broke through. The woman gasped as the katar pierced her. Her mouth opened, as if she would dispute the fact of what Ambessa had done to her. There was no disputing death. Ambessa pulled her blade free and pushed the dying woman to the ground.

She heard the whistle of wind before the second bolt hit her in the side.

My baby. Her first thought. Then came the pain. The pain in Ambessa's shoulder was nothing to the agony that tore through her side. It bit deep. Still, she raised her katar again. Her next step faltered, though. Her knee went weak and she fell to the ground. She tried to catch herself on her hands, but her wounded shoulder gave out, too. She cried out as she fell onto her belly and rolled onto her back.

Every breath was agony. There was not enough air in the whole world.

Ambessa fought to stay awake as her vision narrowed, but the world around her was closing off, fading to blackness. Beside her, the woman she had killed stared up at the gray sky. Like Ambessa would, soon.

Then, instead of the woman, she saw a wolf, its muzzle low to the ground as it studied her. A harbinger of Kindred.

It came for her.

Ambessa steps through the darkness—and she is no longer on the bat-tlefield she left. She wipes away the muck that covers her—afterbirth

is the only way she can describe it, though she knows this is the oppo-site of birth. She walks upon a path of thick stone blocks. All around her rise broad pillars of the same black stone, and the room is satu-rated with a red glow. Figures are etched upon the walls, but they aren't clear. She knows not where she is, but she knows what she is doing: She is waiting. For what? No, *she thinks, for* whom.

"Hello?" she calls. No one responds. Her voice does not echo.

Ahead, the gloom lightens slightly. She glimpses a throne in the dis-tance, and someone is sitting on it.

"Hello!" she calls again. But the person on the throne doesn't respond. No one stops her as she approaches the throne and its occupant.

A sudden eruption of stone to her left makes Ambessa crouch defen-sively. There's no enemy to fight, though. There's a figure amidst the rubble, which floats around her, around the—figures. Ambessa sees herself among them, in the center of them.

She watches herself, apart from herself, watches this other Ambessa dancing in a room full of others, lost in the feel of her body, of its strength, its beauty, its hungers and the beautiful hunger of those around her. This is what the body is for, this is what she is. *Her feet carry her closer. She wants to join them. She reaches her hand out—*

No.

That is not why she is here. Some part of her knows this. She feels a pang of loss. That life is gone now. That body. She knows where she is now. Volrachnun. Where the Wolf takes great warriors after death.

She holds her hands out in front of her face. She can feel them more easily than she can see them in this penumbra, their certainty. Their strength. They are still hers.

"Who are you?" Ambessa calls to the throne, turning away from that vision of her own ecstasy. "What do you want with me?"

She quickens her pace, half jogging to get closer. All the while, she wishes for a weapon. Her hands are still hers, but she feels naked, unarmed and unarmored. She is *naked.*

And then, as if obedient to the logic of this dreamlike death-world, Ambessa is suddenly clothed: a sash that drapes across one shoulder, a breastplate that leaves her midriff bare, and a battle skirt with golden hip guards.

At the throne, she knows she will find her purpose. She continues . . .

. . . and is interrupted again by another scene, this one—a young Ambessa, a child, holding a lamb in her arms. She can't remember ever having carried a lamb like this, and yet—there is something familiar. She is so young, so innocent— When was she last so innocent? She doesn't know and she weeps for it, this gap within her like the socket of a tooth.

She steps toward this smaller self and sees, too, her faithful drakehounds, Quench and Temper. No matter where she went, they followed her until they died. That loss is more tangible—she can place that pain directly, and the adjacent pain: the loss of another friend, a friend who could be here now.

Ambessa turns to look for her, but instead, she sees the throne again. It is closer, but she still cannot see the figure who sits upon it. And her hands are no longer empty. Two half-moon blades, the same gold as her armor, gleam in the dim room.

She frowns. Armor. Weapons. What good are these things with nothing to fight? She is on her guard now, and approaches the throne more carefully.

Though the journey should be short, it is interrupted over and over again by these visions of herself, moments she recognizes and moments she does not.

A young Ambessa on the battlefield, holding a dead woman's sword.

Ambessa and Azizi with their first child on her lap, holding Kino against her breast.

Ta'Fik and Zoya, surrounded by drakehounds.

Ta'Fik and Ambessa, surrounded by drakehounds.

An older Ambessa in a great chair, with a young woman and young man at either side.

Ambessa and that same young woman standing opposed, each ready to attack the other.

An entire life, lived and unlived, that she must pass by. Ambessa pulls herself away from the images of her past and of futures not to come. They will not come, they cannot come, because she is dead.

She stands at the foot of the stairs to the throne.

She cranes her neck up. She should not be surprised, and yet, she is.

High above her, the figure on the throne is her.

Ambessa swells with pride. This is what her valor has earned her. She takes the first step toward the dais, and her bare foot sticks.

"You must earn the right."

The voice comes from everywhere and nowhere, pressing in on her ears and echoing in her mind. Two voices speaking at once, deep and high, gentle and forceful.

"How?" she asks.

"How do you think?"

From the shadows, a creature emerges, walking on two hooves. Their maned head dips and searches, as if sniffing her. They have four ears, two erect like a wolf's, and two that hang to their jaw.

Kindred.

"I have earned my place in battle, have I not?"

It is, perhaps, impertinent, but the throne is right there. She is in Volrachnun. What more must she do to prove herself?

"You have earned your place in Volrachnun," *the twin voices say.* "But have you earned your place in legend?"

They hold out a trinket, a three-headed wolf that floats, spinning, between them.

Ambessa reaches for it, but with a gesture, Kindred pulls it out of reach.

"You must face your trials."

Ambessa grows impatient. "I will face any trial you set for me."

And though Kindred does not have a face for smiling, Ambessa senses their amusement.

Suddenly, Ambessa is in a great arena surrounded on all sides by ledges and daises, and on those ledges are her audience. She sees their weapons, their armor. They are her audience and also—her competitors. Though none of them move toward her, she knows this is true.

She hears the shift of metal behind her.

A great warrior with a golden shield stands before her. His chest is bare save for the golden armor that wraps around his shoulders and upper chest. Gauntlets, greaves, boots, helm, all gold. A cloak the color of fresh blood. This is a land of heroes. Ambessa feels drab in comparison.

There is no sign of the throne, but Ambessa understands.

You must earn the right, *says the voice. Voices.*

She runs toward the shielded warrior, striking with the half-moon blades, but suddenly the Shield is behind her. He shoves her skidding across the ground.

The crowd bays for her blood, for the Shield's blood, the blood of all and any, and she will give it to them because this is what the body is for, this is what she is!

Ambessa dodges his spear and strikes again and again, each blow met by a parry, each parry, a counterstrike. For a moment, she thinks they are evenly matched, she and this legendary warrior.

There is not enough time to congratulate herself, though. The Shield cracks his helm against her face, and she staggers back. Another blow from the Shield's spear and she rolls beneath it—belatedly, she realizes that her stomach is small enough to roll; where is her child? There is no time to ponder that, either. She leaps into the air to strike him from above, like lightning from the sky.

He catches her and throws her down like thunder. Her blade skitters out of her hand.

She thinks, This is death? *Because there is cheering. The cheering sounds like mourning, sounds like weeping. It sounds like her grandfather Menelik in the training yard, telling her to* get up!

Someone is watching her. Their voices echo her grandfather.

Get up.

From her back, Ambessa stares up at the Shield. She cannot see his face, and yet, she feels the dispassionate stare. Though she is wounded, Ambessa rolls onto her stomach.

She is not done.

She pushes herself up again. She picks up the half-moon blade. She rises to her knee. Every wound she has ever had is open now, bleeding afresh as the Shield approaches, flanked by more warriors: an assassin with her twin red daggers and her golden breastplate; a rigid man with a whispering arm and a cloak of black raven feathers, his gold pauldrons gleaming; and more, and more, and more. They come for her.

She is not done. She stands. She faces them.

With a nod that Ambessa can only interpret as respect, the Shield lowers his weapon. His golden shield retracts.

"What is this?" she asks.

He does not answer. None of these heroes do. So Ambessa steps toward them—

—and takes another step toward the throne. She is suddenly back in the dark room of stone and memories.

The throne is empty again, and Ambessa climbs toward it, only to find Kindred there, between her and the throne, again.

"I passed your trial. Your heroes have let me pass."

"One trial," *Kindred says.* "We have long known you are willing to kill, Ambessa, war leader of the Medarda clan. Your trials are not over!" *The voices twine together in a great screech, echoing each other, harmonizing and discordant by turns.*

Ambessa shudders and presses her hands against her ears.

"I will face your trials!" she shouts back into the darkness.

And suddenly, she is no longer in darkness at all. The only hint that she was ever in that dark hall is an echo:

"You will shed the blood of others, but what of yours—your own—your heart—will you sacrifice?"

She turns to find Kindred, but they are not there.

The path before her is bright and burning beneath a desert sun, and people, people, so many people—they weep for her in their masks. They sing and weep and scream, and she can feel their grief, and still others do not grieve at all but surround her, all wild legs and wild arms in tattered wanderers' cloaks. There is no space for her except for the space they make, so she steps into it, going where they lead. Above her, drummers in the sky beat the rhythm of her steps.

In her arms, she cradles a golden lamb. It is hard and cold and made of many pieces. There is something familiar about it.

"What is this?" she asks. Where did it come from?

There is no answer but the sense that it is precious, and it is hers and she must protect it, no matter what.

Ambessa struggles forward without knowing what she is looking for, shoving away the creatures wailing at her, with their eyeless faces, their blue skin, their mouths wide enough to devour the lamb she clutches to her chest. She ducks her head down to protect it, to protect herself from the cacophony around them, in this bright, blinding desert.

She is afraid. Ambessa has not felt fear like this in a long time.

Give it to me.

The words come to her, and she clutches the lamb even tighter.

Let it go.

"No," she whispers, shaking her head.

The shrieking mourners in their robes press closer and closer until Ambessa falls to her knees. The lamb in her arms seems to shiver. How is she supposed to let it go? It is a part of her. It is hers. Though it is a *thing of metal, its wide dark eyes are warm and welcoming. It needs to be protected.*

But the echo of Kindred's last question comes back to her.

Sacrifice.

Ambessa holds the lamb up and releases it.

It floats upward, and immediately, she wishes she had not. The lamb rises above her, above them all. It is out of reach now. She will never get it back. The sun burns hotter against Ambessa's skin. The white wraps she wears do not protect her. The dancing guides grow more frantic, encircling her. The drumming drowns out her heartbeat. The wailing, open mouths smother her own cries.

The lamb rises to the mouth of the many-headed wolf. She remembers this wolf. The token, spinning before Kindred, offered to her. The lamb will be devoured if she does not save it.

Let it go.

But I can't, *she thinks.*

You must.

Then the lamb is no more, and the many heads of the wolf bare their teeth, and she screams for the lamb as it is devoured, screams like those who mourn her, raking her nails across her own face, drawing blood, but she does not care. Something is gone, someone is gone, all she has known—

"A sacrifice," *say the twinned voices of Kindred.*

Ambessa is back in the dark hall of Volrachnun before Kindred, and they offer all that she wants most. She reaches for it, it, shapeless, it, untouchable, it— What will it cost?

"I will pay it," *she says.* Whatever the cost, she will pay it.

She closes her hand around the many-headed wolf, and blood-red light sears along her veins like seams in a volcano venting fire. It burns. It is agony.

Ambessa screams as Kindred's light passes through her, and she understands what they are truly offering her for the first time. A possibility. A future: She sits upon the stone throne with a sword at her side. This is her destiny; if she goes back, she can take it.

Or she can die. She can take her place here, in the realm of heroes. She can stand in the arena beside the Shield, dressed in the armor of a legend, her leonine mask in gold, her hair flowing white, a billowing mane, a golden torc at her neck. These warriors would follow her, and she would lead them on the hunt of champions. The hunt of the chosen.

It is what she has always wanted—to die a wolf's death. To be worthy of Volrachnun, and here it is, offered.

Earned.

She will ride with them—a throb pulses in her stomach, heat—*in this land of heroes*—her stomach is flat, but that is not right—*forever with those who have passed the Wolf's tests*—light, white light, and with the pulse comes a cramping spasm—*her victory is already certain, here in Volrachnun*—

Ambessa woke with a gasp from a beautiful, terrible dream. In the distance, she thought she saw a wolf's tail vanish into the fog creeping up the beach. At another agonizing spasm, she reached for her belly. A contraction. She found the crossbow bolt that had taken her—*killed me?* She felt for the edges of the arrowhead. It was deep, but she did not think it was barbed. The echo of the dream gave her strength to grit her teeth against the pain, and she pulled it out with a growling groan.

She needed to get back to Rokrund Citadel. The baby was coming.

With an effort, Ambessa pushed herself to her feet. She supported her belly with one hand, pressed down on her wound with the other, and picked her away across the bodies littered on the rocky beach. The sea's roar had died with the end of the battle. She could barely tell who won; the fallen on both sides were mixed together, but the Citadel's walls still stood.

She looked back over her shoulder for any sign of the wolf she was sure had been there. Her dream had been too vivid to be only a dream. So much of it was hazy now, but she remembered one thing: She sat upon a black throne, atop a mountain of—of what? Stones? Bodies? She didn't know. But she knew she had earned her seat with blood, the blood of her own body and the blood of those who stood in her way. The Wolf had given her this gift, but she had felt a promise in it—

It is yours—if you can take it.

Chapter One

Fifteen Years Later

Ambessa rose to her feet, her katar leaving the body of the Binan captain. The dead man's blood dripped down her weapon and onto his leather armor. He was the soldier who had come to challenge her on her arrival. The feather in his helm had briefly been a beautiful gradient, lively in the wind as he barked orders to his soldiers, other loyal soldiers of the Binan family, here at their fortress-palace near Kumangra. Now that feather lay limp and all one color: the red-brown of a boot-churned battlefield.

He should have surrendered.

Instead, he had wasted his life and the lives of his command against the inevitability of her conquest. Now Ambessa had territory in the east and possibly, just possibly—a connection to Ionia via the Binan family. When Ambessa took her place as the matriarch of the Medarda clan one day, she wanted Darkwill to owe her. She would show him what she had to offer early, so he would understand how indispensable she was. And after that, perhaps…Ambessa pushed aside thoughts of the distant future. There was still the present to contend with.

All around her, her warband rounded up the survivors who were smarter than their captain. They gathered and bound the soldiers in the lush grass outside the palace proper. The yellow-brown stone leading into the palace was littered with bodies that many of them watched fearfully. Most of them followed her with their eyes, though.

The palace itself was more jungle than building, surrounded by trees—not the pines Ambessa knew from the mountains near her home in Rokrund, nor the palms in Bel'zhun, where she and her armies had marched from, but great drooping things that devoured, dripping with vines.

"Ambessa." Rictus, her second-in-command, was dragging a young woman to her by the arm. Flat discs and black cords hung from piercings in her face. The woman was frightened, but he was being gentle.

Ambessa looked the girl in her wide eyes. "You're one of the Binan family?"

"Yes," she said. "Lady Mion of Binan."

Ambessa's sources had described the Binan land as lush and verdant. The exotic fruit would sell well throughout the rest of Noxus, and the positioning was perfect to get ahead of Piltover's canal tariffs. The Binan family itself was an old one, wealthy, though they had left Ionia some time ago for reasons Ambessa did not yet know. There would be time to learn that.

"General Medarda!" A shrill voice broke the moment between them. The messenger skidded to a stop before Ambessa, one hand on her knee and one hand holding out a sealed letter. "Urgent from Bel'zhun."

Ambessa was ready to dismiss the girl from her warband entirely for this interruption, but the last part stayed her. *Bel'zhun.* Her daughter was here, safe with her, but her son, Kino, was there with their father, Azizi, seeing to certain trade agreements. The letter was stamped with the Medarda star, four sharp points of guidance. She flicked a glance to Rictus and Lady Mion. The girl trembled where she stood. Ambessa turned her back on them and flicked the letter open.

She skimmed it and gasped, barely able to hide it. She read it again more slowly and felt a strange twisting in her stomach. She refolded the letter and handed it back to the messenger.

"Put it with my things." Ambessa's voice did not betray her.

She turned back to Lady Mion.

"Where is the rest of your family?"

"My father is dead and my mother is elderly. My sister cares for her," she said. Though her voice was soft, her mouth was set firmly. "I manage the estates alone."

"There were also . . . prisoners." Rictus's pause was weighty.

Ambessa let her glance linger a moment longer on the girl before saying, "Take me to them."

Rictus handed the noblewoman to a pair of soldiers, then led Ambessa into the palace. This was no new construct; the Binan family had been here for generations. Some of the trees the Binans had cultivated within the stone building had to be older even than Ambessa herself. The rooms they passed were, on the whole, uninteresting—no great treasures, though there was a room full of books and scrolls that might have been a library or one person's study, and she made a mental note to have them transported to Bel'zhun. Rictus stopped her at the end of a hall, unlit by the curling sconces that illuminated the rest of the palace. The door was already broken at the handle. Someone—one of hers—had kicked it in.

Slouching against their binds sat a handful of vastaya, some of them with grubby fur, others with limp feathers or dull scales. Ambessa's nose twitched at the stench. They'd been kept here a long time. They watched Ambessa warily as she entered. One in particular stared more sharply than the others, with unnerving square pupils.

She nodded to him. "You. What are you doing here?"

"The Binans are keeping us prisoner," he growled, lowering his horned head as if he would ram a Binan if given the chance.

Ambessa shared a glance with Rictus, who shrugged one massive shoulder. "Why?"

"Because we're tired of the Ionians taking over our homes."

Ah. Ambessa began to understand, and with understanding came a thrill of possibility. Especially now that her accession was painfully closer than she had ever expected.

"If we free you, you will swear to Noxus."

The vastaya swallowed and sat up straighter, his short tail steady though it was still fluffed with tension. "We will make a deal with Noxus."

Ambessa narrowed her eyes. "Yes?"

"The Ionians are destroying the vastaya's magical forests. As our lands weaken, so do we. We're left with nothing. Some Binan men in Ionia caught me as I was trying to—" He shook his furry head, his muzzle wrinkled in disgust. "Our tribes tried fighting back, but something is—happening to us. We're not as—as strong as we used to be. There are fewer of us. But if Noxus came, they could help us overthrow them. Take back what is ours to shepherd."

"You would get Noxus into Ionia?" Ambessa knew how impenetrable the islands were—rumors said the land itself was alive, fighting against any and all invaders. It was unheard-of, enough raw magic to put the bravest, most experienced soldiers on edge.

"If it would get us our homes."

Ambessa nodded slowly. Ionia. The untouched islands beyond the sea, a tantalizing fruit just out of Darkwill's reach.

His greatest ambition. When her scouting bands had told her of the once-Ionian family here, she had come. The vision she'd had that day she had died—almost died—in Rokrund loomed great in her mind. The letter from home made that vision even more urgent. Darkwill would be more than pleased to learn this, and once she took her place at the head of the Medarda family, she would be that much closer to it.

"Good. I will take you to Grand General Darkwill, and you will swear to Noxus. We will see you home."

Before she could do any of that, though, she needed to get back to Bel'zhun.

Menelik was wounded, Ambessa.

He is unlikely to recover.

Return swiftly.

Return to Bel'zhun, where her grandfather would have no choice but to name his heir. And that meant Ambessa needed to prepare her own.

Ambessa stopped in the main hall of the palace and considered the large chair waiting in the middle, raised upon a dais. It was dim and dark, the windows curtained off to block the bright sun as it rose, and more trees stretched from floor to ceiling alongside stone pillars. The throne itself was broken, a streak of blood marring its pale, striated stone surface.

"Rictus. Where is Mel?"

"She has... taken to speaking with some of the Binans, General." He raised an eyebrow, as if to ask if he should stop it.

Ambessa sighed. "Send for her. And ready Lady Mion."

It was time for Mel to know death.

From outside the palace, unseen, Ambessa watched Mel enter the throne room and take in the destruction. Chunks blown out of the stone by black powder, a Rokrund specialty. Blood streaking the walls, the pillars, the floor. The trees, however, seemed untouched. The girl studied it all carefully. At fifteen years, it was past time for her to learn this lesson. After giving her a moment alone, Ambessa followed her in.

Mel turned at the sound of her approach.

"When I was ten," Ambessa said, "your grandfather brought me to the aftermath of the Battle of Hildenard. He offered me a gold coin for every blade I retrieved from the fallen. Said we needed the steel." Loose stone skittered down a pillar. "But I knew it was a lie. He wanted me to know death."

Mel furrowed her brow. "Kino says war is a failure of statecraft."

Ambessa bit back her snort of irritation. "Your brother thinks he can talk his way out of anything. He fancies himself a fox among the wolves. But mark me, child, if you want to last in this world, you must learn to be both the fox *and* the wolf."

Mel considered this, taking in the throne. The wall behind it was shattered in a radial, as if by a heavy blow.

"We'll paint the walls in gold. Import crystal chandeliers. Advisors will enter here." Mel gestured toward a side corridor off the main room as she approached the throne. "But the regent will have her own secret entrance."

Hope rose in Ambessa's chest.

"She should have a kind, fat face," Mel continued, skimming her palm along the seat back of the broken throne. She seemed unbothered by the blood painting its surface. "Clever, to charm her subjects, but pliable so we can mold her."

Ambessa let herself imagine the picture her daughter painted. Already, Mel was poised, and she knew the power of appearance. Her high-collared dress with its pointed sunburst across the chest suited her—elegant, but sharp. The gold holding back her hair, already like a crown. She had mastered one of the most difficult parts of the Medarda Code: *A clever tongue is as valuable as sharp steel.*

"Perhaps she could be my daughter."

Mel's hazel eyes widened in surprise, the first shock she'd shown since she arrived at the killing field that was once a palace.

"You'd give me a throne?"

"I will give you the world, child. If you prove you can take it."

At a signal, Ambessa's soldiers brought in Lady Mion. The young woman was a silhouette highlighted by the bright sunlight of the morning. She seemed to have an inkling of her fate to come; her earlier defiance was gone. She was unwilling to even hold her head up in defeat. The stones of her headdress swayed across her face, and a thick necklace hung at her throat with a pendant made of some sort of bone, perhaps, and beaded with turquoise and coral. That craftsmanship would not do well in all of Noxus, but someone somewhere might buy it. The green of her robes matched the trees in the throne room.

"What should we do with her?" Ambessa asked.

Mel's eyes were wet with the sheen of the Binan noblewoman's pain. Lady Mion raised her pitiful gaze to Mel's, and still Ambessa waited.

"She won't make trouble for us," Mel pronounced. "Strip her of her possessions and send her to the far colonies."

"She's a symbol of the old regime." Ambessa grabbed Lady Mion by the chin. The girl's hair was lank with sweat, and she stank with her fear. Though Lady Mion's holdings were not quite so extensive, Ambessa leaned into the lesson for her daughter's sake. "Kill her now, and only one must die." She released the woman roughly. "Let her live, and you may need to kill thousands."

"We can show the people we are merciful!" Mel's voice rose almost desperately. She looked again to the noblewoman. Mion of Binan pleaded with her eyes. Almost the same green-brown shade as Mel's own.

Ambessa turned to Mel and realized her mistake too late. Lady Mion was too close in age; Mel felt too strong a kinship with her.

She should still be able to do what must be done.

But it was clear she could not.

Ambessa spun and struck the girl across the neck with her katar.

"A wolf has no mercy."

The young woman fell.

Chapter Two

Ambessa was welcomed back into Noxian territory by Bel'zhun's eastern Noxtoraa. The great stone arch not only marked the road for travelers, but served to remind them whose land they trod upon. And, if the arch were not enough, red banners hung with the Noxian crest and thin red streamers waved from poles at intervals on either side of the road, all the way into the city proper.

Bel'zhun itself seemed lively and bustling, but Ambessa led her army around the edge of the city center, the better to avoid the crowded, narrow streets full of hawkers and shoppers, beasts of burden and beasts of labor. Urgency had pushed her to ride hard from the Binan palace, to sail swiftly across the narrow channel.

The somber compound Ambessa returned to contrasted greatly with her internal sense of victory. It butted up against it uncomfortably, much like her grief did. A hush muffled the corridors and the grounds despite the bright warmth of the sun that should have invited garden strolls and games. She left her horse for one of the younger soldiers to take to the stables, and the rest of her warbands dispersed to their barracks, some thousand split across the Wolf's Reapers and the Fists. Only Mel and Rictus accompanied Ambessa farther.

She sighed as she stepped into the main house of the Medardas' Bel'zhun compound. The compound itself was different from their home seat in Rokrund; here, it was a cluster of buildings enclosed by a gateless wall, the top of which curved in a cutout semicircle that ended in sharp points, mimicking the palaces of the Shuriman warlords who once ruled here. The corners of the walls were capped with shaped stone that reminded Ambessa of the hooked beak of a desert eagle. The central building was flanked by blunt Noxian-style pillars cut from pale sandstone, and was capped with a dome the color of the sea. The house itself was large enough to hold any number of visiting Medardas—and with the news, Ambessa was probably not the only one here.

Mel walked stiffly beside her. The girl had been closed off since she'd failed the test Ambessa had given her. The journey back had been uncomfortable, to say the least, but nothing Ambessa said as they traveled had made Mel understand just how uncomfortable *power* was.

Walking into the main receiving room was like walking face-first into a bombardment. The wide and airy space was crammed to the corners with notable Noxians, Medarda and not, come to pay their respects to the great leader. Ambessa made sure none of her worries showed on her face, and despite everything, she was proud to see Mel do the same. The sullen set of her mouth vanished, and she gave Ambessa one last look before going to greet the dignitaries as they cooed over how much she had grown since they'd last seen her.

Ambessa spotted her brother Katye immediately; he was coming toward her, draped in a light silk scarf. Her son, Kino, stood beside a rare black marble vase, tall and handsome and appropriately somber as he charmed Lisabetya, the steward of Krexor. Lisabetya had been adopted into the Medarda family when she was young. She was pale-skinned, with graying black hair and one blind eye, and she was thick about the arms and chest, with heavy hips. Krexor was known for its bladesmithing, and Lisabetya had spent her fair share of time in the smithy. Something Kino said made Lisabetya laugh, head thrown back and mouth wide open.

Steward Ta'Fik was in attendance as well. Ambessa wasn't surprised; he was her cousin, raised beneath Menelik's guiding hand just as she was. Once, they had been close.

As full as the room was, there were many people Ambessa didn't recognize, and some whom she expected to see but did not. Stewards Smik, Dauvin, and Amenesce weren't there at all. She would need to find out why.

Before she could consider her maneuvers further, Katye Medarda took Ambessa's hand and clasped her tightly about the shoulder. "Sister, it's been too long."

"Katye. What is *he* doing here?"

Katye followed her quick glance to Ta'Fik. Ta'Fik was speaking to someone Ambessa didn't recognize, a woman in a loose belted tunic that left her well-muscled arms and legs bare, well suited to Bel'zhun's warmth. Her eyes were narrow, her brows low, as if she squinted into a gale.

"Apparently, he's speaking to Stefana of Kilgrove, Dauvin's niece." Katye sniffed. "No 'How are you?' No 'How is Rokrund?' You wound me." The mirth in Katye's eyes was not unlike his nephew's.

Ambessa gave him a level stare. "Must I ask? With the city in your hands, I always expect to find everything well when I return."

Katye chuckled at the flattery. "We're not doing so bad across the sea. The servants do miss Mel, though." His graying mustache was all the hair he had, and he stroked it almost humbly, which was at odds with his rich flowing robes and soft slippers. His scarf was the color of sand under the noon sun, dyed with a single stripe each of emerald green, blackberry purple, and dusty rose. The craftsmanship of Shurima on full display. Despite his fine dress, he still stood rigid as a spear, and he moved like a man still capable in the fight. He sobered, though, and leaned close. "I suspect it will be some time before you are back, though?"

"That depends. Ta'Fik. My spies have told me that he's been renegotiating some of Darkwill's debts with Piltover." Ambessa squeezed her brother's shoulder, as if they were only exchanging more pleasantries, and forced herself not to glance over again at her cousin, even though her neck prickled with the feeling of being watched. "What do you think?"

Ta'Fik's talks with Piltover were part of why Ambessa had set her sights on the Binan land. Binan land would offer Darkwill a way to bypass Piltover entirely.

Katye took a glass of sunwine from a passing servant and sipped it. "I think he is very charismatic."

"He's no commander." Ambessa kept her voice low as she, too, took a cup. "He hasn't led a warband in decades. Menelik would never choose him."

"You would be surprised, my dear." Katye raised a finely arched eyebrow. The dark kohl lining his eyes and dusted with gold made them seem even sharper. "That is less of a priority to some."

"I see." Ambessa grunted in distaste. "Has everyone grown soft, then?"

Katye smiled, showing his teeth. "Not me."

"Is Menelik—is he well?"

"He's been accepting visitors. Someone's probably already told him you're here, but I can make sure."

"Please."

Katye patted her arm, then floated off to stir up more trouble, leaving Ambessa to subtly scan the room again for Ta'Fik.

Now Ta'Fik was speaking to Azizi, a snake slithering up to the breast, guaranteeing she had no choice but to approach him. A stranger stood beside him, shorter than him with dark skin and close-shaved hair. The short stubble was white. Ambessa made her way over.

"Azizi," she said, taking him by the arm and pressing a kiss to his cheek. From the periphery of her half-closed eyes, she watched Ta'Fik. Saw the flicker of annoyance cross his features.

"Ambessa, my dear. You're back." Azizi took her by both arms and kissed her on both cheeks before kissing her on the mouth. "I've missed you. How was your trip?" He was intelligent enough not to give away more than that.

Ambessa smiled. "We found more than we could have hoped, but not everything could be trusted to a letter."

Ta'Fik's smile tightened at the corners, but his voice was smooth. "Congratulations. I wish we could all be so adventurous. Unfortunately, my responsibilities keep me close to home, but it did mean I could come quickly as soon as I heard. You're the last to arrive."

"I'm sure you've been a great help." Ambessa met his false tenderness with her own. "Introduce me to your friend."

"Inyene has been my advisor for some time; they've proven invaluable in renegotiating azirite deals with some of the more...difficult Shuriman warlords."

"Kind of you to join my cousin on his bereavement, Inyene. Be welcome."

Inyene was beautiful, but slight; they barely looked like they could stand up against a strong wind. Their billowing white trousers only made them look smaller. When Ambessa took their hand, it was uncalloused. And yet, their response was warm and almost—sincere.

"I understand his grief only too well. And yours, perhaps? Though I would not presume." They bowed their head graciously. The gold hanging from their nose gleamed in the candlelight.

Ambessa watched them for a hint of something deeper between them, but they gave nothing away.

"And the children?" Ta'Fik asked. "How are they?"

Ambessa stiffened. Luckily, Ta'Fik didn't give her or Azizi a chance to respond.

"Mine are around here somewhere. Gintara, my eldest, led a band against some Shuriman rebels who took some of our foundry mages hostage. She rescued them and crushed the rebellion. Production has never been so high." Ta'Fik grinned. "Menelik was very pleased to see them."

"That's wonderful," Ambessa said, remembering the shocked horror in Mel's face as the Binan girl fell, dead at her feet, blood pooling around the coral beads. Azizi caught her eye, one of his thick, dark eyebrows raising minutely. Ambessa relaxed her grip on her wineglass. "I'm sure they've done the Medarda name proud."

"General Medarda?" A servant waited politely for Ambessa to turn. "Hostlord Menelik has asked for you."

An opening for a tactical retreat. Ambessa left Azizi with a squeeze of the hand and Ta'Fik with a calculating look that he returned. In truth, though, she wasn't sure if she preferred to stay. Surely fencing back and forth with Ta'Fik as they always had was easier than facing the twisting grief in her gut that had dogged her since first reading that letter.

Menelik's rooms were dark. The servant carried a taper through the anteroom and into the bedroom, where they lit others. Then the servant left, and Ambessa was alone with the man who had raised her more than her parents ever had.

She knelt beside his bed out of respect and took his hand.

"Grandfather." She pressed the hand against her forehead. It was cool, not feverish or clammy. He squeezed in response, and his grip was stronger than she had expected.

"Stand, girl."

More than forty summers and still she was "girl." She smiled at him as she obeyed. She pulled a chair over and sat.

"You've gotten slow, Grandfather."

He chuckled the same gravelly laugh she had always thought only she could pull from him. "I haven't. Everyone else has just gotten faster. And they're cheating. It's not enough to win—"

"*It's how you win.* I know."

Oh, how she knew. Every tenet of the Medarda Code, every quip of wisdom he'd gathered in his lifetime, drilled into her, day after day after backbreaking day of training and studying and scheming. All under his tutelage. He had chosen her, back then, one of the few Medarda scions he'd deemed worthy of his personal attention.

"How are the healers treating you?"

"I taught you better than small talk, Ambessa. Be direct."

"It's not small talk to ask after your health when you've been wounded."

"It is when we both know why you care for my health."

"I care for your health because you are my grandfather." She cared for his health because she hadn't been aware of how drastically it could change—and in mere moments. The closer she looked at him in the dim candlelight, though, the more she wondered how much was recent. He had always loomed so large in her mind that the man in the bed before her was startling. He still had much of his size, but he seemed smaller out of his armor than she remembered. His chest was bare, and bandages peeked up from beneath the blankets.

He pursed his lips and narrowed his eyes, waiting.

Ambessa shook her head, sighing. "Have you decided who you will name heir?"

Menelik nodded once, sharply, the way he had whenever she had offered an acceptable answer to his questions so many years ago. "I have had a vision."

Ambessa looked at him sharply. "Of? Was it about the Immortal Bastion?"

He frowned. "No, why?"

She shook her head again. "Apologies, Grandfather. What was your vision?"

"It wasn't a grand one." His face grew troubled. He scratched at the gray stubble that coated his chin and neck. He had never worn a beard as long as she'd known him. He caught her staring. "They don't shave it often enough for me. I'm half-tempted to get up and do it myself, but they keep the razors tucked away. As if they're afraid I'll kill myself. Me!" He scoffed.

"Let me."

Ambessa found Menelik's shaving equipment in the ornate dresser to one side of the room, and she lit more candles. Azizi liked her to shave him, and Ambessa had never once said no to a sharp blade. She made the lather on his chin and set to work.

"Tell me about this vision."

Something passed over his face as he held her eyes. A glistening in his eyes that made her throat thick before he closed them and let his head tilt back against the pillows.

"I dreamed of a wolf. A wolf with a human body."

Ambessa flinched, and Menelik hissed. "Wolf? *The* Wolf?"

He grunted, neither yes nor no. "A bloody battle is coming, and the Medardas are in danger."

"All of us?" Another swipe of the razor on the towel, another against his chin.

"The clan itself. It begins with the fall of…It begins with a fall."

Ambessa paused mid-stroke, the razor against the apple of her grandfather's throat.

"And then?"

"And then if there's not a strong Medarda at the head of the clan? Ruin."

"There are plenty of strong Medardas, Grandfather. You don't have to worry about that."

"You forgot the battle. Plenty of the strong fall in battle. We need strong lines."

"Where was this battle? In Volrachnun?"

Menelik hesitated. Considered. "No. It was here, on this plane, among the living, but I cannot…" He shut his eyes, concentrating. After a moment, he shook his head, looking even more strained than before. "I don't know. I don't know where."

Ambessa held him still to finish. "I was in the east, south of Piltover. I found a stronghold with old ties to Ionia. What I found there will secure Darkwill's friendship for a long time to come."

She didn't tell him about Mel's failure to kill the princess.

"Good. We'll need all the favor we can get."

Ambessa scraped the razor on the far cheek. "We could avoid this all if you named an heir now. If you die first, then there will be blood." It was as close as she would come to saying she expected to be named heir and she would fight for it if he named another.

"I know. But the doctors say I have time." He smiled slyly. "Perhaps I exaggerated a little in my notes to make sure you all came quickly. First, we must speak, all of us, about the direction of the family. Besides, I might even make a full recovery."

Ambessa eyed him warily. What was there to say that needed to be discussed before she was named heir?

"Truly? That's good news."

Menelik sighed. "I've shrugged off worse before. Time. Time is what I need."

"And rest." Ambessa cleaned the shaving tools and tucked them away. "You're all finished. Sleep."

"I never planned on dying in a bed," he growled. But he didn't argue with her, and that, more than anything, convinced Ambessa that he was closer to Kindred's threshold than he wanted to admit.

"You've dreamed of the Wolf, Grandfather. He will take you when the time is right."

The reassurance was perhaps less than truthful. The Wolf came to those who died in battle. The wound that had taken Menelik had been delivered by a blade—would that be enough to grant him entry into Volrachnun?

Ambessa thought again of the vision she'd had. Over fifteen years ago. The sword and a dark throne. She still remembered the pulsing golden light that had engulfed her, the golden armor of the Wolf's chosen. Her vision answered Menelik's—she was the solution to the downfall he feared.

Chapter Three

After her visit with Menelik, Ambessa sought refuge where she often did—in the Reckoner Arena she had funded from her own spoils with the blessing of her grandfather. In the chaos of a fight, everything felt clearer, more immediate, more *real*. Even as a spectator, the Reckoner Arena captured that feeling for her. Only this time, she drowned that clarity out with the most expensive wine that she could find.

Rictus stood behind her chair, watching the fight below as she did. He did not drink with her, but Katye more than made up for that; Katye sprawled casually across the sofa in their viewing box, his feet poking out of his sandals as he waved one foot in time with the chanting of the crowd.

"What do you think?" Ambessa asked Katye. She had just told him of Menelik's dream, or vision, or whatever it was. She wanted to think that he'd been delirious. Probably she would have, if the Wolf had not visited her once.

Her brother's attention seemed to be on the field below, watching the champion's first victory of the night. She was growing exasperated when he finally spoke.

"A battle for succession is just about the worst thing I can imagine for our clan. If you recall the schism just after the founding of Noxus, when the lord of House Kythera died with no children? The nieces and nephews fought until all of them were dead."

Ambessa raised an eyebrow. "Is now the time for those dusty old stories? Who won?"

"Those dusty old stories are called *history*. Ignore it at your peril." He sipped his wine to make his point. "The youngest won. But his wife, who was having an affair with the brother he killed, poisoned him in his sleep."

Ambessa snorted. "I have no fear from Azizi on that score. When Menelik names me heir—"

"You're so sure he'll choose you?"

"Why shouldn't he?" Ambessa said coldly to mask the doubt that had been snaking around her like a death-creeper, threatening to pull her down.

"Ta'Fik is making a strong case with some of the other stewards. It's always been the two of you—"

"He's an overstuffed cacklebird—"

"He has two heirs who have proven themselves in battle, as he has made sure to tell every single person he spoke to today."

Ambessa bit her words off and glared at him. The heavy disappointment that Ambessa had been staving off threatened to overwhelm her. Now it was mingled with her fear for the family at large.

"You know Mel came with me on the Binan mission," she said in a low voice. She waited until he nodded for her to continue. "I asked her... I gave her a chance to prove she was ready. That she could be what this family needs." Ambessa shook her head. "If she's unwilling to take the forceful steps necessary, how will she lead this family?"

Katye stroked his mustache in silence. Then, with his finger against his lips, he said, "I'm sorry. She did show so much promise. Perhaps if you give her more time. You're still decided against Kino?"

"Time is promised to no one. I let myself forget that, and now look—Menelik is on his deathbed. I thought I had years to prepare. No, if they cannot be the wolf and the fox, then I will find a wolf for them." Ambessa looked over her shoulder at Rictus.

The large man's expression was solemn. "If you are no longer here to protect your children, then I will have already left this world."

Katye made a considering sound in his throat. "Well said. That, and you are too old." He laughed and tipped his wine cup over his mouth before waving it for a refill.

Ambessa turned back to the dirt pit below. They dragged the victor's bleeding opponent out of the ring while the champion's basilisk thrashed its tail. Navus was his name. He slouched arrogantly astride the basilisk and leered around the arena. He flicked the blood off his glaive. They announced the champion's second challenger simply as "Rell," and Ambessa stood. She had been waiting for this fight, and now she watched with special attention.

Rell rode her horse straight-backed, like a noble's daughter, and the horse, though it was clearly not a noble's horse, was well trained and accustomed to its rider. In one hand, Rell held the reins loosely. In the other, she gripped a spear. The horse's hooves churned up a cloud of dust that obscured Ambessa's vision. By the noise of the crowd, she wasn't the favorite. The basilisk snapped its jaws as the horse cantered around it, and its master's leer widened.

Ambessa beckoned Rictus over. "Tell me what you make of her."

The starting horn blew. The girl rode at her opponent, unfazed by the growl of the basilisk, though her horse's eyes were wide.

She mastered the beast, though, her knees gripping its heaving sides. Navus laughed, loud and arrogant, as he kicked his basilisk forward. The great lizard-like creature needed no urging, digging its claws into the dirt to find speed. Rell didn't waver, only lowered her head in concentration, and the point of her spear.

Katye rose to join them, tapping a fingernail against his glass.

Ambessa winced when she saw the basilisk lunge for the horse's throat. It wouldn't miss, there was no time for the girl to change course—

Rell didn't even try. As the basilisk lunged for her mount, she thrust the spear into the soft meat beneath the creature's chin. Her own horse screamed as the basilisk's teeth and claws raked it, and Rell leapt clear. Both animals' pained screams mingled with the roar of the crowd and Navus's own anger.

When Navus's basilisk collapsed, Navus jerked his glaive back and swiped it across the horse's throat. Then he turned on Rell.

The girl was picking herself up off the ground, but her spear was lodged in the basilisk's head. Instead, she reached for two daggers at her belt.

Ambessa held her breath. "Come on, girl."

Katye eyed her curiously. "Well," he said. "It was a good run." He turned to leave, but Ambessa stopped him with the back of her hand against his chest.

Navus said something that Ambessa couldn't make out, preening and turning his back to get the laughs of the crowd. But Rell was fast, faster than Navus expected. When he turned back to face her, she was already charging him down, blades like sharp fists. He tried to keep her at a distance with his longer reach, but she was smaller than him and wove around the blows. Each time she dodged, she was a little closer, and then it was too late. Rell was behind his blade, behind the worst of the danger to herself—and Ambessa could see the rage on the girl's face as one dagger sliced at Navus's knee. As he collapsed with a cry, she struck out at the opposite arm, slicing a tendon there, too. Navus dropped his glaive and cradled his arm where he knelt.

The girl kicked the champion's weapon aside, and it skittered toward their dead mounts. There was something pure about that fury. Something that Ambessa recognized.

"How's that for a little girl?" Rell spat at Navus in the hush-breath silence of the crowd.

She didn't let him answer. Instead, she flipped her bloody dagger and knocked it into his skull. He collapsed into the dirt.

Katye's eyebrows rose up to his scalp. "Well, now. She wouldn't be the first fighter from the pits who found her way into a warband." Katye gave Rictus a knowing glance.

It was no secret that the Wolf's Reapers were made up of Reckoners. Some fighters sought her out especially, hoping she would come to their matches and claim them. Rictus had been a Reckoner once, too. He'd fought in the Rokrund pit that Ambessa had founded first, almost two decades ago. He'd been one of the first fighters, indebted to the Medardas, but instead of leaving when he'd fought off his dues, he had asked to join Ambessa's warband. Ambessa had been keeping an eye on Rell for some time now.

She looked to Rictus for his assessment.

He grunted. "She's raw."

"We all were, at one point."

He blinked slowly. "Very raw."

"We can hone her."

"If you want to see a real fighter," said a voice behind them, "you should come to one of *my* matches."

Ambessa turned around slowly, carelessly. Behind her, with

Rictus's spear pointed at her chest, Ta'Fik's younger child, Tivadar, stood in a long sleeveless tunic that showed off her ropy arms tattooed in black. She was apparently unarmed but for a long dagger sheathed in her belt.

"You fight in my arena, child?" Ambessa said, turning back to the pit where aides were clearing the unconscious body of Rell's opponent while she strutted. Strength, skill, and showmanship.

"I do. And I'm better than that new upstart by a long shot."

"Hm." Ambessa didn't deign to turn around.

A beat of silence, then—"What about you? You look like you'd do all right down there. How about it? You, me. A hundred gold pieces to the winner?"

Another silence. Ambessa glanced over her shoulder to see Tivadar sizing Rictus up. Rictus was not a small man, taller than Ambessa and half again as broad, and he stood like a predator: no fidgeting, no pacing, just patience, waiting for the proper moment to strike. Nothing about the man was wasted.

And yet, this child looked at him with contempt. Rictus merely watched her, his halberd ready. As the silence stretched, she grew more agitated, glancing between Rictus, Ambessa, and Katye, and flexing her empty hands.

Finally, she scoffed. "I suppose you're big but not bright, is that it? Aunt, is this the best you could come up with?"

Ambessa raised an eyebrow at Rictus. The man shook his head slightly: no need for her to humiliate the child on his account. Perhaps on her own, however.

Ambessa turned fully in her cushioned chair, one leg crossed over the other. "If you're so talented, child, why are you playing messenger for your father?" She beckoned with her empty glass for the pretty serving boy, and he replaced it with a full one. "I came here to find peace, not to be pestered by a pup yapping at my heels."

"I'm not my—" She flushed red. "I just thought I might find

my cousins here. But Kino and Mel don't have the taste for physical arts, do they?"

Not a messenger, then, exactly, but a goad—which was a message from Ta'Fik in itself.

Ambessa hummed again and sat back in her seat. The new fight had already begun. "When is your next match, child?"

Tivadar stammered, surprised by the turn of the conversation. "Er, next week. Why?"

"Very good. I will look forward to your performance. Good luck." She didn't look back at her, a clear dismissal.

After a moment, she heard the quick footsteps departing the box. The fall of the curtain behind them.

"Are you sure you don't want to take her up on her offer?" Ambessa asked Rictus when she was certain they were alone again.

Rictus grunted. "She is young."

"Bah." Ambessa waved a hand dismissively and drank deep from her cup. "Ta'Fik sent her to irritate me. I won't give him the pleasure."

They waited for Rell at the fighters' rooms, where the champions prepared for their bouts, nursed their wounds, polished their weapons, and picked their petty squabbles before the real games began in the pit above. When the girl came out, a man and woman were berating her, and though she'd just beaten the champion and surely won a sizable purse, she hung her head.

"Rell," Ambessa interrupted. "You fought well today." She held her arm out, and Rell clasped it, brightening immediately.

"You came," the young woman said excitedly. She was of an age with Mel, Ambessa suspected, with dusky skin and a flare of blond hair.

"Of course I did. You know your fights are always my favorite. I saw you took my advice about committing to a course. Not quite how I expected, though."

Rell grinned. "If they don't expect you, they can't defend against you."

She was brash, and full of energy she could barely contain. It was as if she'd forgotten her parents entirely. Ambessa shared a glance with Rictus. *Raw.*

"Rell, dear, aren't you going to introduce us?" The man who had been speaking to her earlier pushed his way between Rell and Ambessa. He had a limp. He was a plain man, but he had quick, observant eyes. He knew exactly who Ambessa was.

Rell's enthusiasm was snuffed out. She looked at the ground as she said, "Father, this is General Medarda. General, this is my father and my mother. Father was an infantryman before he was wounded. And Mother—"

"How do you do?" Rell's mother jumped forward to clasp Ambessa's wrist in a soldier's clasp, but Ambessa drew back. She had the edges of a genteel accent. Stymied, the woman put her fist to her chest in salute instead. The father matched the salute, though he bowed his head more deeply. "I'm Dahlia of House Canwell. Rell has spoken so much about you. We can't thank you enough for your interest in our girl."

"We knew she had potential—"

"—we've always known, she's always been so special—"

"Any mentorship you could offer—"

"—any support, we'd do more for her if we could—"

There was a gleam in their eyes, something beyond the joy of supportive parents, and Rell's shoulders slumped further. It wasn't shame—or at least, it wasn't only shame—but resentment. Ambessa tried to place the family name Canwell, but couldn't—it was either too small a noble house or long fallen out of favor.

"Can we go now?" Rell finally snapped. She turned on her heel and left without even looking back at Ambessa.

The father's expression darkened for a moment as he watched Rell leave, but when he turned back to Ambessa, he was all smooth smiles again.

"Please excuse our daughter's outburst. I hope you won't think less of her. She has always been..."

"Volatile," the mother said, shaking her head.

Volatile. Ambessa considered that, too. She didn't trust these parents, though, and she wondered what layers lay beneath this exchange.

"Young fighters have a certain fire," Ambessa said. She turned her back on their continued attempts to ingratiate themselves with her, and Rictus followed.

"Raw we can work with," she murmured as they wound their way from the arena back to the Medarda compound. "But volatile?"

She thought of the girl, striking with barely restrained anger at Navus. The bridled rage as she stalked away from her parents. No, she couldn't be sure that Rell was the iron she needed. She would be a strong addition to the Wolf's Reapers, though.

"You were never volatile?" Rictus asked. Though his face never changed from his stoic expression, there was laughter in his voice.

Ambessa chuckled. *"A controlled fire is more dangerous than a wildfire.* And you? What was young Rictus the Reckoner like?"

Because Ambessa had seen the man on the battlefield. A more perfect rage had never existed. She was always glad that he was on her side, and doubly grateful that he had survived the arenas.

Now the big man did smile. "Volatile? Me? Never."

Chapter Four

Instead of retiring to her own rooms as she should, where she knew Azizi—and his hurt, accusatory stare—waited, Ambessa knew where she needed to be.

"You're going to see him again," Rictus said flatly. It wasn't a question.

Ambessa nodded. She couldn't even say why, exactly. Maybe seeing Rell, wanting to guide the girl, had her thinking even more about her days with her grandfather. They had been hard, but she also remembered them as some of the best times of her life. What she wouldn't have done for his quiet approval. The reward was always *more*—more fighting, more studying, more responsibility. Because she had proven she was up to the challenge.

"Do you want me to come?"

Ambessa shook her head, but she put a hand on his arm as he walked away. "Thank you."

She walked the corridors to her grandfather's rooms alone. The halls were quiet, only a few candles left to light the way, but she knew the path well. Though Rokrund was her home, she'd spent a fair amount of time here, too, where much of the Medarda power was concentrated. It paid well to be close to

Piltover, where the Medarda military presence in Bel'zhun ensured favorable rates on trade through the Sun Gates.

A soldier stood outside Menelik's door. He saluted her, but did not let her pass.

"He's with someone, General."

"At this hour?"

"Ma'am." He looked apologetic, but didn't move out of her way.

"Very well."

She stood on the other side of the hallway and retreated into her thoughts, trying to ignore the man standing guard as he stared adamantly into the empty space in front of him.

Menelik Medarda was dying. The star by which Ambessa had charted the course of her life would blink out soon, just when she most needed the guidance. She hadn't let on to Katye how much it had shaken her, Mel's failure. The look on Mel's face... horror. Fear. And not fear of death, no—fear of Ambessa herself. She had always felt a distance between her and her children, but never had it felt so great as in that moment.

It had never been like that with her and her grandfather. Her parents had taught her the history of the Medardas, how her ancestor Eskender had risen from merely guiding merchants through the Shuriman deserts to leading one of the most powerful clans in Noxus, in the earliest days of the Noxian empire—when they were still warring Noxian Houses, barely unified. Her father died shortly after the Battle of Hildenard, when Ambessa was young, and then she immediately started training with Menelik. By the time her mother died, she was on her own campaign. She'd been too busy to truly feel their loss, but they had shown her their legacy.

Menelik had taught her how to continue it.

She would never forget the first wound she'd ever received on a battlefield. She hadn't been fighting. She'd been collecting the weapons, and had cut herself on one of the enemy blades. She'd taken the wound to her grandfather, expecting him to take her hand gently and wrap it with ointment as her father's healers would have.

Instead, he'd taken the blade that had cut her and made her hold it, wrapped her fingers around it and made her squeeze tighter, deepening the cut just enough—not enough to ruin her but enough to leave a scar she would never forget. He'd stared down at her, his hard, clean-shaven jaw grimly set while she tried not to cry.

"This will be your lesson," he'd said.

"Yes, sir," she had whispered.

The door opened, drawing Ambessa out of the past. Ta'Fik stepped out quietly, pulling the door closed behind him.

"You," Ambessa hissed.

Surprise flitted across Ta'Fik's face before he could mask it. "Cousin. How are you?"

"What are you doing here?"

"The same as you, I'm sure. Spending the last moments I can with the grandfather I love."

"He needs his rest."

"Indeed." Ta'Fik folded his arms across his chest. He was a ropy man. He had always been rather bookish, and when he fought, he preferred to fight from a distance. Even Ambessa could admit that he was one of the best shots she knew with a bow. He had been ever since they were young. Menelik had often praised Ta'Fik's skill.

She thumbed the scar across her palm.

"I'll watch over him while he sleeps. It's good to have a familiar face as you heal."

Without looking at the guard, Ta'Fik flicked a hand. "Leave us."

When the guard was out of earshot, Ambessa said, "I've been leading his warbands for decades now, Ta'Fik. He's been grooming me to lead this family since I could walk. No amount of whispering in his ear will get you what you want."

"How do you know what I want?" He stepped close to her, circling like a hungry drakehound. He was taller than her, and his curled lip showed his teeth.

Ambessa scoffed. "What else could you want?"

Ta'Fik smirked. "You see? How can you lead this family if your vision is so narrow? But I've always had the best eye."

"Go back to Tereshni." Ambessa folded her arms across her chest. "You're not prepared for the fight you're trying to pick. You are my cousin. *Medarda over all.* We are stronger together, *nothing* is worth shedding Medarda blood. Ionia—"

"Nothing?" Ta'Fik interrupted. He laughed darkly. "I know just how well you prize Medarda blood, especially when it's in your way."

He pulled at the leather thong on his neck, drawing Ambessa's attention to the necklace of drakehound teeth. At the nadir of the necklace was a tooth encased in azirite. The blood glass gleamed sharp and red, the color of a fresh wound.

A wound that Ambessa had long since let scab over.

"She knew the risks, Ta'Fik." That's what Ambessa had told herself in the days, months, years after. All of them knew the risks. They came with being a Medarda.

"Zoya trusted you. Stronger together?" Ta'Fik scoffed. "As if you wouldn't stab me in the back the moment you found an advantage."

Ambessa bristled. "She should never have been there. I tried to protect her, but she was too stubborn."

"A Medarda strikes their own path," Ta'Fik said mockingly.

The second line of the four-pointed Code that Menelik had

emblazoned on Ambessa's heart, the star that lit her path. It was meant to encourage Medardas to look at the larger picture, to be bold and take risks—but even she could hear the contradiction in the words tonight.

Zoya had tried to strike her own path, and it had cost her.

"Zoya was my sister." Ta'Fik's voice was thick with restraint. He stepped up to Ambessa so they were almost chest to chest. Ambessa put a hand between their bodies, the other on the knife at her hip, but he made no move to attack her. "We are not the same, Ambessa. I will show you that. Take your 'Medarda Code' and bury it like the fossilized shit that it is."

He enunciated each word carefully, then knocked past her as he left.

Ambessa was still standing in the corridor trying to slow the thudding in her chest when the guard returned to his post.

"General?" he asked. "Is everything all right? Do you still wish to visit with Hostlord Menelik?"

Ambessa straightened her shoulders. "Yes."

Chapter Five

Another man might be insulted that his wife comes home from a long campaign and barely deigns to speak to him."

Ambessa closed the door behind her with a quiet snick. "Azizi. I've had so much on my mind. So much to attend to since I returned."

"You smell like wine. You were at the arena, weren't you?" Azizi sat on the couch in their receiving room in his nightgown. He'd been waiting up for her. The room was lit with low-burning lanterns.

She waved her hand dismissively as she sat beside him. "Earlier. I had to see someone. Then I...couldn't leave Menelik. I went to see him again."

Without waiting for her to ask, Azizi opened his arms to her. If his anger wasn't gone, he at least stowed it away as he tucked her head in the crook of his neck. He had been scrawny in his youth, and Kino took after him, but now Azizi was soft in ways that pleased her. She let herself relax for just a moment but not so much that the tension in her stomach overcame her.

"How is he?"

Ambessa shook her head. "Not well." The tightness in her stomach moved to her throat, lodged there, a solid lump that choked her silent. Her nose burned with the effort of pushing it away, and she blinked quickly.

"I'm sorry, my dear."

"A warrior does not fear death. Death is the gate to Volrach-nun. It is…it's the sight of him in that bed." She couldn't voice the words herself, though she knew they matched Menelik's own thoughts. He should have died on the battlefield. But then, she thought, the war of succession that Katye warned her of would surely happen. Hopefully tomorrow Menelik would make his decision known to the whole family. She would finally take her place as heir.

Azizi made no answer to this but kissed her on the forehead. "I take it Mel did not pass whatever test you had for her?"

Ambessa looked at him sharply, and he laughed.

"She's my daughter. No matter how she hides it behind her young elegance, I can tell when she's pouting."

"Perhaps she is too much your daughter. She faltered when it was time. She is afraid to spill blood."

"That is a bad thing?"

"It is when you must lead *this* family. That kind of responsibility requires ruthlessness, and neither she nor Kino has it."

Azizi leaned into the opulent sofa, and it swallowed him. He dragged Ambessa deeper with him. He took off her boots and began to rub her feet.

Ambessa moaned with pleasure despite herself. "You spoil them," she grumbled. "That's why they're not ready."

"*I* spoil them?" Azizi raised an eyebrow, but his hands never stopped their work.

To be truthful, Azizi also spoiled her. Though they had not explicitly chosen each other, they had found an easy camaraderie, and affection had grown quickly. Azizi was a good Noxian, though his strengths leaned toward commerce, not battlefields.

Like Kino and Mel, he was good with words. He could charm the gold out of a mine.

Ambessa snorted and let her head loll back onto the pillows.

"That's why I went to the arena tonight. I've been thinking—" She shook her head. "Later. It's not important right now." Even though it was all she could think of.

"Before you get too comfortable"—Azizi paused to press at a particularly stubborn knot in Ambessa's arch—"do you want the bad news now or later?"

"Ta'Fik."

Azizi's hands stilled. "How did you— Never mind. Of course you know."

"When I went to see Menelik just now, he was just leaving. I don't trust him."

"Because he wants to sit at the head of the family."

"Yes." Then Ambessa shook her head. "He still hates me. He's never stopped."

Azizi nodded somberly. "Ah. His sister."

"Zoya," Ambessa whispered. Ta'Fik had stirred the loss in her chest to life, dormant embers.

Ambessa wasn't ashamed, never had been. She had only done what needed to be done. One sacrifice among the many she had made to become who she was today—one of the strongest pillars of the Medarda name. And as Menelik himself had taught her, a Medarda did not apologize—especially not for winning.

Azizi hummed gently against her. He didn't push, and she was grateful.

"While you were at the Reckoners, I saw Ta'Fik and that advisor of his getting rather cozy with a few more of the clan and some of the eastern Noxians as well. Dauvin of Kilgrove's daughter—niece? I forget—for one, and someone from the Du Couteau family. Even Lisabetya."

Ambessa sat up abruptly, yanking her foot away from Azizi. "Lisabetya? We need her weapons."

Azizi pursed his lips. "So if Menelik chooses him, you will fight?"

"Menelik won't choose him. Ta'Fik couldn't be in charge of his own arsehole."

"He is the steward of Tereshni. He oversees the banks there—where even *we* have some of our resources—and azirite sales have been profitable."

"Will you take his side, then?"

Azizi furrowed his thick, dark eyebrows at the warning in Ambessa's voice. His own voice grew hard in response. "You know I won't. But he has more than enough in his favor. Don't take him lightly." He sighed and sat back. "If I noticed that Mel left the reception early and upset, he would have, too—and others."

"Katye already knows." Ambessa swore. "Others will have heard by now, too."

A servant arrived with tea, and when he had poured it and departed, Azizi brought Ambessa a cup. It warmed her hand pleasantly, and she breathed in the fragrant steam, trying to still her exhausted mind.

"Are you sure?" Azizi said quietly. "Rather, I mean to say— are you sure Mel is unfit? She is so young. There is time to prove herself yet, time to learn, to grow—"

"No." Ambessa sipped her tea. "I'm not sure. But this is Noxus; half of these Houses are run by spineless vipers, and the other half are starving drakehounds. One wrong step and they'll bite. If Mel isn't strong enough to fend them off—" Ambessa sighed and let her teacup clatter against the saucer. "I asked her what we should do with the Binan leader, and she gave me soft-hearted drivel. If she can't be the wolf, then she cannot lead this family. How will she handle rebels in Bel'zhun or the raiders in the Varju Mountains? How will she help Noxus expand its borders? When I was her age—"

When Ambessa was fifteen, she had been one of the most promising young warriors in the clan. She closed her eyes, remembering the battlefields she'd walked on. Her first uniform, the little red pauldrons made of leather. Her dark boots, and the dirk at her belt. She'd been so proud.

Was that where she had gone wrong? By protecting them, had she made them too soft?

Azizi scratched his beard in contemplation. Then he sighed. "I would have you home more."

The lines in his face were growing deeper, and there was more gray in his hair than Ambessa remembered.

She smiled tenderly and said, "This is why they're so spoiled."

Pounding on the door woke Ambessa, and she was out of bed, sword in hand, before Azizi had rubbed the sleep from his eyes.

A frightened servant stared at her wide-eyed—stared at the point of her sword, rather, and then pointedly lowered his eyes to Ambessa's bare feet. She hadn't bothered with clothing, and she didn't bother for modesty now.

"What is it?" she asked, though she knew what was coming.

"Hostlord Menelik is dead."

It was like a blow, no less powerful for expecting it. She closed her eyes.

"I thought we had more time," she murmured as Azizi draped a robe over her shoulders.

"General?" The boy finally dared raise his eyes up above Ambessa's ankles.

"Nothing. Thank you."

He ran off to finish his rounds before Ambessa remembered—
"Wait." The boy skittered to a halt. "Did he say anything before
he died?"

The boy shook his head. "He was— They found him when
stewards Ta'Fik and Lisabetya went to visit him."

Ambessa dismissed him again and slammed the door shut.

"Ta'Fik. Of course he was there. And if he's pulled Lisabetya
to his side—"

Azizi's calming hands were on her shoulders again. "Nothing
is binding without witnesses. If he was dead when they found
him, that means there's no heir."

Ambessa left his embrace and started dressing. She hesitated
before pulling on pieces of her ceremonial armor. Azizi helped
her secure her pauldrons without speaking. He knew as well as
she how important it was to look the part you needed to play.

They found other members of the family and its allies outside Menelik's room. A corridor of crows come to feast upon the
corpse. They parted for her and Azizi, making space for her to
reach the door. Menelik's anteroom was as crowded as the hallway. She made her way to the bedroom, which was guarded by
two of Menelik's own soldiers. They stepped apart for Ambessa
and Azizi.

Ta'Fik was inside, of course. His eyes were red rimmed, but
he had dressed himself well, in all black, tailored so the breadth
of his back made a strong triangle. His fingers were taped and
he wore a bracer, as if he were going shooting. The drakehound
teeth stood out starkly against his clothing. His advisor was
with him—Inyene. They looked suitably solemn, just a step
behind him, their hands clasped behind their back. Katye was
also there, and Lisabetya. Lisabetya gripped the bedding with
one heavy-knuckled fist.

Menelik looked more peaceful than he had last night when

Ambessa watched him sleep. Someone had pulled the coverlet up his chest, tucking it neatly. The bandages weren't even visible. That tidiness said it all—only death was this tidy, this orderly. A rigid line you couldn't come back from once you'd crossed it.

"What have the doctors said?"

"His heart. The blood loss and the medicine combined..." Lisabetya growled low in her throat.

"He wasn't a young man," Katye finished.

Ambessa studied her grandfather. He wasn't young, no, but he'd been hale. His grip had been strong, his eyes sharp and his mind sharper. But things were not always as they seemed. She took his hand and squeezed it tight. She bent over and kissed him on the brow.

Goodbye, Grandfather.

To the rest of the room, she announced, "He made this family strong, and I will follow in his footsteps as the new matriarch of the Medarda family. He will be buried with every honor a warrior deserves."

She headed back to the corridor where the visitors who weren't family waited, to make the final pronouncement, but Ta'Fik stopped her in the anteroom.

"*You* will follow in his footsteps?" he said.

The quiet murmuring from the crowd in the hallway and in the anteroom hushed.

Ambessa faced him. His eyes were alight with anger, not grief, and Ambessa felt so heavy.

"When I left our grandfather last night, he was sitting up and eating. Even the pain was leaving, he said. Then you were there."

Ambessa laughed out loud. "You wouldn't dare—"

"Dare? I don't have to dare." Ta'Fik raised his voice. "You were the last to see Menelik alive, and now he is dead."

That was a line too far. "How dare you accuse me of murdering *my* grandfather!" Ambessa reached for him, but Azizi caught her wrist in a surprisingly strong grip.

"Do you have a witness?" Ta'Fik asked.

"Everyone here can look at his body and see—no marks upon his throat, no wound but the one he returned home with."

"There are plenty of poisons that leave no outer mark."

Ambessa made a disgusted sound in her throat. "Poison is not my weapon."

"Then provide your witness."

"The soldier on guard that night." Ambessa cast a glance around her. "He'll tell everyone that you are a snake."

"Then we'll find him and question him. Until then, while I don't know what you *would* do, I know what you have done. Everyone here knows you're capable of sacrificing another Medarda on the altar of your ambition."

Ambessa exhaled sharply, holding herself back from squeezing his neck between her hands. Zoya's death was not a secret, but it was rarely spoken of. The sacrifices made in the family name often weren't. Especially if they came in a moment of weakness.

"*Family is more important than the individual,*" Ambessa growled. "Did he warn you about his dream? That a bloodbath will follow if we don't stand united?"

"He warned me that *you* would lead us to destruction."

"You liar." Ambessa shook off Azizi as he tightened his grip. "You will not blacken my name. Challenge me in combat, if you wish, but don't try to tie us all in knots with your lies."

"So you can murder me, too, with some cheap cheat? I think not." He looked around the room, making eye contact with those watching. Everyone in the corridor could hear their argument. "It's clear who they should stand with."

A chill shivered up Ambessa's spine. All around her, people

were considering Ta'Fik's words. Any justification she could make would be a hollow excuse without evidence. She had misstepped. As Azizi had warned, she had underestimated Ta'Fik.

She inhaled deeply and set her shoulders back. "You've turned a time of grief into petty squabbling, Ta'Fik, before the very body of our grandfather has grown cold. I will honor him alone, if I must, and those who wish may join me. After, we can revisit the matter of the succession."

She left him standing behind her, his restrained fury barely showing through his haughty composure. The others opened a path for her again, this time hushed as she passed. Ambessa would earn their confidence by proving she had nothing to do with Menelik's death. Then she would wipe Ta'Fik off the map entirely. There would be no question then. To do that, though, she would need allies, and to gain allies... a well-placed, circular trap he had laid. It had been a long time since Ta'Fik set foot on a battlefield, though.

Ambessa would outmaneuver him yet.

Chapter Six

And where are *you* going, child?"

Mel whirled around, her dress spinning around her ankles and panic pulling her heart into her throat.

It was only Kino, doing a frighteningly good impression of their mother.

"Kino!"

Kino's eyes were closed as he laughed silently, clutching his side. "Your face!"

Mel stalked over to him and pinched the soft meat above his elbow, and he yelped. "Your face when I have you gutted! Then we'll see whether a wolf has mercy or not." She added the last in a low mutter as she abandoned Kino, continuing the way she'd been going.

Kino sobered and fell into step beside her, catching up easily with his long strides. Like Mel, he was tall and slim—his grace the grace of ballrooms, not battlefields.

"She used that line on you, too, did she?"

Mel made a noncommittal noise in her throat.

"Don't take it too hard. It happens to the best of us." He held his arms open to indicate himself, and offered her a smile that was meant to be charming—doubtless it worked on everyone else he turned it on, but Mel was too deep beneath the cloud of her mother's disappointment.

"Not to her, though. Not to a proper Medarda."

"Now, you see here—" Kino skipped in front of Mel and put his hands on her shoulders, stopping her. "You *are* a proper Medarda. You have her strength. Her resolve. My cleverness and stunning good looks." He chucked her under the chin. "If she can be a little"—he lowered his voice conspiratorially— "narrow-minded about her definition of strength, it's our job to remind her what we're really capable of."

"She doesn't think we're capable of running the family."

"And yet, I have friends in every quarter of this city, high and low, wet and dry." Kino buffed his fingernails on the lapel of his fine coat immodestly. "We all have our strengths, even you. No matter what Mother says, we have our role to play in this family."

"She was right," Mel said dryly. "You have an answer for everything."

"Yes, she was. Though if I know Mother, what she actually said is something far less complimentary, so you've shown just how necessary your skill set is."

That coaxed a chuckle from Mel, the dark pall that had covered her the last few days easing—slightly. "You mean tact?"

"Precisely." Kino tapped her gently on the nose. "You could lead this family as well as anyone, and better than most."

Mel sighed. "Thank you, Kino."

"Would you like to join me and my friends at the new noodle-house? I'd like to show the owner a little favoritism and get a feel for the patrons there, and I've heard the fire noodles are to die for."

Mel raised an eyebrow at him. It would also garner the restaurant a significant amount of attention and even more patrons, which would make the owner grateful—and potentially in Kino's debt for his favor. And then the owner would be yet another coin in Kino's pocket, jingling with all the other people Kino danced around so effortlessly. But even Kino wasn't good enough for their mother. How would *Mel* ever be? The despair returned.

"What about Grandfather?" Her great-grandfather's death was a pall that blanketed the compound.

"Well, he, may Kindred watch over his spirit, is gone. I don't think he cares at all, and he certainly didn't care for me. I'll celebrate him with a drink. As for Mother..." He shuddered. "I don't do well with all this formal funereal business. I'm sure she'd rather me out from underfoot. I take it you won't be joining me?"

"No, thank you. I'd like to spend some time alone. I...also need some time away from this." Everyone radiated tension, especially her mother and Steward Ta'Fik. And the way they looked at her, pointed and considering, just reminded her that she hadn't lived up to her mother's expectations. It made her feel like *she* had done something to Grandfather Menelik.

Kino nodded knowingly. This was not the first time he'd caught her sneaking off to explore the city alone. "Well, if you change your mind, it's on Kirak's Row, just near the Dawn Gate. I plan on being there until late."

Before Mel could stride past him, he looped an arm about her shoulders and swept her into a hug. "No matter what," he murmured into her hair, "I'm proud of you. She is, too. Even if she doesn't show it."

Pressed tight against her brother's chest, Mel blinked away the sudden influx of tears. Unlike him, she didn't have the words for everything. She surreptitiously wiped her eyes on his coat, and released him.

She composed herself and said, "If I get bored, I'll find you there."

Mel made her way to the Shimmering Market, passing under the small arch that was almost an imitation of the greater Nox-toraa on the road into the city. The Shimmering Market wasn't the largest marketplace in Bel'zhun, but it was Mel's favorite. It was the artists' market, named for the Bel'zhun glassblowers whose work was prized throughout not just Shurima but also Noxus—and beyond. It was also home to stoneworkers, paint-ers and their canvases, mosaicists and their painted tiles, and so many more. It was beautiful.

It was also the perfect place to get lost. She roamed the streets with the hood of her cloak up, as if protecting her eyes from the sun. It wasn't too odd; there were a number of people doing the same. Her mother would not look for her here, though; none of the Medardas would. Not after her great-grandfather's death. They would be too absorbed to go art shopping. Here, she was safe.

Here, she could forget, for a moment at least, that she had failed.

"Hello, young miss. Has something caught your eye?"

Mel jumped at the call of the peddler. She looked around, but she was the nearest to him. He nodded at her. She realized that she had stopped in the middle of the winding maze that was the market path, her attention zoning in on his wares—mostly paintings but also a few clay jugs and a very small carpet.

The salesman was a handsome older man, dark of skin and hair, his long locs piled in a bun atop his head. He wore a scarf to hold them back. He wore nothing else but a long wrap around his waist, and his bare chest and arms were covered in swirling gold tattoos. A sun worshipper from Targon.

"Rare, to see Rakkor so far from their mountains," she said, while studying one of his paintings. An impression of a mountain at sunrise, with the rays of the sun limning the peak in spikes of gold.

"Is it?" The man blinked in surprise. "I'm surprised you recognize one, then."

Mel glanced up at the teasing smile in his voice, then the man continued.

"There are always wanderers among us. The sky wanderers, for example, traveling the earth to trace the sky."

"Are you a sky wanderer?"

He smiled again and shook his head. It was a warm smile. "Simply an artist. To honor the sun, I like to see what she looks like from as many places as I can. She is different everywhere, you know."

"The sun? It is always the sun, no matter where you go."

"Mm. But how cold she is in the Freljord, amidst the clear blue sky, reflecting off the snow and blinding. There, she offers little warmth, and yet, she is salvation—but in the deserts of Nashramae? She shines with an intensity that will blister the skin, golden and radiant. There, she could mean death." He rotated his arms in a practiced way, making the gold ink on his body flare bright. "The bloody sunsets on the ever-spreading Noxian borders, the bashful sunrises off the coast of Basilich. She may be one thing, but she offers each of us a different face."

"You speak like a poet," Mel said, but that was not all. His eyes had grown misty, his voice soft. There was longing and grief and joy behind those sunrises.

"Anyone can become a poet if they are devout enough." His warm smile crinkled his eyes.

"I'm not allowed to devote myself to anything like this," Mel murmured, more to herself than to the stranger. She traced over the mountain rays without touching the painting itself.

"Not allowed? Do you need permission to devote yourself to beauty?"

"I don't think my mother knows what beauty is."

She wasn't sure why she even let the bitter words slip from her mouth, but there was a comfort in their anonymity.

The artist hummed quietly in understanding. "Are you sure? Sometimes our parents simply don't understand what *we* call beauty, but they hold something else dear to their hearts."

Mel scoffed indelicately. "Not my mother." Despite her words, she suspected her mother probably did find violence beautiful. When Mel thought of Lady Binan, though, her blood pooling on the stone floor of the throne room, all she could see was *waste*. Waste, and pain. *It doesn't have to be this way.*

"It doesn't matter what I think. My mother...she's a powerful woman. I'm her daughter. I have duties. Every child has a duty to their parents. To their family."

The artist lowered his head to look up into her downcast face. The beard cropped close to his face was speckled with gray among the black.

"Perhaps you could show her. Is there something of mine that you think she would like? Or something that *you* like, something to show her who you are? Because I think that is too often the trouble with parents. They see only what they want for us, and not what we are in front of them."

"Or how we're right," she muttered.

The man chuckled. "No, they'll never admit when we're right, not even on their deathbeds."

Mel examined the other paintings on display—a raging fire, turning into smoke, into sunset. An ocean, with the sun mirrored in the blue sky above and watery ripples below. So many more, in all the ways the artist had spoken of, in great paintings the size of her outstretched arms, and some that were no bigger

than her palm. What *would* her mother think if she brought one
back?

The artist came around his stand and stood next to her, looking down at the mountain painting that had captured her attention first. He towered over her, but he was slim, with the body
of a dancer, the grace of his every movement the same as the
grace of his paintings. She noticed, too, how his tattoos also
echoed the brilliance of the paintings.

"The thing about power," he said softly, "is that, once you
have it, the thing you fear most of all is losing it. It's been the
way of the mighty since time immemorial. It can make us do
things we're...not proud of. Things we never thought we'd do.
Take that one, if you like. A gift."

Mel blinked up at him, her mouth open in surprise. "No,
please—I'll pay you for it."

He smiled indulgently. "I don't think a girl alone can afford
what I tend to ask for my work."

Mel raised her eyebrows. He still didn't know who she was.
The sudden freedom made her feel energetic and reckless.

"Your tattoos. Who did them?"

Taken aback, the artist looked down at himself. It was almost
comical. "I did some of them. My brethren did others."

"What if I don't want a painting?"

He narrowed his eyes suspiciously.

"Would you give me tattoos? Like yours?"

"Like mine? Will you join the Rakkor, then?"

Mel flushed. "Not quite, but—you said you'd give me something to show my mother that I am my own. Something to
make her appreciate beauty. Your tattoos—they *are* beautiful."

An unreadable expression crossed the man's face. Then he
cocked his head.

"You don't even know what they mean."

"Explain them to me, then."

He knit his brow at her demand, and though his face was serious, Mel couldn't fight the feeling that he was also amused. She straightened and said more delicately, "Please. You're right. I would like to understand."

That faraway look returned to his eyes. "Each tattoo marks a part of my journey. The glare of a burning noon. A glint of sunlight off glass. Moments in time long gone, moments yet to come." Almost self-consciously, the man traced his shoulders, and Mel followed his fingers. The tattoos had the look of a celestial map.

"I understand. I'm not part of the Rakkor, but I know what I would ask." It surprised her, how immediately the vision came to her, but once she realized it, she knew her tattoos could be nothing else.

"They will hurt. Let me give you one of my paintings instead—"

"I am not afraid of pain." Mel held her hands at her sides and raised her chin. She was glad that he wasn't going to deny her, at least.

What did she know of pain, though? Her cheeks flushed at the thought. She had been raised at the top of Noxian society, protected by her family name, her mother's reputation, and her father's money. Had she ever even scraped a knee?

No wonder her mother thought her incapable. It was as if Ambessa knew *only* pain. Ambessa was covered in scars, scars she had earned through trial after trial. A part of Mel wanted to understand. Another part of her simply couldn't bear yet another person implying that she was weak.

"The tattoos," she said firmly. "Please."

The man looked around his stall and then out to the wider market and blew out his cheeks. "I can't—"

"I can handle—"

"I can't do it here. I don't have the materials, and unless you want to lie on the ground in front of everyone in Bel'zhun, it would be best if we did it inside. I have lodgings nearby. I'll ask the matron if she has a spare room I can work in. I'll need to pack my things here. Meet me at the Golden Drake in an hour?"

Mel stopped herself from leaping in excitement. With as much dignity as she could muster, she clasped her fingers together in front of herself and nodded.

"An hour, then."

She left him there, and hoped that he would not renege on the agreement between now and then.

She hoped she would not lose her courage.

Just over an hour later, Mel hovered beside a table in the Golden Drake while the artist—she still had not asked his name—mixed a bright gold ink that almost seemed to glow. He murmured to himself as he mixed it, as if he were praying over it. A Rakkor ritual, perhaps.

A young woman who worked with the inn staff was serving as his assistant, getting Mel ready by cleaning her skin and wrapping her in a cloth dress that bared her back and shoulders. Mel tried not to look at the sharp implements the man pulled out of a leather case.

"Do you do this often?" she asked nervously.

"I do, actually," he said, offering her a reassuring smile. "Don't worry. Are you ready?"

Mel clenched her jaw. "I am."

"It's a long process. Usually, people will come for more than one session while we work on it."

"I'll do it all today," Mel said quickly.

The man raised an eyebrow, but nodded. "We'll see how you go. Lie down. I'll start with the back."

Mel lay down on the broad wooden table covered in blankets and pillowed her head on her arms. He picked up one of the sticks with its cluster of needles so tight it looked almost like a paintbrush, and dipped it in the ink.

"Stay as still as you can, miss," he said. "This is going to hurt."

Mel returned home late in the night. As much as she tried to be circumspect, she was barely into the main corridors, headed toward her room, when she heard furtive footsteps coming around the corner. She pulled her cloak closer to her body, wincing as it moved over her raw skin. She had walked almost hunched from the artist's lodging house in the city, partly to keep the cloak from brushing her new tattoos and the shooting pain that came with it, and partly to keep from stretching them, and *that* shooting pain. The mysterious artist was right: It *had* hurt. And she felt…different, somehow. Tired. Almost as if she had a fever.

She recognized the figure who emerged. Inyene, Steward Ta'Fik's advisor. Despite the late hour, they were fully dressed and heading away from the guest rooms of the compound. They were dressed in dark trousers and a long overcoat, with a simple dagger at their belt. They startled when they saw her.

"Ah, Miss Medarda. What are you doing out so late?" The assistant smiled conspiratorially.

Mel straightened, hiding her wince as she did. She clutched the cloak tighter around her shoulders to cover herself and hissed sharply as the cloth scraped against her skin—what had felt so well-made and luxurious this morning felt like the roughest canvas—sending pain like a wildfire. As he had given her the markings, each stab had blended into the next, creating a monotonous song of it. She had gritted her teeth and bit her lips to keep from crying out.

She could still taste the blood in her mouth and feel the teeth marks on the inside of her cheek.

"Inyene. Hello. I was out."

"Your mother has been looking for you. She sent—Rictus, is that his name?" Though their voice was friendly, they studied her carefully. Their eyes narrowed briefly as they skimmed over her shoulders, and Mel pulled the cloak tighter. "I'd be careful, if I were you. She didn't look very generous."

"Thank you for your warning."

In her rooms, Mel undressed and washed the mess of blood and ink oozing from her skin, the blood and the gold swirling together like a potion. This, too, was a new kind of pain, one she had no choice but to inflict on herself or risk infections, the artist had told her.

Then she stared at herself in awe as the candlelight of her bedroom flickered against the gold in her skin. Her shoulders were covered in gold, like pauldrons, and the ink braced her neck like a gorget. She ghosted her fingers over her shoulder, her neck. Her mother had her armor. Mel would show Ambessa that she could fashion her own.

Chapter Seven

The morning after Menelik's death, Ambessa went hunting for Katye, but he had already left his rooms. The great dining room where all the guests were breaking their fasts was another option. Ambessa would never have said she was . . . afraid to go there, to see the Medardas and their allies look askance at her, but she wasn't eager. She also couldn't let them think she had anything to hide. *She* had not killed Menelik. Hiding would only make her seem guilty.

When she went to the dining room, however, Katye wasn't there. Lisabetya was, though, and the representative from Trannit; Steward Smik hadn't been able to come. His representative was a nervous-looking man, plump, with a tendency to glance sidelong at the people he thought were the most powerful in the room. Today, he kept flicking his eyes toward Lisabetya.

Under normal circumstances, Ambessa would have been sure of Lisabetya's support. The older woman had fought beside Menelik in their youth. She had sense and skill, and though she had retired from the fighting to be the steward of Krexor, no one could argue with the victories she'd had as a leader of her own warband.

However, Lisabetya only looked Ambessa up and down, her eyes cold, before turning back to her porridge and expensive tea without a word. So be it. Ambessa made sure they heard the disgusted sound in her throat before she turned on her heel.

There was only one more place Katye could be. She found him in the library, sipping something—probably the same tea Lisabetya favored; Ambessa preferred coffee—while he turned the pages of a large book slowly.

"Katye."

"Shh." He patted the air before him without looking up. "This is a library, you know."

Ambessa hissed. A lesser Medarda perusing one of the shelves looked at her as she stomped in. Their eyes went wide, and she bared her teeth. For a moment, they stood, still as a rabbit under the eagle's eye. Then they scampered, leaving whatever search they were on.

Katye watched the exchange, his lips flat. "Was that necessary?"

"I didn't do it, Katye."

Katye sighed and placed a green silk ribbon in his book. He folded his hands atop it. "I believe you. You're my sister. I've known you for a long time. Poison is *not* your weapon, and more importantly, I know how much you cared for him."

Ambessa didn't know how to respond to that. "Menelik was my grandfather and my mentor."

"Mmm. I also know that you were quite certain he was going to announce you as heir, which means there would be no need for you to kill him before that announcement."

Relief, cool after the humiliating heat she'd felt under Trannit's and Krexor's gazes. "Thank you, Katye."

Katye grunted delicately. "Unfortunately, I think I'm in the minority of those with sense—either that, or I'm simply the only one who cares for the truth. Ta'Fik has many things that many people want."

"I'll take it all away from him, starting with his balls."

Ambessa paced in front of Katye's table, squeezing her fist in her palm.

"Admirable, I'm sure. Menelik would approve. However, has it occurred to you that you're outnumbered?" Katye nodded his head toward Rictus, who was behind her. "You and your shadow, however well-appointed he is, against Ta'Fik and whoever else he's called to his banner?"

"My warbands are worth ten of his."

Another delicate grunt. "Come to Rokrund with me. Bide your time. Strike back at him when he grows complacent. Knowing Ta'Fik, that won't be too long."

"I will *not* run away. Because of *him*? No. Never."

"It's not running away. It's strategic. History is littered with the broken armies of those who were too good to retreat when necessity required." He tapped the pages of his open book with one long finger. "Even if you don't come home to Rokrund, you can use that time to find allies. Trannit, Kilgrove, and Krexor still have representatives here. Speak to them."

Ambessa snorted. "Ta'Fik has his hooks in them already. What about Vindor? I could use Amenesce's cavalry."

"I haven't heard any word from the north. There's also Darkwill. He could be invaluable."

Ambessa thought of Lady Binan, and Caprian, the leader of the vastayan rebels on whose behalf she'd promised to speak to the Noxian Grand General.

She shook her head. "I'm not running from that sack of mwatis dung."

She glanced over her shoulder at Rictus. He hesitated, then said, "Katye might be right. No matter how well-appointed I am." He shrugged his broad shoulders for emphasis.

"You two don't understand. It's as good as surrender to run away from a fight."

"No, it isn't."

Ambessa expected the rebuke to come from Katye, but it was Rictus again.

"Only surrender is surrender. Better to gather your strength and strike with all of it, than swing half-hearted and leave your opponent able to hit you again."

The two men couldn't have been more different, the large warrior and the small historian, but both of them wore identical grim lines for mouths. Ambessa scoffed. "I'm going to make my rounds. I'll throw Ta'Fik into the channel by the end of the week."

She left the library, followed by the sound of Katye's sigh.

"Are you sure about this, Ambessa?" Rictus murmured.

"Will you stand beside me and guard my back in this? Whatever happens?"

"Of course, but—"

"Then that is all I need."

Rictus nodded solemnly. "Of course, Kreipsha."

The dining room was empty when Ambessa returned, looking for the Trannit emissary while simultaneously keeping an eye out for Ta'Fik. Odd, that he would make himself so scarce after this coup of his; she would have expected him to be crowing from the highest rooftop. It showed too much restraint in the face of victory. It gave Ambessa the creeping sense that he wasn't done yet.

The Trannit emissary was in the courtyard garden that was central to the Bel'zhun Medarda compound. He was speaking with the woman Katye had called Stefana, niece of the steward of Kilgrove. She wore the Kilgrove symbol along with the Medarda ring. Ambessa forced herself to smile.

"Trannit. Kilgrove. I regret that I haven't had the pleasure of making your acquaintances. I was away when introductions were made."

"So we heard. In fact, I met you before, when I was a child." The Kilgrovan stood. "Disappointing, to know someone I looked up to would flout the Code like this." Her tattooed muscles rivaled Ambessa's, and she had the swaying gait of someone used to spending too much time at sea. She scowled as she took in both Ambessa and Rictus, then left the Trannit representative on his bench alone.

Ambessa struck Kilgrove off her mental list. No help would come from that quarter, at least not if that was the only Kilgrovan she could speak to here.

The man from Trannit tried to get up also, but Ambessa stood her ground in front of him, and with Rictus at her side, they hemmed him in. For a moment, Ambessa let him stew in his fear. His eyes flicked from her to Rictus and back again, as if he couldn't decide who was the greater threat. Then she let her smile soften and sat down beside him in the Kilgrovan's spot. The stone bench was warm with heat. The smell of jasmine wafted strong and sweet.

She pulled her ankle up over her knee. "What is your name?"

"I'm Gessik."

"Smik's... heir?" He didn't look like one of Smik's children; Smik was a dark man with a cap of tight black curls Ambessa last remembered seeing woven with gold. This man was pale and blond, with blue eyes and a smattering of freckles across his face. Nor was he quite so young. Adopted, maybe.

"No. But I am his right hand. He's given me permission to speak with his own voice." Gessik raised his chin.

Ambessa reconsidered. Though he didn't look impressive on the surface, that sort of trust wasn't given lightly. However, it could be bought, and Smik wasn't known to keep the cleanest of ledgers.

"And if he were here, what would he say?"

Another nervous glance to Rictus. He licked his lips and mustered all his courage to say, "We don't support kinslayers."

Ambessa smiled sadly. She waved Rictus down, and the large man relaxed a fraction of a hair. "I'm sorry you believe that of me. I would never kill a member of my own clan. How can I prove to you that I only ever wanted what the clan needed? That my only law was Hostlord Menelik's?"

Gessik snorted. "The Code? Without him here, who will uphold it?"

Ambessa looked down her nose at him. "We uphold it. Every Medarda, wherever they are. It is in our history, in our blood."

"And you hold it so closely that you would murder him for it?" Gessik swallowed. Ambessa admired him, at least, for having the courage to speak—though she doubted these words were his.

Ambessa continued to glare at him until he looked her up and down again, taking account of her weapons, the ease with which she sat, the power of her body. He swallowed, as if realizing what she was capable of for the first time—and that he was very alone with someone he believed had already murdered one person who stood in her way. Ambessa allowed her mouth to turn up at one corner, then changed tactics.

"Do your master's debts grow too heavy again?" Ambessa asked. "If Ta'Fik is his creditor, we can deal with that, too. We can pay more for Trannit ships."

Gessik narrowed his eyes.

"Or is it blackmail? Some new vice that Smik has picked up? I can snuff out those who hold the secrets and make him safe again." Everyone knew Steward Smik spent less time attending to Medarda interests in Trannit than he did sampling every pleasure herb and spirit that trade brought through the city—and being so close to Bilgewater, quite a few things slipped from pirate hands to his.

Gessik stood in a huff, an indignant pink tingeing those pale cheeks. Or perhaps it was the heat. His forehead was dotted with sweat. "Steward Smik is above reproach. I shall add this insult to the reasons we support Steward Ta'Fik, among many. If you will please excuse me, General." He said the last through gritted teeth and then spun away in a flurry of fabric streaming from his long black coat and the red ribbons attached to it.

Alone on the bench, Ambessa stared around the garden. The sun hitting the peak of its arc, warming the skin of her bare arms. Bright little birds flitted from flower to bush to the dirt, chirping and pecking for bugs, as cheerful as if their world hadn't been turned upside down.

"What now?" Rictus said, dropping onto the stone bench beside her.

She rose as soon as he settled. "To the training yard. And then to the arena." She should have gone to see her children. To explain what was coming. "I need to hit people, and then I need to watch people be hit. And have something good to drink. A lot of something."

Rell was not fighting in the arena tonight. She wondered how the girl was faring with her parents and their naked hunger. They drooled over their daughter's potential. The money Rell could bring as a fighter. The connections she could make, *had* made, used for their gain. All the more reason to invite Rell to join one of her warbands before her parents ruined her with their scheming.

The fights of the night passed in a blur of screaming and cheering from the crowd, weapons clashing in the sand, the roars of the beasts the champions rode. Ambessa filled herself with Bel'zhun honey wine and, more than once, fantasized about skewering Ta'Fik on the blade of her katar in the arena below.

Once, in another box, she thought she saw Lisabetya, and she rose to go tell the woman exactly what was on her mind, to give her one chance to stand beside her. The older woman—she was only a handful of years younger than Menelik himself—had been one of Menelik's war leaders, maybe even friends, or at least as close to friends as a clan leader could have.

She left her box in the middle of one of the fights, with Rictus at her elbow. The corridors above the crowd's tiered seating were empty. It was eerily quiet there, compared to the crush of noise below. When they got to the spectator's box where Lisabetya had been, though, she was gone. Dauvin's sailor niece from Kilgrove was there, but Rictus put a hand on her shoulder. It was firm, and in it, she could read his feelings: *I don't think this is wise, but I will follow you if you do.* She took a deep breath and decided to respect his wisdom. She wouldn't pick a fight. Still, she stepped into the box and took the empty seat beside the young Kilgrove woman. The young woman pointedly stared down at the fighting pit, but the tic in her clenched jaw belied her insouciance.

"Stefana."

The young woman started to get up, but Ambessa put a hand out to stop her. Slowly, Stefana sat back down.

It was Ambessa's turn to focus on the arena below. Ta'Fik's younger daughter was finally fighting. "Tivadar is too impulsive. She's won her last battles with sheer speed, but she has no tactical awareness."

Stefana grunted. With no small bit of pride, she said, "Leda is a thousand times more clever, and patient as a mountain."

Ambessa crooked an eyebrow, but she didn't look at Stefana. "You know Leda well?"

"Perhaps." A tinge of embarrassment in the young woman's voice.

"Well. You have a good eye." Ambessa made a mental note to attend more of Leda's fights. Another Reckoner she could make better use of in a warband than in the gaming pits. She raised her hand for one of the workers in the box to bring them drinks. Begrudgingly, she added, almost to herself, "Tivadar does have potential, though."

Stefana took hers but didn't drink. "What do you want, General?"

"I'm sorry I didn't recognize you earlier. You've grown. I hear you're a sailor. Captain of your own ship. That's quite a feat at your age."

Ambessa turned just enough to see Stefana's shoulders shift uncomfortably.

"It's not impossible. You did it. When you were my age, you had a fleet."

"If you can call a few ships a fleet. They were a gift from Menelik. He was more than my grandfather. He was my instructor, my tutor in the arts of war, my mentor in all things. Much like your uncle is to you, I think."

Their eyes met, finally. Stefana's eyes were dark beneath thin eyebrows. Creeping up her neck past the band of her collar and down her bare arms were black tattoos that evoked the motion of a turbulent sea.

"I owe Uncle Dauvin everything."

"No, you don't." Ambessa thought of her own obligations to the people who had helped her become what she was. Menelik, yes, but also her parents. Her brother Katye, and even Rictus. "You never owe anyone everything. No matter what gifts they give you, you are the one who has to build yourself. You can make a name separate from him, if you wish to." Ambessa turned her hands up in invitation. "My fleet has grown some. I could always use a good captain."

Stefana's face went stony. "It's that kind of disloyalty that shows me I was wrong to ever admire you. My uncle has his own reasons for believing Steward Ta'Fik is best for the Medarda family, and I will support him in that, but make no mistake, General—I have my own reasons, too."

Instead of lashing out, Ambessa stood. Looking down on Stefana, she said, "You're a child still, and you haven't been on your own enough to know what it means to have true responsibility— but if that changes, send word to Rokrund."

Without another glance, Ambessa began to leave. Rictus waited for her at the door to the spectators' box, and it was only his widening eyes that warned her. She turned in time to see Stefana's boot knife speeding toward her stomach.

Ambessa caught the young woman's wrist, twisted her arm, and shoved her against the wall near the worker with the drink cart. He leapt out of the way, and the trolley tipped with a clatter and crash. Ambessa yanked Stefana's arm until the blade Stefana had intended for Ambessa was pointed at her own throat.

Stefana struggled but couldn't break the hold Ambessa had on her. She didn't lose the determined set of her jaw, though.

"What, then?" she spat. "Are you going to kill me, too?"

"I did not kill Menelik, child," Ambessa growled. "And not a witness here would argue against me killing you now—not only am I family, but you tried to strike me in the back." Ambessa sneered in disgust, but more than anything she felt pity. "Ta'Fik has tricked you into doing his dirty work. By killing another Medarda, you would make yourself a pariah, while he gets the benefit. Reconsider where you place your trust."

"What's this, Stefana?" barked a deep voice from behind.

It was Lisabetya. Ambessa could feel her approach, but didn't turn. She trusted Rictus to have her back if Lisabetya made a move against her. "*A Medarda fights with honor.* Yet you dishonor all of us with this behavior."

The third tenet of the Code. How loose was Dauvin's interpretation, if this behavior is what he'd taught his niece?

Ambessa eased her weight off Stefana marginally. "You're young, and you're hasty," she said in a low voice, "but you are loyal to those you care about. That's commendable. One day, though, you'll have to grow up and let go of their coattails."

Then Ambessa released Stefana, but kept the boot knife. The sailor glared at her, fists clenched, as if she wanted to say something else, or take an unarmed swing at Ambessa.

"Girl!" Lisabetya barked again. "If you have any sense in that thick head of yours, take your good luck and run."

Stefana looked between both of the older women and, belatedly, at the other spectators in the box. While some looked pointedly away, others were watching avidly, making their own calculations. Stefana paled. Without another word, she shoved her way out of the box and into the winding corridors of the arena.

Lisabetya grunted. "Too much heart and not enough brains." She tucked away the tiny knives she'd been holding in her great fists. She saw Ambessa notice them and grinned. "My milk teeth. Wasn't sure *how* foolish she'd be."

Ambessa tucked Stefana's knife in the back of her belt and held out her hand. "You have impeccable timing, Steward."

Lisabetya didn't take the offered hand. She started to leave, and Ambessa followed her into the corridor. Rictus trailed them.

"I know what you want, Ambessa, and I cannot give it to you."

"Why not? I didn't kill him."

Lisabetya nodded gravely. "I know."

"Then support my claim. You know this is the last thing he wanted—divided, we are weak. I can bring Ta'Fik to heel now if I have your support."

But the steward shook her head. "I won't get in the middle of this. It would have been better if he'd named his choice, but—"

"Do you know?" Ambessa asked sharply, suddenly suspicious. "Who he meant to name?"

"No. I asked him to tell me for just this reason, but he refused. So we'll figure this out as Noxians do. Good night, Ambessa." Lisabetya pressed a fist to her chest in salute, then turned down a different corridor.

Ambessa paused at the stairs that led back to her own box. "Never mind. Let's go home."

Rictus grunted his assent, and they made their way out of the arena. The streets were darkening with sunset. The last match would be over soon, and then the crowd would stream out like a river bursting its dam to every drinkery and eatery within a mile. For now, though, it was blessedly deserted.

In the distance, she could see the Noxtoraa at the northern edge of the city. It filled her with a certain pride. Her people had done that. It was a long time since they'd won something so great. Ionia. That was still a possibility. She could hand Ionia to Darkwill and deal with Ta'Fik in one blow by getting Caprian to the Grand General. With Darkwill on her side, Ta'Fik wouldn't stand a chance.

"Maybe Katye was right." She did need to find more allies, and she would have to look in some unexpected places.

This would be war, and war would not be won with words alone.

Chapter Eight

Ambessa, what happened?" Azizi rose from his place on their couch, searching her face in concern. He took in the weary set of her shoulders. "Kino, send for the healers."

"No, I'm fine." But Ambessa touched his shoulder as Kino hovered by the door. "Fetch your sister, though. We need to speak as a family."

Kino, his face somber for once, nodded.

Ambessa gestured for Rictus to be at ease. He picked a chair from which he could easily see and reach the door.

Azizi stroked her back, but Ambessa wasn't in the mood for comfort.

"What is it?" he repeated.

"Dauvin's niece. She attacked me at the arena."

"A knife in the back," Rictus added in disapproval.

"The sailor girl?" Azizi frowned, the lines in his forehead growing deeper. "That's...bold. By Ta'Fik's orders?"

"If not his orders, she believes in him enough to try to gain his favor."

Kino returned soon, with Mel at his side.

"Mother? Are you all right? Kino said you'd been hurt."

Despite their recent trouble, Mel hugged her, and that made

what Ambessa had to do even harder. She wished she could stay to guide her—to protect her.

With a start, Ambessa noticed the stripe of gold peeking from the neck of Mel's gown. She pulled it back just enough to see the gold extend against Mel's brown skin. Inflamed. The tattoo was fresh.

Ambessa narrowed her eyes, and Mel straightened under the scrutiny. The child had come prepared to do battle. A part of Ambessa was proud of her.

Another part, a larger part, was stricken with a terrible longing, almost like homesickness.

Smaller still was a part of her full of sudden dread.

Ambessa reached out and touched Mel's chin gently, tilting it away so that she could better see the art that graced her daughter's body. *Familiar* art. She was aware of the eyes on the pair of them. Azizi would have questions, and Ambessa was not sure she was ready to answer them.

"Who gave you these?" Ambessa whispered.

"A Rakkor artist in the city."

In the city. *How dare he come so close?* The dread in her grew urgent, her heart beating faster. Unless something was wrong, and he came to warn her. If *they* knew about Mel—

"What was his name? His work is—unique."

Mel bristled. "I didn't say it was a man."

Ambessa didn't answer, only waited until Mel sighed.

"He didn't give me his name, and I didn't give him mine. I thought it better that way."

"Good," Ambessa said, though she knew it was no accident that Rudo had found Mel in all of Bel'zhun. *But why now?* Just as she was dealing with Ta'Fik. She didn't need additional *complications.*

And yet. She wanted to see him. It had been so long.

Mel still stood there, though, as if she were waiting for something else. When Ambessa offered nothing, Mel asked, "What do you think of them?"

Something within her softened. She glanced at Azizi and Kino, who were watching them curiously, but without comment, Azizi's face unreadable. Oh, yes, there would be questions.

"I think that you were reckless, and endangered yourself needlessly," she said, and Mel's face fell. "But. They are... beautiful. You are beautiful, child."

Mel looked up at her, her hazel eyes wide with surprise, a hesitant smile on her lips. Then she remembered why she had been summoned in the first place.

"Endangered by whom?"

Ambessa finally sat on the sofa. Mel sat beside her, and Azizi on Mel's other side. Kino folded his arms across his chest and remained standing. She spoke parallel to the truth.

"When your great-grandfather died, he neglected to name an heir." His children—her mother and uncles—were long since gone, on this campaign or that. "He's always had his favorites, though. Those of us he trained up from the ground. Ta'Fik and I are chief among those."

And Ta'Fik had hated her for decades for what happened to Zoya. He wouldn't roll over easily; this was too personal to him.

"I have to leave Bel'zhun." Ambessa held up a hand to forestall the protests on her family's lips. "Rictus and I."

"Alone?" Azizi said, alarm turning his voice shrill.

"With the Fist and my ships. Some of the Wolf's Reapers. We're going to speak with Darkwill, the steward of Vindor, and anyone else we can convince to join me."

"You mean a civil war," Kino said. "You want to start a civil war in the clan."

Ambessa bristled at the accusatory tone. "If Ta'Fik didn't

want to start a war, he should have thought twice before accusing me of murdering Menelik and stealing my rightful place in this family. He knows what that means. Not to mention setting his amateurs on me." She cut her hand through the air. "This is not a debate. You will return to Rokrund with your uncle, where you'll be safe. Perhaps it won't come to war. If enough of the stewards support me, our warbands will outnumber Ta'Fik's, and he will have no choice but to surrender."

"I want to come with you." Mel sat on the edge of the couch, her hands folded on her knees, back straight as a pillar.

"You will go to Rokrund and stay there."

"You're going to make allies. I know you and I do things differently, but I can help you create diplomatic ties—"

"You'll be no help in the kind of diplomacy I need to do," Ambessa growled with finality, her hand on her belt knife.

Kino glanced, worried, at Mel, then said, "I want to stay here. I have interests in the city, and friendships to cultivate. They could be useful to you."

Ambessa considered Kino a moment, then nodded slowly. "Yes. Stay with your father. You and Azizi can attack Ta'Fik's interests closer to home. A throttle on trade in and out of Tereshni could cripple his resources." Then she rounded on Mel. "But you will return home with Katye."

Ambessa couldn't keep herself from looking at the gold tattoo peeking from Mel's collar. If Rudo had come, there was the possibility that much more was moving here than just Ta'Fik's petty power grabbing. She wanted Mel beyond Rudo's reach. Beyond *their* reach.

She tried to explain to Azizi when the children had gone and Rictus had gone to his own room next door.

"There may be worse than Ta'Fik after me. After . . . the children. Promise me you'll watch out for them."

"What do you mean?" His brow furrowed. His hair was shot through with more gray—when had that happened? She ran a hand through it. "What's worse than Ta'Fik? Shouldn't you stay, then?"

Ambessa shook her head. "I can't explain it, and it's dangerous to speak of. The more you know, the more you become a target."

"I don't understand."

"You don't have to. Just protect them." She kissed Azizi, then stood. But Azizi caught her hand.

He hummed thoughtfully. "I've been working on certain deals with some of the Shuriman caravans. Ta'Fik makes a lot of money on goods that travel from Bel'zhun to Nashramae. I will cut a hole in his purse for you." His crooked smile was so like Kino's that Ambessa's heart ached with affection.

It also ached with fear. "Fine. I'll leave half of the Wolf's Reapers." They were her most elite warband, five hundred warriors picked from the best of other warbands or hand selected from the Reckoners' pits. They would watch over her family. "Promise me you'll keep him safe, and make sure Mel gets to Rokrund."

Azizi kissed her fingers. "I'll keep our children safe. I promise."

Despite the stress of her new resolution, Ambessa woke with the afterglow of pleasant dreams. Sea spray on the cliffside, a long-limbed dancer, his body painted in gold, his smile broad and his hands strong. She pushed the thoughts away and began her preparations as quietly as she could. Bitter as the pill was to swallow, she told herself that she was doing this for her children. Everything was for them, she told herself as she wrote to the captains of her warbands, of her ships. They would be safer with her gone, she told herself as she wrote to Katye that he was right.

"You're up early," Azizi said, coming into Ambessa's study in his robe. The softness of his belly bulged adorably beneath the fabric. "How soon do you have to leave?"

Ambessa set her pen down and rubbed her eyes. "As soon as possible."

"Before the funeral?"

She sighed. Nodded. Ta'Fik would use that against her, but she had already turned her gaze to the next campaign. There was no further victory to win here, and every day's delay would make a difference.

Azizi kissed her temple. "I'll speak to the quartermaster."

"Be discreet. Please."

Azizi hummed, then went back to the bedroom.

Ambessa finished the letter to Katye, then dressed. This time, she wore her knife and a sword, as well as the light armor the Medardas were known for.

She met Rictus outside her room. She had two stops to make today, both of them out in the city. On the way out, she handed Katye's letter to one of the servants.

How many of them are in Ta'Fik's pay already? she wondered. Just in case, she'd written it in code.

First, Ambessa led them to the Shimmering Market. To see. She told herself that if she saw Rudo, she wouldn't speak to him, but she would know he was in her city. It was good to gather information.

Then why not have one of your people find him? You could do that without gathering suspicion. But Ambessa couldn't release the hold on the thing she had kept closest to her heart for over fifteen years. If someone else went, Ambessa would not get to see him with her own eyes.

People saluted her as she walked through the market, calling out her name: *Medarda, Medarda, General Medarda.* Some only whispered it, but that was all right, too. Awe and fear.

Fear makes allies. Awe will keep them.

Ambessa searched the part of the market where most of the artisans set up their stalls, but he was not there, nor was he in the area where the performers cleared spaces and danced or sang or performed plays and puppetry for coins.

Seeing Mel with her tattoos had been like seeing a ghost. Ambessa had thought she was imagining it—Rudo, walking back into her midst. They had met in Basilich, the biggest port city in eastern Noxus. She had caught him dancing. She had always wondered if he'd *let* her catch him dancing, bait upon the lure.

"Ambessa?" Rictus asked. "What are we doing?"

Ambessa startled out of her memories, her face growing warm.

"Nothing," she said sharply. Frustrated at her girlish foolishness, she asked a nearby puppeteer who had just finished a show.

"Have you seen a tall man, brown skin, hazel eyes?" Oh, those eyes. Ambessa held her hand up to indicate Rudo's height. "Rakkor, with golden tattoos all over?"

"It's General Ambessa Medarda!" the puppeteer said in a squeaking voice, pulling up one of the puppets they'd been putting away and making it salute. It wore what was clearly supposed to be a Noxian soldier's outfit, with a tiny red cloak, though its carved wooden sword was curved like a Bel'zhun scimitar. Then, with the other hand, they brought up a different puppet, in a ragged combination of Freljordian furs, and made it cower. "Don't talk to her, hide, hide!"

Ambessa frowned. "I'm only asking a question. Have I done something to you?"

The first puppet fell to its knees. "No, no, Ambessa Medarda! We are humbled. *You* speak to *us*!"

The second puppet covered its amber-bead eyes. "We know nothing about the golden man with his painted fingers."

She caught the puppet master's intentional slip. "Do you know where I might find this man?" Infuriatingly, Ambessa found herself addressing the puppets. She scoffed in disgust and brushed the puppets aside. "Tell me, or stop wasting my time."

Both puppets hung their heads and shook them abjectly, and their puppeteer imitated them.

Ambessa stormed away, this time more angry with herself than anything. And feeling humiliated.

She whirled around at a tug at her cloak, just in time to snatch at a young pickpocket's wrist. They slipped away from her, but ran into the wall that was Rictus's bulk. He held the narrow forearm in a grip like iron while he squirmed.

"I know you're not foolish enough to try to steal from me, child."

The boy's eyes glowed with intensity. He couldn't have been more than thirteen, but there was a keen intelligence in his eyes. As if out of nowhere, the boy manifested a small piece of paper between his fingers.

"For the Medarda clan."

Ambessa stared down at the paper, then at the boy. A small smirk tipped the corner of his mouth. Ambessa's own mouth went dry. Perhaps this was all worse than she thought, and it wasn't Rudo whom Mel had met at all, but one of *them*. *The order.*

"From whom?" she asked.

The boy shrugged, even with his captive arm. "The gold man. He said to give it to you."

Hope—fear—longing—frustration—all of it lanced through her, one after the other, and then back again. She jerked her head around rapidly, hunting.

"If he was here, you think I'd have a note?" The messenger sucked his teeth. "Look, you gonna tell your giant dormun to let me go or what, lady?"

She nodded to Rictus, who released him, plucking the piece of paper out of his hand. She looked him up and down. He was young enough to be in one of the Noxian student halls. Truant, or something else?

"Would you like a job?" she asked.

He looked up at her dubiously. "No?"

"Let me rephrase that. If you want to become part of my household, go to the Medarda compound. Ask for Azizi and tell him Ambessa sent you."

The child gave Rictus a once-over and rubbed his arm. "Nah. I'll pass."

"As you like. Go then." She shooed him away, but her attention was already on the paper in her hand.

It was folded many times to make the small square that it was. When she finally saw the message, something went out of her, like a punctured mwatis bladder.

Keep a low profile. All is well.

It was his handwriting; she recognized it well enough from the few cryptic letters they had exchanged over the past almost decade and a half. But there was so...little of it, and it opened more questions than she already had. The sense of dread that had followed her since her return from the east grew darker.

They had agreed to keep their distance for Mel's sake. What could be so important that he would break that? And without explanation.

Ambessa had not gotten to where she was without listening to her instincts—instincts her father and grandfather had honed from the moment she could toddle on two feet.

Trouble *was* coming, and Ta'Fik was the least of it.

Chapter Nine

Rictus's stare sat heavy on her shoulders as she led them out of the Shimmering Market—not toward the compounds of the war leaders and the steward and the merchants wealthy enough to share the same space, but toward the humbler neighborhoods. No marble here, no old Shuriman palaces. Shuriman buildings were the majority, though—not as many new Noxian buildings erected in the less desirable sectors of the city. Bricks of sandstone littered the ground where they had fallen from buildings; they had been repurposed as seats outside homes, or ledges to climb to higher levels. She even saw two old women playing a game of dice on one. People covered the empty spaces with diaphanous curtains in red or turquoise or gold, as if the holes in their homes were windows and had been all along. She made a mental note to speak to Steward Dorrik. This was unacceptable, and it would only give the discontented factions in the city stronger motivations.

"Where are you taking us?" Rictus finally asked. His thick eyebrows were low over his eyes, and he watched everything and everyone around him with suspicion.

"To pick up supplies."

Rictus narrowed his eyes at her, but said nothing else.

In the neighborhood colloquially called the Barrel, Ambessa stopped in front of a large building in the old Shuriman style, the clay pitted but strong nevertheless. The arched doorway was draped with a colorful cloth.

"Hello?" Ambessa called. "Rell Canwell, are you home? Lady Canwell?"

A man passed them by, carrying a basket on his hip. He eyed them warily. Another moment, and Ambessa called again. Even with Rictus at her back, she couldn't help but feel like another knife was coming her way. At her third call, a small girl barely at Ambessa's knee peeked around the curtain. She peered up with wide dark eyes.

"Hello there." Ambessa smiled and dropped to the girl's level. "I'm looking for Rell. Does she live here?"

The girl nodded, her mouth parted in an O as round as her eyes.

"Are you her sister?"

The girl closed her mouth and shook her head.

"Could you go and get her for me?"

The girl shook her head again. Then she shrugged and stepped into the building. She looked over her shoulder, waiting for Ambessa to follow.

Ambessa murmured to Rictus, "Keep an eye out here for me."

"This could be a trap."

"Trust me."

Rictus gave her a doleful look, but he turned his back on her to better watch the street. Ambessa twitched the curtain closed, then followed the girl up the stairs, past the curtains of other families, some worn threadbare. So many feet had trod the path up that the stone was worn smooth and the stairs sloped slightly in the middle.

The girl stopped them at a blue curtain that was thick and

vibrant compared to the other tattered ones, with a gold embroidered lion in the center. The girl skittered away, but she stopped up the stairs, peering down at Ambessa from the heights with her large eyes. She must have belonged to one of the other families in the building. Or maybe Rictus was right.

She's just a girl. Paranoia is worse than no instinct at all.

"Rell?" Ambessa called again. "Lady Canwell?"

"What do you want now?" snarled Rell's father as he jerked open the curtain. As soon as he saw her, though, his entire demeanor changed. He saluted. "General Medarda! At our home! What an honor!" He glanced over his shoulder. "I'm afraid we aren't—ah—ready for visitors, especially not someone of your—ah—that is to say, while we keep a better home than many here, we—ah—" He cleared his throat and raked his hand through his short brown curls. His brown skin flushed darker.

Ambessa fixed him with a steady gaze. "Is Rell here?"

"Yes, of course. She hasn't left for the arena yet." He shouted over his shoulder. "Rell! General Medarda wants to speak to you!"

There was a fumbling clatter from within and then a shrill "General Medarda?" Then Rell skidded into the doorway. Her blond hair rose from her head in a great tuft like the white-hot heart of a flame. "General! What are you doing here?"

Rell's mother joined them, hovering just behind Rell.

Ambessa folded her hands behind her back. "Rell. Hello. Would you like to join me on my next campaign? In my warband?"

Rell's mother's eyebrows rose into her pale hair. Hesitantly, she said, "What an opportunity, Rell."

"You would join the Wolf's Reapers, starting as a—"

"Yes!"

"Take time to think about it. Discuss it with your parents."

"I want to come. Please, General, I'm ready." Rell was like a horse straining at the bit to go faster.

"Well—the general's right. It's quite a big decision, though, don't you think, Rell?" Rell's mother pulled Rell back by the arm, hard, making her daughter stumble backward. Her father seemed not to notice. She took Rell by the shoulders and made the girl look in her face. "If something were to happen to you..." She stroked the flare of Rell's hair.

Ambessa understood the pang of a mother's fear. She tried to assuage it. "My parents were honored when I was chosen for my first warband. They were eager to see how far I could rise."

"This is an honor, General, but Rell is our only child." Rell's father stepped between Ambessa and the girl. "This is entirely too risky."

"Riskier than the Reckoner Arena?" Ambessa looked down her nose at him.

Rell's father straightened under her regard. "With all due respect, I have been to war, General. We both know that they are not quite the same."

Ambessa inhaled slowly and nodded to concede the man's point. "You are correct. War is even more deadly, and Rell's comforts will not be guaranteed." She turned back to Rell. "Which is why you need to consider this carefully. Your compensation will include not only your regular pay, but also, should you fall, a portion for your family. Coin is not worth a life, but I tell you this so you understand the reality."

Finally, Rell seemed to pause long enough to take in the magnitude of the moment.

"How...how often do you make these payments?" she asked.

Ambessa tightened her mouth and shook her head. *Too often.* Perhaps the girl wasn't ready after all.

Rell looked over her shoulder to Lady Canwell, who gripped her tight against her body. Her parents exchanged a look.

Then Rell pulled away from her mother and pushed past her father. Lady Canwell reached out again, but Rell shrugged away.

"I understand, General."

"Rell—" her father warned.

"If you join me, you will live and train with the Wolf's Reapers and act as my aide. When I deem you ready, you will join the battle line, but not before then. I will do my best to safeguard you, but as your father says—war is not an arena."

"As her parents, we—"

"She is just a child—"

Ambessa drew herself up to her considerable height. Both of Rell's parents went quiet. "If she comes to fight for me, she is no more a child than you. This is her choice. Rell?"

"I'll come."

"Good. I'll send someone to collect you and your things this evening." Then Ambessa would send her to the quartermaster to get armed and armored.

"I can come now," Rell said quickly. "I don't have much to pack. Just give me a minute."

She pushed past her parents and back into the house, leaving Ambessa with the indignant sputtering of her parents. Neither of them had the courage to protest further, though. When Rell came back with a small rucksack slung from one shoulder, they forced her into a hug that she returned without enthusiasm.

When Rell was finally free, they walked down the stairs in silence. Rell kept her eyes on the ground, and her pale brown cheeks were tinged with color. Ambessa took in the cobwebs and the cracked sandstone.

"There's no shame in coming from humble origins," Ambessa murmured.

For a long moment, the only sound was the scuffing of the stairs beneath them. Then Rell said, "I'm not ashamed of *where* I've come from. It's *who* I came from."

"They love you. A parent will always worry about their child."

Rell snorted and shook her head, but didn't elaborate.

They stepped out into the sunlight. It barely filtered through the shaded warren of this quarter of Bel'zhun, but it felt like stepping back into the world. Rictus kicked himself off the wall where he was leaning.

"Well." Ambessa clapped a hand on Rell's shoulder and inhaled the relatively fresh air. "That doesn't matter, either. From now on, you make your own destiny."

The girl looked up at her with eager hope, and the hunger in that gaze was as familiar as a mirror.

Chapter Ten

Ambessa considered sending Rell back to the Medarda compound, but thought better of it. Better not to let an inexperienced girl enter that den of drakehounds for the first time alone. And if she came with Ambessa now, Ambessa could see how she held up under other environments, beyond the brute strength of the arena. The fox *and* the wolf.

This time, Rictus only raised an eyebrow, and when Ambessa said nothing, he accompanied her wordlessly alert. They were headed into more dangerous territory, this time by the docks. Blocky Noxian customshouses squatted among the bright awnings and domed roofs. The dark gray stone was splashed with graffiti—and little was complimentary to Noxian leadership. While Rictus watched the streets, Ambessa hunted for a particular sign—

"There," she muttered, steering them to a tavern with a bright blue awning. A sign called it ANY PORT. Beneath the awning, a stone table was surrounded by two stone benches, and dockworkers sat with their lunches and a drink to stave off the afternoon heat. On the side of the building, almost hidden by shadow, was carved graffiti in the shape of a Shuriman sun with spears as the rays. The Suns of Bel'zhun. They carved their graffiti because it couldn't be cleaned away or painted over. They weren't always done on the sides of eateries, and they didn't always signify a loyal rebel, but in this case, Ambessa had her sources.

They were confirmed when the patrons at the tables outside stopped drinking and talking to stare at her as she walked into the place.

The inside was well-appointed. Many of the bars near the docks catered to the low types, sailors and dockworkers who were only in for trouble before moving on, but this was a different sort of clientele, and Any Port didn't hurt for custom. Inside, too, the patrons stopped their conversations to stare warily.

Ambessa grinned as she took everyone and everything in. Counted the potential opponents she and Rictus would have to fight if this all went wrong. *And Rell*, she added. There was no doubt the girl could handle herself, even with the simple belt knife she wore at her hip. A man and woman sat on cushions at a low table in one corner, holding hands while they drank tea from clear glass cups. A man with a gray-striped black beard and spectacles was eating a crunchy fried dumpling at a table in the back corner while reading some sort of pamphlet or broadside. Three youths in sailor's short pants were playing some sort of chance game at another table.

The proprietor came over, sweeping an escaped curl back over her forehead. "How may I help you . . . ma'am?" She looked Ambessa up and down nervously. "Our permits are all paid up, I can bring you—"

Ambessa leaned down to the woman's ear and said, "I want to speak to Valif." Then she straightened and pulled out a pouch of coins. "I'll wait here until then. Bring whatever food and drink you have."

The woman swallowed but nodded. She hurried back to the

kitchen. Ambessa led Rell and Rictus to the low table in the center of the room. The lovers downed their tea quickly and left. With a nervous look between Ambessa and the proprietor, so did one of the gambling youths.

"What are we doing here?" Rell whispered.

"Sometimes, you learn more from observation than asking questions," Ambessa said, raising a finger. "Besides, when you ask a question, you betray your ignorance."

Rell nodded her understanding, and her glances around the room became less nervous and more curious. More studious. From the owner of Any Port, who was intent on cleaning the bar with a rag, to the man in the corner who, alone in all of the tavern, hadn't looked their way once.

When food and drinks were brought out to them, Ambessa paid with the coins from the pouch at her hip. Rell dived for the spread immediately, but Ambessa held her back with another raised finger. Rell frowned at the bread and the warm dips and steaming stews, then crossed her legs on the cushion and draped her hands in her lap.

"Tell me, Rell. How did you get started in the Reckoner Arena?"

The proprietor was gone from her bar. Ambessa picked up a grape and rolled it around in her fingers before putting it down. Rell followed the action with longing, then sighed.

"Always wanted to. My family's from Qualthala, but things didn't go well for my mother and father. When I came along, things only got harder. That's how we ended up here in Bel'zhun. I think they saw it as an opportunity.

"It was always a fight for me, down in the Barrel. I got good at doing what I did. My friends and I would sneak in to watch the arena fights from the penny stands." She looked at Ambessa sheepishly. "I think it was my mother who saw me fighting once.

Nearly killed someone with a broomstick. I...got in trouble." She broke off and looked away, as if remembering something too painful to share.

From the corner of her eye, Ambessa saw movement, and reached for the knife in her boot. It was only the man in the corner, beckoning for the staff.

"I don't know when my parents realized there was prize money in Reckoner fighting. I was excited at first. For once, they were letting me do something that *I wanted* to do. Then they pushed me harder and harder. I couldn't see my friends anymore. I spent all my time practicing, practicing, practicing."

"Your prize money goes to them, I take it."

"Mm-hmm." Another embarrassed, downcast look.

"What do they spend it on?" Clearly, they hadn't used it to move.

Rell snorted with disgust. "Clothes. Drink. Going up to the Bells and rubbing elbows before coming down with their pockets empty, waiting for me to fill them up again."

The Bells were what locals called the neighborhoods where the rich merchants and war leaders lived, where Steward Dorrik held his parties. Steward Dorrik, at least, had enough sense to claim neutrality while both Ambessa and Ta'Fik were in his city. Perhaps, if Azizi stayed long enough, he could change that.

Ambessa exhaled her rising anger slowly. "I'm sorry to hear that, Rell. With my warband, everything you earn will be yours—all the glory, all the rewards. But also," she added, "all the consequences. None of this will be easy. You should understand that before we go."

"Where are we going?"

Instead of answering, Ambessa glanced around the room. It had emptied. The remaining youths had gone. It was just them now, them and the man in the corner. He met Ambessa's eyes and smiled. His own eyes crinkled warmly. He stood and came over.

Rictus reached for the weapon at his side, but Ambessa shook her head.

"You've been here awhile, friend," the stranger said. He pointed to the last empty cushion at their table. "May I have this seat? I don't think you'll get to speak to whoever you wanted to find."

"Don't you?" Ambessa eyed the man up and down. He moved with confidence—the kind of confidence that came from a leader of men, not just from never having been knocked down before, or entitlement. "A pity. I had an offer for the Suns."

The man laughed. "The Suns? And what would the Suns want with the Medarda who left them licking their wounds five years ago?" He stroked his gray-speckled beard.

"Was it five years?" Ambessa leaned back and tilted her head thoughtfully. "I forget."

The man grunted. "Give or take. These things pass me by like a dormun fart in the wind." He waved his hand in front of his face.

"They do. I was hoping that our past disagreements might blow away as easily."

"I wouldn't know." The stranger shrugged. "Seems a hard grudge to wipe away for a fighting man. The Suns...Young fighters are prickly."

"And older ones? Intelligent leaders with a sense of strategy?"

The stranger stilled, and his jovial expression transformed into one of canniness. He was a handsome man, his face lined with rough years. He had been the hagyos of Shuriman Bel'zhun before Noxus came. Before Menelik came. There was little blood spilled—at least, not at first. Other leaders of the city, rich merchants and influential families, betrayed Valif, preferring Noxian stability, and it was almost easy after that. Even the warlord who had protected him was easy to buy off after a brief meeting with Noxian steel. But Valif never sat easy with that betrayal and had quietly built up a band of rebels he called the Suns of Bel'zhun.

Ambessa continued. "I know someone was sent to get more of your people. Mine are already here, already watching. They always were. However, I am open to making a deal with you, Valif."

This time, Valif's laugh was bitter. "Ah, Ambessa Medarda. It's good to sit across a table from you at last. I am sorry to hear about your grandfather's death. Whatever else he did, I can admit he was a formidable enemy."

Ambessa accepted the condolences with a gracious nod.

"What do you want from me?" he asked. "As you say, if you wanted me and my people dead, it could be done."

"Exactly what I said. A deal. I know you want to bloody Noxian noses, and I know you've been trying to get your hands on our black powder."

Valif narrowed his eyes in confusion. When he realized Ambessa was serious, he laughed uproariously. "I don't know what you're talking about. Eat." He pointed to the food as he grabbed some himself. He made a show of eating it. "It's not poisoned."

Rell didn't wait. Ambessa almost chastised her, but she supposed it was for the best. Either the girl would get some meat on her bones, or she'd spend her first day in the warband learning where the latrines were.

"The Suns are planning an attack on Noxian ships, taking advantage of the funeral proceedings for my grandfather." Ambessa took the wine, finally, and saluted Valif with it. Then she drank deep. It was sweet and cool and, indeed, expensive.

She had half expected the woman to take her money and give her something cheap.

If Valif was surprised that his plans had been discovered, he made no indication. He plucked up a grape, tossed it into his mouth, and chewed thoughtfully. "As hard as the Medardas have worked to scrape us out of the city—and failed, I might add—why would you arm us now? You would only make it more difficult to put us down later."

"Perhaps this is the first step toward building a certain amount of trust between us. An accord between the Suns and the Medardas. We could come to understand each other better."

Ambessa felt the heat of Rell's stare, but the girl learned fast—she didn't interrupt.

"What then? You want us not to attack the ships? Is that it?"

Ambessa laughed. "Oh no. I want you to attack them all—all of them except mine. I won't stop you, and you can have whatever goods you find on them. All you have to do is leave the ones I say. The harbormaster will be able to tell you which belongs to whom; I'm sure one of your clever little sunrays can figure it out."

"I see. Is that all?"

"No. In particular, you're to target any of Steward Ta'Fik's ships. Keep tabs on his people in the city and disrupt them and any of his business however you can. You're good at that. If he starts sinking claws into the city, pry them out."

Valif inhaled slowly, rolling a grape backward along the table toward himself. He ate it and took another. "Why?"

"That's my business."

"This is still my city. I still care for my people. I deserve to know."

"This is Noxus's city," Ambessa said sharply.

"A certain amount of trust, you said." Valif frowned, but he wasn't angry in a hot-tempered way.

Ambessa relented. "He is a usurper."

"Ah. What makes you think I won't make him a counteroffer?"

"Because this is the best offer you're going to get. And when I destroy him, you're going to want to be on my side." Ambessa stood. She had said enough. "Do we have a deal?"

Valif stared at the plates of food on the table. Rell alone had devoured most of it. He looked up at Rictus, too, who now towered over him. Valif didn't seem cowed at all. He rose and straightened his bright green over-robes and adjusted his spectacles on his nose.

"Very well. We have an accord, Ambessa Medarda."

He extended his hand, and Ambessa took it.

Chapter Eleven

The next day was full of leave-takings.

Ambessa said her goodbyes to Azizi in bed the night before. A passionate goodbye, driven by the anticipation of knowing she marched to war. His own goodbye, knowing that she might not come back to him, and his anger at that.

They had lain in the darkness after, naked and sweating, and he had asked her.

"Are you sure you must go?"

The answer was the same as always.

"Glory is never found at home." Another thing her grandfather had told her. Not part of the Code, something from their nomadic Shuriman forebears, perhaps, but Ambessa found it true nonetheless. "Look after Kino."

"Some glory isn't worth it, Ambessa." Then he had rolled over, but his breathing never slowed into sleep.

Katye's farewell was simple. A letter sent to his rooms, and a young girl in Medarda livery returned with a folded piece of paper before disappearing. She recognized the neatly spaced handwriting instantly. *Rokrund will remain.* She crunched the paper in her fist and shoved it in her pocket. One of the tightly wound, invisible bands around her chest loosened.

The next ones were harder.

She had a servant find Kino and tell him it was urgent. She should have gone to speak to Mel while she was waiting, but she needed to gather herself before that conversation. She went to one of the training rooms to wait.

Half an hour in and sweat dripped down Ambessa's forehead as she backpedaled, absorbing Rictus's blows on her dull practice blade. He swung the lower half of his haft at her ankles and she spun into him, using her own blade to protect herself from his halberd. Before he could cover himself, she jabbed at the exposed side of his ribs, but his cover was already in place, suppressing her.

This was where she preferred to be. The hours in between were torture to her. She preferred to act. To feel the exertion of her muscles as an extension of her will. A well-laid plan required patience, though.

Before Rictus could hold her in place, Ambessa circled her hilt around his wrists, locking the haft of his halberd in place. Her own blade was too far from his throat to do any damage. She shoved, inching closer and closer to his exposed skin as he strained with all his strength against her—

Until suddenly, he was gone, everything she was striving against. He had dropped his halberd to the ground, and her own momentum sent her stumbling into him, and he turned all his strength to throwing her to the ground.

Ambessa stared up at his offered hand, trying to catch her breath. She brushed her sweat from her face with her arm guards as she let him haul her to her feet.

"Thank you." She patted him on the shoulder. He'd brought her a moment of clarity that she could find nowhere else. He nodded somberly, and she knew he understood.

She had never known anyone like Rictus. She had discovered him, a man deep in debt, in the Rokrund Reckoner Arena, the first one she had commissioned. He had impressed her with his calm before the battle began, and his utter annihilation of his opponents. It had taken only a moment for her to understand how he was wasted in the arena. She'd bought out his debts, and when he paid them off fighting, he asked to stay, as impressed with her leadership as she was with him. It only took one battle before she made him a lieutenant, and she had only grown more certain of his value as time went on.

But he's not fit to be my heir any more than Mel or Kino. And she wasn't sure he would accept even if she asked.

As if summoned by her thoughts, a voice called from the edge of the training room.

"Mother. You sent for me." Kino stood at the edge of the padded training floor, gazing curiously around the room with its racks of training weapons sharp and dull, as if he had never been in such a place.

Perhaps she had been too lax with him. Too late now for those regrets.

"Have you come to spar with your mother?" she teased.

"I'm sorry, Mother. I didn't come prepared." Kino smiled ruefully and pointed to his immaculate knee-length coat, bright yellow with red embroidery, and matching slippers.

"Come, sit with me, then." Ambessa stowed her practice weapon and went to the wooden table where there was water waiting.

"What's got you so serious, Mother? It's only a short good-bye." Kino grinned, bright and winning. He had his father's charm, with an irreverence that was all his own.

Ambessa chuckled despite herself, then said, "You should reconsider going to Rokrund. There are strong currents moving around the family. I've been doing my best to make sure they don't touch you and Mel."

"Ta'Fik."

Ambessa thinned her lips. "Among other things."

"I'm more worried about *you*, Mother. He's been rallying the others. I don't think you have long before he sends them after you with fire and steel to drag you from your bed."

Ambessa gave Rictus a silent nod, and the man stepped out of the room to guard it against eavesdroppers and intruders. Kino watched him as he left, but Rictus didn't go far. The room was warm, the light was warm, dim—lit by lanterns on the walls between the weapon racks.

Ambessa rested her elbows on her knees. " 'War is a failure of statecraft.' You told Mel that."

"Ah." Kino laughed softly. "So I did."

"Thanks to you, she couldn't do what needed to be done."

Kino raised his head sharply. "This is not my fault, Mother."

No, she thought. *It is mine.*

"Blame is not important," she said aloud. "The standing of this family is. Don't waste time on words when actions speak more loudly—and are much harder to forget. Actions give us results. Actions protect us."

"Words can protect us. Friends protect us. Deals and favors protect us. Even money protects us, Mother."

"But words are soft. Words have as little substance as the wind and can turn just as quickly—and there will always be people with more money. I will never say you aren't strong, Kino. But you and Mel both must be backed with steel or your words will crumple. They cannot turn a dagger."

"And you expect daggers from Ta'Fik while you're gone."

"Of course I do." She looked at the ground, imagining Ta'Fik and his allies converging upon her.

A frown line deepened in Kino's forehead. "There have been…missing people. Some of the usuals at my parties. They haven't come for a month or two. Do you think this has anything to do with that?"

Ambessa felt a chill across her neck. "Make sure Mel returns to Rokrund with Katye," she said abruptly.

Ta'Fik would attack Rokrund. He wanted to hurt her out of revenge. Ambessa was sure of that. What better target than her home and her children? But at least if Mel was there, she would be behind Rokrund's walls, with all her warbands, with her uncle. And Katye could keep her safe from *them*, too.

Kino's frown deepened. "Why? She'll be safe with Father and me. You said you'd leave some of the Wolf's Reapers. Surely that's enough. Besides, she's quite capable of taking care of herself."

Ambessa made a disbelieving sound in her throat. "She's fifteen, Kino. She sees everyone's potential for good but not their potential for danger. If there are young people going missing—"

He exhaled sharply. "She's my sister. Of course I'll look out for her. What would Ta'Fik want with them, though, any of them?"

"I don't know," Ambessa said. "Alert me if anyone else disappears."

Kino snorted. "It'll take days to reach you, wherever you go."

"Send a message anyway. Send it to Katye."

Ambessa wasn't thinking of Ta'Fik. She was thinking instead of a beautiful man with long dark hair and rays of gold upon his skin. He had *promised* Mel would be *safe*.

"You should at least carry protection. When was the last time you practiced here?" Ambessa gestured to the room around them, the weapons.

Kino laughed again, his humor biting. "Too long, Mother. Too long." He stood and pulled her to her feet. He wrapped her in a hug. He was as tall as her, but he felt so fragile in her arms.

In her mind, he was still the toddling child who tugged at her gold earrings when she carried him.

"Goodbye, Mother. I'll see you when you come back." He kissed her once on each cheek, then left her alone in the room, blinking away the dampness in her eyes.

And so Ambessa's heart was heavy when she knocked roughly on Mel's door. All ambient sound ceased, and she knew that Mel was in.

"Mel. It's me. We have things to speak about."

The silence behind the door stretched, and Ambessa imagined her daughter debating with herself whether to stay silent or to open the door. No matter. Ambessa would not leave without having this talk.

Finally, Mel opened the door, her young face wrinkled in anger, pursed lips and furrowed brow, but she met Ambessa's eyes full on.

"Yes, Mother?"

Mel wore a gown that bared her shoulder and neck, with long sleeves tapering past her fingers. Wherever her brown skin was bare, gold ink traced her in arcs and coils. The tattoos had healed. Slits along the sides of the skirt revealed more markings on her thighs.

Ambessa narrowed her eyes, and Mel straightened under the scrutiny.

"May I come in?"

Mel stepped away from the door, ushering her in.

"Would you like refreshments?" she asked, as if her own mother was a visiting dignitary.

Ambessa felt stung. Azizi was wrong, though. Some sacrifices *were* worth it.

"No, thank you, child."

Mel led her to the small couch in her sitting room. A painting of a mountain at sunset with golden spikes pointing out from behind the peak leaned against one of the walls. It snagged Ambessa's attention, and Mel noticed.

She cleared her throat. "I can be helpful here. While you're gone."

Ambessa pulled her gaze away from the painting—it *had to be* Rudo's. "No. This is not up for discussion. You're going to Rokrund."

Mel's lips pursed tighter. "There are other ways we could pull the other Medardas away from Ta'Fik. I think that—I suspect—I know why some of them might be unhappy enough to go to him, and what we can do to win them back."

"And?"

"Well, take Steward Dauvin. He owns a substantial share of the Noxian grape crops, but he sees good profits only when the warbands are at home. More people to drink his wine. And then there's Steward Dorrik, and he claims neutrality right now, but I know he thinks more should be done with regard to the schools in Bel'zhun—he thinks that we won't begin to make inroads with the rest of Shurima if we don't make it more attractive."

Ambessa bristled. Dauvin was a soft man and had always been jealous of her own recognition. At least Ta'Fik *had* made the effort to distinguish himself in combat. Dauvin wanted only the spoils and none of the work. Even now, he sent his niece to do his fighting for him. Dorrik had always had a bit more of Ambessa's respect. Mel's information surprised her, but Dorrik did have a point—it would make inward conquest easier when the time came. But that was something Azizi could attend to, not Mel.

"That doesn't mean we won't need to fight," Ambessa said.

Mel looked away and murmured something below her breath.

"Speak up, child, or don't speak at all."

"I said, you've named no heir. You aren't the only one looking for stability."

"You think I don't know that?" Ambessa hissed. "But I will not surrender to the man who framed me as a murderer for my own grandfather's death."

Mel pressed her lips shut again and looked away. She didn't have the same habit of looking down as Rell; her expression remained defiant.

"Mel. Have you seen the man who did your tattoos again? Since that day?"

Mel startled at the abrupt change of subject. "No," she said, guardedly, hand rising to her throat. "Why?"

"He hasn't contacted you? Tried to get information from you?"

"You think he'll use me because he knows I'm a Medarda?"

"Yes," Ambessa lied smoothly. It wasn't even entirely a lie. It was naive to think that Rudo would come just to see them, to visit. Too great a risk. If he was here, it was probably for the Rose. That could be very dangerous indeed.

Mel looked troubled, but she shook her head.

"Good. If he does contact you, send word to me through Katye. I don't think he meant you harm," she said, to soothe the worry from Mel's face, "but we can never be too careful."

"As you wish. Will you consider what I said?"

"No," Ambessa said simply as she rose to her feet. "I'm sorry, child, but this man has forced me to run like a thief in the night. He will answer for this with steel. Words alone are not enough for this kind of enemy."

"Not words alone—we would be stripping him of possible allies—"

"*It's not enough.* You will have to trust me on this. I have been here before. I have seen the way this plays out, every time."

Ambessa shook her head. "I didn't come here to fight with you. I wanted to say goodbye. I'm leaving tonight."

"Before Grandfather's funeral?"

Ambessa nodded. Another wound Ta'Fik would answer for. Suddenly, Mel launched herself into Ambessa's arms. After a moment of shock, Ambessa held the girl close. She breathed in the scent of her, the oil in her hair, the perfume she wore.

When she pulled herself away, she reminded herself: This was what she fought for.

Her family.

Part II

Chapter Twelve

Rudo was tired. More tired than the backbreaking journey from Bel'zhun should have left him. Instead of sailing from Bel'zhun to Tereshni and *then* riding inland to the laboratory he shared with Inyene, they'd had to travel overland through the desert because *someone* had set fire to their ships with explosives while they were still in the harbor, coincidentally after Ambessa's ships had departed. Though the rebellious Suns of Bel'zhun took credit for it, Ta'Fik swore it was *her*.

Because Rudo was tired, exhausted, even, he was easily distracted. His mind, well honed in the arenas of magic and self-discipline, kept wandering against his will—

To the memory of a girl with his eyes and her mother's spirit. She was so beautiful with the gold of his art upon her. The only gift he could give her, and it felt more like a gift to him—to adorn her with his love for the first time. He had had to study her from a distance to understand her habits, the time she spent in the Shimmering Market. It had been everything he could do not to weep when she finally wandered past his stall. He could only hope the protection he'd laid within the ink would hold. To keep her safe from harm and—more importantly—safe from the Rose.

Mel.

"Rudo." Inyene snapped their fingers under his nose. "Are you listening? What do you think of this one?"

Rudo blinked Mel's face from his mind's eye and focused on his present surroundings. He and Inyene were in the "laboratory" that the pale woman had discovered for their experiments with magical transference.

The laboratory was more like a bunker, hidden deep underground beneath what appeared to be the ruins of an ancient sandstone keep. The wall above had long since crumbled to nothing but a few great bricks, whittled down by sandstorms and time. The surface ruins had long been picked clean of anything of value, but the true treasure was beneath.

When Inyene had led Rudo to this site the first time, Rudo had grumbled, asking why it had to be so far away from Tereshni. Then, with their magic, Inyene had revealed a passage beneath the sand. It opened like a mouth into darkness, and Rudo felt it: There was power here, something ancient that he had no name for. His own magic hummed in response to it as he followed Inyene down the corridors of jagged, broken-off stone—pearlescent gray, cold, completely unlike the stone above. Someone, or something, had built this place long ago.

Ta'Fik could only pretend at owning something so ancient. In return for the "generosity" of offering this space, Rudo and Inyene would provide magically enhanced soldiers for Ta'Fik's takeover of the Medarda family. Another part of the pale woman's plan to dominate in Noxus—control the most powerful families in Noxus, and she would control the empire.

"What's wrong with you?" Inyene said sharply, pulling Rudo from his thoughts. "Did something happen while we were in Bel'zhun?"

Rudo wiped the slate of his face clean. "What? No. Why?"

"You don't have the attention span of a cat with a mouse. Haven't since we got back."

Damn it. He needed to pull himself together. "It's nothing. I'm just getting old. Travel agrees with me less and less. Especially on a skallashi's back." He stretched for show, and his back offered him a gratifying crack.

"You are lying." Inyene raised an eyebrow.

Unfortunately, they had known each other too long and too well. They had both been raised in the Rose, sent on missions for the pale woman to find artifacts, to find students, to eliminate targets. Rudo had rescued Inyene from persecution during a mission in Demacia. Their ill treatment lingered in the scars on their body—their arms and hands were ravaged. Ever since, Rudo had felt almost protective over the other mage.

"I am not."

"I can practically smell it on you." Inyene softened. "Rudo, what's wrong? Let me help."

"I—" Rudo cast about quickly for the nearest lie he could tie neatly. "You know as well as I that sometimes we have work that even other members can't be privy to."

A deep line wrinkled above Inyene's nose as they frowned. They opened their mouth to speak, but they were interrupted.

"Inyene!" An imperious voice sounded from the entry of the deep chambers, echoing along the hallways like the ghost of some slain king. Inyene had fashioned a single key for non-magical users to enter, and its owner had arrived.

"Ugh." Inyene's lip curled.

For once, Rudo was relieved by Ta'Fik's presence. He wasn't sure how well he could keep Inyene away from the truth, and he would do anything—everything—to keep Mel safe. He had promised Ambessa. He had promised himself. He didn't want killing Inyene to be on that list. And anyway, if he did...it would be hard to explain to the pale woman why their initiative with Ta'Fik had suddenly failed.

"A pity the old man died before he could name his successor. Now we're stuck with this pompous parrot," Inyene muttered.

"We were always going to be stuck with him," Rudo said. "That's the point of the assignment."

Inyene huffed.

Ta'Fik arrived with a flourish, his boots clicking on the oddly resonant stone floor.

"Ah, Rudo. You're here, too. Good."

Inyene inclined their head politely. "What brings—"

"I want to see one of these soldiers you promised me."

"But, Steward, I haven't perfected the runes yet—"

"Tsk, tsk. *If you wait for the perfect weapon, you will fight empty-handed.*" Ta'Fik held out a flat, open palm, then clenched it tight on the air. "Show me what you have." He enunciated the last words carefully, a warning.

The steward had a temper, and though he tucked it away for public appearances, he was showing it more and more behind closed doors. Especially since Ambessa had escaped his clutches in Bel'zhun. Rudo wasn't the only one who didn't travel well these days. (And perhaps Rudo felt more than a little wry pride at his onetime lover. It did *sound* like Ambessa. But he smothered his smile. Not so hard, given the pain in his own back.)

Inyene shared a worried glance with Rudo. Rudo shook his head minutely, but Inyene widened their eyes. Rudo took their point. They didn't really have a choice. Perhaps an example would show Ta'Fik how volatile this process was.

"We need a soldier," Inyene said slowly. "We're out of... appropriate subjects."

Ta'Fik looked over his shoulder at his personal guards flanking him. He pointed to the one on the left. "You."

Without hesitation, the chosen soldier obeyed, stepping up to Inyene. It was almost comical how tall the soldier was in comparison with the other mage. And yet, Inyene was in their element. Rudo stood behind the soldier. He met Inyene's eyes, and as one, they began.

Rudo had perfected his own use of runes after long study—the celestial runes of protection he'd developed lay under Mel's own tattoos. At the pale woman's behest, he'd been working with Inyene on something similar: runes that could be seared into flesh, just like the runes burned into weapons. If they worked properly, these new flesh runes would deaden pain, lend endurance and power to soldiers' sword arms, to their legs. Feats reserved only for the greatest warriors would become habit for these enhanced soldiers. They had been working on this project for some time. It was not impossible—there already were powerful rune mages, like Ryze, whose body was covered in runes. None of the Rose knew how he'd gotten them, but Inyene had been inspired. Why couldn't they transfer this power to soldiers?

And yet, all the tests so far had failed. The runes weren't ready yet.

Still, they obeyed Ta'Fik. They outlined the runes with their hands in the pattern Inyene had developed, Inyene on the man's front and Rudo behind. The runes took shape in the air: Rudo's came in flares of golden light; Inyene's magic was the bloody, deep red of a wound. Then the light sank into the soldier, through the leather of his armor and the cloth of his under-tunic.

The soldier screamed. His cry echoed through the stone chamber until he fell to the ground. He curled on his side and twitched in pain.

"What's happening? What have you done to him?" Ta'Fik snapped.

Inyene held up a hand against Ta'Fik's questions. The three of them watched the pained man for long minutes. Rudo didn't think he imagined Ta'Fik's other guard taking a step back.

Slowly, the twitching subsided and the man's breathing grew easier. He pushed himself up to one knee of his own accord, and held his own hand up before his face. He flexed it open and closed.

"How do you feel?" Inyene asked.

"I—better."

"Compared to before the magic?"

He nodded slowly. "Better."

Inyene began to run through the usual post-experiment health checks, but Ta'Fik interrupted them.

"Excellent," he said sharply. "Let's put it to the test, then."

"Test?" Rudo asked.

"We need to see if these enhancements actually work."

"We need time for them to settle—"

Ta'Fik was already walking back toward the surface, his footsteps echoing through the stone corridor. They followed him outside, the newly enhanced soldier muttering in awe all the way as he felt the difference in his limbs. Ta'Fik called over a squad from the warband he had brought with him from Tereshni. Not the full company, but enough to escort him through the desert safely. Six came at his order, with short swords and large shields. About fifty more waited at attention.

"Fight them," Ta'Fik ordered. "Consider it a training exercise."

Inyene glanced nervously at the group of soldiers. "I don't know if that's wise, Steward."

"If not for this, what have I paid you for?"

Inyene ground their teeth, their jaw flexing.

The enhanced soldier looked toward his oncoming cohort. "All of them, sir?"

Before Ta'Fik could send the man out to be slaughtered, Rudo stepped in.

"First, let us see how you do with one. Then we'll go from there." He added quickly, "No weapons."

The enhanced soldier squared up against his first compatriot, who cracked his neck and flexed his fingers open and closed.

Ta'Fik said, "Now!"

The two soldiers surged together.

The rune-strengthened soldier reached the other blisteringly fast, and the impact of his fist on the other soldier's body resounded with a crack. The normal soldier flew back across the sand and didn't get up again.

Rudo ran to him immediately—the man still had a pulse, but blood trickled from the corner of his mouth. He opened the man's shirt and saw the deep bruising on his chest, the catch as it rose and fell. Broken ribs, maybe even a punctured lung.

"Are you satisfied?" he called to Ta'Fik.

The steward didn't look at Rudo, or the injured man. He stared at his new prize instead, a slow smile spreading across his face. The enhanced man looked back to Inyene and Rudo, his awe turning into a thrilled grin. He looked back at his own hands.

"Again," Ta'Fik said. He gestured sharply toward the rest of the soldiers watching. "All of you, now."

Despite the clear advantage in numbers, the five soldiers remaining hesitated.

"Are you cowards?" Ta'Fik growled. "You outnumber him five to one. Are you Noxians? Fight!"

"We will if you give us what he got, sir," said one woman. She clutched her sword and shield protectively in front of her. She seemed to settle unconsciously into a defensive stance, her copper-studded leather boots digging into the ground. Whether her voice trembled with fear or awe, Rudo couldn't quite say.

Ta'Fik strode up to her and stared hard into her eyes. "If you want these gifts, then prove you deserve them."

The soldier sucked her teeth, but looked at her fellows. A silent signal passed between them, and they put aside their weapons. Then they charged the enhanced soldier as one.

It was still carnage, but at least together, they managed to land a blow on him. Finally, it was just the woman who had spoken up remaining. Her expression as she stared at her fallen comrades was unreadable. She readied herself for the final onslaught, her fists raised. Her leather bracers matched her boots, copper glinting in the sun.

"Incredible," Ta'Fik muttered.

Rudo couldn't help but agree.

Then, just as the enhanced soldier leapt for the woman, he collapsed. If his screams were awful when the magic was placed upon him, they were a thousand times worse now. This time, he spoke.

"Please!" he cried. "Make—it—agh!—stop! Please!"

It made Rudo nauseous. So did the grotesque way the man writhed on the ground, flinging his limbs backward, arching to crack his spine in half.

The other soldier cringed back, all discipline forgotten.

Inyene ran forward and sent a tendril of magic into the man to put him to sleep. Rudo knelt over him, heaving as if *he* were the one who had just been fighting.

Ta'Fik came over to him and examined the unconscious man dispassionately.

"How soon can you do that to an entire warband?" Ta'Fik asked Inyene.

Inyene hesitated. "I— There are clearly things we need to correct in the process."

"Nonsense. It worked fine. He managed five at once, and due

to the nature of the open battlefield, I don't expect he'll need to do quite that much. I'll be able to take the field with a fraction of the fighters *she* has."

"Unless they collapse from pain halfway through the battle," Rudo growled.

Ta'Fik fixed him with a cold glare, taking him in top to bottom. "Then they'll be motivated to end the battles quickly."

"Steward, if you'll allow, I'm sure I can fix it so that there are *no* repercussions; it will just take an extra month or two—"

Ta'Fik took Inyene by the collar, raising them up on their toes.

"I want this ready *now*. I've already given you months. You promised it would be ready."

Inyene visibly swallowed their retort, inhaling deep to keep their own temper in check. Ta'Fik was lucky that he couldn't feel the angry swell of their magic.

"You don't understand how complicated this balance is to achieve. If you don't want your soldiers to collapse mid-battle, it's best that we are certain. Besides," they added, "you have more allies than Ambessa Medarda. You can afford to be patient."

Ta'Fik's nostrils flared with irritation, but he released Inyene roughly. "You'll show me another before the month is out. They'd better be ready to sail then."

"Sail where, sir?"

"That's my concern."

"Of course," Inyene said through gritted teeth. "Will you be leaving more...volunteers?"

"Take what you need from the warband." Ta'Fik pivoted on his heel, his gray cloak swirling like a cloud of ash behind him. The rest of his soldiers fell into line behind him.

"Why do you let him treat you like that?"

"We have commands from higher places." Inyene glared up

at Rudo as they straightened their collar. "Puppets are easier to control when they think they're holding the strings."

Rudo tongued his teeth as he watched Ta'Fik stomp back to his opulent tent. The man would fold it up and head back to Tereshni in the morning, and good riddance. He would find some way to delay, no matter what Ta'Fik threatened. He owed Ambessa that much.

Chapter Thirteen

Ambessa had always loved the sea. In her youth, her grandfather had given her different tokens of his approval at this victory or that proving. Above all, she had prized her first ships, the beginning of her fleet. He had given them to her on her majority. Ambessa's boots didn't touch solid earth for a year after she received them, she was certain of it. The pitch and tumble of the ship during a storm was just another battlefield. She'd jumped to the challenge and found herself equal to it. Controlling the ship felt no different than mastering her hounds; another magnificent creature with a mind of its own that demanded respect and strength. Show any weakness at all, and it would know you were inferior. It would devour you.

This ship, her flagship, she had called the *Golden Dancer*. Braced on the railing, Ambessa inhaled the sea salt air, let it caress her scalp, cool against her tight braids. Clear blue sky and blue waters, as far as she could see, with one of her ships trailing behind her and one ahead. They were a speedy flotilla of five ships, the better to sail quickly, without sacrificing too much attack power. To their north lay Krexor, Lisabetya's land. They'd already passed Kumangra and its song-market to the south. The first week of their journey had passed quickly; there had been so

much to do. Now, several days on the other side of Piltover—
they had made it through the canal expeditiously, due in large
part to Jago Medarda's influence and the not-so-subtle flash of
coin to bump them to the front of the queue—there was nothing to do but wait and let the wind take them, or if the wind was
too slow, to drop oar and row.

"You're sure he'll help us?" Caprian asked. The vastaya looked
nervously toward the horizon. Toward Ionia. He didn't seem
troubled by the sea so much as by the future.

"The Grand General is...hard to read." Ambessa tried to
form a description that would give Caprian confidence in her
plan. She couldn't afford to have him grow skeptical. It was no
longer a simple matter of Darkwill's favor for some nebulous
future—she needed his aid now, against Ta'Fik. It could be the
difference between taking her place at the head of the family
and watching Ta'Fik take everything she'd worked for. "We
simply have to show him how your interests align with his, and
he'll give you all you need. He's a powerful man."

Caprian still looked uncertain, his long ears twitching.

Heavy footsteps signaled Rictus's arrival.

"How is the girl?" she asked him.

The railing creaked as he draped his heavy upper body over
it. "She's got a worse tongue on her than some of your veterans."

Caprian bleated laughter. "Aye, she does."

"I take it she's not feeling better."

A slight smirk curled Rictus's mouth. "No."

Rell had not taken so easily to the sea. She'd started vomiting
practically the minute her feet touched the deck.

"She likes it with the horses," Rictus said. "Says it's the closest thing to land."

"Probably on account of the vast quantities of manure they
drop."

Rictus chuckled and shrugged. "Smells like a farm."

They hadn't come with many horses, just enough for a small foray if they needed to go on land. Her stable was not her strong suit in any case. After she met with Darkwill, she would go to Vindor. Amenesce of Vindor had a reputation as a masterful horsewoman, and the best steeds in all of Noxus came from her stables. Even the prized Noxian warmbloods were a Vindoran breed. Strong cavalry would give her an edge against Ta'Fik. She just had to convince the woman—if she hadn't already been turned to Ta'Fik's cause.

With favorable winds, it would be easier to get to the Immortal Bastion by sea. It might take a little longer, but they wouldn't have to hope the passes in the Great Barrier were clear. Only a few weeks left, at best.

And at worst?

At worst, they could be on the seas for much longer. It was a gamble, but war was full of gambles. So far, the gamble had paid off. There were no ships in pursuit yet, and the way ahead was clear.

The problem with gambling, though, was that luck was never permanent.

That is why we make our own luck, Menelik would have told Ambessa as she was woken from her bunk by an explosion on deck.

She launched out of her bed and into her boots. Rictus did the same. She hesitated only for a moment over which weapon to take—her twin drakehound gauntlets or her sword; she opted for the sword to keep her hands free.

The alarm bell on deck was ringing now, the thunder of sailors running on the wooden planks in their bare feet. Most of them wore the lightest version of the Medarda woven armor—too heavy and they'd be sure to drown under the weight of the fabric. Some didn't wear even that, preferring to go bare chested or in sleeveless tunics beneath temperate skies. Ambessa emerged from her cabin just as her ship shook from the first volley of cannon fire.

"Are we under attack?" Rell shouted, running full tilt into Rictus, unable to keep her feet.

The big man steadied her. "Yes."

"Who?" asked Caprian, skidding up beside them.

"I can't tell yet," Ambessa growled, more to herself than to the others. "Stay safe, you two, and stay out of the way. Rictus, stay with them."

She ran to the forecastle and pulled out her spyglass, but the night was dark, illuminated only by the stars and bursts of cannon fire.

"They've sunk one of our ships, General!" Zishani, the captain of the *Golden Dancer* pointed frantically ahead, her own spyglass clenched in one white-knuckle fist. "The *Silver Mwatis* is going down!"

Ambessa didn't need her spyglass to see the flare of a fireball engulf the ship. She looked anyway, and saw the small figures of men and women leaping over the side to escape the flames. She cursed beneath her breath. *Mages.*

"Who are you?" she growled. Trannit had a strong navy and was already against them, but how would they have word already? They could be Krexorian. Even Mudtowners, though she had never thought they had this kind of firepower, let alone the gall.

"Shall we attack or land, General?" Zishani waited. Her face was pale in the moonlight. "They'll likely trap us if we turn toward land, but at least we could control the circumstances. We'd save more lives and possibly even the ships."

Attack or land? If they landed to the south, these ships would trap her. But the closest place to land on the north continent was Trannit. And she wasn't going to turn back. They didn't have *time*.

"We attack. Break through the blockade."

"Aye, General."

The captain's mate took his signaling horn and blew it in a pattern of two sharp calls and one long. The ships left and right took it up until it sounded like a hundred sea monsters bugling their war cries.

Captain Zishani set her sailors to rowing, the better to reach the vanguard ship where it struggled against the blockade. The other was heavily on fire, now a deadly obstacle for every ship to avoid. Ambessa's rightmost ship fired another volley of cannon at the nearest enemy, taking down a mast. The enemy ship began to list. Ambessa could only clench her teeth together as she watched, too far out of range to help. Through her spyglass, she watched as her own sailors leapt across the railings with grapples and hooks to do battle hand to hand.

"Incoming!" Zishani pulled Ambessa down as a fireball from another enemy ship shot over their heads. Even though it went wide and missed the wood itself, flames caught the sails and burned with unnatural quickness.

"Archers!" Ambessa shouted. "There's a mage on the ship to starboard! Shoot them! Drop that sail into the water, now!"

While a pair of sailors shimmied up the rigging to untie the burning sail, she grabbed a bucket of sand herself and threw it on a flare of embers that threatened to catch on the deck. The *Golden Dancer*'s sail dropped to the deck with a *whomp*, and the weight of the material smothered the flames. Ambessa didn't have time to breathe a sigh of relief.

She kept her head low as she peered around to take in the

battle. They were close enough to the enemy ship that Ambessa could make out the unmarked sail. *Pirates?*

A streak of bright light and wild heat lit up the night.

"Brace!" she warned at the same time as the captain. The ship beneath her shuddered and buckled, and Ambessa caught the scent of burning wood and polish. They had been hit.

The crew's shouts confirmed; they were taking on water and losing maneuverability.

"General?" Rell shouted. She ran across the deck and skittered to her knees beside Ambessa and the mate. "General, what do we do?"

The girl's eyes were wide and uncertain, but her grip on the spear Captain Zishani had given her was sure, and the light woven armor fit her well. The fear was normal. The girl had probably never met an enemy she couldn't point a spear at; you couldn't stab a burning, sinking ship. You could jump, or you could wait to die in it, trapped in the flooding hull. Ambessa scanned the deck for Caprian and Rictus, but she couldn't see them anywhere.

"Can you swim?" she asked the girl.

"Yes?" Rell asked in return, as if she didn't know for sure.

Ambessa stood, bringing the girl up with her. "Hold on," she said quietly. Then, for the whole crew, "Prepare to jump ship! Aim for the northern coast!"

Another gamble. They could all drown. They could be hit by the ships. The crew members gathered only the most useful things, including things to help them float—like planks of wood they hacked off the *Golden Dancer* herself. Ambessa considered running back to her cabin for her drakehound gauntlets, but they would only drag her into the depths.

They waited in tense quiet until the enemy came. Closer. Closer. Just before they engaged, but not so close that they could loose arrows into their backs...

"Now!"

Her sailors and what remained of her Reapers, some two hundred fifty fighters, leapt into the water, their splashes so long to come until suddenly they were all around her. Still, she hunted for Rictus and Caprian among them, but they weren't there.

"Rell, stay with me."

"But—"

"With me! An order!"

The girl didn't protest again, but her fear was written all over her. Ambessa ran belowdecks. The ship pitched as another fireball crashed into them, slamming her into a bulkhead. Rell tumbled down the stairs. Ambessa grabbed for her shirt as she caromed past her.

"Rictus!"

Boots sloshing through calf-deep water, Ambessa followed the sound of angry shouting until she was in the crew quarters. Caprian clung desperately to a hammock.

"I'm not going out there!" Caprian screamed. "I'll die!"

"You'll die if you stay here," Rictus said in a low, calming voice.

"Rictus, we don't have time for this," Ambessa shouted. "Caprian, if you don't move now, what will happen to your people?"

The vastaya looked between Ambessa, Rictus, and the shuddering bulkhead behind him.

"You promised we'd help them! Instead, we're going to die at the bottom of the sea!"

Ambessa glanced at Rell to see if Caprian's fear was contagious. The girl clung to another hammock on the verge of panic.

"We won't drown if you face the sea! Show her you can earn her respect." Ambessa was running out of patience—and they were running out of time. The water was crawling up to her knees. "The sea is part of the natural world. The world you're supposed to protect. Not fear. Come with us. We'll swim for shore."

For a moment, Ambessa thought she'd reached him. His ears twitched toward her. Then they lowered tight against his skull, and he shook his head stubbornly.

They didn't have time for this.

"Rictus, grab him."

Ambessa pushed Rell ahead of her, back up the stairs. Behind her, she heard Caprian's cries and once even the crack of his horns on something hard—but when she turned, Rictus was still standing and it was Caprian who was dazed, slung over Rictus's shoulder.

On deck, there was no one on the ship but the four of them. The *Golden Dancer*, her prized ship, listed to stern, and it was hot with the blaze eating up her planking. She spared a moment for the grief, a different kind of wave.

They leapt.

Ambessa hit the water with a lung-breaking crash. The water chilled to the bone, and it was heavy—*so heavy*. The sword at her hip threatened to pull her down. She floundered for wooden flotsam, gripped the wood for her life as the sea churned her upside down, now one way, now another. She held her breath even though she thought her chest would burst. Then the water calmed enough for her to feel the tug as the wood bobbed for the surface. Now that she knew the direction, she kicked.

She broke the surface with a gasp. Shaking her eyes clear, she oriented herself. One of the unmarked ships was sailing toward the *Golden Dancer*. They would probably try to board her just long enough to bring over worthy salvage. Pirates, then. She hoped her ship would bring them all down with her.

Her other ships were gone, as far as she could see—the two

behind the *Golden Dancer* had retreated, and with them, their troops. The ones ahead were sinking or had been apprehended.

Whoever commanded these unmarked ships would pay for this.

But there was a right order to things.

"Rictus! Rell!" she shouted. "Rictus!"

She swam with one hand and kicked her feet while she let the wooden plank take much of her weight. In the darkness, the swim felt interminable. The wet clammed her skin, and her feet were numb in their boots.

Ambessa swam and she shouted, but no one made any answer, though she saw here and there something bobbing close to her. The first time, she swam to them even though they were parallel to shore, her hope lending her a burst of speed. When she arrived, though, her heart sank. The sailor was dead, their face pale, eyes unblinking, their lips already blue. But it was not Rictus or Caprian, and it was not Rell. She turned herself back to shore and swam.

By the time she reached the shore, cold and exhaustion had sapped everything from her but the last of the adrenaline. Even that had left her with burning muscles and a desperate heartbeat. She tried to push herself to her feet but fell back down immediately.

As Ambessa's body succumbed to weariness, she passed out with vengeance on her lips.

Chapter Fourteen

She woke to a hand on her cheek.

"Rudo?"

She had been dreaming. Of a golden dancer, his dark hair whirling about him in ropes. His face had changed, though, to a woman's face, a face she didn't know, and then another man's, and someone else's—it flickered through a hundred faces until it settled back to Rudo.

Ambessa, he whispered. *I am coming for her.*

As soon as she remembered that dark hiss from her lover's lips, she jerked awake.

It wasn't Rudo's hand but Rell's. She held her in her lap, one hand patting her cheek softly, but frantically.

"General?" The girl's face brightened in surprise and utter relief. Her eyes were bright with tears, and Ambessa couldn't tell if the streaks of salt water on her face came from the ocean.

Ambessa reached for the girl's hand and clasped it. "Rictus? The vastaya?"

The brief smile disappeared and the fear returned. Rell shook her head.

Ambessa swore and pushed herself to her feet. Was she cursed? Was this what she deserved for the arrogance before

Kindred those many years ago? Should she have taken her reward then, instead of craving more?

Reading the bitter thoughts on Ambessa's face, Rell scrambled to her own feet.

"What do we do now?" Rell asked.

"We look for them. For any survivors."

They had washed up on a rocky beach, not the pleasant pale sands on the other side of the Conqueror's Channel. The sun was just starting to lighten the horizon. Ambessa picked up some of the rocks and stuffed them in her pockets. They were gray and sharp. *Anything can become a weapon.* They would need to take care of their actual weapons as well, drying them as best they could, but that would have to wait.

"Rictus!" Ambessa called. "Caprian!"

They found Rictus approaching them, empty-handed. When he saw Ambessa, his face was conflicted.

"Kreipsha," he whispered. His beard was salt-crusted. "Forgive me." His voice was heavy with the ballast of his failure.

"We have to find him" was all Ambessa said.

They kept marching along the beach. They collected half a company, about fifty warriors, most of them weaponless and waterlogged, but still uninjured. One of them had broken an arm in the jump, and only supreme will had kept her clinging to the wood she'd chosen with her broken arm. Ambessa made a note to keep an eye on that one's progress. Captain Zishani was not among them.

Caprian's body sprawled spread-eagle across the jagged stones. The thick fog that clung to the beach almost completely obscured him. Like most of them, he was bedraggled and scratched. A despair deeper than Ambessa had ever known threatened to overwhelm her. Without Caprian, all was lost. Ambessa knelt at his side.

"Shall we bury him?" Rictus asked softly. "We can make the time."

"Not yet," Ambessa whispered, blinking hard. The cuts seemed fresh, the blood bright on his fur.

She applied pressure to the vastaya's chest. It tried to inflate, but the water inside prevented it. Another push. Another.

Then a gush of water burst from Caprian's mouth, and he coughed and sputtered. Ambessa pushed him onto his side so that he could vomit up more seawater, but the vastaya, barely conscious as he was, clutched at Ambessa's hand. Ambessa didn't let go.

After he'd purged himself and was breathing regularly, if raggedly, Caprian looked around. He saw Ambessa and realized he was clinging to her arm like a child. He quickly released her. He ducked his head. "General."

Ambessa patted Caprian's back, then helped him sit up. "Are you hurt anywhere else?"

Caprian patted himself clumsily, then shook his head. "Only my head. I think...I think I hit my head on something—then water, water, water." He winced and scowled up at Rictus. "Where are we?"

"We haven't figured that out yet," Ambessa said.

Ambessa heard the crunching of boots on rocks before the fog parted enough for her to see those approaching.

"Who's there?" She rose from her crouch and placed herself between Caprian and the newcomers. Rictus was at her back, his halberd fitted to its full length.

"Your hosts, of course."

Ambessa drew her sword. Three figures emerged from the fog: a soldier in a pointed steel helm that mimicked the steel covering the muzzles of the drakehounds whose leashes he held, a dark-skinned woman with tight black curls held back from her face with a golden headband, and the pale Trannit advisor from Bel'zhun.

"I thought we left you in Bel'zhun," Ambessa said to the blond man.

He smiled in the dawn's light. "Ah, yes. That would have been my twin brother, Gessik. But don't worry. We knew enough to prepare you the proper welcome." Though he was identical, this twin had none of the fear his brother had oozed back in Bel'zhun. Quicker to smile and much more smug. He wore armor instead of a robe and slippers. "My name is Geskir."

"You're responsible for this 'welcome'?" Ambessa asked. "The attack on my ships?"

"I follow the orders of my steward. My next order is to take you to him."

"I'll take you to Kindred first," growled one of the sailors behind Ambessa.

She was inclined to agree, and she readied herself to spring— there were only five of them, and one wasn't even armed for battle.

Then the fog shifted, revealing the rest of a warband, and Ambessa knew there was no hope for them if they fought here, now.

"Will you drop your weapons, or will we have to take them from you?" Geskir asked. His pleasant expression didn't change.

Ambessa memorized his face, the pink of it, matching his brother, the thin mustache, the smug, thin lips. He would account for his role in this. But first, she would see Smik.

She threw her weapon on the ground at Geskir's feet.

"How kind of you. I needed an escort to the steward."

The smile on Geskir's face flickered away for a moment, but returned quickly. Ambessa turned to her crew and nodded. Though they were confused and some of them openly angry, they surrendered their weapons. Rictus alone seemed confident in her.

Make a decision and see it through, consequences and all.

They were bound with rope by the wrists and handed off to a basilisk rider and left to trail behind it while they walked for at least two hours, dodging the dung it dropped. Intentional humiliation.

Closer up, Ambessa could see that the Noxian holding the leashes of the drakehounds was very young. He had caught Ambessa's eye because of the way the hounds seemed to drag him instead of walking at his side. A new handler, or an amateur. Ambessa scoffed. She would never have assigned a new hound-handler on a mission like this. Too many things could go wrong. She considered heckling the youth, but she wanted to see Smik. Besides, that was beneath her, and they were already being forced to endure indignities.

They arrived at the small castle Ambessa assumed was Smik's as the day burned away the last of the morning fog over the city of Trannit. It was a home in the old Noxian style, tall stone, oddly shaped, as more buildings and wings were added as needed. More than a home, it was a small keep, like an imitation of the Immortal Bastion.

The whole city was at the top of a bluff that overlooked the sea, and Smik's home stood at the top of it with those of the other highly influential residents—the Trannit governor, other members of the Great Houses, and those who had clawed, schemed, or manipulated their way to the top. Like many of the older Noxian cities, it was a warren of stone—as with Smik's house, other buildings were added to as necessity dictated, torn down and rebuilt, always aiming to be the most efficient structures they could be. In Trannit, the stone was water-stained and salt-crusted from the sea spray blowing in from the south. Moss grew thick.

"Welcome to Steward Smik's home, General Medarda." Geskir untied Ambessa's rope from the basilisk. "Will you please follow me?"

"And the rest of my band?"

Geskir smiled. "They'll be shown to their accommodations, of course."

Prison.

"At least let me take my lieutenant, then, and my pages." When Geskir's smile threatened to drop again, she said, "I've walked behind the tail of a lizard all day. At least let me maintain some dignity and have my attendants. Or has Smik fallen so low that he is afraid of a woman and her attendants, even a child?"

Geskir narrowed his eyes. He turned to the dark woman, whom Ambessa had not heard speak yet. She wondered if she was Smik's daughter. She had his complexion, and the same narrow frame, but the resemblance ended there. The woman made an impatient sound in her throat and walked inside. Geskir cleared his throat.

"Take your attendants, then." After a few more sharp orders, two other soldiers came bearing the ropes holding Rictus, Rell, and Caprian. Some of the warband filed into the house behind them, while others marched the rest of her squad away. Geskir bade the drakehounds stay outside the main building—no doubt to catch her if she tried to make a run for it.

They were taken to a grand dining hall, and in it was Steward Smik. His dark curls were gone now, his scalp shaved close to hide his balding. To make up for it, he'd grown out his beard and braided gold through that instead. His coat was a rich, bright purple that suited his dark complexion. Gold embroidery slashed horizontally across the chest. Flamboyant. Extravagant.

He was breaking his fast with stewed pepper beef and a thin

flatbread. He scooped the sauced meat with the bread, and the juices dripped down his hand. Ambessa's stomach growled against her will, but he was too far to hear it. He didn't look up from his food.

Ambessa didn't wait for Geskir to announce her. She approached the table. "Steward Smik. Menelik Medarda has died and announced no heir. Your advisor and your actions both say that you support Ta'Fik Medarda's claim. Is this true?"

Geskir pulled back on the rope attached to her hands. Smik continued to eat, taking his time chewing and tidying his face and then his hands with a cloth. He waved for a servant to take it away.

"You say so yourself," Smik said. His voice carried, clear and imperious, and he looked over Ambessa and her entourage with disdain, lingering over Caprian. "My advisor and my actions speak plain. Why do you ask, then?"

Noxus had only one Grand General, but it seemed that Smik had forgotten that. He behaved as a lord of the kingdoms to the west, spoiled and arrogant.

"I wanted to hear your foolishness from your own lips, that's all. To make sure that no one has lied in your name or taken control of your forces."

Smik's face pulled distastefully. "And why would you care about that?" He laughed. "You can't think to save me from some kind of—insurrection? From blackmail?" He laughed harder, incredulous.

Ambessa made no answer but to hold his gaze until he grew visibly uncomfortable.

He cleared his throat. "Take them away," he told Geskir. "See how you enjoy my jail while you wait for Ta'Fik to do what he wishes with you."

The woman bent down and spoke into his ear. He nodded, but Ambessa couldn't tell what passed between them.

Geskir led them back out, shoving Ambessa roughly ahead of him. The young hound-keeper was where they had left him, sitting on his heels. He jumped to attention when he saw Geskir. Morning had come. It didn't seem that the day should be as bright as it was.

"Come on," Geskir snapped at the young handler. "To the Hold."

"The Hold?" Ambessa asked.

They wound through the city, opposite the way they'd come, away from the sea.

"Shut up." Geskir jerked her rope, cutting into her wrists. But he couldn't help gloating. "The jail here isn't in the keep. We've got a special place for people like you. Even *if* you got out into the tunnels, you'd never escape the mages."

Mages? Ambessa tucked that bit of information away. A mage-guarded prison wasn't something to take lightly.

"People like me? You mean war leaders? Leaders of the clan you serve?"

"I serve Noxus." Geskir straightened himself up. "It's a place for people who think too highly of themselves. No fighting your way out of the Hold."

Ambessa grunted. She would see about that.

Chapter Fifteen

Mel found it strange to sit in her mother's box at the Reckoner Arena without her and watch the blood sport below. It had never been Mel's favorite entertainment. She didn't understand the thrill of watching people fight for coin. It seemed a waste.

Kino thought the same thing. "I just don't see the point," he said. He swallowed the last of the wine within his glass. "Why would you want to get hit for fun, when you could sit up here and drink instead?" He held his cup out, and a silent servant refilled it for him.

And yet, they were both here, watching the match below, for their own reasons. Mel thought, perhaps for both of them, missing their mother was one such reason.

As much as she missed her mother, though, Mel couldn't help but breathe more easily without her mother's glower over her shoulder, ready to find fault with everything from her ideas about diplomacy to the delicacy of her step. She felt as if she could finally stand up straight again.

Which was why Mel was watching *this* match.

Below, in the dirt of the arena, their cousin Tivadar fought like a blur. Her two azirite-edged scimitars flashed like fire in the light. It was as beautiful as a dance. Had her mother been here to watch, she would have respected it, no matter that Ta'Fik was Tivadar's father. Mel was not jealous, though.

Tivadar's opponent was the reigning champion; the new champion, after her mother's favorite, Rell, abandoned the arena to join Ambessa's warband. Mel wasn't jealous of *her*, either.

Their mother had been gone for a month now, and they had had no word since—probably, Mel told herself, because she was not in Rokrund, where her mother expected her to be. Not because she was hurt. A part of Mel wished she could have gone with her if only to know that she was well.

"Tell me why you're so interested in her of all people," Kino drawled. "She's not the sister that Ta'Fik would tell all his secrets to. She's the youngest. There's a reason why she's still here."

"I'm the youngest," Mel said sharply. "She could be here for the same reasons we're here."

"Because her father thought she was useless, like our mother thinks we're useless?"

"That's not why we're here." Mel's face warmed. It was not why *she* was here, anyway. "I know she thinks I'm better off in Rokrund, that I can't take care of myself, but she's wrong. I'm going to help her, and I'm going to do it my way."

Kino waved away her protests, laughing softly. They had already had this fight when she refused to leave on Katye's ship. Kino had threatened to carry her over his shoulder himself until their father said heavily, "If you can stay here, so can she." She'd felt her father put the mantle of duty on her shoulders then. By letting her stay, he was giving her a chance: *Prove yourself.* So she would.

"Your way." Kino laughed softly to himself. There was a tinge of bitterness in it. "Speaking of *your way*: You're entitled to your secrets, but—those tattoos. You didn't get them from Inyene, did you?"

Mel reached self-consciously to her throat. "Inyene? Steward

Ta'Fik's advisor? Inyene isn't from Targon. They're Noxian, I think."

"So you've been asking, too."

Mel flushed again. "Of course. *Information is the most valuable currency.*" They spoke the words together, a saying their mother had drilled into them.

"*Because a smart man will give up gold to get it.* Maybe you're right. Maybe we're not useless here."

"What did you find out about them?"

"Not much. That's what's got me curious. They're new to Ta'Fik's inner circle, and yet, he seems to take their advice exclusively. Before Grandfather died, I'd see them whispering together like old gossips."

"Maybe I can learn more from Tivadar. I think I can win her over. As you say, she and I have a few things in common."

Kino laughed, this time with actual mirth. "I'm sorry. You're not useless. But, sister—be careful."

Mel and Kino waited for Tivadar at the champions' exit. When she saw her cousin, Mel waved and called out. Tivadar jerked back, lip curled, and she looked around her before approaching, as if hoping Mel was calling out to someone else. When there was no hope, however, she came warily, expecting an ambush.

Tivadar had scrubbed herself clean of the sweat and dirt; her pale brown skin was slightly pink. Her casual clothes imitated her fighting leathers, all belts and a rigid shoulder pad.

"Cousins," she said tersely.

"Congratulations on your match, cousin!" Kino said. "What a fight! I'm glad I laid odds on you." He tapped the purse at his pocket, heavier now that he'd collected his winnings.

"We wondered if you'd like to come get a drink with us. With

Gintara gone, we thought you might be—" *Lonely* wasn't a word Mel thought would go over well with this warrior, however much she suspected it to be the truth. "Bored. Kino, where are those noodles you mentioned? Kino knows the best places in the city; you must let him take us." Mel put her hand on her brother's arm and held on to it, smiling disarmingly.

Tivadar grimaced and looked back toward the arena. Perhaps she had friends there whom she was loath to leave, but Mel didn't think that was what was holding her back.

"Is there someone else you'd like to invite to join us?" Mel asked.

"Oh, come on. There's no harm in getting to know your cousins. It's just one night, and you can go back to hating us in the morning." Kino's smile was just as disarming, and he seared right to the core of Tivadar's hesitation. That was enough to banish it.

"Fine," she grumbled. "But you're buying."

Kino grinned. "I'm sure you'll find that's *not* the case. Let's go, then, double time."

Kino did not, in fact, move double time—he was already somewhat drunk, and his long strides were leisurely as he pointed out the different landmarks of the city and how he'd made his stamp upon them. Tivadar listened with unconcealed annoyance.

"He really doesn't know when to stop," Mel muttered conspiratorially. "But you'll see why I keep him around in a minute."

"I heard that, sister mine."

"I have no idea what you mean, brother." Mel turned to Tivadar. "Is Gintara like this?"

Tivadar frowned. "Like...what?" It sounded like she was keeping herself from saying something insulting.

Mel sighed in mock exasperation, gesturing at all of Kino.

"No," Tivadar said. "I admire Gintara very much. Though I'm almost as good a fighter as she—I'm not as strong as her, but

I can beat her four or five times out of ten—she's a better leader. It's why I spend so much time in the arenas. She has taught me very much." Her voice grew wistful.

"Why didn't she stay?"

The brief openness in Tivadar's face shuttered. "She's a leader. She commands warbands. She doesn't have time to drink and play games on fake battlegrounds."

Mel missed neither the bitter shot at herself and Kino, nor the self-loathing in Tivadar's words. "You're an excellent fighter," she said. "It was amazing to watch. Normally, I don't."

Tivadar glanced at her suspiciously, looking for the poison in the compliment.

"Here we are!" Kino interrupted, throwing his arms wide. "Welcome to Jahven's Noodles! Spiciest noodles in all the empire!" He threw open the door and ushered them inside. They were greeted as warmly by the owner as they were by the delicious smell of fresh noodles and stews.

"Thank you, Lord Kino, thank you, here, sit, sit." The woman led them to a large table as if it were waiting just for them.

"Please, Madam Jahven, it's just Kino. Remember?" The grin had a much better effect here than it had on Tivadar. Madam Jahven, who had to be as old as their mother, blushed and waved him away.

Without their asking, a bottle of yellowish liquor and bowls of steamed and salted beans and vegetables were sent to their table before they'd even had time to settle in their seats.

"You see?" Kino poured them each one of the small cups. He raised his. "To my excellent skills of procurement."

Mel laughed, but she raised her cup anyway. From the corner of her eye, she saw that Tivadar crossed her arms over her chest and didn't touch hers at all. Kino shrugged and drank his in a gulp. Then he took Tivadar's and drank that, too. Mel swallowed hers more delicately. It was a smooth liquor, stronger than the wine she took occasionally with dinner. She shuddered, and cleared her throat to cover it.

A few moments later, three bowls of coiled noodles coated in a slick red oil slid steaming in front of them.

"Allow me to show you how it's done." Kino took a pair of eating sticks and plucked the end of a noodle up and into his mouth. Then he slurped it up steadily, noisily, until his bowl was empty, and Mel realized that the bowl of noodles was actually one single noodle. Kino smacked his lips, then patted them with a cloth napkin. "Delicious."

Before Mel or Tivadar could say anything else, Kino waved to someone across the room. A very pretty woman with skin the color of clay and thick, dark hair falling in waves beckoned him over.

Kino stood and bowed to Mel and Tivadar with a flourish. "I do hate to drink and run, but"—he cleared his throat—"I'm sure you understand. Duty calls, and I am a Medarda. I always answer. Ask dear Madam Jahven for whatever you like. It will go on my account."

Then he glided away to the woman and her friends. For a moment, the two women watched Kino as if he were an exotic animal exhibiting absurd mating rituals.

"If he were my brother, I would have stabbed him already." Tivadar didn't uncross her arms. "So what did you drag me all the way out here for? I know it's not because you like the way I fight."

Mel met Tivadar's gaze. Her eyes were a cold brown, her jaw sharp. No matter what, Tivadar was still a Medarda. Mel couldn't underestimate her.

"You're my cousin. It's good for us to get to know each other. I don't want us to be like our parents, with whatever ill blood lies between them."

"You don't even know, do you? She never told you."

"Told me what? If there's something I don't understand, help me."

"Why should I waste my time?" Tivadar slapped her palms on the table and pushed herself up. The untouched noodle in her bowl wobbled.

Mel grabbed her cousin's arm, which was a mistake. Tivadar escaped her grip with a twist and captured Mel's forearm in a vicious grip.

"Don't touch me," Tivadar growled.

"I'm sorry." Mel swallowed. "Please. Tell me."

Tivadar threw Mel's hand away. Hands still flat on the table, she bent over.

"Your mother bastardized the Medarda Code, but Menelik went along with it. So fuck her and fuck him."

"Wait—" Mel reached out again to touch Tivadar, but withdrew her hand just before she did. "You don't— You disagree with the Code? You don't follow it?"

Tivadar scoffed. "What's there to agree with? You're either strong enough that you're always following it, or you're so weak that you can't and you die for it."

"Is that what your father told you?" Mel said quietly.

"What would you know about it?" Tivadar looked down at Mel, taking in her gown, her pinned-up hair. Tivadar kept hers shorn close to the scalp. She left without waiting for an answer.

"More than you know," Mel whispered quietly to herself.

Fortunately, Mel was as stubborn as every other Medarda. A few weeks later, she waited for Tivadar at the Reckoner Arena after another one of her bouts. She was alone this time, and determined not to feel unnerved by that.

A ring was already purpling around Tivadar's eye. She had lost tonight, and her anger filled every motion of her body, from her glares up and down corridors to the protective hunch of her shoulders. Tivadar was also alone, but then she always was.

It was something Mel had noticed about her cousin. Where Kino had his many admirers and connections, Tivadar held herself apart from everyone. At first, Mel thought it was just arrogance, and that Tivadar thought no one was worth her time. She didn't spend time with any of Kino's sort, nor did she spend time with the Reckoners outside of bouts and training. But the more she watched Tivadar, the more Mel caught the longing on Tivadar's face as Kino's friends gathered and passed her by.

After that day in Madam Jahven's noodle bar, Tivadar hadn't approached Mel, either. She studiously ignored Mel anytime she tried to catch her eye. So it was time for Mel to make herself unavoidable. She stepped out into the fighters' corridor where it met the spectators', on the way out of the great arena.

"Tivadar! Hello!" Mel stopped right in Tivadar's path.

Tivadar jerked back, scowling before she realized who it was. When she did see Mel, the scowl deepened. "Mel." She brushed past Mel, trying to outpace her, but she was limping and Mel matched her easily.

"You're hurt," Mel said softly.

"I'm fine."

"And you're a liar."

Tivadar's back stiffened, and for a moment, Mel thought she had misjudged. If Tivadar decided to fight her...but no. Tivadar kept walking.

"Leave me alone."

"You're already alone," Mel said. "Every day. Would you like company tonight?"

"If I wanted company, I would find it."

"Hear me out." Mel reached out for Tivadar's arm, but remembered what happened the last time. She didn't touch her, but Tivadar stopped long enough for Mel to stand in front of her. "Have a drink with me. We don't have to talk about our parents at all. I just— Maybe I'm projecting. I've been lonely. I could use some company."

"You have plenty of company. Your brother. Your father." Tivadar flicked her hand dismissively. Bitterness colored her voice. "All the nobles you flit about with. Even the servants at the compound."

"I know. But they're not . . . friends. Kino and my father treat me like a child, and the nobles—well, that's more political than anything. You know how that is." Mel smiled ruefully.

"I don't." Tivadar brushed past her again and into the cool night air.

"We have more in common than you think," Mel called after her.

Tivadar didn't stop, so Mel followed her, pulling her shawl tighter around her. Tivadar shivered once but ignored it and kept walking. The sky above was clear and littered with bright stars. The sound of carousing seemed more distant than it was. It was like they really were alone in the world, just the two of them.

"Are you following me now?" Tivadar asked dryly.

"I told you I was lonely. At least this is company."

"So you're desperate as well as pathetic?" There was a quirk of laughter behind the barb.

"And some of us are cruel in our loneliness." Mel shrugged. "A matter of personality, I suppose. Kino is the one who makes easy companions. He gets it from our father. He has every chef in the city ready to make him a meal."

Tivadar grunted. "Gintara's the same. Her soldiers line up for her like hounds in a kennel. I can't even get a warband to put their practice weapons away."

It wasn't exactly the kind of confession Mel had been hoping to elicit, but she went with it anyway.

"I've fallen short of what my mother hoped, too." She didn't have to pretend at the ache in her voice. For a moment, she wondered how wise it was to share any of this. How much would get to Ta'Fik? But she wouldn't get Tivadar at all if she didn't offer her something of herself. "She took me all over Noxus to teach me to be useful, and in the end, she left me behind. I wasn't good enough."

"Neither was I." Tivadar gave a soft, bitter laugh. "It's always been Gintara. She's the golden one. The better warrior, the better strategist. I thought I could win his attention in other ways, but…"

Mel tensed, wondering if she had misstepped after all. She was, after all, very alone with Tivadar, and not even Kino knew where she was. She'd even slipped away from the Wolf's Reapers, who followed her almost everywhere. Many of the shops lining the street had their lights out, but if she ran fast enough, surely there would be a tavern she could seek refuge in.

Tivadar noticed Mel's hesitation and realized what she said. She looked abashed.

"I'm sorry, that's not what I meant. I meant in the arena. I'm—I'm not going to hurt you."

Instead of pushing, Mel said, "Would you like to get that drink? It sounds like we have even more in common than I thought."

Tivadar snorted. "I don't drink."

"Tea, then."

"Fine."

"And Tellstones. I may not beat you in the arena, but I bet I can beat you at Tellstones."

Tivadar's bruised mouth pulled up in a half smile. "I would like to see you try."

Chapter Sixteen

They picked up horses for the guards from the city stables. This time, Ambessa would have the pleasure of walking behind horseshit instead. Ambessa waited for the right opportunity to overpower the guards, but it never came. There was no way they would escape the soldiers on foot and those on horseback. Then there were the drakehounds, with their steel masks over their muzzles, over their thickly muscled chests. Fast as wolves, and deadly hunters. Their eyes gleamed red behind the metal. Their spines were sharp, their whiplike tails lethal. She had seen them turn their teeth to humans before. She did not want to be one of them.

Rictus and Rell marched beside her, their wrists bound, held by other, less talkative guards. Rell's face was pale with fear, but she governed herself well. She locked eyes with Ambessa only once, and when she did, she straightened her shoulders and walked as if Geskir were leading them to opulent chambers. Caprian, on the other hand, seemed to have been cowed by his near-death experience in the sea and displayed none of the bold-ness he had when Ambessa had found him in the Binan prison. Despite his great horns, he seemed to shrink as he ducked his head into his shoulders.

The opulent chambers in question turned out to be a system of caves cut into the bluff that Trannit sat upon.

Now she understood Geskir's cockiness. She would be forgotten, and no one would find her there. The thought brought her as close to fear as she had come in a long time.

Ta'Fik will come, she reminded herself. He wanted to see her brought low. He wouldn't deny himself the chance to gloat. Then, if he were smart, he would kill her.

What would that mean for her family?

It wasn't until Geskir and the other soldiers dismounted that a plan began to form. If she bided her time, locked in the prison belowground, her options would shrink.

She locked eyes with Rictus. Their glance needed no words. To Rell, though, she mouthed, *Be ready.*

They had only this chance, a slim one: Ambessa knew drakehounds. She respected them, respected their power, their autonomy. They were obedient only to greater power. This young handler had none, and she could see the hounds' distaste for him in their lack of attention, how they roved as far as their leashes would allow, how they hung their heads low and growled to each other. Even their armor needed better attention—the shifting plates caught and stuck where they needed to be oiled.

She knew also that most of the Medarda drakehounds came from the same kennels before they found their owners, and at those kennels were trained with the same basic commands. Give chase. Come. Kill. Stop. Each command a particular whistle that their unique ears could pick out.

The soldiers tied their horses to the stakes outside the jail. The young hound-keeper looked to Geskir for orders, and in his inattention, the drakehounds clawed the dirt in boredom.

Now.

Ambessa gave the sharp two-part whistle for "give chase,"

and the drakehounds perked up. One of the three tilted its head, while another sniffed the air, looking for the prey in question. The handler jumped, looking wildly for where the sound had come from.

It *was* the right command. She whistled again, sharp and certain.

"No!" the handler cried. He jerked at the leashes, but the drakehounds pulled harder. One of them even snapped back at him. He fell onto his backside, squealing.

Rictus timed his move perfectly. While the soldier holding him was distracted by the drakehounds and their handler, he took his rope between his bound hands and pulled his guard off-balance. As the guard toppled toward him, Rictus took his two hands clasped together and bashed them into the other man's face. He flew backward with a nasty crunch, blood spurting from his nose.

Rell caught on quickly, jerking her own captor.

"Stop them!" Geskir cried.

Ambessa focused on the drakehounds. At the scent of blood, they grew even more agitated.

Frantically scrambling to his feet, the handler tried to whistle the "halt" command, but his lips couldn't form the shape—he was too scared, every whistle turning into a desperate whimper. With a great tug, the largest drakehound pulled away and sprinted into the distance. The rest clawed and whined after it. In his desperation, the handler crawled to his knees and cuffed one behind its plated ears.

That was the wrong thing to do. The drakehound he'd hit turned to snarl at him, and that was what Ambessa had been waiting for. She whistled the single low-pitched command: kill.

This time, the remaining hounds didn't hesitate. They launched themselves at the handler who had hit them. The youth screamed as one buried its teeth in his hand, the other, his arm.

Time to go.

Ambessa knocked Geskir to the ground and launched herself toward the horses tied up to the post. She climbed onto one, and it shied beneath her. The new rider made it nervous—or maybe it was the drakehounds in their savagery. Rictus had taken down another two of the guards and was unceremoniously throwing Caprian onto a saddle. Rell's guard was now wrapped up in the same rope with which she had held Rell, and the girl was backing away from the angry beasts.

"Up, child, up!" Ambessa cried, kicking her horse on and pulling Rell's mount behind her.

The cry stirred Rell from her horror. Ambessa began to slow the horses for her, but she didn't need to. Rell took a running leap, caught the saddle, and threw herself onto it.

It was beyond impressive. It was masterful.

There was no time to admire, though, not if they wanted to live.

They kicked the horses to a gallop, but they weren't so fast that they didn't hear the handler's last cry, shrill and piercing in the afternoon.

Only Rell looked back.

At first, they rode without thinking where, just away. When it seemed they had gotten enough clearance, Ambessa slowed.

"We must turn around," she said. "We've been riding north."

"Vindor is north," Rictus rumbled.

"And Smik is south." Ambessa reached for the weapon at her side and found nothing. All she had for the journey was on those ships that *he* had taken. Along with her warband and her crew. She wheeled her horse toward the south. "I have unfinished business with him."

"You have unfinished business with Ta'Fik."

"He's Ta'Fik's hand."

"Exactly. If you have an opening, do you strike the hand or the head?"

Ambessa bit her tongue. She didn't turn her horse back to the mountains, though.

Rictus put a hand on Ambessa's arm. "The bigger picture, Ambessa. Vision. Remember?" He jerked his head toward Caprian.

Ambessa closed her eyes. Oh, how sweet it would be to thrust her way back into Smik's inner sanctum like a blade, and from there, into his heart. But Rictus was right. There were greater things at stake.

But, said a voice in the back of her mind, *wouldn't it be more prudent to deal with this threat at your back now? Eradicate it.*

There was reason in that, too. However, she could see Rictus's point. She needed to get to Darkwill with Caprian. Vindor was a step toward that. To take down Smik in his own home, and to escape—that would take time to plan, and it would only gain her so much. Ta'Fik would come at her even stronger.

No, her vengeance against Smik would have to wait. It would come, though. That much, she vowed.

"What about the rest of the band? The ones in the prison?" Rell frowned. "We're not going to leave them, are we?"

Ambessa raised her eyebrows at Rictus, as if to say, *See?* She could use another fifty of her best.

Rictus huffed. "We must."

"But that's not fair, they're *our* fighters, we have to go back for them! Smik might—I don't know, he might torture them when he finds out we're gone! Or worse, they'll think we abandoned them."

"It's possible." Ambessa sighed. "This shall be another lesson. Vision means seeing the sacrifices that must be made. They are soldiers. They will wait until we arrange an exchange, or I have freed them with Smik's or Ta'Fik's blood. And if Smik hurts them, I will avenge them."

"Blood either way, then?" Rell asked, growing somber.

Ambessa tilted Rell's chin up and stared down into her eyes. "Strength. Strength either way. Sometimes we express that strength in blood. A Medarda does what it takes. No matter what it takes."

Rell ducked her chin away to nod, but Ambessa took it back. "Do you understand me, child?"

"Yes, General. I do."

"Will you follow me?"

"Yes, General. I will."

"Then come. We ride for the mountains."

Finally, with the city far behind them, it seemed best to pause and let the horses drink. Rictus riffled through the animals' saddlebags, organizing the useful things into piles. Those piles were unfortunately small.

"What?" Ambessa asked him. He was squatting on his heels, studying the piles. Rell squatted just behind him, studying but dumbfounded.

"The good news is, they kept weapons strapped to their saddles." He pointed to a bow, a sword, and a spear. "Bad news is...no food."

"Hmph. A short journey from the city to the jail."

"What do we do, then?" Rell asked. "How do we get all the way to Vindor with no food?"

Ambessa and Rictus shared a glance, and then laughed.

"We hunt, child. Just like the drakehounds." Ambessa took in the daylight filtering through the trees above. "But first, we get as far away from pursuit as we can."

They rode through the afternoon and into the early evening. As dusk came on, Rictus reined them all in. While he and Caprian went to find food, Ambessa taught Rell the finer points of setting up camp in the wild: the right wood and tinder for a fire, how to make a shelter if you needed one. The girl was a quick and eager study, and by the time Rictus had returned with one rabbit and a fistful of fresh herbs, Rell had started a fire for them to cook it on. Caprian, on the other hand, held two rabbits in each hand. He strutted back into the camp, chewing on the long stem of some kind of grass, a spark of his old self returning as he cracked through the cocoon of fear he'd built around himself.

"Just the one?" Ambessa teased Rictus.

"I did my best," he grumbled. "Don't worry. I left a couple traps for overnight. I won't let you starve."

They would begin the crossing of the mountains tomorrow with all haste. The Great Barrier was a dangerous place for four travelers alone, and not because of outlaws.

Ambessa took the first watch. She stared into the darkness, imagining red-eyed, snarling drakehounds. It wasn't the young handler's scream she heard in her memory, though.

They doubled back through the mountains, following goat tracks until they found what might have been a hunter's footpath—that is, only slightly more defined than the goat tracks. Caprian followed them nimbly, always with a stick or some piece of foliage to chew on. They kept a nightly patrol, too, everyone in pairs. Ambessa made sure Rell had plenty of practice; even in spring, crossing the Great Barrier was no mean feat.

The deeper into the mountains they went, the twitchier Caprian became.

"What's wrong?" Rictus rumbled.

Caprian scented the air, his ears perked and alert. He paused his chewing. After a moment, though, he shook his head. "Nothing. It's nothing."

But they tightened the nightly watches anyway.

And so they trudged on. They'd been traveling for nearly two months when Ambessa was shaken awake roughly.

Ambessa went immediately for the sword beside her, but Rell stilled her with a hand to her lips. The girl crouched low over her and turned slowly, indicating with her fingers one direction, and then again, toward the other side of the cold fire where Rictus lay, Caprian crouched over him. Though Rictus was still, Ambessa could tell he was no longer sleeping. The horses, however, were agitated, whinnying and shying away from the outer trees.

She was about to ask the girl what was wrong when she saw them.

Eyes glowing red in the darkness. Several pairs of eyes. They were surrounded. And unlike the drakehounds in the kennels, these wild ones wouldn't respond to her whistled commands. Drakehounds were distant relatives of dragons, and it was always dangerous to come across a wild pack, where that ancient blood was volatile and untamed. Even tamed drakehounds were only a half step away from their true natures.

Though the drakehounds originally came from the mountains of northern Noxus, packs were not completely unheard-of in this region, especially if competition for territory grew fierce.

Slowly, Ambessa unsheathed her stolen sword. Slowly, she rolled her legs beneath her. Slowly, she rose to a crouch. Rell followed her lead.

One, two, three pairs of eyes to the left. Four, five, six, and seven were on the other side. It wasn't even close to a fair fight.

She thought of Zoya. If only Ta'Fik could see her now. *Is this justice?* She almost laughed.

Somehow, she knew there would be no offering from the Wolf this time. When she died this time, it would be true and final.

The drakehounds launched themselves as one, and Ambessa kicked the coals of the fire. The banked coals at the bottom flared as they flew—one drakehound whimpered as sparks flew into its eyes, but the others weren't delayed.

The first one that leapt for Ambessa's throat gored itself on the point of her sword raised between them, but another went for her ankle. Her roar of pain rivaled the hounds' growls of fury and hunger.

She stabbed down, but it was agile and dodged away from her strike.

"General!" Rell cried. The girl was backing up. The hounds had picked her as the weakest target, the best option for their nighttime meal.

Ambessa couldn't get to her, though. "Fight them, Rell! *Fight!*"

"There are too many!"

Had Ambessa chosen wrong again? "Think of the arena!"

Rell struggled to gather her courage. She didn't do what Ambessa expected. She jabbed with her spear, forcing the drakehounds circling her to open a gap. Then she sprinted for the horses.

"Rell!" Ambessa screamed. This *cowardice*— She didn't have time to watch the girl flee. She would account for that loss when she had a chance—if she had a chance.

Her leg burned with the bite and her arm with another, but

she had killed two. With Rictus and Caprian at her back, they faced another trio. The other two—

Rell hadn't fled. On horseback, she looked like the fighter Ambessa had watched eagerly, winning and basking in the applause of the audience as she rode circles around her enemy in the arena. This horse wasn't as confident around the drakehounds, but it obeyed Rell's commands, and her spear darted as quick as the drakehounds' tongues.

But Ambessa's distraction had cost them. Rictus buckled to the ground, one drakehound teeth-deep into his shoulder. Before Ambessa could reach him, Caprian let out a loud bleat and rammed his head into the drakehound's skull. It fell to the ground, stunned, but another drakehound was already lunging to take its place. Ambessa tried to help him, but another hound demanded her attention, biting for her sword arm. She cracked it with the pommel and it skittered away, whining before turning back, fangs bared.

A piercing horn broke through the night. It made Ambessa and the drakehounds alike flinch and look around. Torchlight flickered through the trees, and then there was the unmistakable hiss of arrows.

The archers' aim was true. Three drakehounds fell, almost at once, arrows in their eyes or throats or ribs. Another ran, followed by its remaining wounded companion.

Ambessa didn't relax her grip on her weapon. "Show yourselves."

A woman leading a group of mounted scouts rode slowly into their camp clearing. Amenesce of Vindor glared down at her from horseback, the scar on her face making her menacing in the torchlit night.

"Is that how you greet your saviors, Ambessa Medarda?"

Chapter Seventeen

W ho's your horse girl?" Amenesce asked Ambessa in a low
voice. She glanced over her shoulder at Rell, considering. The
girl was riding beside Rictus and taking her own surreptitious
looks, studying Amenesce's renowned horsemen.

After they had dealt with the drakehound corpses and packed
up their meager supplies, Ambessa and her warband of three
accepted Amenesce's escort to Vindor. The first night, they had
ridden in silence to one of the stowed camping spots that all
Vindoran scouts learned. Now they were riding in earnest, several days out from the city.

"No one."

The denial came too quickly. Amenesce raised a black
eyebrow.

"No one in particular. She, Rictus, and Caprian are the only
ones in my crew who escaped with me."

"Caprian is the vastaya? Part of your warband?"

"Mmm."

Amenesce grunted at the nonanswer. "And your children?
Fate send that they are well."

"They were when I left. If you know something, don't toy
with me. Tell me."

"I know nothing. If something has happened, it hasn't made it this far north, you have my word."

"Then how did you know to come looking for me?"

Amenesce laughed. It was a warm sound, though her scar pulled her mirth into viciousness. "Some news *has* made it this far north. We heard about Menelik, of course. I am sorry. I know you were close." She met Ambessa's eyes, and she did look remorseful. "That man shaped the world. Probably in ways we can't even know yet. But"—she turned back to the road—"I came looking for you because Smik's men are crawling all over Vindor and the nearby towns. They've been asking my people after you. And a vastaya." She flexed her hands in their riding gloves as if they were claws. "I really don't like other stewards running roughshod in my jurisdiction. Rather rude, don't you think?"

Ambessa froze but tried to keep her voice from betraying her. "Terribly. Did they say why they're looking for me?" She pretended she hadn't heard the second bit.

"I can guess. I'm more interested in why *you* are looking for *me*."

"Surely you can guess that, too."

"Better to hear you say it. What did Menelik always say? Something about assumptions making everyone a fool?"

Ambessa grunted. Amenesce wasn't born to the Medarda blood, but she was as much a part of this family as any blood kin. She had been under Menelik's tutelage, the same as Ambessa and Ta'Fik had, though she had never quite thirsted in the same way for his seat. She had been content to lead her warbands of cavalry, and years later, when she was injured, she'd taken advantage of a steward's seat. Now she turned her expertise in horseflesh to breeding and training steeds with every possible specialty—horses that could survive the Shuriman deserts, warhorses that were as fearsome as any basilisk or drakehound on the battlefield. She was formidable and had more than earned Ambessa's respect. The real question was if she would keep it.

"I need a warband of cavalry. Specifically, if you can spare them—your Light Vindorans."

Amenesce chuckled. "To do battle in the desert."

Ambessa tilted her head in answer to the question that was not a question.

"And why should I support either of you? No matter who wins, you'll need me. Darkwill needs me. Why should I risk my people, my beautiful horses? Better yet, why not let the two of you fight until there's nothing left? Then I'll just ride in over the corpses and take over the Medarda name myself." She motioned said riding with her hands.

"Because you're too smart for that," Ambessa said dangerously.

"Hmm." Amenesce tapped her fingers across the horn of her saddle. "I suppose we'll see."

They didn't revisit the subject until they were in Vindor, in Amenesce's home. Another city on the coast, it couldn't have been more different from Trannit. Where the southern city was situated on cruel bluffs, spattered by storms and wracked by winds, Vindor was low to the water, nestled between river and sea. South of the river, the mountains and their forests rose in a dark swath of green. The rolling lowlands north of the river allowed for the cavalry Vindor was so proud of. The sea air was cooler here, and yet, there was a vibrancy that she felt was missing from Trannit. The river brought traffic from the busiest parts of the empire, like Basilich; its citizens were connected to the latest in politics and fashion. The Noxtoraa here were carved more artistically than most, patterns of triangles almost like mosaics, and the pattern was repeated throughout the city, on buildings, on the roads at major intersections. There was appreciation for a hard type of beauty here, as well as function.

Amenesce's home was no different. Amenesce sent them to opulent guest rooms, one suite for her and Rell, and another for Rictus and Caprian—much better than the oubliette Smik threatened them with. First, the drakehound bites on her leg and arm were cleaned more thoroughly and bandaged with clean linens. Then the baths. It was a pleasure to bathe, to have attendants who washed and braided her hair, scenting it with oils and weaving in strands of pure white horse mane that gleamed amidst Ambessa's dark curls. There were fragrant oils for her body, too, and provided she kept her wounds out of it, she was allowed to soak in the oiled water with ever-flowing wine until she wearied of it.

Ambessa didn't think she would ever weary of it, but from the neighboring tub, Rell's questions were unceasing.

"Do you think the steward will help us? How long has she ridden? Did you see her with the drakehounds? Do you think she'll give us the Light Vindorans? Will she at least let us see them? Ride one?"

"Child, peace! Please." Ambessa closed her eyes and sank lower in the water.

"Sorry," Rell mumbled. Her hair had also been washed and braided. It was odd to see the young woman's flare of bright hair so tamed. It made her seem smaller.

However, the questions on Rell's lips were the same in Ambessa's mind, and so at dinner, Ambessa brought it up again.

Amenesce plucked a bite of heavily salted swordfish with her fork. She had also requested baked naaps in Ambessa's honor, a nod to her hometown of Rokrund. She held the fish in the air.

"I don't mean to be rude, Ambessa, but do you have *anyone* on your side?"

"Does it matter? I intend to win, whether I count you among my allies or if every one of you is arrayed against me."

"Truly noble, I'm sure. However, I didn't get to my position through nobility and fighting for lost causes. I fight to win. I've already won all I care to. Why should I risk losing?" Amenesce popped her fish into her mouth and held Ambessa's gaze as she chewed.

"I have my brother Katye on my side. Several of my warbands remain in Rokrund with him. And...certain factions in Bel'zhun."

Amenesce choked with laughter. "Katye? That crusty old historian? How is *he* going to help you?"

"Don't underestimate him. I value his counsel, and you can't ignore the contributions of extra soldiers. Then there's Darkwill."

Now Amenesce narrowed her eyes. "You have Darkwill?"

Ambessa glanced at Caprian. He had also been pampered; his white-and-black splotched fur gleamed, and the fine goatee at his chin had been braided with small beads that clacked gently when he chewed. The vastaya was examining the table offerings enthusiastically even as he chewed continually on the fresh greens, but he perked up when he heard Darkwill mentioned. He met Ambessa's eyes.

"I have information that will be invaluable to him."

"What kind of information?" Amenesce leaned over her plate, looking between the two of them.

"So that you can present it to him yourself?" Ambessa leaned back. "I think not."

"You accuse me of such low behavior in my own house?"

"Others have done worse," Ambessa growled. She thought of Ta'Fik's smug face as he accused her of killing her own grandfather while his body lay cooling. Her fists tightened on the knife and fork in her hands until the fine silver left marks. She didn't notice until Rictus nudged her with his boot under the table. She forced herself to loosen her grip.

Amenesce, too, collected herself. She relaxed back into her tall chair and took another bite of her fish nonchalantly. "So I take it you'll present this to him at the tribute?"

Ambessa froze with her wineglass halfway to her lips. Amenesce's smile sharpened, and she cocked her head.

"Have you forgotten?" she asked.

"I've been traveling for so long that I lost track of time." Ambessa drank deeply from her cup. "Yes. It will be the perfect time. And I'll be there to represent House Medarda."

"Do you have an outfit picked out?"

"If you won't support me with cavalry, will you at least let me sail with you to the Immortal Bastion?"

Amenesce tapped her fork casually on her plate. "Perhaps. Who else is arrayed against you?"

Ambessa cocked an eyebrow. "Ta'Fik. Smik, as you can guess. And Kilgrove. At least. Maybe Fallgren as well."

A muscle twitched in Amenesce's jaw. She wasn't looking at Ambessa. She was staring vaguely at the table, as if seeing something else, something far beyond the present. "And *when* you defeat them, what do you plan to do with them?"

"That is my concern."

"Will you kill them?"

"That is my concern."

Amenesce asked nothing else. Ambessa returned to her food.

"Lend me the girl tomorrow."

Ambessa paused. She had expected Amenesce to angle for Caprian. "What?"

Amenesce regained her focus, but it was on Rell instead of Ambessa. "I have some things I'd like to teach your young charge."

Ambessa glanced at Rell, whose eyes were wide with shock or

with hope—Ambessa couldn't tell. "You refuse to aid my cause, you won't lend me a ship, but you want to take my trainee?"

Amenesce shrugged.

When Ambessa left Amenesce at the table, Rell and Rictus followed.

Rell skipped to catch up to her. "General," she said softly at Ambessa's elbow. "I could serve you better if I had even a day's lesson with a rider like her."

If Rell were to be the strongest warrior she could be, she did need teachers who could foster her strengths. There were many things Ambessa could teach her, but Ambessa had seen the girl's instincts. She had a gift for horses, an affinity with them. It would be folly not to nurture it. And Rell was right: She would serve Ambessa better.

"Fine. But one day only. We don't have time for games."

"Yes!" Rell shouted, punching the air in glee. "I'll go back and tell Steward Amenesce."

"Jealousy doesn't become you, Ambessa," Rictus murmured, laughter teasing in his voice. His lips quirked amidst his beard, which, like Caprian's, had been oiled and intricately braided. The drakehound wound in his shoulder had also been bandaged.

Ambessa scowled and flicked one of his beaded mustaches. "Be careful, or I'll make you take lessons, too."

But his words had left a mark.

In truth, Ambessa was grateful for the extra days in Vindor. She made sure Rictus stayed near Caprian, but otherwise took the brief respite to catch her breath, to let her body recover before what promised to be a long campaign. It would also give her time to think of a way to win Amenesce to her side. What could she want that Ambessa could win for her?

She pondered the thought as she accompanied Rell to her lesson with Amenesce the next day. In the stables, Amenesce showed Rell some of the choicest steeds and let her pick one to ride that day. It was a beautiful beast, with a shimmering gold coat and a mane the same white-blond as Rell's own hair. A pretty stablehand helped her saddle the mare, and Rell blushed.

The horsewoman led the horses to a large paddock, and Ambessa watched Amenesce put Rell through her paces, testing her strengths and weaknesses. She huffed quietly to herself and went back into the stables.

She was *not* jealous.

Ambessa meandered through the stables, limping, admiring the horses. No matter how irritating she was, Ambessa couldn't deny Amenesce her expertise.

"...steward'll have a right fit over that, she will..."

Ambessa paused to better overhear the stablehands gossiping as they tended to one of the horses.

"She'll have a right fit if she hears you lot gossiping over her affairs," said a louder voice. The head of the stables, Jako, was a carthorse of a man and lumbered to the stall where the gossips were chatting. "Brushing out a coat ain't a job for two. You know what is? Stable-mucking. Go to it. See how much breath you want to spend for gossip then."

A chorus of groans, and the two youths emerged. One was the stablehand who had helped Rell with her tack.

While the youths took their shovels to bend to their chore, Ambessa sidled up to Jako convivially. "What was that about?"

"Oh, General, hello. It's nothing, I'm sure. Harmless. They just get it into their heads what's not their business."

"What's the news today?" she asked wryly.

"Oh, nothing. Just some ships from Fallgren spotted among the Trannit ones, and the lady's been irritated enough about *them*, so she's gonna be in a piss-poor mood all right, the kids weren't wrong about that."

Ambessa recalled the steward's tension when she brought up Fallgren. Time to dig a little deeper.

"Why? What's wrong with Fallgren ships?"

The stable master's face flushed ruddy beneath his scruffy beard, all the way to his ears. "Oh, well, I shouldn't say, or I'm just as bad as them."

Ambessa smiled. "Of course, of course. Tell me, the young stablehand, the one who was helping my page—what's her name?"

"Oh, you mean Tora?" Jako's voice went fond. "She's a good lass, better rider. She'll make a name for herself, mark me, but I can tell you one thing," he laughed, "you watch your girl around her."

"Oh?"

"Let's just say, I've seen one or two chambermaids leave the stables crying."

"Mmm. Perhaps I'd better speak to her. Gently, of course."

"Aye, maybe so. Or tell your lass to be careful while you're here. A little fun's all well and good, but you don't want her moping the rest of the way to the Immortal Bastion, I reckon."

"I certainly don't. Thank you, Jako." Ambessa slipped him a gold coin as she left him. It was good to be back in a city with a bank. "For the advice."

Ambessa found Tora outside at another paddock, looping a horse in a training circle. She stood at the center of the paddock holding one end of a long rope, while the horse, attached to the other end, cantered around her. Her focus was completely absorbed by the great beast, and she startled when she saw Ambessa.

"General." Tora came over and saluted her. "Did Steward Amenesce send for me?" Her voice was eager, expectant.

"No," Ambessa said. "You're quite good with horses, aren't you?"

Tora puffed out her chest. "I've been training in Steward Amenesce's stables since I could walk. She said she'll let me join the Scar's Rangers once I've proved myself."

Ambessa raised her eyebrows appreciatively, and it was only slightly feigned. The Scar's Rangers were one of Amenesce's warbands, her elite scouts. If the girl wasn't exaggerating, that would be quite the feat for a young woman her age.

"Jako was also telling me you have quite the way with the young women."

Tora's swaggering pride vanished immediately, replaced by wide eyes and flushed cheeks. "What— I didn't— I haven't done—"

"Easy, easy," Ambessa said. "I'm not worried about Rell. She's more than a match for you. Just be careful, for your own sake." Then, as if she were making casual conversation, she asked, "What's going on that's got the whole compound stirred up? Fallgren ships?"

Tora leapt for the new topic like salvation. "Aye, but it's not the ships themselves that are the problem." The girl lowered her voice, as if she thought Jako was near enough to chastise her again. "But everyone knows Steward Amenesce and Steward Jeon were...involved." She trailed off and her flush deepened, as if she realized she was straying too close to dangerous topics again.

"I take it that it ended poorly?" Ambessa coaxed.

"Oh, aye. The whole compound hid itself near a month. She was out riding every day, left at sunup alone and didn't come back until well after dark. The horses were exhausted, and Jako said the final batch of mounts she sent to the steward was nothing but nags, the worst-tempered horses we had." She paused.

"Course, it's nothing but hearsay. If you'll excuse me, General, plenty of work to do. Let me know if you need any of the horses saddled. It would be my pleasure." Tora saluted and went back to her charge, who was grazing lazily.

The threads of a plan began to come together.

That evening at dinner, Ambessa watched Amenesce's face as she pronounced, "Steward Jeon of Fallgren. He's in league with Ta'Fik and Smik."

It was Amenesce's turn to be caught flat-footed. She didn't even have time to conjure a deflection. "How do you know?"

"His ships were seen among the Trannit ships, messages passing between them by dinghy." The last was, perhaps, a fabrication. Amenesce's sudden pallor was enough to tell Ambessa she had struck true.

"That bastard," she muttered.

"I heard his ships are on their way here?"

Amenesce glared. "Not anymore. I've asked some friends of mine to make a blockade. If he wants to set foot in Vindor, he'll need to get in a damned rowboat."

"So you will help me?"

"My arguments from before remain the same. But you can sail with me. I was going to leave at the end of the week."

"I thought you hated ships."

"I was made to have a beast between my legs and the earth beneath my feet," Amenesce said flatly. "But I also have tribute for Darkwill, and I'd rather it didn't show up winded and ill-used."

Ambessa grunted. She turned to Caprian, who had stopped his chewing and stared at Amenesce with dread.

"You're sure we can't ride? Even walk?" he asked. "I was also meant to have the earth beneath *my* feet." His eyes were wide with the terror of another sea attack.

Ambessa gave him a warning look. "The faster we get to Darkwill, the better. You know this." She turned to Amenesce. "Thank you for the offer, but we'll look for earlier passage. If you'll excuse us. We have plans to make."

The steward of Vindor flicked her hands dismissively, scowling at the table before her.

Chapter Eighteen

Despite her attitude the night before, Amenesce was courteous enough to see them off the next morning. They headed to the docks early, as soon as the sun was high enough to see by and the tides were favorable. With at least a few weeks of sailing and less than two months before the tribute, Ambessa could waste no time.

While Ambessa and Amenesce walked at the head of their small train, Rell hung back, talking to another young Vindoran. Tora, the gossiping stablehand. She was jaunty and bowlegged and turned her crooked smile on Rell.

"Not a moment too soon," Ambessa muttered wryly.

Amenesce followed Ambessa's gaze and then snickered. "I can't say I'm surprised. Tora has a reputation. She breaks horses and hearts."

"She'd better be careful. Rell breaks things, too. Usually in a more permanent fashion."

"Well. Young love and all that…" Amenesce trailed off, frowning.

Ambessa followed her gaze, out into the harbor. It took her a moment to see the problem. When she did, her own fury rose to match the rage building in the steward's face.

The ships from Trannit and Fallgren had surrounded Amenesce's ships. Even though the Vindoran ships were keeping the other ships out of the harbor, the Vindoran ships couldn't get out of the harbor, either. They were effectively trapped. If Ambessa wanted to leave by ship, she would have to get past the dozen warships they had scattered through the Guardian's Sea.

A young boy came running up from the docks. "Steward!" He hunched over, hands on his knees as he struggled to get his breath. "Captain Royson sent me—Steward Jeon—wants to speak—but Captain Royson didn't let him through—only said he could come in if he took one of the dinghies in—"

Amenesce didn't let him finish. "That *bastard*."

She strode down the docks to get a better look, the long coat she always wore billowing behind her, her boots ringing out on the wood, her saber jangling. She stopped abruptly as five men climbed out of a small boat.

"*You.*" Amenesce's lips twisted in disgust.

A handsome man in his forties, sporting the lanky build of a sailor who spent his time in the rigging, strolled up with a rolling gait, as if he'd forgotten how to walk on ground that didn't shift beneath his feet. His brown skin was weathered by the sea. He smoothed his mustache, then tipped the edge of his three-cornered hat.

"Amenesce. It's good to see you again." Jeon of Fallgren's voice was warm and slightly apologetic.

"If you don't get back in that boat and get your ships out of my harbor, I swear—"

Jeon's voice hardened. "Don't start with threats, Amenesce. Especially threats you can't keep."

"I'll show you what threats I can keep." Amenesce put her hand on the hilt of her saber, but didn't draw it.

"For the sake of our friendship, I came in person. Will you turn Ambessa over to us?"

Amenesce flexed and unflexed her fingers. The tension between the two stewards was palpable. No wonder the rumors had made it all the way to the stables. It was the best thing Ambessa could have asked for—if Jeon pushed Amenesce the wrong way, she would be sure to support Ambessa. Ambessa held herself ready, just in case. She was well-fed now and her injuries had healed some, but she didn't want to have to kill Amenesce as well. She had enjoyed getting reacquainted with the horsewoman. And she wanted that cavalry.

"For the sake of our friendship, you blockaded my harbor? Smik has had his soldiers crawling all over Vindor like lice. He's lucky I haven't plucked them out and squeezed them." Amenesce drew her steel. "For the sake of our *friendship*, you should go. Now."

Ambessa drew her sword, too, and behind her, she felt Rictus shift into readiness. He'd taken a wicked-looking halberd from Amenesce's armory that was taller than he was, and it gleamed sharp and deadly in the early light.

"Are you sure?" Jeon asked. He stopped moving closer, and the warmth in his voice had turned to condescension. He sneered at Ambessa. "There are stronger allegiances you could make."

"Ta'Fik, you mean? Or you and Smik? You're barely home long enough to grow your little rubber plants, and Smik is so corrupt that he's probably only siding with Ta'Fik to keep his own ass safe."

Jeon flushed in anger. "You'll regret this, Amenesce." Then he nodded to the soldiers he'd brought with him. They jumped back into their rowboat.

"I regret a lot of things," Amenesce said to his retreating back.

Jeon scowled over his shoulder. There was a deep hurt there, but his face hardened, and he ordered his men to row.

Ambessa watched them all the way out to sea. Only then did she turn to Amenesce.

"Thank you."

"He's a coward. He always has been." Amenesce cast her gaze to the side, but her voice was hard. "I suppose that's that bed made." She extended her hand begrudgingly, and Ambessa took it.

"So." Ambessa raised an eyebrow. "Do you have a horse fast enough to get us to the city in time for the tribute?"

Amenesce grinned mischievously. "Oh yes. In a manner of speaking."

Amenesce took her to a different stable, just outside Vindor proper. There was a wide paddock with a herd of odd creatures, grazing. Pronged bony horns jutted out of their heads and down the length of their necks, and they had shiny brown-and-gray brindle-patterned coats. They looked up as Ambessa and Amenesce approached.

"You have swifthorns." Ambessa looked between Amenesce and the placid animals. "*Tame* swifthorns."

The horse master gave a quietly proud smile. A much different expression from the pure hatred she'd worn as she faced down Jeon of Fallgren.

"They'll shave off a quarter of the journey from here to the Immortal Bastion, if we travel light. I was going to show these to Darkwill, but now I'll really get to test them out."

Amenesce made a clicking sound with her tongue and pulled out a palmful of mashed naap from a pouch.

"In the meantime, I'll send my riders in the Bloody Thunder west to Rokrund to await you. That's three hundred of my best cavalry on Light Vindorans. Will that be enough?"

"I'm sure," Ambessa said, relieved though she didn't show it.

"You're sure Rokrund is loyal?" Amenesce asked dubiously.

"Rokrund is my home and I would trust Katye with my life."

"I mean no insult. It seems that loyalties are...fragile, these days."

The closest swiftthorn sniffed the air and trotted over. Warily, it examined the two of them with large gray eyes. Up close, its horns were massive. They were meant for goring predators, but they would gore a rider just as easily if they weren't careful.

Ambessa considered the long-legged creatures. "Is it like riding a horse?"

The wicked grin returned. "Nothing like it."

They left the next day. Rictus was as skeptical of the new mounts as they were of him, and it was a struggle to find one large enough to support him. He ended up on a stout male with a bad temper, and Caprian laughed as Rictus and the swiftthorn grumbled in mutual dissatisfaction.

"Never trust anything with horns," Rictus said in a mock whisper to Rell.

"I heard that," Caprian said.

Rell's young friend, Tora, was also along for the journey, this time in a new leather riding coat, lightly armored at the chest, but with the arms free for her bow. She sat on her own swiftthorn as easily as she swaggered on the street. Something she said as Rell climbed into her saddle made Rell blush again.

It made Ambessa think of Rudo. Surely she had never blushed so much around him. They would have to pass through Basilich on the way to the Immortal Bastion. Where she and Rudo had met. Where they'd fallen in love.

Where was he now?

Ambessa had received only one note from Katye—it had been waiting for her when she arrived—and that had been to say that all was well in Rokrund except for the small, minute fact of Mel deciding to stay in Bel'zhun with Kino and Azizi, and Ambessa was *not* to blame Katye for that, and anyway, she would be safe with her father and the Wolf's Reapers, and make sure she wrote when she got to Vindor safely.

Ambessa had sent a terse response after reading it, but today, she sent another to update him on their alliances, and to expect the Bloody Thunder.

The best way to take care of your family is to take care of Ta'Fik.

"Are we ready to go?" She was suddenly taut as a cocked crossbow.

Amenesce leapt onto her mount gracefully and turned it in a tight circle to take in the small band that would accompany them. She let out a whoop, and they echoed her, kicking their mounts forward.

Ambessa's own swifthorn felt odd beneath her. She was very aware of the bony plates of its neck and the sharp horns. She made herself sit it like any other horse, but she felt stiff compared to Amenesce's fluidity.

No matter. Ambessa had always learned fast.

Rell was riding in a warband. Rell was riding in Ambessa Medarda's warband. She was also riding with Steward Amenesce, who worked with the legendary horses of Vindor. Finally, it felt like the adventure she'd only imagined in her wildest dreams.

She'd been so eager to get out when General Medarda had come to her in Bel'zhun—to get away from her parents and their overbearing demands. She'd been making a name for herself in the arena, but she'd never been able to escape her parents' lurking shadow. With Ambessa, it would be different. Then Rell had gotten on the *Golden Dancer*.

It was the worst thing she'd ever experienced, and she'd

almost begged to be let back off. She'd go back home to her parents, just so she didn't have to throw up over the railings again. Then came the attack, and it was one turn of bad luck after the next. Not an adventure at all.

But Rell was starting to think that maybe her luck had changed.

"You're a really good rider," Tora said, trotting up beside her. The young rider's swifthorn snapped playfully at Rell's, and Tora chided it with a gentle nudge of her thighs. "I thought all you southerners learned on dormuns."

Tora's smile was as teasing and playful as her swifthorn was, and Rell felt her face warm embarrassingly.

"You're—um. A really good rider. Too, I mean." Rell wished she could vanish immediately. "I mean—obviously you are, you wouldn't be in the steward's warband otherwise. And anyway, look at you—"

Unfortunately, Rell did look at Tora right then, and not only was she gorgeous, with her bright smile and her laughing eyes, she had strong shoulders and she really *did* sit on her mount like a warrior. But she was also definitely smirking at her.

Rell turned away and closed her eyes. "Right. Dormun. No. I'm not from Bel'zhun, not originally. I learned to ride horses at my mother's estate in the Bloodcliffs, back when we had one."

"What happened?" Tora no longer seemed to be laughing at her, but her curiosity was almost as embarrassing. Especially about this.

She was saved having to answer by a cry up ahead.

"Deer!"

"Left!"

There was a scramble as everyone turned in their saddles. They were a large band of fifty riders, and they'd been eating nothing but salted meat and hard bread unless they caught a few rabbits when they camped, but it seemed like most rabbits had heard the clomping of their hooves and vanished for miles. Fresh meat would be worth a celebration.

Tora unlatched her bow from her saddle and had an arrow nocked and pulled to her eye in half a moment. Rell searched the woods to their left, but she couldn't see the deer. Then, out of the corner of her eye, she saw a flurry of movement in the leaves. Tora's bow loosed with a snap.

A moment later, there was a crash in the underbrush.

With delight, Tora turned to her. "Let's go get it! We'll get the first cut if that was my arrow!"

While the line halted, Rell and Tora dismounted. Rell brought her spear with her, just in case. A few others tramped through the wood with them, their bows hanging ready in their hands, but it was Tora's arrow that had pierced the heart, with her blue-tipped fletching.

Rell stared at her. "That— How did you do that?"

"I've been practicing since I was young. Have you ever used one? I could teach you."

"Sure," Rell said, but she gripped her spear tighter. It was slick in her palm. "I usually use this."

Tora smirked again, eyeing the spear dubiously. "But how good are you with it at a distance?"

The challenge burned away some of Rell's shyness. She smiled grimly, then turned to find a likely target.

"There, that tree, with the knot?" Rell pointed with her spear at a tree some distance away. Not as far as Tora's deer, but far enough to make her point.

Tora crossed her arms. "No. Impossible. Not with a spear."

Rell didn't say anything else. She'd learned that from Ambessa. No one listened to what you *said* as much as to what you *did*. She pulled her arm back, reveling in the tension before letting it fly.

It stuck just above the knot she'd indicated, wobbling.

Rell turned back to Tora smugly. The other girl's mouth was hanging open.

"Oy, Tora, you going to flirt all day, or help us get your kill back so we can have some dinner?"

Tora turned, chastened, back to the kill, and Rell went to fetch her spear. Ambessa would give her an earful for blunting it just to show off.

Tora found Rell again when it was time to eat. With a portion of venison to go with their bread, everyone was in a good mood, even their war leaders.

"May I?" she asked.

Rell shrugged and made space in the dirt.

"I wanted to apologize," Tora said, sitting down gracefully. "I interrupted you. You were saying, about the estate in the Bloodcliffs earlier?"

"Nothing," Rell said quickly. "But I loved it, riding. Now I ride in the Reckoner Arena in Bel'zhun. Or, I did. Now I'm with General Medarda."

Tora glanced up ahead of them, to where their mentors were eating and talking with their heads close together.

"What's she like, the general?"

Rell studied Ambessa, too. It was hard to put into words everything she'd learned about the older woman in the time since leaving Bel'zhun.

"She's . . . different," Rell said honestly. "I mean—she's amazing. She's generous, but she's also exacting. I've never seen anyone fight like her. And if you watch her and Rictus sparring together—there's no chance Ta'Fik can beat the two of them. I don't think anyone can. I want to be like Rictus one day. He came out of the arena, too. He gives me lessons, sometimes."

"I bet you will." Tora's voice was soft with admiration.

Rell felt a swoop in her belly.

Chapter Nineteen

True to Amenesce's word, they arrived in the capital of Noxus with a week to prepare for the tribute. The road took them through the lower city first—not even the Immortal Bastion proper, but the sprawling outgrowth of city that had gathered and hardened around the outer walls like barnacles on a ship's hull. It started as tents and shabby lean-tos, which became shacks, and then shady travelers' lodgings and then the more respectable ones, and finally more permanent dwellings butting up against the outer wall.

The outer wall was split by a great Noxtoraa—this one, the southernmost one, was the Conqueror's Gate. They rode through it and into the empire's sprawling capital. It was a warren of a city, where the old buildings butted up against the new, and the new was built over the crumbling, and where everyone everywhere, no matter what land they came from, fought to scramble as high as they could, through might, vision, or guile.

Above it all loomed the Immortal Bastion, the great fortress that the city had risen around, a monument to their glory and success. It originally belonged to the Iron Revenant, Mordekaiser, whom the Noxii tribes defeated many centuries ago. No matter where you stood in the city, you would see it rising above the walls of the inner keep. And deep within that ancient citadel lay the haunted inner sanctum, eerie and almost sacred, where no one dared to tread.

While Rell and Caprian turned their heads up to the grand city above them, their eyes wide and their mouths hanging open, Ambessa's dread kept her focused. She needed to know if Ta'Fik was in the city. Amenesce left to see her swiftthorns to a stable where they would be well taken care of before offering them as tribute. Ambessa led Rell, Rictus, and Caprian to the Medardas' seat in the Immortal Bastion.

Because the capital was so tightly packed, the Medarda residence in the Immortal Bastion was smaller than the Medarda compounds elsewhere—rising vertically, attached to its neighbor on one side, instead of sprawling and taking up space. It made Ambessa miss the wide-open plains in Rokrund. But she could feel the power swirling about in the Immortal Bastion. She could practically smell its metallic tang—the smell of coin and blood and blades.

The Medarda house was in the Steel City. Early on in the city's life, it had been where the proudest warriors lived, within the inner wall, close to the fortress. Over time, the residents became those who fought their way to the top—and not just with blades.

"This is also your house?" Rell said, quietly awestruck as she craned her head up to look at it.

"It is. In a manner of speaking. It's a Medarda house. Any Medarda may come here and stay when they're in the city. Just like the compound in Bel'zhun."

Rell's brow knit in concern. "Even—"

Ambessa shook her head to cut the girl off. She shared a glance with Rictus, who tightened his grip on his halberd.

Ambessa knocked, and a servant opened the door. He was a thin man with an upright posture—when he bowed, he bent in half exactly.

"General Medarda," he said. "We have been expecting you. Please come in. I will have tea made for you and your guests." He ushered them in. Ambessa's boots sounded heavy as she followed him into the sitting room.

The room was opulent; the stone outer walls were draped in sheer red and gold hangings, made to glow by the warm lighting. A painting hung on another wall, one of a single man leading a Noxian merchant and his caravan through the desert. *Eskender.*

And at the center of it all, Ta'Fik sat in one of the deep chairs, one leg crossed over the other knee, holding a cup of steaming tea. He was wearing an asymmetric robe that buttoned beneath a stylish but clearly false pauldron. It wouldn't hold up under a solid blow.

"Ta'Fik," Ambessa growled. She reached for the hilt of her sword, ready to test her theory.

"Ah-ah-ah, Ambessa. We're on neutral ground. Not that that means much to you." He gestured to the other man in the room. "I was just explaining to Hanek that he would have to be careful when you came."

"Brother." Ambessa greeted her elder brother with a slow nod. "I hope you received word of my coming?"

She searched his face for any deeper indication that he believed her and not Ta'Fik's lies, but Hanek's frown was turned equally on both of them.

Hanek was older than her by several years, and his hair was more gray than black now, slicked in waves against his head.

"There will be no bloodshed in my house," Hanek said. He looked slowly from Ambessa to Ta'Fik. *"Medarda over all.* You will both agree to this now, or you will leave. Do you understand?"

Ambessa exhaled slowly. "You cannot trust him, Hanek."

"*Me?*" Ta'Fik said in a low voice. "*I* didn't—"

"Do you understand!" Hanek's voice cut through Ta'Fik's words.

"Of course, brother." Ambessa nodded once.

Ta'Fik was slower to assent, but he did.

Ambessa noticed something, though. "Where are your daughters? I hope they're well? And that advisor who was following you around in Bel'zhun. Did they finally realize you weren't worth their talents?"

He smiled wide, his white, even teeth gleaming. "Tivadar is still in Bel'zhun. She prefers the arenas. Gintara is busy taking care of affairs while I'm away, like any good heir. So is Inyene. How are Kino and Mel?"

Did Ambessa imagine the bite in his words?

"They're well." Ambessa left it at that. "Hanek. Ta'Fik. It's been a long journey." Without waiting for her tea, she turned on her heel and left.

She bade a servant show them to their rooms, and so Ambessa and her small entourage followed them up the stairs. They had an entire floor to themselves, with two bedchambers, a sitting room, and a bathing room.

"This changes things," she told them when they were alone. She gave Caprian an especially hard look. "Stay on your guard, always. Rell and I need to go out to get suitable clothing for the tribute. Rictus, stay here with Caprian."

Caprian shook his head in disgust. "Why should I stay here? I want to see the city, and it's probably safer than anywhere near him." He shuddered. "He looked at me like he wanted to roast me over a spit."

"He'd do worse if he had the chance. But as long as you're here, in the house, he won't touch you."

"Nothing will happen to me with the world's biggest nanny

goat following me around." Caprian slapped Rictus's thick chest with the back of his hand. The larger man scowled.

"Nothing will happen to you because you will stay *here*."

Caprian opened his mouth to protest again, but Ambessa interrupted. "That is an order. I've brought you this far safely. Trust me to get you in front of Darkwill. Then your life is your own."

At Ambessa's words, Rictus put a firm hand on Caprian's shoulder. Caprian's turn to scowl, this time.

"Fine," the vastaya grumbled.

When Ambessa took Rell out, her first stop was at a bank to pull more funds. Enough that she could also hire the pleasant company of a masseuse—a pretty young man or a woman with strong hands. It had been a very long journey.

Then she took Rell shopping.

The shops in the Steel City catered to those with power and influence—or those who had enough money to pretend they had power and influence. Instead of hawkers with open stalls, the merchants were specialists with shops as established as the neighborhood itself. Names of artisans marked the doors, not trades. If you wanted armor, you went to Jani Lucas or Vex Cathor; if you wanted a tailor, you went to Lisam Taana or Nika Fallow; and so on.

They went to Nika Fallow first, lingering over styles draped on mannequins or sketched in books. While they browsed, Rell kept up a streaming patter about the city. It was her first time in the Immortal Bastion; could they go to a Reckoners fight? Would they be able to see the great champions? Could *she* fight in the arena here? And why was the Immortal Bastion *like that*? Her eyes were wide, and her mouth hung open in what might have been a smile but never quite was. It tugged a string in Ambessa's heart to watch the girl's hesitation despite her clear excitement. It also reminded her how young the girl was, despite her prowess. Young or no, there were things they needed to discuss.

"Rell. Now that we're alone, we should talk about some things."

Rell stopped with a length of burgundy silk caught between her fingers. She glanced nervously at Ambessa and then studied the silk even harder.

"What things, General?" Her voice came out a squeak.

"What ambitions do you have for your life?"

Rell looked up at Ambessa, both eyebrows raised. "Oh. My ambitions?" She laughed nervously and scrubbed a hand over her hair. "I thought you were going to explain *the ways* to me."

"The *ways*?"

Nika Fallow, an older woman with her gray hair pulled back in a tight bun, chuckled as she eavesdropped.

"You know..." Rell's face burned. "The *ways*. The things people do together. I don't need to be told. You should hear what they said in the changing rooms at the arena."

Ambessa cleared her throat and shot a glare at Madam Fallow, but it only made the woman grin wider. "Yes, well. Good. How well have you considered your affections for the young rider?"

"So this *is* about the ways?"

"It's about your ambitions."

"I—I like Tora. She's good with a bow." Rell looked down at another bolt of cloth, this one dark green, the color of a pine forest. She stroked it absently. "Really good. And with horses. And swiftthorns."

Ambessa lowered her voice. "You need to be careful who you

trust. These sorts of entanglements are always a risk. As you saw with stewards Amenesce and Jeon."

A cloud passed over Rell's open features. "Why? Do you know something about her? She's always been nice to me."

"It hasn't been all that long. Things change, and sometimes before you realize."

It hadn't been long at all before she pulled Rudo to her bed in Basilich. Who was Ambessa to lecture Rell? The girl looked stricken, and Ambessa felt a twist of remorse. She pulled Rell around and placed a hand on each shoulder.

"Be happy, child. Enjoy yourself. The life of a war leader, though it is full of its own passions—the glory on the battlefield, the thrill of your own pumping blood, of victory, of a strategy laid well—there are softer passions that come fewer and farther between. Enjoy them when they come. But be careful. Every entanglement becomes a snare around your heart, unless you know how to cut it when you need to."

Rell bit her lip. "I think I understand."

They left that shop and passed through a lesser-known artisan's shop in silence. Then, while lingering over an impressive display of weapons in a window, Rell asked, "General, what about you? Aren't you married?"

Ambessa smiled, though Rell couldn't see it. "I am. Azizi. I love him dearly." Though what she felt for him was not like what she'd felt in Basilich, it was not a lie. Even now, she missed him. "He is the father of my children. Our marriage was arranged, however. To strengthen the family."

"Oh." Then: "Did you meet on the battlefield?"

Ambessa laughed out loud, then covered her mouth. "Oh no, child. Azizi's strengths lie elsewhere."

Instead of laughing, though, Rell asked quietly, "Does he ever worry you'll die when you fight?"

Ambessa sobered, remembering one of their last conversations in Bel'zhun. *Some glory isn't worth it, Ambessa.*

"I think he does. But I could no more stay home and mind the books and records than he could put on my armor and swing my sword."

"Did you . . . Were you always a fighter?"

"My father put my first sword in my hand before I could stand. My first steel sword by the time I was five. I smelled the blood of my first battlefield before I was ten. I trained with him and my mother until he died, and then she gave me to the care of my grandfather. It was relentless."

"It sounds hard," Rell said simply.

"It was." For a moment, Ambessa wondered what it would have been like to have an easier life. A softer one. She couldn't imagine it. A softer body, with children all around her? Fewer scars and calluses? It wasn't her. "I wouldn't have been better for it. Would you have been better off if your parents hadn't pushed you?"

Rell didn't say anything for a long time, and when she did, it was so quiet that Ambessa almost didn't hear her.

"Speak up, child."

"Yes. I think I would have." Rell spoke in a bitter whisper, choked with tears. Her fingers lingered over the edge of a sharpened axe-head. "They didn't push me because they wanted me to be good, like you and Rictus. They pushed me because they wanted something out of me. They wanted to use me as their passage to . . . I don't even know! Somewhere better than where we were. They never saw *me*. Who I am; what I want."

A thickness rose in Ambessa's throat. It was clear how deeply Rell had been hurt by her parents, how she *still* hurt. She ached for the girl. And yet, it wasn't just Rell she thought of, but Mel and Kino. She thought of Mel's face, so different from Rell's, and yet, they had this same expression of hurt.

Ambessa put her hand on Rell's shoulder as they walked into Vex Cathor's armory.

"Don't worry, Rell. I see you."

The next days passed in a dance of feigned politeness, every courtesy as sharp as a dagger. Ta'Fik lounged in the common areas of the house with his personal guards, making sure Ambessa couldn't forget he was there. Rell was all puffed-up bravado, but she also spent some of her time in the barracks where the rest of Amenesce's warband—and Tora—was. Caprian grew sulkier every day. But Hanek did nothing, and so Ambessa didn't, either. She simply had to wait until the night of the tribute. When she handed Caprian off to Darkwill, she would have the support she needed to move on Ta'Fik.

Patience. It was a core part of vision. Without the patience to see it through, it was nothing but fantasy.

The day before the ball, Ambessa and Rell went to pick up their clothing from the tailor. Amenesce had come with them to get something for herself as well.

They returned to the Medarda residence to find Ta'Fik in his usual place in the lower floor's sitting room. He and Hanek were playing a game of strategy that Menelik had taught them. Anger and grief burned in the pit of her stomach. Silently, Ta'Fik taunted her, knowing that she had not even been there to lay their grandfather to rest. He raised a lazy eyebrow at her.

She ignored it and followed the servants carrying her things upstairs.

Their floor was oddly quiet. She gripped the hilt of the sword at her belt.

"Rictus?" she called.

No response. *Damn it.*

"Caprian?" Again, nothing.

Ambessa pushed past the servant, drawing her sword, expecting the worst. In the vastaya's room, however, there was nothing—no blood, no body, but also no living Caprian.

Amenesce came up behind her. "What is it? What's wrong?"

Ambessa didn't answer. She went to Rictus's room next.

Also empty. Where could they have gone? Caprian might have disobeyed her, but Rictus would not have. She wanted to storm back down the stairs and demand their whereabouts from Ta'Fik, but that would have given too much away. If he didn't already, he would *know* for certain how important Caprian was to her plans.

"Come on," she told Amenesce. "We're going back out—"

Below them, a heavy door slammed.

"Ambessa!" Rictus bellowed.

Ambessa sprinted down the stairs, not waiting for Amenesce and Rell to keep pace. She found Rictus holding the lanky vastaya up, one of Caprian's arms draped over his broad shoulders. There was blood.

"He snuck out," Rictus murmured for her ears only. "Wanted to 'see the city.' I told him no, as you ordered. I followed as soon as I realized. The two who attacked him are dead, but they should never have gotten close. Forgive me, Kreipsha."

Ambessa didn't know who she was more angry at—Ta'Fik or Caprian or Rictus. She checked Caprian's wounds, but none of them looked fatal. A gash across his shoulder that could have been a knife across the throat if it had landed just a handspan to the right.

"My, my. What's this?" Ta'Fik asked from the doorway of the salon. He clicked his tongue in concern.

"Hanek, send for a healer!" Ambessa shouted. "Or will you let one of your guests bleed out in your own foyer?"

Her brother scowled at her, but snapped his fingers at one of the servants, who scurried quickly.

As Rictus carried Caprian upstairs, Ambessa gave Ta'Fik a long, hard look. He watched her ascend, a slight curl to the corner of his mouth.

Later that night, when Caprian was asleep and stable, Ambessa knocked on the door of Hanek's study.

"Enter," came an annoyed voice.

Ambessa went in and closed the door tight behind her.

"Brother."

Hanek looked up from his desk. He frowned at her, his lips pursed.

"Why are you acting like none of this is your concern? Can't you see what Ta'Fik is doing?"

"I'm acting like it's none of my concern, *sister*, because it isn't."

"He's trying to shred the integrity of our family. He's doing it under your roof, and you'll do nothing to stop it?"

"Whatever grievance you two have between you has nothing to do with *my* integrity." Hanek dipped his quill back into his inkpot and returned to his papers. There was a map spread across the desk, and he scratched a small note in one corner.

"He's trying to turn the other Medardas against us. He claims I murdered Menelik! That *I* broke the Code, so that *he* can take my place as heir of the family. How does that have nothing to do with you?"

Hanek's grip on the quill tightened so much that Ambessa thought he would snap it. He governed himself and glared at the splotch he had made on the map.

"My ties to Menelik ended long ago, Ambessa. He made certain of that when he cast me out." He blotted the spot of ink with unnecessary fervor. "I'm only lucky that my talents are so suited to life in the capital." He said the words mockingly, as if quoting something he'd heard often, but they were an understatement. There was no one else in the family whom Ambessa would trust to steward the Medarda interests at the beating heart of Noxus's power.

Ambessa sat in the chair across from him. "When I'm head of this family, I'll welcome you back. You don't have to stay here if you don't want to, though your work here is appreciated. You've kept the family high in Darkwill's good graces, and we're respected among the other Houses."

"You don't get it, Ambessa. I don't *want* to be welcomed back. When Menelik kicked me out of his warband, he made one thing clear: I wasn't good enough to be part of this family. I was a coward, and he'd wasted his time on me." He sneered at her, but behind it was the pain and anger of a younger man. "Why do you think Mother sent you to Grandfather so young? She needed you to make up for my mistakes." He snorted.

"He called you a coward for running from one fight," Ambessa said softly. She held his dark gaze in her own. "So now you'll run from another?"

Instead of shouting at her for disrespecting him, or demanding that she leave, Hanek only laughed sad and soft, shaking his head.

"Oh, Ambessa. You can't goad me. I'm old enough that I know which fight is mine and which isn't. I've given you enough—this house is neutral ground, and the house guard will maintain that. Anything else . . . including what happens in the city streets . . . it's between you and Ta'Fik."

Ambessa stood. "So be it, Hanek. But I will remember this."

"I'm sure you will."

"Before I go—the city isn't as . . . crisp as it once was. There are more veterans in the lower city than there used to be. They look broken, Hanek, and not just them. What do you know?"

Hanek frowned again, but this time, it wasn't directed at her. "Darkwill is..." He tilted his head back and forth. "Well. I'm sure you'll see tomorrow. Let's just say, the money he takes in taxes from the empire isn't going to maintenance and upkeep," he said dryly.

Ambessa's heart beat harder. If he couldn't afford to send her aid, then all this would have been for nothing. She kept her voice calm, though.

"Thank you, Hanek."

"Good night, Ambessa."

Chapter Twenty

They were allowed one page and one guard—and absolutely no weapons. Wise, given that this gathering would pull together bitter rivals and hated enemies. It would be a miracle if no blood was shed. In fact, Ambessa was sure that was part of Darkwill's plans. A chance to force the constant churn of power that was Noxian politics.

Amenesce descended with Ambessa, wearing a long black coat embroidered with silver, the collar standing tall. Over it, stylized silver armor capped her shoulders and lined her spine. Because she was long and lean, the effect made her resemble one of her swifthorns. Her black hair had been freshly cut, sharp at her chin. Tora accompanied her, as Rell accompanied Ambessa. Rictus stood close to Caprian, who was somewhat worse for wear, moving stiffly with his wounded shoulder. The bandages were covered by the coat Ambessa had bought him, and he wore a pauldron on the opposite shoulder. The curls of his horns were tipped with gold.

For Ambessa's part, she wore an elegant red dress that imitated the cut of a uniform across the shoulders and slit at the hips down to the floor, showing her powerful legs in the fitted gray-black trousers. The collar dipped low, the better to show the jewels and stones of an Ionian necklace she'd taken from the Binan hold. A second layer of proof.

Ta'Fik was not in the house; he hadn't been there all day, but she would be alert to his tricks.

"You're not coming, Hanek?" Ambessa asked her brother as she left.

From his seat in the main sitting room, Hanek gave her a flat look, his lips pursed. "There will be more than enough Medardas spoiling for a fight without me." He tilted his glass of strong spirits at her, and then turned back to the book he was reading.

It would be just the six of them, then. Her only allies in the capital. For now.

Darkwill's home was guarded by two of his Baleful Guard, soldiers from the general's prized fighting force, and more frightening than either of them, one elegant but unpleasant woman who scowled at everyone through her pinched face.

"Name?" The woman's voice was just as pinched as her expression.

Amenesce bowed sweepingly and showed her ring: the Medarda star, four silver points set in a circle like a compass. It was different from Ambessa's own, which was cut in a gold octagon, thick and brutal like Menelik's iron one.

"Steward Amenesce of Vindor. I received permission to keep my tribute in the stable nearby with my handlers. I hope you don't mind."

The woman's eyes widened in apprehension, but she cleared her throat. "Very well." She let Amenesce, Tora, and their guard inside. "And you?"

"Ambessa Medarda, matriarch of the Medarda clan." Ambessa bowed with less flourish and proffered her own ring.

The gatekeeper's lips pinched impossibly tighter as she looked from Ambessa's ring to Ambessa's face and back again.

"There's already a head of the Medarda clan here," she said shrewdly.

Ambessa smiled slowly. "I'm sure there is. Family discussions are . . . ongoing. You understand."

The woman inhaled slowly. "Check her for weapons. The big one, too." As one of the Baleful Guard came to search Ambessa, the woman said to her, "There's to be no bloodshed in the Grand General's house."

Ambessa smiled generously. "Of course."

She swept into the raucous noise of Darkwill's home and understood immediately what Hanek had meant.

Everywhere Ambessa turned there was a splash of gold, a spray of red azirite, a dazzling streak of magical lights for no purpose Ambessa could tell. Paintings of Darkwill hung in sequence along the walls of the main gallery—Darkwill, stepping forward to the edge of a cliff, commanding warships into the face of a storm; Darkwill, his great axe poised over an armored soldier on the ground; Darkwill, a wise smile on his face, seated on a throne with a gleaming sword in his lap.

It had the look of a man who desperately wanted to believe something about himself that wasn't true.

In the main gallery, the guests mingled in their finery. The theme, of course, was battlefield glory, but it was clear immediately which guests had ever set foot on a battlefield and which had not. Oversize shoulder pads stretched one woman into a perfect triangle, but instead of approximating armor, Ambessa thought it made her look ridiculous. The woman could barely raise her goblet of wine to her own lips, let alone a sword. By contrast, she was speaking to a man who was wearing leather armor—and not much else. Layers of leather plate covered his shoulders, but he wore no cuirass—only bracers and greaves and a codpiece that covered just enough. Ambessa was not the only one who caught herself staring.

It wasn't glory; it was a mockery.

"Let's go in," she said to the others.

Rell followed close at Ambessa's heels. She stopped at the entry to the ballroom and gaped at the red banners streaming from the ceiling, dripping with gold tassels. Gold gleamed in the hands of scantily clad jugglers, flashing back and forth as they threw knives at each other with incautious speed.

"General Darkwill lives *here*?" she asked.

"Where else would he live?" Amenesce said dryly.

"I mean, I knew it was a palace, but I didn't..." Rell trailed off, lost for words, but Tora finished for her.

"Know a palace could look like this." The young horsewoman was just as awestruck.

"In my home," Caprian murmured, sorrowful, "there are trees larger than this place, and more beautiful."

"We'll get them back for you," Ambessa said.

"Is he here?" Caprian's eyes darted around them.

Ambessa scanned the ballroom as they drifted farther in. Not yet. But there were others worth noting—Jericho Swain was glaring with sullen disdain at the hall and its trappings. Someone else with enough wisdom to see through Darkwill's gilding. Swain's clothing was simple, muted colors and a thick breastplate beneath a dark cloak. He stood upright, and his eyes constantly scanned the room as if for threats. He was a true general.

"When it's time for the tribute, we'll speak to him. Patience."

They mingled briefly, Amenesce and Ambessa greeting those they hadn't seen in some time. More than a few offered condolences for Menelik's death.

Ambessa hadn't seen Ta'Fik yet.

Then the musicians who had been playing quietly in the background erupted in a fanfare of trumpets and drums beating out a marching cadence. Everyone around the ballroom door stepped back as a column of twenty soldiers marched through in lock-step, accompanied by even more trumpets and children in felt caps drumming a rapid tattoo. They wore matching uniforms, though the colors alternated, red and black, red and black.

Then the column broke apart—those in the second row jumped onto the shoulders of the soldiers in front of them, and from there leapt in synchrony onto the streamers hanging from the ceilings, weaving their legs deftly around the fabric and hanging upside down.

The guests below gasped and cooed. Even Ambessa had to admire the strength of the lithe bodies. But they were not the only display. The third row of "soldiers" broke rank next, and the first row turned back to face them in a beautiful choreography of combat, each strike a beat of the drums, a stamp of the feet, faster and faster as the music sped. Then came the last two rows of "soldiers": mages, this time, firing harmless bolts of color at one another, dodging and swirling with the shifting music. Occasionally—intentionally, Ambessa was sure—the bolts of light streaked over the heads of the attendees.

Right when the music reached its height, when Ambessa was certain the dancers couldn't move any faster, the thunderclap of an explosion burst from the entry. Gray smoke rose from the ground, thick and impenetrable.

Ambessa wasn't the only one who reached for a weapon that wasn't there.

Grand General Boram Darkwill emerged from the smoke. He cut an impressive figure in his shining boots and silver shoulder caps, Ambessa could admit that. A long, fur-lined cloak swayed behind him. He gave the illusion of a man ready for battle at a moment's notice. He smiled with self-satisfaction as he walked through the aisle of dancers, who now stood at attention, and toward the throne in the middle of the room.

"A pretty show," a man murmured nearby.

Ambessa turned. General Marcus Du Couteau. Elegant in dark gray tunic and trousers, his cloak black as the night sky, Du Couteau could have disappeared in the slip of a shadow. Even his soft boots were a dull leather that refused to catch the light. He did not need steel to be dangerous. The Du Couteaus were one of the most ancient Noxian houses, a family of assassins, masters of guile, the domain of mages and spies and cheats. Ambessa rarely saw it as a virtue, but she could acknowledge that it was useful.

It was impossible to know what thoughts lay behind Du Couteau's words.

Soon, the tributes began.

"I'll be back," Amenesce murmured. "Time to see how well the door woman likes having a thousand pounds of bony animal flesh at the door."

"And swifthorn shit on the marble," Tora snickered as she followed her steward out.

The line to offer Darkwill his tribute was almost informal—some rushed to be first, but only the most insecure. Others lingered over the dishes the servants offered, turning up their noses at this dish or that, from one conquered Noxian territory or another. Ambessa took a snail poached in dunpor milk from a pretty young man and sucked it from the shell with relish.

"Ew," Rell said.

"Try it," Caprian said. He crunched through the first one, shell and all, and took another.

"I'll pass." Rell side-eyed them both, and Ambessa heard Rictus's deep chuckle.

Then Rictus cleared his throat and nodded to the dais—there was Ta'Fik, already speaking with Darkwill.

Caprian looked up from his snails worriedly.

"It's fine," she said, and she made herself feel it. Ta'Fik couldn't offer Darkwill Ionia.

When she reached the dais, Darkwill leaned forward.

"General Ambessa Medarda. One of Menelik's best war leaders. Welcome."

"Grand General Darkwill." Ambessa bowed, though not as deeply as others had. Rell followed suit, if somewhat clumsily. "An honor I would not miss. Your dancers are...very talented."

"They are, aren't they? From every corner of the empire, only the best. Now. The news I hear from the Medarda clan is confusing. Menelik is dead. Ta'Fik says he takes his place, and yet, here you are—ah, and here he is, again!"

Ta'Fik appeared at Ambessa's side. "Cousin! You made it." He smiled with false cheer.

"Succession has not yet been determined," Ambessa said smoothly. She smiled at her cousin, whose lips froze in a rictus of politesse.

Darkwill looked between them both, studying their expressions, from Ta'Fik's rigidity to the relaxation Ambessa tried to cultivate.

"I understand." Darkwill was a noble in his own right. He would be familiar with the rise and fall of families, within families. The only true law in the empire was strength above all. The fall of a war leader or a steward would not be a surprise. "I will look forward to your decision."

He seemed to consider the matter settled, already looking to the next in the line, but Ambessa said, "My lord, your tribute?"

Darkwill's eyes brightened. "Ah, beyond the soldiers Ta'Fik has promised me for the Ionian conquest? Forgive me," he chuckled. "I thought you were gifting together as one family."

"No, Grand General. I have something more useful against Ionia than soldiers." Ambessa had sent a letter ahead of them from Vindor, hoping that he would deign to give her a private audience, but this might be the only opportunity she would have.

Darkwill was dubious. "Go on."

Ambessa glanced pointedly at Ta'Fik. "It's a sensitive matter."

Ta'Fik sneered. "Whatever you need to say to Grand General Darkwill is clearly a family matter. I'll—"

Ambessa pressed her lips together and looked to Darkwill, who shooed Ta'Fik away impatiently, saying, "Leave us."

She bowed her head to Darkwill to hide the satisfaction in her face.

When they were alone, Darkwill said, "Ta'Fik offers me soldiers stronger than any I yet command. How can you beat that?"

Ambessa frowned. What could Ta'Fik mean by that?

She stepped to the dais and beckoned Caprian closer. She put her hands on both of his shoulders. "My gift to you, Grand General, is a way *into* Ionia."

The vastaya bowed his great horned head. "There are secret ways, Grand General, if you help us take back our home."

"And you, Ambessa?" Darkwill raised his gaze from Caprian to her. "What boon do you expect from this tribute?"

"You said it yourself, Grand General. The matter of succession is undecided."

Darkwill cocked an eyebrow. A low laugh started in his throat before growing loud enough to draw the attention of those around them. Aware of their eyes, Ambessa smiled, too, but she could no more tell if she were about to be rewarded or executed on the spot.

The smile he turned on her was cold, but he clapped a hand on Ambessa's shoulder. He squeezed hard, nails digging into her for just a moment. Rictus twitched, and Darkwill turned his smile on him, too.

"Easy, great wolf," he said to him. "I understand you, Ambessa, and I admire you. But I do not get involved with these silly squabbles between family members. I run an empire. However," he said, tilting his head from side to side. "The vastaya will stay with me. If I find him useful, you both will have the power of my favor."

Ambessa clapped a fist to her shoulder in salute. "Grand General. You are generous."

Darkwill snorted. "Yes, yes. Enjoy yourself tonight. Expect word soon."

He turned to speak quietly with Caprian, in clear dismissal, and Caprian had time for only the briefest glance of farewell before Darkwill monopolized his attention.

Away from the dais, Ambessa exhaled in a thin stream of anger. She never let her mask of confidence drop, though. Every moment at an event like this was pure performance—everyone here trying to remind the others where exactly they stood, to tell them who was on the rise, who would make a strong ally, and who was ripe for the picking.

"Not as conclusive as I hoped," Rictus murmured.

"No," Ambessa agreed. It was worse than nothing—it was a promise of air, and for it, she had lost her bargaining chip. With Caprian out of her hands, she wouldn't be able to *make* Darkwill do anything. She wished she could have left Caprian at the Medarda residence until Darkwill agreed, but it was too dangerous to leave him alone, no matter what Hanek said.

"Will you dance, then, or is there someone else you'd like to speak to?"

On one side of the ballroom, a display of dancers and musicians took pride of place. They were dressed in the clothing of the northern mountains, voluminous knee-length trousers that billowed when they performed their particular high-kneed style of dance with flaring arms. The music was characterized by heavy drumbeats interrupted at times by a bugling horn made from one of the native rams.

Ambessa frowned and shook her head. "Better not to get distracted. Where's Amenesce?" It would have been impossible to miss the steward and her swiftthorn.

She scanned the crowd, looking for Amenesce and any other key players in the Noxian games of power, those who might support her. She started when she spotted Lisabetya from Krexor. Lisabetya, who had refused to support Ambessa's claim to innocence. She headed for her, but at that moment, the music stopped and the dancers tromped off the central floor, making room for the next troupe. Ambessa wove through them and the colorful trousers and tunics that were common among the farmers and shepherds who lived in the plains. By the time she emerged where Lisabetya had been, the older woman was gone.

Ambessa cursed. "Rell—"

She swallowed her words as she saw Amenesce headed her way. The steward smiled her crooked smile as other stewards and nobles caught her eye, and she didn't run, but there was an urgent cadence to her steps that put Ambessa on alert.

"Is everything all right?" she asked when Amenesce reached her.

"I was in the stables getting the swiftthorns, and you know how stablehands gossip." Beneath her urgency, there was still a wry sharpness. "There's news from Rokrund. Soldiers. Ta'Fik's, if the rumors are true."

Ambessa stood frozen.

"Where is he?" Rictus growled.

"No." Ambessa took his arm. "We need to go. Now. Amenesce, I won't ask you to come with us, but can we borrow—"

"I'll be right behind you. Me and my riders."

"You already spoke to Darkwill about the swifthorns?"

Amenesce shrugged. "He'll have a few less than he's expecting. The details will keep until later."

The hints started to piece themselves together: Gintara and Inyene, seeing to his affairs. And these soldiers he promised Darkwill; did they have anything to do with this?

She wanted to stay, to demand another audience with Darkwill once he'd spoken to Caprian, but she couldn't risk it. That Ta'Fik would dare to strike at Rokrund, at her *home*, was more than an insult—it would shake all of Noxus's confidence in her. All of these smiling people with their hidden daggers, like jaullfish circling for the smell of blood.

"It will take a long time to get to Rokrund," Amenesce said doubtfully, voicing Ambessa's own fears. They could be too late by the time they arrived.

They could be too late already. It had been a long time since she'd heard from Katye. And if Katye and Rokrund Citadel fell...

She didn't let herself think it. Rokrund would not fall. She would not let it.

Ambessa smiled to force a confidence she didn't feel. "I thought your swifthorns were the best mounts the empire could buy."

Amenesce smiled back. "Let's put them to the test."

Ambessa led the way out, only to be stopped just before she reached the door. Lisabetya, wearing a wolf pelt over her broad shoulders. Ambessa drew herself up.

"Steward Lisabetya. If you'll excuse me."

Lisabetya stepped in her way as she tried to pass. "What did you discuss with Darkwill?"

Ambessa bristled. "How audacious. Do you not think me a patricide?"

Lisabetya searched her teeth with her tongue. "I told you, I do not."

"You never said you didn't when it might have counted for something."

"True. That's true. Whatever it is, he looked pleased."

"Then let that satisfy you. Write to me at Rokrund if you decide you're done sitting on fences. *Patience is prudence—*"

"*But indecision is cowardice.* I knew Menelik as well as you, Ambessa. You're going back to Rokrund?"

"Why? Do you know something of it?"

Lisabetya looked down at her through heavy-lidded eyes. "No. Only ride fast."

Lisabetya stepped out of their way, but Ambessa felt the steward's gaze on her back well after she was out of the Grand General's home.

She felt the weight of all of their expectations following her. Ta'Fik, satisfied that he had made her move to his music. Darkwill, waiting for her to end victorious or to fail. And Lisabetya. Even Rell and Amenesce. Even Rictus.

She would bear the weight. She was made to bear it.

Chapter Twenty-One

Several months after their mother left, their father summoned Mel and Kino. Mel went eagerly. There had to be a letter, finally. Mel had been desperately anxious, though she hadn't let it show as she coaxed Tivadar into a standoffish companionship that was held together primarily because they were the only ones of a similar age and status (and because Tivadar's arrogance in the Reckoner Arena *had* alienated her from the peers she might have found there, which Mel had pointed out).

She was also desperately frightened that her mother had found out that Mel had disobeyed her, which she would as soon as Katye wrote to her. So she practically ran to the rooms her father shared with her mother whenever Ambessa deigned to be held captive by her family.

Kino was already there, lounging like a lazy cat over the arm of a couch.

"Is it a letter?" Mel asked breathlessly. "Did Mother write?"

Azizi smiled warmly and patted the couch next to him. His eyes were tight at the corners, though, and shadows bagged beneath them.

"Is something wrong?" she asked.

"He hasn't opened it yet. We've been waiting on you, your

majesty, so please, do sit down."

Mel picked up a pillow and hit Kino in the head with it as she sat down.

Azizi rolled his eyes and opened up the letter. If he realized his hands were trembling, he made no sign, not even to still them.

"Oh," he said softly, eyes round. "She made it to Vindor."

"Read it, Father, or else what's the point of us staring at you?" Kino drawled, but even his laconic attitude couldn't hide that he was just as anxious as they were.

"Of course, of course, forgive me, O peacock prince." Azizi cleared his throat as an orator.

"Azizi. Kino. Mel. Yes, I know you're still in Bel'zhun. Unless, of course, you've found your sense and sailed to Rokrund. But if not, I hope this letter finds all of you well. I have made it to Vindor. Amenesce is an ally. Smik is not. His ships sank and scattered my fleet. Was captured but escaped and forced overland. Will sail to strike deal with BD. Send return to Katye in Rokrund.

"Azizi—convince Dorrik that bolbo-head soup is out of fashion. I want to hit Smik's purse as well as his warbands.

"Kino—speak to the Suns of Bel'zhun. They're our only allies in the city. I've made them assurances. Be their friend.

"Ambessa"

"BD?" Kino asked.

"Boram Darkwill," Mel said automatically. She had seen him in the Immortal Bastion once, when she was touring the great cities and meeting their leaders with her mother. She'd seen Darkwill only from a distance, but he'd struck her as a larger-than-life man, so grandiose that he must have been hiding something. "Was there nothing else for me?"

Azizi looked from the letter to her, then went back to skimming the letter before shaking his head apologetically.

"Well, she certainly won't waste paper." Kino swung his legs off the couch. "Do you know what assurances she made to the Suns, Father?"

Azizi shook his head, but he didn't look away from Mel. Mel looked down at her lap to avoid both men's gazes, so they wouldn't see how hard she had to work not to cry.

"I see," Kino said. "I'll just go get started on that, shall I?"

He left and Mel got up to follow him.

"Mel. Wait."

She stopped but didn't turn, trying to dry the dampness at the corners of her eyes surreptitiously.

"Mel?"

She heard her father rise from the couch, heard the gentle tread of his slippered feet.

"I'm supposed to meet Tivadar at another one of Kino's taverns," she sniffed.

"Spare your old father some company." He draped an arm around her shoulders and turned her into him for a hug. "Spying on Tivadar can wait, can't it? I've missed you."

"I—I'm not spying on her."

Azizi laughed softly. "You are a Medarda. I know exactly what you are doing, and what she is doing to you, to us. So come. Let us drop the pretenses for a little while. We can speak honestly for once." His voice was dressed in irony that, somehow, managed not to be bitter.

He held her away from him and raised his eyebrows, waiting for an answer, unlike her mother, who would simply have commanded and waited for Mel to obey. He was shorter than her mother, and slight, with a small belly pressing against his tunic. His smile was soft and sad, but his eyes laughed. In short, he was everything that her mother was not. Uncharitably, Mel hoped she took more after him than her mother.

"Yes, Father."

They were silent in the carriage for some time before her father spoke.

"Do you want to tell me what's wrong?"

Mel looked away, out of the carriage window. The horses' hooves rang on the stone road. On either side, hawkers sold street food and trinkets, and her thoughts flitted toward the Rakkor man who'd given her her tattoos.

"It's all right." Her father chuckled, and Mel heard a twinge of sadness in it. "She and I fought before she left, you know. I swear, when she smells a fight, it's like watching someone dump black powder on an open flame."

Mel wasn't sure she was supposed to hear that last part. Her father shook his head as if to clear the thought.

"Your mother is the strongest person I know. I'd never known someone so single-minded, so determined. Until, of course, I met you."

"Me?" Mel whipped her head around in disbelief. "I'm nothing like her. That's why she thinks I'm useless. Weak." Her voice cracked, proving her point. "She won't even let me help her. She just wants to bundle me out of the way."

Azizi winced. "She didn't say that."

"She doesn't need to. She has something important for you and Kino to do, but she doesn't trust me with anything. What else could it mean?"

Her father sighed, and for a few seconds, they sat in pained silence, both tonguing the wounds left by Ambessa's sharp edges. Then he wrapped an arm around Mel and pulled her close against his side. He kissed the top of her head and held her there.

"I think—and she'll never admit this—that your mother is

scared. And when people are scared, they can be crueler than they might normally be, to those they love and those they're— those they think might hurt the ones they love. She might do things that she regrets, and struggle to make amends after."

"Mother doesn't have regrets." Mel stated it like a fact, no bitterness. It was a truth she had accustomed herself to. Medardas didn't regret—they simply took the results of an action and made a new plan. Apologies were never part of those plans. *A wolf does not apologize*, she would probably say.

There was the bitterness.

Her father laughed aloud then. "You may not know them, but she does. She hides some of them from me, too, I'm sure." He squeezed Mel tight. "No matter what she says, though, she says it out of love. The reason she wants you to be so strong is because she wants you to be safe. She wants you to be stronger than anyone who could ever hurt you. You understand that, right?"

Though Mel didn't pull herself out of his embrace, she stared out the window instead of meeting her father's eyes.

"She doesn't mean to hurt you."

Again, Mel remained silent. How could she explain to him that she wasn't hurt because her mother thought she was weak but because her mother thought she couldn't *help*? Because her mother wouldn't *listen*? All Mel wanted to do was to show her that she could do what the Medarda family needed her to do, but that she could do it in *her own* way.

And yes, there was the part of her that saw the Binan woman's face as her head fell away from her body in her dreams. The necklace, broken beads scattered through the lake of blood. There had been so much of it. The haunting was just another sign that Mel was the wrong choice.

"Someone told me that people with power only fear losing that power."

Mel had turned the artist's words over in her head and heart since that day. He was wrong, for certain, though, on one point: Ambessa had never done anything she wasn't proud of, something she didn't think was worthy of her cause. No matter what the artist said, no matter what her father said about regret. *Medarda over all.*

Azizi made a quiet sound in his throat. Slowly, begrudgingly, he nodded. "That's not far off, perhaps. I think your mother is more complicated than that, but perhaps that is a part of it."

"If she's so afraid, why doesn't she let us *help* her?"

Azizi gave her an odd, startled look, then he smiled. "You're very wise for someone so young. And compassionate. I'll say you got it from me." His smile widened, and he jostled her in the ribs with his elbow until Mel couldn't help smiling herself, then giggling, and then they were both laughing.

Suddenly, they were slammed into each other as the carriage lurched wildly and the horses screamed and squealed outside. Mel clutched at her father's arm as they careened from side to side.

Then the entire thing tilted, and Mel felt herself falling in slow motion from one side of the cab to the other. Her father fell, too, his arms reaching in vain for something to hold on to—no, *he was reaching for her*— She closed her eyes tight as the cab crashed onto its side. Her head slammed into something hard.

A flash of bright white light, and then—darkness.

When Mel woke, she was still on her side, her arm crushed beneath her. She tried to wiggle her fingers, and though it hurt, they obeyed her command. It took longer for her vision to cooperate—it was nothing but blurry shapes, and everything spun.

"Father?" she called. Her voice was raspy, her throat raw. She must have been screaming.

She blinked until her vision solidified. Shapes were still blurry, but she could see the outline where her father lay.

"Father, are you all right?"

Nothing. She reached over and shook him, wincing as a lancing pain shot up her arm. "Father." He didn't respond to her rough touch, and her breath quickened.

Slowly, her sight sharpened. Her father lay on the floor, like her, which was actually the side of the cab. One arm was bent at an odd angle, and— Mel gasped. His neck—no neck should be bent that way. She clenched tight on her stomach, holding back the sudden urge to vomit. Holding back the urge to scream, as much as she wanted to. To scream for help. To scream for him to wake up.

What would her mother have done?

Mel calmed her shuddering breath. Rolled closer to him, double-checking his breathing—but when she turned him, his eyes were open and staring. She held back a sob.

Outside, urgent voices shouted around their overturned cab, but they sounded muffled from inside. Where was their driver? Gingerly, she pushed at the door that had become their ceiling, but it wouldn't open, and her body hurt too much to force it.

"Help!" she finally called. "Help! My father!"

The carriage shook as someone wrenched the door above open. A man with thick arms reached in to help her climb out of the cab. Mel emerged onto a crowded street. Someone else rushed over to help the man, and Mel recognized her—the girl from the hostel the artist had stayed at.

"You," Mel said, still not functioning properly.

The girl looked at her in surprise, but only nodded. "Are you all right?"

"My father, he's—" This time, the sob escaped.

The girl looked down into the cab and gasped. "It's— Come on, we'll get you out."

The whispers now carried a different tone—that of gossip. *Medarda*, they said. *Medarda, Medarda.*

"Please," she rasped. "Send for Kino Medarda." Someone else hurried to obey, but her attention was already elsewhere.

Two more men were dragging her father out as carefully as they could. The voices of the crowd hushed as they realized he was dead—it grew quieter still as they realized who the man was.

Ambessa Medarda's husband was dead.

Mel's father was dead.

Oh. She would have to write to her mother. *Oh no.*

She tried to hold herself upright, but then she felt herself tilting and her vision blinking out again. Only the girl at her side kept her from hitting the ground as she fainted.

She woke several times in a second carriage on the way to the healers at the Medarda compound, each time certain that this was all a bad, blurry dream (that pain in her arm was surely only because she was sleeping poorly on it, the pins and needles translating into something worse in her imagination).

At least, she thought this until she woke, finally in her own bed, covered in blankets against the autumn night chill.

"Mel. You're awake." Kino startled from his chair at her bedside. He scrubbed his face. "How are you feeling?"

"My arm—"

"Is broken. Only reason your head wasn't is because it's too thick." His relief gave way easily to the mask of humor.

"Father?"

Kino shook his head, his lips tightening. "Are you well enough to see a guest? They've been waiting in the corridor for quite some time."

Mel frowned. Who could want to see her that badly? The last person in the city whom she cared for was in this room.

"I suppose?"

Kino's voice darkened. "It's Tivadar."

Mel's mind was too fuzzy to understand. "Is she angry?"

"She wasn't with you and Father? You didn't see her outside the carriage?"

Slowly, his meaning came to her. "You think she did this?"

It hadn't even occurred to Mel that the carriage accident had been intentional, but now she could see it from Kino's perspective. A chance to take out two of Ambessa Medarda's immediate family—ripe fruit for an enemy.

Kino looked away guiltily. "She asked where you were when you didn't show up for lunch. I told her you'd gone riding with Father."

"But she wouldn't—" Mel broke off, chewing her lip.

Only, she would. It was against the Code, but Tivadar didn't respect the Code. It was the kind of thing Mel wasn't strong enough to do, but exactly the kind of thing Ambessa wished Mel could do.

"Let her in," Mel said, her voice tight. "Let me speak to her."

Kino sensed the change in Mel and opened the door. Tivadar came in, hunching her shoulders as if frightened, for once, of her height. She held a small package tight to her stomach.

At the sight of her, a fury like Mel had never known lit her up from the inside.

"Did you have anything to do with this?" Mel snapped at her cousin.

Tivadar jerked back as if Mel were a striking pit viper. "No.

I was waiting for you at Kino's noodle place, but you stood me up!"

"I know you're here spying on me for your father! How do I know he hasn't given you orders for—for something worse?"

"I'm not doing anything you aren't!" She scoffed in disgust and threw the small wrapped packet on the bed in Mel's lap. "I just came to bring you this and make sure you were all right. I guess you are. My father was right about you all." With a glare for Mel and for Kino, she stomped out.

Mel immediately felt the hot scourge of regret, even before Kino made a considering sound in his throat.

"Ah, the wolf pup bites! I thought for certain you were going to get up and strangle her yourself, broken arm or no."

"Shut up, Kino." Mel crossed her good arm over her chest and glared to the side. She was remembering what Azizi had said to her about regret. About her mother's.

Her brother sighed and came to sit on the foot of Mel's bed. He squeezed her ankle beneath the blankets, then started to unwrap the packet Tivadar had left. It smelled like food, but Mel had no appetite.

"He's gone," she whispered, throat thick.

Kino's face contorted in pain, and he closed his eyes, hands still. Nodded. Swallowed. His voice was hoarse when he said, "I'm going into the city tonight. Mother said to speak to the Suns. Maybe...maybe they'll know something about what happened today."

"Aren't they rebels? They hate Noxus. Maybe *they're* the ones who did this." They had *so many* enemies.

Kino sighed. "It's possible. I won't know until I speak with them."

Maybe not even then. Mel was stricken with a sudden fear that beat hard in her chest. "It's not safe."

Kino stared at the ceiling as if trying not to cry, but the dried tracks on his cheeks and the redness of his eyes told all Mel needed to know.

"I'm so sorry, Mel. I should have been with you both. I could have . . ." He shook his head, at a loss.

"Could have what?" In a small voice, realizing it with a shudder, "What if I'd lost you both?"

"Never." Kino shook his head fervently. "Never." He leaned over and kissed her on the forehead. "Rest. I'll take plenty of guards. Don't worry. I'll get to the bottom of this."

After Kino left, Mel stared at the ceiling, with nothing but the last memories of her father to keep her company. Her head ached from crying, but there was no possibility of sleep—every time she closed her eyes, she saw his empty eyes. She needed a distraction. She called for ink and paper and began trying to write to her mother with her off hand. A knock at the door interrupted her unsuccessful attempts.

"There's a young woman here, Lady Mel." The guard looked skeptically back over her shoulder. "She says she knows you."

Wary, Mel said, "I'm not expecting anyone."

Then she saw the face peering around the guard's arm. The assistant at the inn. The girl who had found her and her father after the accident. It was an unfortunate coincidence. Still. Kino's words had struck a chord in her. She did not *want* to be like her mother.

"Come in," she said gently.

The guard let the girl approach but followed her, lest she attack Mel in her bed. The girl saw what Mel was struggling to do and, without asking, turned the lamp brighter.

"Can I help?" She pointed to the pen Mel held awkwardly.

Trust. It was the thing her mother lacked. Perhaps because people in their position—*so many enemies*—could not afford it. But without it, they could not have friends, either.

I will be careful, but I will not be closed.

"I'm trying to write to my mother. To tell her...what happened." Mel handed the girl the pen and a fresh piece of paper. The girl took it, nodding. "Did you see? What happened, I mean?"

The girl frowned as she tried to remember. "Not really. I mean, I watched the carriage roll, but I didn't see anything that could have caused it. The horses just jerked in one direction, and the carriage driver—" Her frown deepened. "I didn't see a driver anywhere." She met Mel's eyes. Her own weren't scared, exactly, but wide with the same realization that Mel was having.

Intelligent, and not easily frightened. Mel found herself assessing the young woman just like her mother would. She could be a good person to keep around, if she could be trusted.

Mel smiled tentatively. "What's your name?"

"Elora."

"I'm Mel. Thank you. For helping me today."

Elora's smile was warm and genuine, and Mel hoped that it was real.

Chapter Twenty-Two

They rode hard, eking out every ounce of endurance that Amenesce swore the swifthorns could give them. Only a few weeks, she said, were all it would take to reach the mountains bordering the Rokrund Plains. Even so, Ambessa didn't think it was the beasts that would give out first, but their own bodies. They stopped just long enough for the animals and tried not to fall asleep in their saddles. More than once, she saw Tora jab Rell in the side to keep her awake as they traveled through the dark of the night.

Still, it was taking too long.

They were in the middle of one of these too-brief pauses, a day or two from the Varju Mountains, when one of Amenesce's outriders came galloping back to them. Amenesce's voice darkened as she took their report.

Ambessa gulped water from a skin and splashed some of it on her face. Rictus brought her some coffee, brewed with the grounds over the quick fire one of the riders had made. She sipped the hot drink, attempting to clear her mind until Amenesce was finished.

"It's Trannit," Amenesce spat. She tongued her teeth, hands on her hips. "He's got soldiers headed to Rokrund. Or trying to intercept us. Unless they change course, we'll meet before the Varju Mountains."

Ambessa drank her coffee and exhaled slowly. "He's probably been planning this since we left Vindor."

Tora brought Amenesce a cup, too, before running off to sit beside the fire with Rell, who watched them with concern from bleary eyes. The girl was exhausted. They all were. But she'd never been pushed so hard.

"We could outrun them," Amenesce suggested, but even she sounded dubious and weary at the prospect. "If we reach the mountains before they do, we could set traps. Everyone knows how treacherous the Varjus are. An unfortunate rockslide... tragic."

Ambessa nodded. It could work. But the odds of them outrunning Trannit's soldiers, in this shape, were low. She'd already planned on slowing through the mountains, taking the time to rest, and then catching a barge at the base of the mountains on the other side, riding the river all the way down.

The only other option was to stop and fight, and that was a delay—and a risk—that could be devastating for Rokrund.

"Did they see your rider?" Ambessa asked sharply. "Is there any chance at all that this is a coincidence?"

Amenesce sniffed. "I don't know about my scout, but it's hard to miss fifty riders racing at top speed. They've got lookouts just like we do."

"It's me they want, though."

"Aren't we cocky?"

"You know it's true. The mountains would be just as good for an ambush."

Amenesce shook her head. "We're cavalrymen, not assassins."

The assertion, however, gave Ambessa a better idea. "Pull back half of your riders. Take the long way around Smik's people so that you're behind them, but keep back so his scouts don't see you. What direction are they marching?"

"He said southwesterly."

"Then we'll keep going south, me and the other half of your riders."

Amenesce nodded slowly, a wry smile pulling her scar. "Make yourselves as appetizing as possible while we ride over his ass?"

"Exactly. And when he runs from you…" Ambessa snapped her fingers, the crack silencing the conversations around them. "We finish him."

It was past time to rid herself of this thorn in her foot.

The only hope echoing in her mind was that the warband of three hundred heavy cavalry that Amenesce had sent from Vindor were already in Rokrund, holding the line.

Rell hid behind an outcropping of rock, her back flush against it so she would be out of sight when the Trannit warband came running. Around her, the pass was full of hidden warriors, tucked away like deadly little secrets the mountain kept. Except the mountain wasn't the Varju Mountains. The mountain was Ambessa. Her will had dispersed two dozen of them, and it was her signal they waited for.

The cold of the stone seeped into Rell's back. She tried to slow her breaths to keep them quiet, but that only made her want to gasp. The sun was setting. Everyone had blacked the steel of their weapons with ash to keep the glare of the sun from giving away their location. They'd gotten into position in the afternoon, hidden their swifthorns out of sight. Rell thought she would die of anticipation. It was half like waiting to go out into the arena, and half something else. Her stomach was tight with nerves, but she was—she couldn't deny it—*excited*. Finally. It was the moment she'd been waiting for.

Before they'd taken their places, Rictus had come up to her.

"Are you ready?" he asked.

Rell bristled. "Of course I am. You've seen me in the arena."

"Battle is different." He cocked his head as he looked down at her, taking in her armor and the spear she was covering in ash.

"People die in the arena all the time." Rell hadn't killed any; she'd managed to win by disabling her opponents or knocking them out, but she'd always known it might come to that. She could have. She just hadn't.

"Dying in a game is different than fighting for your life."

"I know," Rell said, though she didn't really see how. The goal was to win, no matter what.

Rictus sighed. The thing he always wore on his weapons glowed faintly around his halberd. He told her it was called a rookern, but he ignored her anytime she pressed for more.

"Remember what we practiced." He held two fingers up beside his right eye and moved them to the side of his left eye. "See everything around you."

He looked as if he were going to say something else, but one eyebrow rose at something behind Rell. It was Tora, come to say goodbye.

"Could we have a moment, Captain?"

Rictus grunted in amusement. He refused any title. Still, he left, but not before giving Rell a tight squeeze on one shoulder. He held her gaze steadily, but whatever he was trying to say, Rell didn't understand it.

Then she and the cavalrywoman were alone. Tora took her by the hand. She pulled Rell's palm open and thrust something warm and metal into it. A small, misshapen hunk of metal with a leather thong through it. She recognized it as the thong that was always around Tora's neck.

"What is it?" Rell asked artlessly.

"Good luck charm," Tora said. She smiled her crooked smile,

and Rell's stomach fluttered. "Bit of the first shoe of my first horse."

"I—uh—" Rell didn't know what to say. She blurted out, "Are you sure it works?"

Tora only laughed. "Course it does. I was wearing it the day I met you, wasn't I?"

"But—you need it."

"Me? Ha. I don't need luck. Not with this." Tora patted her bow and quiver on the swifthorn's saddle.

It was Tora's first battle, too, and her undaunted swagger goaded Rell to match it. And why shouldn't she? She'd done this before. It was going to be just like the arena.

"What makes you think I need luck?" Rell jabbed back. She spun her spear in a tight circle in front of her, forcing Tora to jump back, laughing.

Behind them, Amenesce quietly snapped orders at the riders who would go with her, looping wide and then chasing Smik and his warband into the gap where Ambessa waited.

Tora grabbed her swifthorn's reins and started jogging away with it. "Keep it safe for me, then. I'll see you soon." Then, while the swifthorn was at a trot, she leapt onto its back and rode after Amenesce and the others.

"Show-off," Rell muttered to herself affectionately, against the stone. She touched the metal lump where it rested against her sternum and smiled.

Night had fallen by the time she felt herself begin to tremble—the very earth beneath her feet and the rock at her back shook. She looked to Ambessa, who held her blackened sword low at her hip. The general listened carefully, raised the sword horizontally—the "get ready" position. Rell gripped her spear and waited for the final signal, listening to the growing roar of hoofbeats.

The closer they came, the more she could hear the shouting of men and women—shouting in anger, shouting in fear, shouting at their beasts, urging them faster. Then came the roar and tremble of rocks that shook Rell even more in her protected position. Ambessa had signaled the first trap, a slide of boulders arranged to fall toward anyone riding up the pass.

The shouts turned to screams as riders tried to turn their mounts away, screams of the horses as they broke their legs, unable to spin around fast enough, screams as soldier and beast alike were hit by the heavy stone like cannonballs. Another signal from Ambessa and arrows flew down, swift and deadly, silent compared to all the other noise. Even if some arrows lost their targets in the dark, many did not.

Rell waited and she waited for the final signal with her heart in her throat. Suddenly, she wondered what it might feel like to have an arrow in her. She'd never been shot before— *No. Not now.* She hunted for the calm she took up before she walked into the arena.

She was so absorbed in trying to find it that she almost missed the signal. It was the rush of the other soldiers around her, sprinting down toward Smik's broken warband, that pulled her out of herself. Their war cry carried her with it until even she was yelling wordlessly.

The first Trannit soldier she found was picking himself up from the ground where his horse had thrown him. The beast was flailing on its side, as dangerous to Rell as to its rider. Rell's spear took him through the ribs before he realized what was happening. Her momentum drove the man back onto the ground, staring up at the night sky. Her momentum carried her, too, so that she stood over him, staring into his blue eyes as he groaned in pain.

He bared his bloody teeth in a snarl at her before he died.

Bile burned the back of her throat. She had to twist and jerk the spear out of his ribs where it had stuck.

There. That was easy. Her first bout, won.

But the noise around her was nothing like the adoration of the crowd. There would be no victory lap here.

She charged at another Trannit soldier, one who was already up on their feet. They spun at her with a curved sword, deflecting Rell's first thrust. When they tried to get in closer, though, Rell swung the butt of her spear into their gut. When they doubled over, she brought the blade back around, and this time, it found a mark. The blacked blade cut across their eyes, and they fell back, screaming with their hands pressed over their face.

Two, Rell thought smugly, just as a silver dart streaked across her peripheral vision. She turned with her spear out, reflexes honed in training leading her into a roll just as another sword pierced the spot where she'd been standing.

For every one that Rell fought, though, there was another, and another, and another. This wasn't like the arena at all. No single opponent, no clean and certain victory, no judge to call it final—after the initial surprise of the ambush had worn off, the pitch of the battle changed. The soldiers were ready for her. She had to dodge bodies and riderless horses rearing up, or riderless swifthorns, their horns as lethal as any sword. She careened from one desperate scrabble to another. She wasn't even sure if the people she left behind her were properly dead.

Where was Tora? Was she out there, still? Was one of these riderless swifthorns hers?

She couldn't ask that, not now.

Rell was fighting in a warband. Rell was fighting in General Ambessa Medarda's warband. She was part of an ambush with the legendary riders of Vindor, with their deep teal tunics and their leather riding coats streaming behind them and their hooked sabers flashing. It was nothing like the adventures of her daydreams.

This was a nightmare.

A vicious knock sent Rell sprawling to the ground, and she wasn't even sure what had hit her. She scrambled to her feet in the patchy grass. Her hands stung where gravel had ripped them—her hands were empty. Where was her spear?—there, in the grass, just a pace away. Rell dived for it only to be pulled back.

A large man, as big as Rictus, had caught hold of the back of her riding coat. Only he was not Rictus. There was none of the wry stoicism, no hidden amusement, no steady guidance—just dark eyes, intent on their object. Like many of Smik's riders, he wore heavy studded armor that Rell wouldn't even be able to lift. He yanked, and she had no choice but to fall backward.

Rell saw stars when her head smacked earth and rock. She clutched for a weapon and found only grass. *No,* she thought. She tried to roll onto her hands and knees, she had to get away, get to her spear—*I can't die here.*

But she was going to. A wave of dizziness dropped her back down, and the man pulled back his arm. The steel glint of his sword caught the moonlight.

Time seemed to slow as she watched the blade fall. Then two arrows flew into the man's chest, one after the other. It wasn't enough to kill him, but he staggered. He looked after the ones who'd had the audacity to hit him, but Rell did not. She lurched toward her spear and spun it up into his chest, right between the two arrows, and she twisted and shoved and twisted and shoved until he fell to his knees and the light was gone from his eyes.

Oh gods. Rell hunched over on her hands and knees, gasping for breath. She tasted copper in her mouth. Her muscles burned with exhaustion. She'd thought—she'd almost—she needed to find Ambessa.

Like this? said an angry voice in her head. *You want to crawl to the general on your knees, like a scared little kitten?*

She didn't. She didn't want Ambessa to change her mind and send Rell home. She didn't want to tell Tora that this was what she'd done during the battle.

Rell struggled to her feet but fell back to her knees. Her legs were shaking that badly. Her spear was slick with blood. She crawled through the darkness, flinching away from the sounds of battle that still clashed around her.

Then she heard Ambessa's voice. Self-assured, cultured, it made Rell feel safe immediately. She followed it until she saw the general, standing over a thin man whose bald head gleamed in the moonlight. She recognized Steward Smik. His riding clothes were fine, a coat all lined in fur. No armor that Rell could see. Except for the odd gauntlets on his hands, she would say he hadn't expected to be anywhere near battle.

"Were you looking for me?" Ambessa growled. "Or just your courage?"

He'd been crawling away, just like her. The thought filled Rell with shame.

The man jerked back, but the gauntlets slowed him. Ambessa's boot rose and fell on his outstretched arm.

"Kind of you to bring these all the way here for me," she said over Smik's yowl of pain.

He screamed again as she bent down to pull the gauntlet from his broken arm. He swiped at her with the other gauntlet, but he could barely raise it. Ambessa merely batted it aside as if it were no more than a fly. Then she took that one off him, too, and fitted it on. She closed her eyes and sighed, as if, instead of picking up the great weights, a heavy burden had fallen from her.

Rell saw then that the gauntlets weren't gauntlets exactly; they were shaped like drakehound heads with curved blades resting in their mouths.

Smik crawled backward on his backside as fast as he could, cradling his broken arm against his belly, wincing and whimpering when he jostled it.

Ambessa advanced. Rell stared, too enraptured to make a sound.

"Please," Smik begged. "Please. You don't understand. He made me."

"Ta'Fik?" Ambessa's voice was cold and disinterested. It made Rell shiver.

"Yes! Ta'Fik made me. You don't understand."

"What's to understand? You chose him in the succession. You sank my ships. You tried to jail me." She flexed her arms, raising the gauntlets to catch the light of the stars. Unblackened by ash, the half-moon blades gleamed sharp. "You stole my drakehounds."

Smik gulped. "We— To call us allies discounts the nature of our relationship, you see, he blackmailed me, otherwise, of course I would have supported your claim, you have every right, *every right*!" His voice rose as she stepped closer. "Please!"

Ambessa hesitated. "Blackmail?"

"I—might have been indiscreet with—my coffers. He promised—" Smik cleared his throat. "He promised to erase my debts, and then to make Trannit the prime source of azirite in the north. I was only doing what I thought my people needed, and he threatened to reveal the extent of—my debts."

"Temperance would have served you better." Ambessa raised her arm as if to deal him a fatal backhand.

"Please, have mercy. Please!" He rolled onto his knees and bowed his head in supplication. "You'll have all my warbands at your disposal. You'll have my support, my funds—such as they are, only have mercy on me."

For a moment, Rell felt sympathetic relief. Her own breath sagged out of her. They would take him hostage, and the general would have a new coin to bargain with in this war against the steward of Tereshni.

Ambessa tilted his chin up with the horizontal blade of one drakehound, tenderly, careful not to cut him. She gazed down at him and said, "A wolf has no mercy."

Rell closed her eyes against the silver arc of the second drakehound blade as it descended.

Was she a coward?

Rell sat away from the grassy area right before the pass, away from the torchlight of Ambessa's and Amenesce's soldiers as they separated the wounded from the dead. It was the closest to being alone that she could get. She closed her eyes tight to hold back the tears that threatened, but when she did, she saw the man who'd almost killed her. She saw the crushed body parts she'd tripped over. She heard the crunch of cartilage and bone as Ambessa's gauntlets cut through Smik's neck. Ambessa hadn't seen her.

She didn't know how long she sat there, growing colder as the heat of battle fled. When she heard voices calling her name, she knew she should heed them, but she couldn't. She didn't want to face any of them. If she went back to them, they'd know she was weak. They'd see how scared she was, and how scared she would be to go into battle again. They would reject her, all of them, Tora, Rictus, Ambessa. They would call her worthless, just like her parents had whenever she lost in the arena.

In a moment. She would go in a moment. Clean herself up

and face Ambessa like a warrior. Rell sniffed hard and went to wipe her face, but her sleeve was just as filthy as her blood-sticky hands.

"Rell?"

At the sound of Tora's voice, so close, Rell couldn't help but turn to it. A fresh wave of tears broke past her defenses. Tora was still alive.

Tora ran over and crushed her in a hug. "You're safe. You're here! We thought— General! Steward! She's here!"

"No," she said. "I don't want them to see me." Rell buried her face in Tora's coat. It was cleaner than her own.

Tora didn't seem to understand her, but she rubbed Rell's back and murmured softly with none of her old bravado. "I'm so glad you're safe. I didn't know what to do when we couldn't find you. Are you hurt? We'll get you to the healer's tent." It was a nervous sort of patter.

Rell pulled away from her. "I'm—" She started to say she was fine, but saw that Tora looked as bad as she did in the light of the torch she held aloft. Tora's dark curls were frayed, her eyes shadowed and cheeks blood-speckled. Though her coat was mostly clean, her trousers were drenched in blood from her riding boots to her thighs. One thigh had a gash that had already been sewn shut and bandaged.

Rell gasped. "Me? What about you?"

Tora sagged onto the ground beside her with a pained grunt. "That was the worst thing I've ever lived through." Tora's voice cracked as she spoke. The usual cocky lilt of her voice was tinged with something else now, something that Rell felt deep in her bones. Tora sniffed hard.

"Me too," Rell said quietly. She took Tora's empty hand.

"Rell!" Ambessa's frantic voice broke harshly through the quiet as the general and Amenesce jogged over to them.

Rell stood up quickly, straightening her clothes with one hand and holding her spear with the other. She saluted. "General. Steward."

Ambessa's empty hands reached out as if to grab Rell by the shoulders, but she hesitated, hovering above her. "You're well?"

"I—" The words wouldn't come out. They would have been a lie.

Ambessa looked down at Rell's hands, so Rell did, too. They were stained red, darker in the cracks of her palms. Ambessa's brow creased, and she opened her mouth as if to speak but stopped. Rell felt Tora's and Amenesce's gazes on them.

Ambessa lowered her hands and nodded once. "Well done."

Then she turned and left, shouting more orders. Amenesce lingered a moment longer, an expression almost like pity on her face. Rell straightened her back and nodded to the steward. Then she, too, left Rell and Tora alone with what they had done.

Chapter Twenty-Three

After the ambush against Smik and his warband, Ambessa's forces crossed the Varju Mountains, which took nearly a month. Ambessa then sailed into Rokrund on a commandeered river barge, passing a military encampment. At first, she thought it was Ta'Fik's forces; then she recognized the standard of the Miners, her artillery warband.

"Here," she commanded the bargeman to stop along the banks. When he found a shallow enough spot, she disembarked along with Rell, Rictus, and just over a dozen of Amenesce's swifthorn riders—all of those who could fit. Amenesce and the other few dozen remaining were riding down from the foothills, with the spare swifthorns. There wasn't enough space on the barge for the forty surviving fighters, let alone their mounts.

"Ho, there! Halt!" A lieutenant marched over to the riverbank as Ambessa approached. "What's your business in Rokrund?"

A fistful of soldiers followed him, their spears bristling at her.

Ragged and sleep deprived, Ambessa could see that her group might have looked, if not formidable, deeply suspicious.

She spread her shoulders back and looked down her nose at him. "I am General Medarda. Take me to your war leader."

"General Ambessa Medarda?" The soldier murmured doubtfully

to the soldier beside him. The other soldier shook their head. "Leave your weapons and we'll escort you—"

"I will *not*." Ambessa bulled forward. She thrust her ring out but barely gave him a chance to see it. "I do not have time for this, and neither do you. Where are Ta'Fik's warbands?"

Spearpoints lowered and swords were unsheathed.

"Ambessa Medarda?" came another voice. A familiar one.

Gareth Burnside, war leader of her Fists, cut through the small crowd that was forming. He limped more than Ambessa remembered.

"Captain." She clasped his forearm.

"General. What are you doing here?"

"I'm here to save your backsides." Ambessa grinned, then sobered. "What news?"

Burnside shook his head and tugged at the bushy gray mustaches down his chin. "Not good. Come with me; leave these idiots alone." He shot his lieutenant a glare, and the young soldier looked abashed as he saluted Ambessa belatedly.

"Respect has grown lax in the ranks, friend."

Burnside side-eyed her dirty clothes. "So has your upkeep."

"Times are hard."

"Aye, they are. I'm sorry about Menelik. I set my stars by that man. Large boots to fill."

"I know," she said simply. "Ta'Fik?"

"They have the saltpetre mines," he said grimly.

"What?" Ambessa struggled to tamp down her outrage. Control of the saltpetre mines wasn't just about money—it was black powder for her artillery, ship cannons, even food preservation, which meant feeding the armies. Most importantly, it was rare, one of the few mines in Noxus.

Burnside nodded. "Lost a lot of the Fist there. Some heavy cavalry from Vindor helped, but even they couldn't change the way things ended up. Ambessa, it was...nothing like I've ever seen before."

"How big is their force?"

"That's just it," he said softly. "They can't be more than three hundred, and there are even a few basilisks, but the Fist lost an entire company! We're down to two hundred, including the wounded. I'm not used to taking losses like that. Those soldiers—" He cut himself off and shook his head. At Ambessa's frown, he said in a low voice, "In the tent."

That worried her. At full strength, the Fist was five hundred strong, light infantry but especially proficient in getting close, then striking hard and fast. She had lost a few of them in Binan, and some on the journey through Trannit waters, but... If something could do that much damage to them, even *with* Amenesce's cavalry...

Before they could enter Burnside's command tent, however, a boisterous, joyous shout rang through the air.

"General!"

Ambessa turned in surprise. Zishani, captain of the *Golden Dancer*, jogged over and saluted. Then, noticing Rell, Zishani punched the girl in the shoulder.

"Good to see you can swim, little sea pup."

"I can't," Rell grumbled, but she looked pleased nevertheless.

"Good to see you, Zishani. I thought you were lost," Ambessa said. "How many are you?"

"I washed up on the shore, but I'd lost you." Zishani bowed her head in regret. "I gathered those I could, and we made our way back to Rokrund overland. I'm sorry I didn't follow you, but for the sake of the survivors, I thought it better to regroup."

Ambessa wanted to chastise the woman, but she was right—there was no sense in losing every soldier, and she wouldn't have made a difference.

"The *Cacklebird* made it back from Bel'zhun, though! They hit a little trouble but nothing Kress couldn't handle. She's in the city overseeing repairs. Some of her fighters have joined mine. Afraid to say we're not as good on land as old Burnside here." Zishani clapped her hand on Burnside's shoulder. She sobered. "Any others from the *Dancer*?"

Ambessa ducked under the tent flap that Burnside held up for her. Rictus followed, but the lieutenant of her swifthorn riders waited outside.

"Ma'am?" he asked.

"The quartermaster is over there." Burnside jerked his thumb. "She'll see you to a tent and hot meal. Bathe in the river as you like. General?"

"Perfect, thank you, Captain. Lieutenant, at ease. You'll have orders soon."

The Vindoran soldier saluted, and his squad dispersed.

"Rell?" Ambessa caught the girl as she tried to head into the tent after Rictus. "Go with them."

Rell looked up at her. She leaned heavily on her spear. There had been a hollowness to her that went beyond exhaustion ever since they'd ambushed Smik. It was probably the first time she had ever taken a life herself. A heavy thing to do, a life-changing moment on every warrior's path. Ambessa hadn't known what to say when Rell stood before her that night, and she hadn't had the time to coach her through it, not with their breakneck pace through the mountains.

Her own first kill—many kills stood out, but could she remember her first? Perhaps it was that Freljordian scout when she was visiting a cousin in the Ironspikes? No, because she had started her courses by then. It might have been the mercy killing of the wounded woman whose sword she'd picked up. Ambessa remembered the gurgling blood in the woman's chest, the weak raised hand. Beseeching eyes. She had startled Ambessa, who thought she was dead. Ambessa remembered stabbing the woman with her own sword, but was it reflexive or deliberate? Those bits mattered less now. The important part was that the woman was some thirty years dead.

Ambessa gripped Rell's shoulder as comfortingly as she could, and spoke for her ears only.

"We have many things to talk about, Rell. I know I haven't been able to spare the proper time on your training, but when I return, we'll talk about everything that's happened."

Rell's look sharpened. "I'm coming with you."

"You just rode across the continent. You need rest."

"So do you."

"You're not used to this. I've had a lifetime to prepare for a challenge like this." Ambessa was aware of the other commanders pretending politely to ignore this conversation.

"Then I'll become used to it." Rell jutted her chin stubbornly, her brow set. Her eyes, shadowed. "How else will I learn?"

"If you're tired on the field, the consequences are life and death."

"I'm not afraid to die—"

"Not for you," Ambessa said sharply, "but your comrades. Are you prepared to hold their lives in your hands, too? What about your friend, Tora?" Then, in a lower voice: "Rell. You have nothing more to prove to me. Not today."

Rell swallowed. A new gravity settled on her. "I'll take some time to rest, by your leave, General."

As Rell followed the Vindoran riders, her shoulders consciously more erect than before, Ambessa felt something odd spreading through her chest.

Pride. She felt pride. Pride and a stirring sense of potential.

The mood within the tent subdued her immediately.

First, Ambessa answered Zishani's question. "Everyone who survived with me is in one of Smik's prisons. Smik is dead now, but it would cost us more to try to free them right now than if we waited."

"And if we don't rescue them?" Zishani said quietly.

Ambessa had the same answer now as she did when Rell asked her when she first abandoned them to their fate. This was war, and war was not without costs. She would not waste what she'd gained.

She shook her head once. "Captain, explain. What has you with your tail between your legs?"

Instead of laughing with her, Burnside raked his hand through his thinning hair.

"We weren't even engaged long. I retreated as soon as I had a measure of their strength. I needed to regroup and come up with a better plan. They tore us to pieces, General."

"Then let us plan."

Chapter Twenty-Four

Ambessa watched Gintara's forces at the mines from the woods that surrounded them. Rell knelt in the dirt beside her, observing silently. The saltpetre caves were set into a hillside that had once been nothing but forest. When the caves were discovered, though, it became an immediate source of profit, and half the trees were cleared and roads were built to transport the valuable mineral to Rokrund Citadel, and from there, across the empire. There was only one road, the better to keep the profits for Rokrund and her merchants—Ambessa's family.

That single road served her well now. Gintara's sentries focused their attention in that direction while others monitored the mining and loading into wagons that were likely supposed to go to Ta'Fik's ships. Ambessa snorted softly. Somehow, it seemed more like a distraction than Ta'Fik's true aim. It was an insult, but it was not her beating heart. This, more than Burnside's warning, made Ambessa cautious.

"General," came a quiet voice just behind her.

It was one of her Shadowhunters—her small warband of drakehound hunters and their deadly handlers.

"Report."

"All sentries in the woods are cleared. There were only five, ma'am."

"Good. Keep ranging. Send a signal for the Fists to take their positions."

The Shadowhunter saluted silently, and he and his drake-hound dissolved into the trees.

She waited until the Fists had entered the woods. Some two hundred of them, they were not as stealthy as the Shadowhunters, but they did not need to be, now that the sentries were dead. Below, Gintara's fighters and the miners were making enough noise to cover the sounds of Ambessa's soldiers as they surrounded the ones below. They encircled the mining camp like a horseshoe, leaving only the road open.

Gintara's warband was called the Rippers. They were small—ten basilisk riders and two hundred infantry by Burnside's reports. The basilisks were off to the side, their handlers feeding them hunks of raw meat. Ambessa was glad that she was upwind of them. The monstrous lizards alone would account for hefty losses, but they weren't responsible for Burnside's apprehension. *Stronger than any man or woman I've ever fought, stronger even than minotaurs*, he'd said. It was hard to credit, but Burnside was a trustworthy captain, not some green boy clutching at his general's sleeve.

When Burnside's signaling mirror told her he was in place, she sent Rell to Rictus and the local Wolf's Reapers. He would lead them up the road and straight into Gintara's camp.

Wind rustled in the trees. A peaceful sound, despite the war beating in Ambessa's chest. The ground was soft beneath her feet, a combination of loam and leaves. The wind brought the smell of campfires and camp meals—comforting smells. It made her think of Menelik, and the years she spent campaigning with him, learning from him.

Medarda over all. It was against the Code for Medarda to war against Medarda. She knew it in her heart and was ashamed at what Menelik would think to see her arrayed against Ta'Fik like this—but it would be a greater dishonor to her grandfather for Ta'Fik to take over the family and turn it into nothing but merchants and schemers. She would do what she could to keep from killing Gintara—the girl was only doing a daughter's duty—but Ta'Fik had struck the first blow by sending her to Rokrund in the first place.

Rell returned. "He's going, General."

Then Ambessa heard what she was waiting for, and so did Gintara's fighters. At the sound of marching boots coming up the road, the cook fires were doused, formations were taken. The basilisk riders took to their mounts.

Rictus made a convincing show; it helped that the Wolf's Reapers looked formidable enough that anyone would believe they were all you needed to take a small force like Gintara's— two hundred men and women, forged in Rokrund's arenas and tempered on the battlefield.

Rictus didn't offer a parlay. The Wolf's Reapers hit Gintara's infantry hard.

They should have buckled under the onslaught almost immediately. These were Ambessa's shock troops, her elite warband. Instead, she watched Gintara's fighters hold them—and then begin to push back.

How was that possible?

Ambessa flashed her hand mirror to signal Burnside. Then she slid her hands into her drakehound gauntlets. The leather grips within made everything feel more certain. She felt more *real*.

She wanted to turn to Rell and ask her if she was ready, but it would shame the girl, and moreover, it would introduce doubt.

There was nothing more dangerous to a warrior on the battle-field than doubt. Instead, she signaled the soldiers in the Fist behind her. *Now.*

Time to tighten the noose.

She charged out of the woods, soldiers following her, and they took Gintara's fighters in the left flank while Burnside and his squad took the right. For a moment, quick as the flutter of memory, she saw golden greaves on her shins, golden bracers covering her forearms. Then they were gone, but the promise of their strength remained.

The first woman she crashed into was too focused on the Wolf's Reaper in front of her to guard against Ambessa's attack in time. Ambessa barreled into her, the half-moon blades first. With both fists and the full force of her momentum, she launched the other woman upward. She crashed to the ground in a broken heap, but Ambessa had already turned to find her next opponent.

The next opponent, however, was already swinging for her. The curved blade of her gauntlets caught and held the man's sword. The force that would normally have sent him flailing barely budged him. A subtle light burned in his eyes and from beneath his collar. He smiled at Ambessa, showing straight, fierce teeth, and pushed his weapon down harder, forcing Ambessa's arm down. Her shoulder ached with the strain of holding against it.

So Ambessa gave, letting her arm drop and rolling to the man's outside. She struck at his unprotected back—only for him to twist around. He was fast. Unnaturally fast. Burnside's fears came back to her.

The only thing that saved Ambessa was the man's poor skill—he was strong, but when she feinted, he focused too much on parrying the false blow and not enough on the fist that punched into his gut.

The eerie light in his eyes guttered and died.

Ambessa hunted in between gaps of the battle for Rictus, but the Rippers were fierce—too strong, too fast, and all of them glowing with that same odd light. Every time she clawed herself a gap, she was pressed again. She had already lost track of Rell, too.

Gintara was easier to find. She was at the back of the warband, sitting astride a young basilisk. She watched it all smugly. The beast was armored just as she was, the spines of its back and tail as sharp as Gintara's spear.

Ambessa ducked another incoming blow and only narrowly got her gauntlets in place before the falling axe could cleave her. She roared in defiance, slashing her arms before her to gain space.

Too many of her own were falling. Burnside had been right. These soldiers weren't *normal*. If Ambessa didn't end this quickly, they would all be lost.

Or you could retreat.

She could still win this. If she captured Gintara, it would be enough.

Ambessa chased the screams of her own soldiers to the twisting tail of Gintara's basilisk, dodging past the wild swing of one Ripper. There was only one fighter in her focus. She was almost there, could smell the stink of the basilisk as it snapped at three Fists, when something barreled into her from the side, driving her to the ground.

One of her gauntlets flew off her hand, skittering away. Ambessa and her opponent rolled in the grass, slick with blood-churned mud. They were on top of her, their own bearded axe rearing back over her head as they held down her arm with the remaining drakehound blade. Ambessa bucked and jerked her hips, but the enemy was steady above her, their eyes glowing with that same pale light. Their grip on her arm was unshakable.

Would she die again, so near the plains where the Wolf had found her last?

Let it be clean, then.

Just as she bared her throat to claim her fate, Rell cried out. Ambessa recognized her voice immediately, though she had never heard the girl in this kind of pain or fear. The soldier above her was also distracted. In that split second of opportunity, Ambessa broke her arm free and punched her drakehound fist through their throat, nearly severing their head.

She shoved their deadweight off and raced toward Rell's voice, scooping up her other gauntlet as she ran. Within the gloves, she unhooked the catch that held the half-moons in the drakehounds' mouths.

Rell was scrambling to her feet before Gintara and her basilisk, trying to dodge the beast's vicious snapping jaws and the sweeping of its claws. Someone else cried in agony as its tail spines caught them.

Ambessa took her moment. She flung one of her blades forward. It unspooled on its thin chain and collided with Gintara's chest, ringing against her armor and catching. Ambessa pulled, and Gintara toppled off the basilisk's back.

The basilisk turned its burning eyes toward Ambessa.

"Run!" Ambessa shouted at Rell, who had frozen in shock. She saw Zishani nearby and cried out to her. The ship captain fought well even on land, but only with the help of two more sailors could she kill one of Gintara's Rippers.

"Zishani!" Ambessa yelled. When the woman saw her, Ambessa pointed to Rell. "Run!"

Then Ambessa had no more time to see what Rell or Zishani did, because the basilisk was bearing down on her. Instead of letting it strike her with those great claws, though, Gintara commanded the beast to halt with a chirruping signal. Gintara pushed herself to her feet, wincing, her hand on her chest.

"Look around, Aunt. We've beaten you. Tell your band to surrender, and I'll take you to my father alive."

Ambessa did look around. The fighting continued, but her superior numbers weren't bringing her the victory she'd expected. Burnside's fears were well-founded. But she would not surrender to be taken to Ta'Fik.

"I'll kill you!" From Ambessa's periphery, she saw Rell hurl a spear at Gintara.

"Rell, no!" Ambessa shouted. Gintara jumped backward, pressed flat against her basilisk. The beast rounded on Rell, and Gintara did, too.

"Zishani, take her! Go!"

The captain pulled at the back of Rell's coat, trying to drag her away. Not that the rest of the battlefield was much safer. Zishani swung her cutlass toward the basilisk in a dissuading arc as she backed away.

"Rell?" Gintara smirked. "I know you. You're the little runt from my sister's arena games. Welcome to the real world."

"Runt?" Rell growled. She dodged one of the basilisk's backhands. She was weaponless now. Even through her anger, Ambessa could see the fear as she backed away. There was nowhere to run now, basilisk on one side, Gintara on the other. She saw Zishani recognize it, too. The captain stopped backing away and turned to put herself between Rell and Gintara, Rell and the beast.

"Gintara, your fight is with me. If you want me, come and take me."

Gintara turned. Her basilisk did not.

It lunged forward, and Zishani sidestepped it, cutting at the side of its head. Her blade rang uselessly against its armored helmet, and it turned its maw on her.

"No!" Rell cried.

Beneath Zishani's scream of pain, Ambessa heard bones cracking. The basilisk threw Zishani aside like a doll. It slashed at Rell again, and she stumbled back, tripping over a dead man. She scrambled back on her hands, but she never lost the expression of rage, even when the next claw swipe came.

Ambessa swung her chained blades and knocked Gintara aside. The other woman fell in a clatter of armor, and Ambessa dived between Rell and the basilisk. Rell's eyes widened in shock as Ambessa intercepted the beast's attack. If any words came out, Ambessa didn't hear them, only the whistle of the claws splitting the air behind her.

A tearing sensation at her back as armor and skin alike ripped. Beneath her, Rell screamed wordless fury.

Then Ambessa hit the ground. The pain dazzled and dazed her. Where was the girl? Where was Rell?

Here, beside her, kneeling protectively over her with a broken spear haft in one hand as she screamed.

And then something miraculous happened. As Rell screamed, Ambessa felt a wave ripple across the field. Her steel gauntlets became immensely heavy. The blade of Rell's spear bent in half. Gintara, in all her steel armor, couldn't push herself up from the ground.

And the armor on the basilisk... it crumpled in on itself, with no regard for the basilisk at all. The beast howled in pain as the metal carapace dug into its flesh, tightening and tightening until it pierced it, and then tightening further still. The protective guard on its head clamped down on its skull and squeezed.

It was a mercy when the metal reached the basilisk's brain and silenced its screams.

"Kreipsha." Rictus was beside her, and Ambessa felt him pick her up in his arms. His breathing was as ragged as hers. "Kreipsha, call the retreat."

All Ambessa could do was nod, so he shouted the order himself. Searing pain ripped through her body as he carried her away. She growled against the scream she wanted to let out.

"Rell," she gritted. She clawed at Rictus's armor, trying to turn him. The motion made her vision go black with pain, so she shut her eyes. "Go back for her."

Rictus ignored her.

Chapter Twenty-Five

Rudo wished he was asleep in his borrowed bed.

No, he wished he was in Basilich again. He'd been wishing for those halcyon days more and more these past months. He'd been drawn back into the past, second-guessing his decision not to stay with Ambessa, and every time he'd chosen not to see her. He'd done it to protect her, he had told himself each time, then and now. To protect their child. Now it only felt like cowardice.

Instead, Rudo was in the laboratory beneath the abandoned ruins with Inyene. The deep halls of the hidden bunker were not quiet, not at all. They echoed with the moaning and screaming and pleading of their test subjects. The newest was a boy whose magic could shape the clouds; Rudo had found him playing with puddles near the docks in Bel'zhun. Now he wept bitterly for his mother, and there was no magic in his tears, only fear.

Inyene had insisted they work late into the night. There was a manic fervor in their eyes, and Rudo kept returning to what they'd said several months ago—*We have commands from higher places*. What commands had they been given? And what were the consequences of failure? Why were they pushing so hard?

The Black Rose might have been their family, but the pale woman was not known to be a gentle master.

"I think I have it," they muttered to themself.

They were working on yet another trial with the runes. A new project. Rudo had only managed to delay finishing up the flesh runes for a few months. Though the side effects on the soldiers were the excuse he gave, his true motivations were more self-ish. Every month's delay was another day to spare Ambessa, a day for her to prepare. How, he had no idea. That was up to her now. He couldn't stall forever. Eventually, Inyene and Ta'Fik both had rounded on Rudo and pushed the project to the next phase, applying the flesh runes to Ta'Fik's soldiers. That took another few weeks, and after that, the rune-soldiers were ready for battle. He'd sent them immediately with Gintara to Rok-rund. Then Inyene had moved on to what Rudo realized was the real goal all the time.

The adolescent beneath Inyene's hands groaned through his teeth and bucked at his restraints. He lay shirtless on the stone slab, a sacrifice. Rudo had found him in Bel'zhun when they had been there to handle Menelik and Ambessa. He wasn't certain what powers the young mage had, or if the boy even knew that he had them, but Rudo had marked him, and when Inyene was ready, others in the Rose brought him here. He had been the first, but now he was one of many mages, scouted and brought here for Inyene's experimentation.

"Be ready," Inyene ordered. "I'll need your strength."

Inyene shaped the rune with their hands, and it hovered over the youth. It was a different shape to the ones they'd given Ta'Fik's soldiers. It was spiky and seemed almost...alive. Hungry. The tendrils reached out and drew back upon themselves like tentacles grasping.

The last time they had tried this technique on this youth, it had failed. The boy still had his magic, despite the pain it had caused him.

Rudo joined his own magic in the tracery of the odd rune, bright gold overlaying the red-gold of Inyene's power.

"Now!" Inyene pressed their hand to the youth's bare chest, and Rudo did, too.

As with the soldiers, the rune sank into the boy's skin, but this time, it didn't dissipate. It burned there like a brand, and the boy screamed horribly, as if his flesh were truly burning.

"It's working," Inyene whispered, their breathing shallow and excited. They gritted their teeth.

Instead of the rune fading to a glow, a different color surged up from within him in the same shape—but this was a purplish yellow. As this new energy surged up, it pulled with it a scream beyond bearing from the youth's lips, pain so sharp that it brought tears to Rudo's eyes.

"We have to stop," he said.

"No, not yet, it's working. I can feel it."

Rudo could feel it, too, though he felt distant from it. He realized with a stab of heartache that this was not his magic, nor was it Inyene's—it was the boy's. Their rune had taken his magic from him, and that was why he screamed as if he were being torn apart.

Because he was.

Then his eyes rolled into the back of his head, and his body went slack. His mouth hung open, silent.

Was he—

"I have it. Quick, I need—" Inyene clenched their fist as if holding on tightly to a living creature trying to escape. "Will you take it?"

"What?"

"His magic, will you take it?" They shook with the effort, and sweat dampened their forehead. "We need to see if it works."

Rudo jerked back in revulsion. "No."

Inyene gritted their teeth and growled in irritation. "Get— that other boy. The hydromancer. Quick, I can't hold on to it much longer, and I don't know what will happen if I let it go—"

Rudo sprinted from the experimentation room, relieved to be doing anything but watching that boy writhe on the stone table. His heart thudded madly in his chest, railing against everything that he was doing.

The pale woman wanted this. It was for the good of the Black Rose. To strengthen them, to protect them. But Rudo wasn't a fool. He knew that some of that "protection" was for her own machinations, and whatever they may have been, more were about power than the safety of mages. And what was safe anyway, when their own kind would do what Rudo and Inyene were doing to the young mages they'd found?

Rudo unlocked the cell of the boy who'd just arrived. Hydromancy. Powerful magic that could manipulate water, even weather, but raw and untrained. His magic was deadened now, held in place by Rudo's own dampening runes.

The boy looked up at Rudo when he entered. His eyes were dry, his voice listless. "I want my mother."

Rudo shuddered. "What's your name, young one?"

"Skira," he said simply.

"Come with me, Skira. It'll be all right." The boy didn't fight when Rudo picked him up by the arm. He led him to Inyene, who still held the stolen magic in their grip. Their skin had taken a grayish hue.

"Hurry," they whispered hoarsely.

Rudo lay the boy on top of the stone slab. He overlapped the youth, but not by much. Skira was so small. Rudo bound him with magic to the slab.

"Keep your hold on his magic," Inyene said, and then they released the rune onto Skira with a groan of relief.

Skira shot upright as the new power surged into him. The tendons in his small neck strained as his back arched. His mouth opened to scream, but no sound came out.

Rudo felt it all through his own magical hold on the boy—it pushed and battered against him, and for a moment, he felt his grip slipping. He was...fighting him. With the new power. He didn't even think the boy was doing it on purpose. But Rudo was one of the most powerful mages in the Black Rose, and he'd had decades to hone his art. He pushed Skira's efforts aside and tightened his grip on the boy.

Then he felt the powerful wave of magic diminish suddenly— before surging back, battering against him like a wave in a storm. Then, like a wave, it drew back again.

"Inyene? What's happening?"

"I'm trying—"

The rune settled into Skira, and Inyene sagged against the stone table, holding themself upright. They were shaking.

"Did it work?" They turned to Rudo. "Did you feel it?"

Rudo tried to catch his breath, but he didn't dare step closer to the table.

Inyene's lip curled. "Don't look at me like that. He was weak enough to be disposable. And the boy...?"

He looked hesitantly at Skira.

Skira lay on the table, his small chest rising feebly. Rudo could feel only the faintest flicker of the boy's magic, a struggling pulse, and then, even as he tried to hold on to it, it faded. Then nothing.

Inyene watched the boy breathe his last. They waited a moment for his chest to rise again. When it didn't, they cursed and slammed their fists upon the stone slab tables.

"No! It should have worked this time!" they roared in frustration. They gripped their shorn head and paced away on unsteady legs.

"It's too much, Inyene. No one is meant to take this." *He was just a boy.* "Even one of us—"

"It's not impossible, Rudo. We just—we just need a stronger mage. They have to be strong enough to hold that much power."

Most of the mages Rudo and Inyene had been brought were weaker, low-level. They might be capable of something more than parlor tricks, but they would never be like the two of them. They would never rise in the ranks of the Black Rose. Skira had had more potential—he might have grown much stronger, if he had lived.

"I need you to find me more. Older than the boy. Stronger—not just in their magic but—" Inyene groped for the word, clutching furiously at the air. "Robust. They need to have stamina. Does Ta'Fik have any mages in his warbands?"

Rudo didn't know. Even now, most of those warbands, including the rune-soldiers, were in Rokrund, moving on Ambessa's home. When they'd known each other so briefly in Basilich, they had known better than to make promises to each other, but he was meant to be the instrument of her destruction. The mother of his child.

He had done what he could to give her a chance to claim her place in this succession, even though he'd killed Menelik rather than have the old man make the pronouncement that would break Ambessa's heart. Even though she would hate him for it, he had done that for her.

But this . . . it was too much. All he could think of was Mel. He had hidden dampening runes beneath the tattoos he'd given her; any latent magical ability she had would be masked. But what if something *slipped*? What if another of the pale woman's sniffers, someone like him, *found her*? What would he do then, if they tried to separate *her* from her magic?

He stumbled away from Skira and the unconscious young man on the table. The youth who was Mel's age. He sprawled over the stone, limp. His fingers dangled off the edge, curling delicately, no longer clenched in agony. When he woke up, though, what would he feel, knowing that his magic had been taken from him? And all of it was for nothing. Inyene's rune hadn't even worked.

"This isn't right." Rudo reached for their shoulder in an effort to calm them.

Inyene threw his hand off their shoulder. "What's wrong with you lately, Rudo? You balk at every turn. First, you held back the rune-soldiers. Now this. You're tiptoeing where you used to dance. *Tell me what's going on.*" They finished with a plea.

Rudo wanted to tell them. He wanted to trust them.

"Whatever your orders are, maybe—" He hesitated before voicing something he'd only touched the edges of in his mind. He finished softly, "Maybe we could leave them behind."

"Don't. It's not your place to tell me what's wrong and what's right. This has nothing to do with *her*—" Inyene caught themself, breathing heavily. Instead of finishing their sentence, they shook their head and glared at Rudo. Then their face went slack. "You mean leave the Rose?" Inyene laughed in disbelief. "Are you mad?"

No. No, for the first time, Rudo felt like he could see things clearly. He just wasn't sure he had the courage to act on that clarity.

"Come with me, Inyene. Enough is enough. How many more mages do we have to lose? It's not worth it."

Inyene was still shaking their head. "Rudo, you don't understand. I'm so close to making a breakthrough like no one has ever seen before. Like Ryze. This could help *us*. Don't you want to be stronger?"

"No," Rudo said vehemently. He chose his next words carefully, to dig where he knew Inyene was weakest. "You're doing this because you're afraid, aren't you? If we go together, no one will be able to hurt you—hurt either of us. I made you a promise when we escaped Demacia."

It had been one of their first missions together, and it had gone badly wrong. Scouting in Demacia for the pale woman, gathering intelligence on the latest mage-taking technologies. But they'd misstepped, and Inyene had been captured.

Years later, and they still hadn't told Rudo what had happened in those three days of captivity.

Now their face twisted in a snarl. "How dare you?"

"Inyene, listen to me." Rudo stepped away from them, putting one of the slabs between them. "Look at these boys. They're children. We're no better than the Demacian mageseekers if we go on like this."

"I'm not the one who's afraid, Rudo. You are."

The words unlocked something in Rudo's chest. The defensive tension that had coiled his body loosened. He straightened.

"You're right." In acknowledging that, Rudo was able to back away.

Inyene frowned in surprise. "What?"

"You're right. I have been afraid. But that shouldn't stop me."

"Stop you from what? Rudo, what are you talking about? Rudo, where are you going?"

"I can't do this, Inyene. Not anymore." Reaching behind his back, he opened the door and walked away.

Chapter Twenty-Six

Ambessa woke lying on her right side in an unfamiliar room. She lay on the floor, on a pallet of woolen blankets. Her body ached, especially the left side of her back. Each breath pulled at the tight skin. A sharp stabbing made her hiss and flinch.

"What—"

"Easy, General. We have to stitch you up." A healer.

She grunted and examined as much of the room as she could. A small stone cottage with long, thin glassless windows that let in the breeze, and angled offspurts for storage. Probably the home of one of the miners. Around her lay other wounded. Her back was to the door, so she didn't see the comings and goings of other soldiers and healers.

"Rell?" she asked.

"The young rider? Yes, ma'am. She's here. Nothing a good meal and a few stitches couldn't help, it looks like. I'll see to her eventually."

Ambessa grunted again. She closed her eyes and paid attention to the pain of each stitch, letting it sharpen her focus. By the time the healer had left her with a tea for the pain, she felt ready to face the loss at the mines.

Because it had been a loss, no matter how it galled her to say the words. She needed to revisit her strategy. She had known something was off, and still she'd let herself be drawn into it.

"Ric—"

Before she had even finished his name, he was kneeling in front of her.

"You're well?" he asked.

"I am. We need to talk—our next move."

"Rell will want to see you."

Ambessa hesitated. "The medic said she was all right."

"She's not hurt. Not like you. But she did see it happen to you, and . . . Zishani." He lowered his voice thoughtfully. "She blames herself."

"That's foolish."

Rictus stared at her, his expression unreadable. "Is it?"

Ambessa sighed. Beneath the pain of her own body, Zishani's loss rang a painful chord. "I'll speak to her."

"Good. She did well, though."

"She froze," Ambessa said tartly. "She disobeyed my orders."

"She tried to save you. And despite her fear, when I pulled you out, she directed the retreat. She has good instincts."

"She needs more training. She should have gone to Rokrund Citadel with Katye like I said."

"Experience will hone those instincts." Rictus kept his voice level.

Ambessa didn't want to argue right now. She sighed. "I'll speak to her. Then we figure out what to do with everyone else. How are casualties?"

Rictus's face was grim. "Not good. Ambessa . . . something was wrong with those fighters. I could feel it in their strength. They were glowing."

Ambessa hissed in a breath. She remembered the gleam in their eyes. She had hoped that it was a dream, a distortion of the pain.

"The girl, first."

Rictus returned with Rell a few minutes later. The girl carried a spear with her, in a grip so tight Ambessa wasn't sure she'd ever let it go again.

"Rictus says you showed good instincts. How did it feel?"

Rell blushed. "It felt..." She hesitated. Ambessa could tell she was struggling to decide how honest she should be. She'd felt it herself, when Menelik had first asked.

"Come, child. Sit." Ambessa patted the spot of blanket on the floor beside her, and Rell sat. "I loved my first battle. The yelling, the fury, the thrill of being beside my compatriots. At least, until we actually met the other army." She offered the girl a small smile. "After that first contact with the enemy, everything changes. You can't say exactly how you'll react. Instincts will serve you well."

"I didn't know what to do. During the ambush. And here— I—I was scared. I'm sorry."

Ambessa recalled finding the girl off to the side, away from the ambush site. She'd been curled up in the shadows, sitting with Tora. Tear tracks had cut down her blood-spattered cheeks. Her hands had been soaked in the blood of Smik's warband, though; she had not cowered the whole time. That had been enough.

"You have nothing to be ashamed of."

"I thought—I thought it was going to kill me. And you. The basilisk. Like it killed Zishani." Rell's voice broke. She closed her eyes, and fresh tears spilled. She brushed them quickly away.

"A warrior must accept death's inevitability, child. Zishani did. I have. We will all die, one day. Do you want to die on the battlefield, or would you rather die comfortable, in your bed, of old age?"

Ambessa tried to ask this without judgment coloring her tone; she needed a true answer if she was going to move forward with the ideas in her mind. Because for all her disobedience on the field, Rell had shown extraordinary courage. She had not run in the face of overwhelming odds and had defended her fellow soldiers. Some things, a warrior could learn—others were innate. If Mel and Kino were two weapons in Ambessa's armory, Rell was an altogether different one.

Rell paled. "I—I don't know."

"Think about it. It will help to know the answer before you next go into battle."

"Yes, General." Rell remained, as if waiting formally to be dismissed.

"You may go," Ambessa said.

The girl looked up at Rictus nervously, and he gave her an encouraging nod.

"General," Rell started. She held her spear across her lap in a white-knuckle grip. "On the battlefield, something happened."

Rell stopped. Ambessa looked to Rictus, but he said nothing to help.

"What, child? I already told you, you have nothing to be ashamed of."

"I did something," Rell said in a rush. "When the basilisk was attacking me, when you jumped in front of me, I *did something*." Rell opened one of her hands in front of her face in wonder. Or terror. It trembled.

Another memory Ambessa had not understood surfaced. The basilisk screaming as its own armor crushed it. Her gauntlets, forced into the ground. "What did you do?" she asked slowly.

Rell jumped to her feet and stepped a few feet back, making space between her and anything—and anyone—in the room. Then she took her spear in one hand, holding the other over it. Her brow furrowed as she concentrated. Ambessa didn't understand what she was watching until the spear haft clattered to the ground and the steel head wrapped around Rell's forearm in a bracer. It must have been heavy, but Rell moved her arm freely, it as if it were nothing.

Ambessa's mouth hung open.

With another look of concentration, Rell lengthened the metal to a spearhead again. She picked up the spear haft and grafted the metal back onto the wood.

"You killed the basilisk," Ambessa murmured.

Rell stared at the weapon in her hand, wary and confused. "I don't know what to do, General. It just happened."

"But you do know what to do. We were just speaking of instincts—you followed them."

"It was an accident."

"With time, you'll hone your skills." Eagerness made Ambessa's heart beat faster. "You'll be able to guide your intention."

Fear still reigned in the girl's eyes. Uncertainty. But Ambessa could tell that a part of Rell was excited by the possibility. Ambessa just had to kindle that excitement. This new power could be the difference between victory and another defeat at the hands of the soldiers lit by strange light.

"People will admire your capabilities. There is a tenet in the Medarda Code: *A Medarda strikes their own path*. It means many things, chief among them that each of us can offer something different to the family. With our unique perspectives and strengths, we chart a course to strengthen the clan. We all have different ones. I excel as a leader, I excel in hand-to-hand combat. I'm even a passable beast-master. But you and I have something in common—I am a terrible shot with a bow. And I'm not a good cook." She smiled, trying to disarm the girl. "This is *a strength*. Every strength you have should be used."

Rell nodded, but she didn't seem convinced. "I don't want my mother to know. When she found out I was good at fighting..."

Ah. Ambessa drew back. She remembered the bright greed in the eyes of the girl's parents. This was different. Ambessa was different.

"Do you wish to fight with it?" Ambessa asked, keeping back her keenness, letting the girl take her time to arrive at the correct conclusion.

"I...guess I would. If I had time to learn how. Someone to train me."

"I will find someone. In the meantime, Rictus will practice with you. He can take quite a lot of abuse."

Rell finally cracked a smile. Then she looked downcast again. "What if I freeze next time, too?"

Ambessa stretched a hand up. She couldn't reach the girl, but Rell came and took it. "You won't freeze again."

Rell swallowed and nodded.

"Good. When I'm better, I want to see what all you can do. Go to the camp armorer and ask for whatever metal they have to spare, and do with it what you will. As soon as I can ride again, we'll return to Rokrund and wait for Amenesce."

"But you won't leave me there?" Rell said quickly.

"No," Ambessa said. "I won't."

When Rell left, Ambessa rested against the pile of blankets. Despite the focus she'd fought so hard to grasp, her body was making other commands. Her eyes began to slide shut.

"We have to send to Katye for reinforcements," she murmured. "And Amenesce. We can make this our base. Where...are we?"

"Still near the mines," Rictus said. He hesitated, busying himself with the blankets beneath Ambessa.

"What is it?"

"Gintara didn't pursue us."

She didn't need him to tell her where the young war leader had taken her band.

"That's foolish," she muttered. She considered what sense there could be in that strategy. With only two hundred and fewer than a dozen basilisks, no warband could hope to take the city, even if they were...*changed* by some sort of magic.

"The attack is coming from both sides," Rictus said. "Maybe Gintara didn't show us her full force."

"Send the Shadowhunters out. Tell them to find every last one of them. When we crush them this time, I'll make sure we've gotten them all."

Ambessa turned her gaze to her gauntlets beside her. She slid one hand into a glove, and even that small motion was excruciating. She tried to lift it, but it was unbearably heavy. Her chest felt bound by iron.

"Kreipsha, don't. You're in no shape." Rictus knelt by her side and pulled the gauntlet off her.

"Rokrund Citadel is my home," Ambessa growled. "As long as I live, I will not let it fall."

"And if it kills you?" Rictus's jaw was tight.

"Then it kills me."

It would not be the first time she had died to protect her home.

Still, she could see Ta'Fik's intent. If he wanted to hurt her, if he wanted to cut off her resources, Rokrund was a certain target. He knew she would defend it to her last breath. As long as he kept her busy here, he would be free to do as he wished anywhere else in Noxus. It left her with a decision to make.

"How long has it been?" Ambessa asked. She clung to the comfort of the gauntlet, an extension of her fist, of the rage she felt.

"From the battle?" Rictus looked up at her from his spot on the ground. "A day. Our wounded..." He nodded to the moaning soldiers around her.

She shook her head. "Since we left." Since she'd left Azizi and Mel and Kino. Since Ta'Fik had run her out of her home, out of her own family.

He paused, calculating. "Over half a year."

Half a year of her life, he had taken.

Ambessa inhaled sharply. "What about Amenesce? Any word?"

"Riding toward the city. She's caught up with the Bloody Thunder."

"Then rally what remains of the Fist and the Wolf's Reapers. Tell Burnside—is Burnside still in command?" When Rictus nodded, Ambessa continued. "Katye can't face this alone. Rell's new...powers. Do you think she can use them? Truly?"

Rictus glanced at the rookern stones wrapped around his forearm. The stones held the names of foes he had killed in honorable combat. They were inert now, but with a ritual, they would have anti-magic properties.

Ambessa nodded to the rookern. "Does it work against these soldiers?"

"Not exactly," he said grimly. "It absorbs some of their strength, but only against me. I saw a rune on one's chest—it doesn't dispel the rune's power, but..."

Ambessa gestured impatiently for him to continue.

"Some of the...*rune-soldiers*. When I pushed them too hard, they collapsed. Screaming. I didn't even touch them."

A tender flame of hope lit within her, and Ambessa set to work turning it into something useful. Strategy. Eagerly, she asked, "All of them? Are they connected?"

Rictus shook his head. No matter. It was still useful information.

They sat together in thoughtful silence for a little longer. Then Rictus said, "The girl will be fine. She's strong."

"I know she is. Her training with the magic begins now, on the road."

"Kreipsha, you can't—"

Ambessa fixed him with an iron gaze.

Rictus bowed his head. "Yes, General." After a moment, he met her gaze again. "Rell could be what you're looking for."

Ambessa's breath tightened in her chest, and this time, it was not the wound but a different kind of pain. She had been able to avoid the reality of her situation beyond the war with Ta'Fik— that neither of her children alone was suitable for the mantle she was trying to win for them. When she thought of Mel, and the vision she'd had on these very plains, disappointment hollowed her.

"An heir."

"If not an heir, she could be a companion to your heir."

As Rictus was to her. It was one possibility. Rell did not lack the courage. With time, she might develop the ruthlessness.

And then there was her power. It was only a small consolation in the face of Gintara's magicked warband. Rell was only one soldier, and she was young. This new power was as raw as the girl was in every other respect, but it was great. It had taken down a basilisk.

"I will think on it. Help me up."

The seed Rictus planted grew unexpected fruit as they rode to Rokrund Citadel. Thoughts of Mel and her tattoos brought thoughts of Rudo. Ambessa had avoided thinking of the Black Rose Rudo had whispered of in the nights against her pillow. The secret cabal of mages that he was beholden to, that might even try to take Mel if they knew she existed, all because she was his.

Would Rell be a target now that she had manifested her own magic? Would she be a danger to Mel because of it?

She wanted to put such thoughts aside, but the Black Rose haunted her nightmares, and the back of her neck prickled when she was awake. It was the warrior's instinct to duck as she felt the wind of the axe coming to cleave her head from her neck. An instinct honed by long experience.

It wasn't something Ambessa could ignore.

Chapter Twenty-Seven

A re you sure you want to do this, Kreipsha?" Rictus asked Ambessa.

He walked beside her mount. It was a messenger's horse, but Burnside decided it could be put to better use elsewhere; their warbands themselves would be message enough. The precious few of the Wolf's Reapers marched in front of her, and the Fist behind her, Burnside at the center of the line. Her Shadow-hunters ranged the area, making sure Gintara wasn't holding any reinforcements back.

Ambessa couldn't urge her horse above a walk without feeling pain ricochet from each hoofbeat into her flesh. Still, she said coldly, "I am certain, Rictus. Do not ask me again."

"Yes, General." He held his shoulders stiff at the rebuke.

Rell marched at her other side. She was still subdued. You couldn't rush this difficult stage in a warrior's life—grappling with what war truly meant. Pain without glory. Sacrifices with no clear reward. The indignities of death and the gaping wound of a lost comrade.

Not everyone is made for this, cousin, but you are, Ta'Fik had said to her once. She had been injured then, too, and he sat beside her, holding her hand while she recovered. *Be strong. Remember that everything you do is for us. For your family. And we will do everything for you. I promise.* She'd squeezed his hand tight until the potent tea sent her back to sleep. It had been enough, then.

And now look at them. What good, a promise?

The crash and cry of battle met them before the sight did, but it wasn't until she saw Gintara's warband at the Citadel's wall that Ambessa's fury truly caught fire. It called her to destroy everything in her path, but that was not the plan she'd made with Rell and her captains.

Several of Gintara's older basilisks were acting as siege engines: They'd been chained to the closed gates, and soldiers were urging the beasts to pull, pull, pull the gate down, and it groaned beneath their effort. On the ground all around them were the corpses of the first waves that Rokrund had sent to fight against these enhanced warriors.

Other Rippers were attempting to scale the walls—they ascended with terrifying speed, the vertical climb too easy. Archers tried to pick them off, but they, too, realized that these soldiers were unnatural, and their shots were not as accurate as they could be. Defenders struggled to push them back over the side.

Ambessa would be the hammer that crushed them against the anvil of the city walls.

"Attack, Wolf's Reapers! Forward, Fist!" Ambessa called. "For Rokrund!"

Despite their last encounter with Gintara's warband, Burnside's soldiers went into battle with a will. Ambessa had spread the word of the rune-soldiers' weakness. If she had exaggerated the possibility, what did it matter? It strengthened their morale and gave them a reason to push. They smashed the back of Gintara's line before the Rippers could make a proper defense. Ambessa itched to ride after them, but the sword in her hand was heavy, almost too heavy to raise. Her gauntlets were impossible to wear.

Focus on your target. Ambessa looked for Gintara, and found the young war leader commanding the rear squads of her warband to face their new challengers. Her long braids whipped about her shoulders as she brandished an azirite-edged axe.

When Gintara spotted her in turn, she pointed her axe silently at Ambessa.

"Rell. Do you see her?" Ambessa murmured. She didn't ask if Rell was ready; she didn't ask if she was sure she could do it. She wouldn't undermine the girl's determination. She would not introduce doubt.

This plan was risky enough as it was. They needed to capture Gintara and get into the city. With Ambessa unable to fight and the enemy's mysterious strength, it was almost impossible. At least the risk would give them a chance.

"Yes, General. But I don't know if I can—"

"You can," Ambessa interrupted firmly.

"I think I'm too far away."

"Then we'll go closer." Ambessa nudged her horse forward, and Rictus led the way.

Anyone who tried to reach Ambessa met Rictus's scything blade. In battle, he was a marvel. In the Reckoner Arena, he was formidable, but it did not compare to the battlefield. For all the strength in the Rippers, Rictus had an unbreakable calm, and though his eyes didn't glow, he was indefatigable. When one Ripper broke past him, he spun from his own opponent, swinging the haft of his halberd up between the new Ripper's legs. While he clutched himself, Ambessa slashed her sword across his throat. He fell.

"Are you all right, General?" Rell asked frantically.

"Concentrate, Rell! Your orders." Ambessa gripped the reins

tightly to keep herself upright. Hot blood trickled down her back, and she sagged in the saddle.

Ahead of them, the Fist struggled to gain ground. Now that the element of surprise was gone, they were simply outmatched. Burnside had gotten nearer to the gate and was shouting for them to open it, as Ambessa had ordered him, but the gatekeepers refused. On the ramparts, archers continued to shoot down at the Rippers trying to climb and the basilisks pulling at their chains, but the arrows pinged harmlessly off hide and armor alike. More and more fighting was taking place on the ramparts.

"Now, Rell!"

"I'm trying!"

And she was. The young woman's face was turning red with the effort. Her hands were outstretched, clawed and reaching. They had discussed this as they rode from their camp—strip the steel away from the enemies' weapons as she had dismantled her own spear. Then she could turn it on them.

But nothing was happening, no matter how the girl strained, and as she struggled, one of the Rippers bowled Rictus into the ground. They became a roiling mass of biting and punching, each of them trying to reach for a blade but not given the chance.

"Rictus!" Ambessa's cry escaped before she could stifle it. She swung down at the Ripper but couldn't reach. Another swing, stretching farther in the saddle, but the horse was skittish—it was trained for swiftness, not courage. It shied her away, and the pain lanced up her body.

She didn't have a chance to dwell on that pain. The man fighting for Rictus's throat began to seize up, his back arching. Rictus didn't hesitate—he took advantage of his opponent's incapacitation. A dagger stopped the man's scream of agony before it started.

There was no time to bask in that small victory. A scream

erupted behind her, raw and loud enough to echo off the city walls. Ambessa turned back to Rell.

Rell's outstretched hands had become clenched fists held tight to her sides, and her eyes glowed silver. Her scream didn't cease, and from the direction of the basilisks came a wrenching screeching of metal.

One of the siege basilisks' metal armor splintered off its back into jagged chunks. The metal shards quivered in the air, as if they were under the same strain as Rell.

The girl was on her knees, and even though she looked at Ambessa, her whole body pleading, Ambessa knew Rell couldn't see her. Around them, most still fought—a handful of the Fists for every Ripper.

"Rell!" *Stop*, she almost said, but she bit the word back. Could this work?

Instead, she slithered painstakingly from her horse's back and bent down to Rell. Just as Ambessa put her hand on Rell's shoulder, the girl screamed again. This time, her yell was followed by cries of surprise and fear and agony.

The shards of metal that Rell had created had only been held in tension by her power. When she released them, they shot forward like hounds, without care for who they struck, enemy or ally. One shard pinned a Fist and a Ripper together into the dirt. Another struck the neighboring basilisk, and it roared once in pain before collapsing. Ambessa ducked behind her horse, pulling Rell with her as steel struck the mount.

The horse screamed and kicked as it died, and Ambessa hunched over Rell to protect her.

She looked into Rell's face, slapping her cheek. "Rell? Are you all right?"

Rell blinked up at her, her eyes unfocused. Blood leaked from one nostril.

"You did it. Well done." She kept the girl close. Rictus helped them both up, then took up his position ahead of them.

"Keep walking," she urged. The gate was still closed. Where was Burnside?

But the girl didn't listen. Her hand was outstretched again, and Ambessa followed her gesture. Gintara stood before them, her teeth bared and her face bloody.

"Ambessa!" she shouted. "Are you afraid to face me? Will you have your little mage do all your fighting for you?"

"I have this, Kreipsha," Rictus said, only loud enough for Ambessa. "Get Rell inside."

"No," Rell muttered fervently from beneath Ambessa's arm.

Even though Rell was concentrating, nothing happened to Gintara or her weapon. She wore no metal at all, and Ambessa wondered if she'd stripped her armor off as soon as she'd realized what had happened to the second basilisk.

Gintara's eyes glowed, and she sprinted at them. Rictus met her raised axe with his own halberd, but she didn't bend to his greater size. For a moment, the light within her intensified. Then it flickered and dimmed, and he heaved her backward. Ambessa saw the first flicker of fear cross the woman's face, but Gintara was already racing toward her again.

"Kreipsha, *go*."

But Rell dug her heels in.

"The—plan—General," Rell gritted through her teeth.

Rell jerked her wrist out of Ambessa's weakening grip, and the metal bracers she had formed shot off her own wrists. The earth seemed to tremble beneath them. For a moment, Ambessa's heart cried out—without control, the steel would shoot straight into Rictus's back. Everything they had gone through together, for this?

But the steel circumvented him, clapping into cuffs around

Gintara's ankles. Rell slammed her bare wrists together, and the metal on Gintara's ankles obeyed: The cuffs joined one to the other.

Gintara roared wordlessly from the ground. She rolled away from Rictus's next blow. She began to glow again as she strained against the binds, but they held. Instead, she reached for Rictus, catching him by one foot and bringing him down with her.

The earth's shaking suddenly distinguished itself. The thunder of hooves came rolling, and with it, the whoops of Amenesce's swiftthorn riders and the rest of the Bloody Thunder. They split around Ambessa and Rell, Rictus and Gintara, as if the four of them were a boulder in a river.

The Rippers were caught in the torrent. Those who hadn't succumbed to the agonizing fits were forced to hold their own against cavalry and deadly sharp horns—no matter how fast or strong they were, it was clear these soldiers were still made of flesh, and flesh could be pierced.

"General!" Amenesce drew rein beside them while her warbands attacked. "You're hurt!"

Tora, Amenesce's young shadow, cried out when she saw Rell, but before Rell could become distracted, Ambessa directed her back to Gintara.

"Rell, her hands!"

Rictus had Gintara in a lock, cradled against his chest while his forearm pressed against her throat.

Gintara sneered at her. "You don't fight your own battles anymore, Aunt?" The power in her words was diminished since she had to choke them past Rictus's strength. She struggled against his grip, but one arm dangled uselessly at her side. She gave one more mighty effort, and a bright light flared from beneath her woven armor. Suddenly, she was seizing, too, her jaw fixed in a snarl as her body stiffened. Steel clanged around both wrists, and both good arm and broken were bound together.

Ambessa kicked Gintara's azirite-edged blade aside. Rictus let Gintara fall to the ground.

"Kill me—then. Isn't that—why you're—here?" Gintara spoke between moans of pain. Her teeth were as red with blood as her blade.

"I will ransom you back to your father when he stops this nonsense. He has made a mockery of the Code, and he will pay for it." Ambessa turned to Amenesce. "Can you carry her?"

"You look like you're the one who needs carrying," the steward said. "Come on."

"Get her inside," Ambessa growled.

Without waiting for Amenesce to protest, Rictus picked up Gintara and threw her over Amenesce's thighs.

"Rell?" Tora's voice cracked with concern, and Ambessa saw Rell's eyes roll up into her skull. Ambessa caught her by reflex. The impact brought them both to the ground.

Tora leapt from her swifthorn and, with Rictus's help, put Rell on the saddle in front of her.

"Inside, now!" Ambessa ordered.

Though neither of them was strictly under her command, Tora and Amenesce obeyed.

And then it was just the two of them, as it always was.

"Shall we?" Ambessa asked Rictus.

Together, they raced for the open gate.

The last thing Ambessa saw as the gate closed behind them was Gintara's warband, looking in horror after their lost captain. They ran after them, but despite their speed, some arrows still met their targets. Others spasmed and screamed on the ground.

Ambessa could not tell if this was a victory or not.

Chapter Twenty-Eight

Even wounded, coming home was a relief. The great walls of the Citadel rose from the earth like the sides of a mountain. The chiseled overhangs, the narrow windows, the pointed corners of the watchtowers rising sharply into the sky like horns. Red banners with the Noxian sigil, black banners with the Medarda compass, both snapping in the wind. The salutes of the soldiers, the awe of the civilians as she walked the familiar paths leading to the Medarda compound. The click of her boots on the paving stones. All of it said *home*. All of it said *power*.

She longed to go straight to her chambers and wash away the past months. Instead, when she arrived at the Medarda compound, she ordered Gintara taken to one of the unused rooms by two of the Wolf's Reapers. Rell and Rictus accompanied her, but Amenesce left to see to the survivors in her cavalry. Ambessa suspected there were not many. Rell was haggard, her face pale. She would collapse at any moment, but she clung doggedly to Ambessa.

Under normal circumstances, the room would have been furnished opulently for guests, but now it was cold, the fire unlit, the bed bare. No comfort to be found.

"Wait outside," Ambessa ordered the Wolf's Reapers.

When they were gone, she turned to Gintara. The young war leader was on her knees, her wrist cuffs melded to her ankle cuffs behind her back, thanks to Rell's magic. Her braids hung in a lank curtain around her face. The glow had faded from her dark eyes, and her golden-brown skin was sallow. Ambessa knelt down beside her. The cloth of her armor was drying in the wound on her back, and every movement of the cloth made her gasp. In a moment. She would see to it in a moment.

Ambessa pulled the knife from her belt. She tested the blade on her thumb, feeling the slight catch upon her skin. It was so sharp, it didn't even hurt.

"What was done to you and your warband?" She made sure Gintara watched the play of the blade.

"Kill me. My father and my sister will avenge me. Can you say the same?"

"It's your father's fault that you're here. You wouldn't need avenging if he hadn't made war upon my home. He's broken the Code."

Gintara sneered. "Father says you've never even held to the Code, not the true Code. He says you're like Darkwill. You say you fight for the family, but you don't care how many Medardas you kill on the way to the top, as long as you get what you want. So prove him right." She tilted her chin up to expose the soft meat beneath. "Kill me. I know you've done it before."

Ambessa gripped the knife until her knuckles hurt. "Your sister is in my daughter's care. Be careful how you threaten me if you love her so."

For the first time, fear shadowed Gintara's face.

Ambessa tucked the knife back into its sheath and stepped into the corridor, closing the door after Rell and Rictus had exited.

To the Wolf's Reapers, Ambessa said, "No one is to come in

or out of this room without my permission." Then, to Rictus, "Have a healer meet me in my chambers. If Katye has a mage, even better."

Rictus hesitated only a moment before obeying.

By the time Ambessa and Rell had limped to the wing where her chambers were, servants were already waiting to take Rell to a newly made-up room, and to help them both undress and bathe and eat.

Before they led her away, though, Rell turned back to Ambessa. "I would avenge you, General," she said quietly.

Caught off guard, Ambessa watched her go in silence, her eyes burning unexpectedly.

A throat clearing brought her attention back. "General. If you please."

The healer. Ambessa followed him into her rooms.

Katye arrived as the last stitches were being placed. The healer had spent more time chastising her than sewing, Ambessa was certain.

Ambessa lay on her stomach while the healer stitched her wounds, making disparaging sounds as he worked. When she turned to see Katye come in, he hissed angrily.

"Do you want these to rip open again? Should I let you bleed to death?" He sucked his teeth, then pressed her back down to the table to finish.

"I thought you used magic for that." Ambessa had felt it, strengthening her body and deadening some of the pain.

"I said the magic would *help* you heal, not that it would do the work for you."

"Easy, Marou. My sister is stubborn. It's best to let her do as she likes."

"I'm sure she will." Marou the healer huffed as he cleaned his tools and put them away.

"Thank you, Marou," Ambessa said.

"Mmm." Marou glared at Katye, then turned to Rictus, who sat in the chair near the bed where Ambessa lay.

Katye cleared his throat. "If Rictus is well enough, could you give us a moment, Marou? I need to speak to Ambessa alone."

Ambessa pushed herself up gingerly. "See to Rictus first. Surely it can wait just a moment."

Katye's expression was grave. "It cannot. If you prefer, Rictus, you can go with the healer."

"I'll stay."

"As you wish," Marou said.

The door clicked shut behind him with finality.

"There's news from Bel'zhun." A chill ran down Ambessa's spine. "Mel? Kino? They didn't come back, did they?"

Katye shook his head, but his eyes remained somber. "The children are fine, Ambessa, but...I'm so sorry. Azizi is dead. Mel wrote to me."

He pulled a letter from the inner pocket of his robes and offered it to her. She took it automatically but didn't open it. He kept talking, as if to soothe himself, but she barely registered the words. The letter was sealed with the Medarda star.

"I looked for you as soon as they told me you were within the walls, but they said you were with the captive. You didn't come to the city first, or I would have told you—"

"How?" Ambessa's voice was hoarse over the thickness in her throat.

Katye clasped his hands awkwardly in front of himself. "Mel said it was a carriage accident."

She closed her eyes, and the tears spilled over immediately. "Katye, could you leave us?"

"Ambessa, you shouldn't—" She heard him step forward, no doubt to comfort her.

"Please, brother. Please."

"Yes, well. I'll be here, if you need anything at all. I'm sorry," he said again.

When they were alone, Rictus said, "I grieve with you, Kreipsha."

Ambessa's breath hitched as she wept. "He was a good man. A good father." She pressed herself to her feet.

"Ambessa, where are you going?" Rictus was on his feet and already moving between Ambessa and the door. "Don't do something that you'll regret."

"They killed *my husband*, Rictus. Ta'Fik will pay for that in blood." She stared him down.

His brown eyes met hers, stern but not uncaring. He folded his arms in front of his chest, but she could tell he was favoring his right leg. A slit in his trousers and the flesh beneath showed dark with blood. She could get around him that way. She feinted with a step toward his left, but he didn't even attempt to move.

"Are you sure it was Ta'Fik?"

"Of course I am. Azizi told me he would wedge himself between Ta'Fik and Nashramae, cutting into Ta'Fik's resources. Besides," Ambessa added bitterly, "he would do anything to hurt me. Just look outside." Ambessa threw an arm in the direction of the gates.

Rictus bowed his head in acknowledgment. "As you say. But killing Gintara—is it what you want now, or is it part of the bigger picture?"

The rebuke in his tone was gentle, but no one else would have dared. She glared but could not deny that she was more rage than strategy. Her eyes welled up again, and she had to look away as a sob wracked her body.

When he reached for her, she let him. In his embrace, though, the anger didn't diminish. It simply took on a new form. Mel's and Kino's faces appeared behind her closed eyelids. She needed to make them safe.

She pushed Rictus away. "Thank you, Rictus. Forgive me, you need to see the healer. Go now."

"Kreipsha—" he started.

"Go. I'll be fine."

As she watched him go, grateful for his strength, an idea occurred to her.

"Rictus, wait."

He turned back, patient as always.

"Do you remember when you said Rell could be what I was looking for?"

Rictus's thick, dark brows knit over his strong nose. "Mm."

"I think you may be right."

He stepped back into the room, listening.

"She's not as raw as she once was. She's had a first battle and looks like she'll recover. She's intelligent, she's trustworthy. Loyal."

"You want her to be your heir?"

"Perhaps." Then Ambessa shook her head. "Or perhaps I want her to guard my heir. Her power with Mel's acumen. Like the two of us."

Rictus nodded slowly. "We should see how Rell recovers first."

"You're right. Thank you, my friend. Go rest."

The next day brought the war council together. Amenesce and Burnside were both there, Burnside with a bandage over one side of his face, obscuring his left eye. Rictus sat beside

Amenesce, quietly fingering the rookern wrapped around his fist. Katye sat on Burnside's right. He alone looked pristine and unhurt, but he made up for this by dressing in muted clothing, loose trousers the color of sand beneath a dark brown tunic and over-robe. He gestured for the servants to leave the hot tea and coffee and food upon the table that was the centerpiece of the war room.

The table had a map of the known world carved into the top by the most skilled cartographer Ambessa could find—her brother Hanek. Cities, ports, trade routes, mountains, oceans, all were carved in the most minute detail. Ambessa could always see at a glance where her next move should be. And right now, her gaze was drawn inevitably to Tereshni. She didn't even know if Ta'Fik was there, but she would take the war to his home as he had done to hers.

"The bad news is," Amenesce was saying, "they haven't given up Gintara for lost. My scouts have seen their camp."

Burnside looked troubled. "The fact that they're still here at all makes me wonder if they expect reinforcements. Not to mention there's still fighting out to sea."

"The combined fleets are pushing them back," Katye interjected.

"Then we hit them now." Amenesce tapped the edge of the table. "While they're licking their wounds. They're less than a hundred. If there are any more cavalry warbands in the city, we can take them easily—"

"Easily?" Burnside snorted. "The Fist is decimated. I only have a hundred men and women left!" The old captain's voice rose.

He was right; it was a catastrophic loss for the Fist.

"The Miners are still in the city." Ambessa tapped the map. "Can you show us where the camp is?"

Amenesce stood, tried to reach her arm out to point, and winced. She laughed apologetically and walked over instead. She jabbed at a spot just within the edge of the forest north of the city.

"I wouldn't recommend sending your artillery in unless you don't mind burning the whole forest down."

"Maybe it would be worth it, if we could take down these monsters from a distance—" Burnside said.

"If you send the artillery away, who will defend the city? Wouldn't it be better to put them right outside the walls?" Katye asked. Burnside laughed unkindly, and the three of them began to bicker.

Ambessa could not think about where to put the artillery. She was still thinking about Azizi. Thinking about Gintara. Rictus had told her to see the bigger picture before she did something that she would regret.

The bigger picture was stopping Ta'Fik. Ta'Fik was not in those woods. Even if he sent more warbands of enhanced soldiers, he would not be with them. That was not his style. Not anymore.

Is that when you stopped respecting him? she thought to herself. *When he lost the taste for blood? Or was it because he knew you too well, and you couldn't hide from him? You were afraid to face the truth.*

She exhaled sharply, and everyone fell silent, watching her. She straightened.

"Ta'Fik wants to keep me occupied. He knows that I won't leave this city as long as there is a threat. Whether Gintara's warband comes for us again or not, whether there are reinforcements or not."

She traced her finger from Rokrund to Tereshni. "This is where the real fight is. This is where I'm going. I'll stop in

Bel'zhun first"—to see Mel and Kino, to make sure they were all right—"and then I'll go to Tereshni."

Ta'Fik had another child in Bel'zhun. Another one to ransom, if she needed to.

"But we can't hold them off if they attack again—" Burnside said gruffly.

"You will. You don't have a choice. With my warbands spent here, I won't have enough soldiers to lay siege to Tereshni, especially not if he has more soldiers like... these. So I'll lead a small group into the city."

"How will you get in?" Amenesce asked, frowning.

"Collateral." The word fell into the quiet like a stone.

Rictus narrowed his eyes at her but said nothing.

"Ah. You plan to use the captive. Your mage girl, with the metal—will she stay and fight with us?" Burnside leaned over the table eagerly. "That could change a great deal."

Ambessa shook her head sharply. "She comes with me."

"But—"

"No. Keep Ta'Fik's eyes on Rokrund," Ambessa continued. "Like any Medarda, he's persistent. Let us hope it narrows his vision. Convince him that I'm still here, fighting, or even better, that I'm too wounded to fight."

Amenesce grunted. "You are too wounded to fight."

"This will cost us." Katye stared at her across the table. He tapped his fingers slowly across the beautiful wood. "It will cost all of us."

"I know. Forgive me. But I will see it paid thrice over when I am the head of this family."

And before that, she would have vengeance.

Chapter Twenty-Nine

Ambessa left the meeting with purpose in her stride. Rictus fell in beside her, as he always did.

"Where are we going?" he asked pointedly.

"I am going to speak with Rell."

The tension in his shoulders eased slightly. "To ask her."

"Yes." Ambessa knew what he feared, and she said nothing to soothe him. The guilt she felt at deceiving him was buried beneath fury and pain.

"She's a good choice, Kreipsha."

His words solidified her path for her. "Thank you, Rictus." When they were outside Rell's door, she said, "I should do this alone."

He held his fist to his chest and bowed, then left.

Rell answered the door with a blushing grin on her face. When she saw Ambessa, however, the grin faltered and the blush faded. She cleared her throat and saluted. "General. Hello."

"Expecting someone else?"

"No, General. I mean, yes—but no, um, come in, General. How may I . . . um, help you?"

"Come with me."

Rell scrambled back inside to get her shoes and her knife belt.

She looked much better than she had the last two days. Color flushed her cheeks again, and the shadows around her eyes had lessened. The spark in her had returned, and Ambessa felt a rush of warm relief. She had not let herself acknowledge how worried she was.

She led Rell back to Gintara's rooms. The corridors were not empty, but Ambessa felt no need to hide. This was her prisoner. This was her war. Servants and soldiers and visitors alike bowed or saluted when she passed. The smell of dinner permeated the compound—there was going to be a feast tonight. Even though it hadn't been a decisive victory, they had made the Rippers retreat and captured the war leader. Ambessa had returned home. There were reasons enough to celebrate, and morale was not the least of them. Tomorrow, she would set out again.

But first, there was this question to settle.

Rell hesitated as they came to Gintara's door. "General?" Her voice trembled, and Ambessa worried that she had guessed wrong again.

"You said you would avenge me. Is that true?"

"Yes, General."

"Then come."

The two Wolf's Reapers stepped aside, and she unlocked the door. Gintara was where they had left her, kneeling and bound. Her pallor was worse now, but she stared fiercely at them when they entered.

"Aunt. Come to visit again? What do you want to know this time?"

Ambessa ignored her. "What should we do with her?"

Rell's eyes widened. "I thought you said we would ransom her?"

Ambessa shrugged one shoulder. "It's possible. She has a sister in Bel'zhun who could also be ransomed."

Rell's eyes darted between Ambessa and Gintara. She bit her

lip as she thought. "Her father killed your husband?"

The words stunned a gasp out of Ambessa. She didn't realize the news had spread.

"Yes," she said tightly.

This was news to Gintara. "What? No, he didn't, he wouldn't have. He wouldn't even let me kill you."

"I suppose your father doesn't trust you with all his plans," Ambessa said.

"*You're* the one who broke the Code."

"Your father is a hypocrite. A Medarda's word is as strong as their steel. Yet he speaks one creed and lives another." She turned to Rell. "What do we do with her?"

Rell held the knife at her belt tight in her hand. "If we kill her, we still have leverage with the ransom. It will also send Ta'Fik a message. He'll know what's at stake with the ransom. You'll also—you'll trade blows with him. Your husband, his child. If she's what he values most."

Ambessa nodded slowly and stepped back. "Blood for blood. Wrath for wrath. I accept this justice. Do it."

Both Rell and Gintara gaped in shock.

Then Gintara's expression hardened. "Like he said you would. Do it, then."

Rell stepped away from Gintara.

"A Medarda strikes swiftly and surely once a decision is made," Ambessa said.

Rell unsheathed the knife at her hip. Gintara's deep scowl told them nothing of fear, only resolution. She would die like a warrior, then. That was not the question Ambessa needed to have answered, however. Ambessa studied Rell, from the flick of her eyes to the tremor of her hands.

The tremor ceased.

Rell drove the point of her blade up under Gintara's chin.

Back in Rell's room, with her hands clean, they sat on the couch. The small apartment was lavish, well beyond anywhere Rell had ever lived, Ambessa was certain. The room was already scattered with bits of armor and weaponry. Untidy as the room was, however, Rell's clothing was sharp, no doubt a gift of Katye's hospitality. If blood had stained the cuffs, it wasn't visible on the dark fabric.

"That was well done. I know it might not have felt good, but you made a strong decision." Ambessa sighed. "Strong decisions rarely feel good. It's hard to do something that you can never take back. Too many people hesitate. But only strong decisions will take you to greatness. Do you understand?"

Rell sat with one foot on the couch, her hands clasped around her knee. She stared at them intently. "Yes, General."

"You showed your capability today, and on this campaign, and during the year that I knew you before this. So I have a question to ask you."

At the formality in Ambessa's tone, Rell straightened. "General?"

"Would you like to formally join my family? I will adopt you as one of my children. I will continue to train you in all things war and strategy. We'll hone your vision, sharpen your wits, and maximize your strengths—all of them. I will teach you the Medarda Code that we all live by, and one day, when I am gone…perhaps you will stand beside my children and lead this family to glory."

Ambessa suppressed a shudder as she remembered her grandfather's foreboding dream. The fall of their family. *Not if I can stop it*, she thought.

Ambessa opened her fingers, revealing a ring with its four-pointed star gleaming golden in her hand. "This star is a guide to remind you of the path—think of it as a compass, or the North Star. Each point represents a part of the Code." She pointed to the top point. "Medarda over all. We will be your family; you will protect your family and the family name above all others." She pointed to the other corners in turn. "A Medarda strikes their own path, seeing the greater picture and daring to tread where no others will. A Medarda fights with honor, and they do not ask for what they can take. With your gift, you can be mighty indeed."

Rell swallowed and nodded slowly. She traced the edge of the ring hesitantly. "And the fourth?"

Ambessa pointed to the last corner. "A clever tongue is as valuable as sharp steel. Sometimes more so. Take this, and whenever you struggle, look back to it."

But Rell did not take the ring. She sat with her mouth opening and closing before she asked, "What about your children?"

"What about them? I have a daughter your age and a son a little older."

"What if they don't want to share?" she said guardedly. "What if they don't want another sibling?"

"They need you, and they'll both see that."

Rell's brow furrowed in confusion but only for a moment. "You mean..." Her hand drifted to her knife, clean and back in its sheath.

"Yes. You are strong in ways they are not. And they have skills that you don't. A lifetime of political training, for example."

Rell glanced up, wary. "No one will take me seriously. I don't know anything about being in a—a Great House. I'm not like the people at Darkwill's ball. I'm just—I'm just a fighter from the arenas. I can't even lead a squad in a warband."

"Not yet, you can't. But you led a retreat even though you'd never been in battle before. You have good instincts. I'm here to teach you the rest. They will take you seriously because you will be *mine*."

But Rell was still suspicious. "Is this because of my powers?"

"It's not. Ask Rictus. You know I've been considering you for a long time—you were the best fighter in that arena." At that, some of Rell's suspicion softened. Ambessa pressed the advantage. "No matter what, take this."

From her pocket, she pulled a cloak clasp, a silver wolf's head. She tucked it into Rell's hand. "You are an astounding young woman, and I would be honored to have you even as just the captain of one of my warbands. You don't have to decide now," she said, trying to delay the swelling of disappointment in her chest. "It is a heavy choice, loaded with responsibility. You may not be ready to bear it, or never want to, and that's all right, too."

Rell nodded. She remained sitting on the couch, cupping the wolf's-head clasp in the palm of her hand, and Ambessa left her there.

"Don't be late to dinner. Regardless of your answer, tonight, you are a guest of honor."

Ambessa pulled the door behind her.

Just before it snicked shut, Rell cried, "Wait!"

The girl ran to the door and pulled it open. They were suspended in that moment, the two of them, Ambessa waiting, and Rell trying to find the courage to change her life. Ambessa remained silent. Some things couldn't be coaxed or pushed. A woman had to choose them for herself.

"You...you'd really keep teaching me?"

"I would teach you everything I know, child." Ambessa cupped Rell's cheek, then settled her hand on the young warrior's shoulder.

Rell inhaled with resolution, straightening her shoulders and meeting Ambessa's eye.

"Then...yes. I will. I'll become a Medarda."

Ambessa took the gold ring back out of her pocket and handed it to Rell. "Welcome to the family." Then she took the wolf pin and fastened it to Rell's cloak. "I know you'll make me proud."

As Rell looked around the feast hall in the Medarda compound, she wondered if this was what her mother and father had meant when they talked to her about "the old days" back before the Canwells lost favor. Rell ate some of every dish until she was bursting; it was good to be back in Noxus proper, eating the meat and spiced stews instead of the lighter fare in Bel'zhun. Dozens of people she didn't know sat at the tables—nobles of the city, leaders of the different warbands, the wealthiest merchants and traders. They were dressed so fine that, even though she'd been given new clothes to wear, Rell felt badly out of place.

And yet she was at the center of it all, sitting right next to General Medarda. Exceptional courage on the field was celebrated, and the fallen were mourned. Rell had wept as Zishani's name was called. Then Steward Katye thanked Rell personally for the role she had played in their victory.

Rell was trying not to think about it.

Instead, she was relieved when the meal was done and the formalities were over. Music was starting, and Tora swaggered over. She bowed in front of Ambessa and Rell, and Rell felt her face heating already. She hated how she could never hide what she was feeling around Tora.

"May I dance with the warrior of the hour?"

Ambessa laughed. "I'm afraid I'm unable to dance tonight, young rider."

From Ambessa's left, Rictus grunted in amusement.

Tora wrinkled her nose playfully. "I meant Rell." She held her hand out to Rell. "Would you?"

"I— If you want to, yeah, I want to, too. Dance, I mean. With you." Rell slammed her mouth shut so she wouldn't say anything even more stupid.

Amenesce, who sat on Rell's other side, grinned at Ambessa over Rell's head. "Don't tease the poor children. Though I don't know how they have the energy for it," she said in a low voice meant for Rell and Tora to hear.

Rell got up as gracefully as she could, the adults still talking around them.

"You remember when you were that age." Even Ambessa's jest was tinged with sadness.

"I grew out of it," Amenesce answered as she slid into Rell's seat. "Didn't you?"

"No," Ambessa said wryly. "I never did."

"Come on," Rell said, tugging Tora's arm. "Let's go before they embarrass us any more."

Amenesce heard and laughed. At their backs, she called, "Don't be like the general. Remember to think with your heads, not what's in your trousers!"

"Oh gods," Tora said, mortified. Even she was blushing, a dark flush against her brown skin.

They left Amenesce's cackling behind them as they found the cleared space where other dancers moved in a complicated step pattern, leaping out and in again, knees high, feet stomping hard. Rell wondered how Amenesce could joke so easily after the last few days they'd had, and yet, something in it was infectious. She laughed nervously.

"I don't know this dance," she confessed.

Conspiratorially, Tora spoke directly in her ear: "Neither do I! That's half the fun."

Together, they hopped and tripped over themselves, finding then losing the rhythm before finding it again. The other dancers cheered them on or moved away from them, but Rell forgot them eventually. There was just the music and Tora—there was no battle, no blood, no magic, no Medarda name. For a little while, she just *was*.

When they stopped to catch their breath and get a drink, though, Rell caught a glimpse of Ambessa at the table, her expression grim. Amenesce was gone—Rell spotted her dancing with a handsome older woman in the line, more gracefully than she and Tora had—but the general occasionally leaned over to speak with Rictus. Her lieutenant was unreadable as usual. Rell's hands suddenly felt slick with Gintara's blood again.

"You all right?" Tora said, handing Rell a fresh cup. It wasn't wine—it was some sort of cordial, made from some flower that grew in the Rokrund meadows. It was delicious. Tora followed Rell's gaze to her mentor. "Oh. I heard about her husband."

Rell nodded noncommittally. She didn't feel like dancing anymore. They edged their way out of the hall and into one of the inner courtyards. There were four of them in the whole compound: one a garden for beauty, another for food, and two training yards. With a start, Rell realized that the compound was shaped like the very ring she now wore on her finger. She spun the ring on her middle finger as they walked through the social garden. It was dark, and the air was heavy with the scent of something night-blooming.

When they were more or less alone, she said, "The general asked me to join her clan. I'm a Medarda now. Or will be when it's official." She held out the ring for Tora to see.

The other girl took her hand and held it up to her face. "Wow. You must have really impressed her."

"I must have. I just don't know if it's for the right reasons."

"What do you mean?"

Rell hesitated. She didn't want to tell Tora about her real parents, but her excitement and her fear were so hard to reconcile.

"My parents aren't dead. I just—don't get along with them," she said, understating dryly. "They...used me. When I was a Reckoner. They'd take my winnings and shout at me when they thought I wasn't training hard enough to win them another purse."

Tora's outrage was immediate. "Those bastards. I bet they don't even have the courage to step into the arena."

Rell shrugged half-heartedly. "What if the general's the same? What if she just wants me for my magic? Everyone's right—it made a difference in this battle." Rell clenched her fist and felt a tendril of power coil up in her again. She didn't have complete control over it, and she still felt depleted, like a well scooped dry. Still, she had enough power to slide a little of the metal armor from her forearms and turn it into an arrowhead. She let it spin in the air a moment before catching it in her palm. She held it out to Tora.

Tora looked at it in wonder. "Thank you."

Then Tora took Rell's hand again, folding it in her own. "She's not like that. General Medarda is admirable. She'll take care of you. This is exactly what you said you wanted, isn't it? To be like Rictus?"

Tora's excitement made Rell smile despite herself. "Yeah, that's true, isn't it?"

"That's better," Tora said softly. She smiled at Rell, her dark eyes tender in the magical lights that fluttered like fireflies along the park path.

Rell's heart suddenly beat faster as she realized how near Tora was—and how much she didn't mind it.

Tora ducked in close but stopped, waiting. "Can I kiss you?"

Rell swallowed. "Um—yeah? Yes."

And then Tora's hand was on her neck and she was kissing her and it was really, really nice.

"Rell? Are you out here?"

At Ambessa's voice, Rell jumped away from Tora and hastily straightened her clothes and tried desperately to look like they hadn't been doing what they'd been doing.

"Here, General!" Rell called, her voice cracking. She glanced at Tora, who stifled a laugh, and punched her in the shoulder.

"Ow!" But Tora didn't stop giggling.

When Ambessa turned onto their path, Rell saluted. The general was as grim as she had been when she was inside, but somehow even stiffer.

"Is something wrong?" Rell asked slowly. For a moment, she had the wild fear that Ambessa was going to say she had changed her mind, that she didn't want Rell after all.

"Unfortunately, but just a small matter. Could you give us a moment, child?" she said to Tora.

"Of course, General." Tora saluted, then said to Rell, "I'll be in my room. Come find me later."

Rell nodded. Tora backed away, a goofy smile on her face as she waved.

Ambessa watched Tora go. When they were alone, she led Rell through the garden and into a different corridor, away from the feast. Rell knew better than to badger the general for information. She would tell Rell what suited her, when it suited her. Through the corridors of the compound, the merrymaking of the feast faded until they'd left the compound entirely and the world was suddenly muted.

They walked down the main road, turning down a poorly lit street. Rell felt a prickle of unease. "General?"

"A little farther, child. With Azizi's death, I find that I can trust fewer and fewer people."

"What about Rictus?" It was odd whenever the lieutenant wasn't following Ambessa.

The general didn't answer. Rell shivered and pulled her cloak tighter around herself. Then Ambessa stopped abruptly. Rell overshot her, then turned back to see what had happened, but Ambessa wasn't alone anymore.

Three shadowed figures flanked her.

"General?" Rell asked tentatively.

Ambessa's mouth curled into an expression Rell didn't think she'd seen in the past days: a smile.

The bolt of magic that struck her in the chest caught her completely unaware. Rell knew nothing after that.

Chapter Thirty

The next morning, Ambessa called the Rokrund Citadel's improvised war council together to relay her plan. Katye and Burnside took their places. Amenesce came in last, complaining of a headache, but her eyes focused sharply on Ambessa.

"I'm going to Bel'zhun," Ambessa announced when everyone was seated. "Tonight."

Katye stroked his mustache thoughtfully, a worry line between his brows. "Fine."

"Fine?" Ambessa had expected him to object.

"Yes. Now is a good time. Our fleet has managed to hold Ta'Fik's ships away from the delta, but I don't know how long that will last."

"What of the prisoner?" Burnside asked. He scratched irritably at the bandage on his face. "The one you said we'd ransom?"

"She's dead. It was necessary."

"Why was it necessary?" Burnside pushed. "It could have bought us time, brought us some relief if you're still adamant that we fight here while you go."

Ambessa bent over the table and met Burnside's good eye. "You question me now, Burnside?" She flexed her fingers into a fist so the Medarda ring glinted in the light.

Silence stretched uncomfortably until finally Burnside shook his head and sat back.

"No, General."

"Good." Ambessa looked around the table. "The rest of you will stay and keep Ta'Fik interested in the city. Don't crush them outright, but don't let Rokrund fall."

"Then hurry," Katye said. Her brother suddenly looked so weary.

As everyone left, she sent servants with orders to prepare for her departure, including someone to fetch Rell.

Amenesce accompanied Ambessa to her rooms. "Do you want me to come with you?"

The idea of another friend, someone she could trust at her back, tempted her. But Amenesce's cavalry was too valuable here, and would do little good in Tereshni. She had a different plan for that.

"Stay here. But thank you."

Tora met them in the corridor, but she was alone.

"Where is Rell?" Amenesce said, teasing. "After you two disappeared together, I'm surprised to see you so easily separated."

Tora furrowed her brow in confusion. "I thought she was with you. I came to find her."

At that moment, the servant Ambessa had sent for Rell returned, looking harried. "Forgive me, General, the girl wasn't in her room."

Ambessa raised an eyebrow at Tora. "Was she with you this morning?"

"No, ma'am. That's what I meant. I haven't seen her since you came to get her last night."

Ambessa frowned. "I haven't seen her since you took her off to dance last night."

Tora hesitated. "But you came to the gardens. You said you wanted to talk to her?"

Ambessa's heart went cold in her chest. "I did not. I sat inside the entire time."

She glanced at Rictus and he nodded.

"General Medarda sat with me the whole time."

Even Amenesce straightened in concern.

"Where did you leave her? Take me there. Now."

Tora grasped that something greater was at work. She seemed frightened as she led Ambessa and the others back to the garden. As they walked, Ambessa sent for one of the Shadowhunters to meet them there.

"We came out here to be alone," Tora said, glancing at Amenesce before lowering her eyes to the ground. "We were— um. Then you came to get her, General. Or, I thought you did. I swear it was you! I mean—"

Ambessa let the young woman stammer as she walked down the garden path, perfect for two lovers looking for quiet and secrecy. There were no noticeable tracks. Then the Shadowhunter came, with his drakehound beside him.

"Do you have something of hers?" Ambessa asked Tora sharply.

The girl flinched at Ambessa's tone. "No, ma'am, we never— Wait." She dug in her pocket and pulled out an arrowhead. It was plain, but beautiful in its simplicity. "She made this for me."

The Shadowhunter presented it to the drakehound. A moment later, the drakehound led them out of the compound entirely until it stopped in a nondescript street. She could smell baked naaps and spices for the coming lunch hour; a yordle drove a team of donkeys the other way. In the distance, she heard the *ting, ting* of hammers on anvils as the Citadel blacksmiths prepared for the battle to come. But there was no sign of Rell.

Ahead of them, the Shadowhunter bent to pick something up from the ground. It glinted in his hand. Ambessa knew what it was before he gave it to her.

A cloak pin in the shape of a wolf's head shone in the darkness. One of its ears was bent, as if it had been stepped on.

No other trace of Rell remained, not even a drop of blood.

Ambessa and Rictus set sail that night without Rell.

"I'll follow up on any leads the Shadowhunters bring," Amenesce had promised. Tora had been inconsolable.

Ambessa was just as heartbroken. She'd made Rell a promise, and already she was turning her back upon it. *It's for her good. Ta'Fik is the root. I will cut him out of the ground.*

"There must be a traitor in the city," Ambessa had told her. "Someone who knows how valuable she is. Find them." She left no question of what to do with them when they were found.

Now she was at sea again, returning to where it all started.

Bel'zhun was beginning to be a place of nothing but pain.

Oh, Azizi. Forgive me.

The ship cut through the waves, water lapping against the wood, the gulls calling overhead. Rictus was belowdecks with a lit brazier, sliding the pieces of his rookern into the small fire in a ritual that Ambessa had never fully understood. Meanwhile, Ambessa watched the ship swallow up mile after mile of sea.

Eskender Medarda had crossed this channel, from Nashramae to Noxus, so many years ago. When she was a child, the stories of his exploits had thrilled her, how he had guided Noxian explorers and merchants across the Shuriman desert, how he had fought bands of Ralsiji to save the cowardly Noxians. She tried to feel connected to that legacy, as she had when her parents passed on those stories, but today, they might as well have been a fantasy.

There were other stories that stuck with her now. How Eskender Medarda had accompanied the last surviving Noxian as a friend, learned the Noxian ways, and then killed him to take the man's land and titles himself.

Ambessa's heritage was strength, and it was cunning, but it was also blood. Ruthlessness. Ta'Fik shared that same heritage, these same stories.

It begins with a fall, Grandfather Menelik said. *And then ruin.* The Medardas needed strength at the head. If she couldn't win, she wasn't the Medarda her family needed.

Cries from the sailors called her back to the present.

"General Medarda!" Captain Felspir rushed over. "The lookout says a ship is making to intercept." He pointed west.

A single ship was angling in their direction. Ambessa took up her spyglass. A war galley. It was impossible to see what colors they flew, but she was prepared to say they weren't allies.

"Then don't let them intercept us, Captain."

"Yes, General."

The captain stirred his sailors to a will, and they scurried like animals before a wildfire, but the humble messenger ship, though swift, wasn't fast enough to stay out of reach of a war galley under oar and sail. Still, they were managing to stay out of boarding reach. Ambessa ran to her cabin to collect her drakehound gauntlets, but she hoped she would not need them.

"Keep pulling ahead!" Ambessa cried when she returned. She pulled up the hood on her cloak. She couldn't risk Ta'Fik learning she had left Rokrund.

"We're trying—" The captain's shout cut off abruptly.

Ambessa turned to see a crossbow quarrel sticking out of the man's shoulder. "Captain!"

The enemy ship pulled alongside them, but they were still too far away for boarding, and without grapples—

But even as Ambessa watched, sailors on the ship mounted their railing. Then, with powerful leaps, they sailed across the gap of flowing sea that no normal human could have contemplated. Ambessa swore.

"Rictus!" she shouted. "They're enhanced. Just like the others."

She shouted a warning to the captain, and he ordered his sailors with courage despite his wound, but Ambessa knew it was no good. Her best warriors had barely stood up to the might of Gintara's enhanced fighters. There was no hope for these poor sailors.

Ambessa closed with one of the first boarders before he had his balance. Her drakehound blades crushed into his chest, and he flew back over the railing, dead before he hit the water. She released the gauntlets' catch and swung the blades free, whipping another soldier off the side.

In moments, the deck was slick with blood, but more of it belonged to her crew than the enemy. It didn't matter. Surrender was not an option.

"General Medarda?" A grin split the face of the enhanced sailor before her. A cruel, gleeful smile. "Look who's fallen into my net."

It took Ambessa a moment to place the bare-armed woman before her. Then she remembered.

"Stefana," Ambessa growled.

The Kilgrovan woman's eyes glowed with the same inner light that Gintara's had. More light limned her arms, almost as if tracing the woman's tattoos.

"You should have joined me," Ambessa said.

"You couldn't have given me this." Stefana swung her saber so fast that Ambessa could barely follow it. Only decades of honed instinct brought the gauntlets up in time to protect her. The strength behind the blow was immense, and Ambessa's muscles burned with the effort of holding Stefana at bay.

Ambessa had wanted to coax her away from Ta'Fik. The girl had the makings of a good Medarda. The hunger, most of all. But it was that same hunger that had brought Stefana to this moment.

As your own hunger has brought you here, said a dark voice in Ambessa's mind.

Ambessa's boots slid on the deck, wet with blood and sea together.

A sudden light appeared near the enemy galley, like flames flickering over the deck. Stefana glanced toward it, fear on her face. Ambessa tried to take advantage of Stefana's distraction, but the light grew brighter and brighter and came from *within* the other ship.

Then the light flared to blinding, and the crack of wood was deafening. Ambessa jumped back from Stefana and shielded her eyes.

"No!" the Kilgrovan roared.

Ambessa peered from behind her forearm. The light was gone now, leaving heavy blackness in its wake, and the ship that had been there a moment ago was quickly capsizing.

Stefana ran to the rail in desperation, but Ambessa swung her drakehound blades in an arc to catch her feet. Stefana crashed to the deck, and Ambessa pounced.

"Surrender," she growled.

"Never," Stefana spat.

The light in the woman's eyes flared again, and she threw Ambessa off her. Ambessa clattered against the deck, sliding into the base of a mast. The half-healed wound in her back ached. She gritted her teeth and pushed onto her feet. She didn't look around to see how many more of these magical soldiers were still on her deck. There was only the one in front of her.

Another light flew from behind Ambessa and into Stefana's

chest. It was like a meteor falling from the sky, and the force of it carried Stefana over the railing. Her scream was cut off by the sea before it even started.

Ambessa whirled around, her gauntlets raised.

A stranger in a hooded robe stood before her, hands folded.

"Who are you?" Ambessa asked. "Show yourself, or you follow her."

The figure chuckled softly, and Ambessa felt a chill down her spine and a flutter in her heart.

"Rudo?" she whispered.

The figure pulled down its hood, and Rudo smiled down at her. "Hello, Ambessa. My, it's good to see you."

Part III

Chapter Thirty-One

Ambessa."

Ambessa stepped back, her gauntlets still raised. She remembered Tora's certainty that Ambessa had taken Rell away. This must be the same thing. Some filthy mage trick. *A lure.*

This creature wearing Rudo's face stepped toward her, a half smile tugging at his lips.

"Whoever you are, tell me what you want before I send this through your heart." Ambessa cocked her fist back. "Rictus!"

"There's no need—"

"General!" There was a splash as a body fell overboard, and then the heavy creak as Rictus sprinted over, his bladed knuckles on his fists. He ran for the stranger, and the man who looked like Rudo spoke quickly.

"Ambessa, please. It is me. Rudo." In a voice low enough that none of the sailors around them could hear, he continued. "We have a daughter together named Mel, and she is the most beautiful thing I've ever laid eyes on. She is the sun to me. And," he added with a chuckle, "it would be difficult for me to say exactly where we made her, but I would guess it was that time after hours in the baths owned by that old woman—"

"Shastine Holinet," Ambessa finished with Rudo, both of

them speaking the name of the proprietor at the same time.

"Kreipsha," Rictus warned.

Abruptly, Ambessa returned to herself, across the distance of time and space. She wasn't in Basilich with its cold blue sea, sneaking into a bathhouse with her lover, but sailing the Conqueror's Channel on a bloody deck. The sailors all looked to her, and then she saw Captain Felspir's body. The hulk of the Kilgrovan galley was fast sinking to the depths, but smoke still came from the charred wood above the surface.

She raised her trembling voice and barked, "Get this deck cleared. Prepare the bodies for sea burial. Wounded, to the foredeck. Get us back on track to Bel'zhun."

The sailors snapped to, eager for direction. There were not many left in the wake of the enhanced fighters Stefana had brought with her.

"Come with me."

Ambessa's back prickled as she led Rudo—*was it really him?*—into the captain's cabin for privacy. She left Rictus guarding the door outside.

When they were alone, Ambessa took off her gauntlets and stepped toward Rudo, fingers outstretched.

Rudo kept his hands at his sides, open-palmed. Her fingers brushed his chest. He felt solid enough. He was no illusion. She skimmed up his chest to his cheeks, hunting for the signs she'd thought she'd memorized—but he was different now, as she was different. Lines now, where there hadn't been. Deep sorrow in his eyes, weariness in his graceful shoulders. Slowly, he brought one hand up to where hers touched his cheek. He covered her hand with his, and sighed into the caress.

"Ambessa, I have missed you."

Ambessa couldn't speak. She swallowed and blinked back the tears she was surprised to feel.

"Do you want me to leave a moment?"

Ambessa shook her head. But she said, "You're not supposed to be here."

"I know."

"Then what—is it about Mel?" Ambessa's stomach lurched. "Do they know about her?"

Rudo glanced back toward the door.

"Whatever you have to say, he can hear it. There's no one in the world I trust more than Rictus. But he will not eavesdrop."

Rudo chuckled. "Your tastes are very... broad."

"Watch yourself, Rudo." Now that the shock of seeing him had passed and she had governed her immediate feelings, Ambessa felt even more the need to be on her guard. He had breached her careful walls before, but there was more at stake now. "Rictus is my second-in-command."

Rudo bowed his head. "Forgive me."

Ambessa scanned the cabin and found what she was looking for on the captain's desk: a heavy bottle, probably filled with alcohol. She opened it and sniffed: pale Shuriman sweet wine, but at least it wasn't grog. She poured for both of them into the glasses she found, and they settled on the edge of the captain's bed.

"Why are you here, Rudo?"

He looked down at the wine she had poured for him and smiled ruefully. "Can't we speak of happier things first? I would like to learn more about Mel. You've raised a beautiful daughter."

A throbbing ache through her heart. She hardened it to stone. "Is this about her?" she asked again.

He sighed. "No, it isn't. She's safe. I made sure of it."

"You met her. In Bel'zhun."

Rudo's breath caught. "I did," he said slowly, carefully, as if he were tiptoeing over a pit viper's barrow. "It's a long story."

Ambessa poured herself more wine. "I have time. You don't. Tell me why I shouldn't have Rictus throw you overboard."

"You probably should." Rudo closed his eyes. "I've been working with Ta'Fik."

"You...what?" Ambessa's voice was a deadly whisper.

"My colleague Inyene and I—we both have different missions from the Black Rose. Ta'Fik is just a piece. The Medardas are one of the strongest families in Noxus, and our leader wants to control that power." Rudo's crooked smile returned. "Unfortunately, you were too headstrong for her to consider you as a puppet."

"Your time. Is ticking."

"Some of us have been looking for young mages. I didn't want them to find Mel, so when I knew Inyene and Ta'Fik would be coming to Bel'zhun and that you would be there, too—it was the perfect chance. I had Mel followed. I disguised myself. I met her." His eyes went misty. "She is so perfect, Ambessa. And she loves you so much."

"The point, Rudo," Ambessa snapped. How dare he? What did he know about her relationship with her daughter?

"Has she shown any hint that my magic was passed down to her?"

"None that I know of." And Ambessa had waited, had watched, never knowing if she wanted Mel to show some strength—or if she wanted her to remain safe and ordinary. She had already seen how dangerous it was to show promise—her enemies had taken Rell the moment they glimpsed her potential.

"Good." Rudo was palpably relieved. "The flesh runes I gave her should keep it that way. They'll act as...a deadener. To keep her powers bound. And no other mage will be able to sense her if she does have them."

"Flesh runes? Like the rune-soldiers?"

Rudo winced. "Not quite. But similar, yes. They're covered by the tattoos."

"Why are they looking for her in the first place? Did someone find out?"

"It's not her." Rudo's lips twisted in bitterness. "Inyene and I have been working on...certain experiments. The runes. To enhance a person's power, to take it away. Ta'Fik's warbands were part of that—"

As he spoke, though, Ambessa was pulling together all the pieces.

"You said young mages," she interrupted. *Rell.*

"Yes. Between mages, the runes can transfer power—"

"Where is she?" Ambessa snarled. The wine spilled onto the coverlet as a knife flashed in her hand, and suddenly she was straddling him with the point at his throat.

Rudo sat calmly beneath her, but his own tattoos began to glow with a faint golden light. Despite his delicate dancer's features, he was not helpless.

"Mel? I don't know what you're talking about—Bel'zhun, isn't she?"

"Yes, you do. *Rell.* My protégé vanished last night, and we found no trace. It was *you.*"

Rudo closed his eyes. "I'm sorry. I had nothing to do with it. I left Inyene weeks ago hoping to find you. But if they have her, I will help you free her. I swear it. All I ask is one thing. Help me stop Inyene."

Ambessa ignored the threatening pulse of golden power and pressed the tip of her dagger to his skin.

"I swear to you, Ambessa. I want to destroy the lab," Rudo picked up in a whisper. "All our searching, our notes. What Inyene is doing to the mages they find— They need to be stopped. It's why I left. I can't be a party to it anymore."

His voice cracked with desperation. Ambessa didn't let the dagger waver.

"Ambessa."

The way he said her name was her undoing. It always had been. She tucked the knife against her forearm and climbed off him.

"Get out."

"Amb—"

"Get out!"

At her shout, Rictus came back inside to *encourage* Rudo, but Rudo held up a hand. Golden light flared and tried to push Rictus away, but it was absorbed by the rookern.

Rudo's eyes widened. "That is fascinating."

Before Rictus could come for him again, Rudo held up both hands, placating. Ambessa looked away, but his gaze still burned.

When Rudo was gone, Ambessa collapsed onto the bed, holding her head in her hands, her breath coming in hitching, tearless sobs. For Rudo—how her heart was torn between rage at what he'd done and desire for him still. For the sick sense that she was grateful Mel had never shown any inkling of magic, lest she share Rell's fate. For the guilt that she still wished Mel had power, so that she could be greater, so that *they* could be greater *together*. She felt Rictus's steady presence beside her, but he made no move to touch her or console her with empty words, and she appreciated that more than he could know.

They sat in silence together until, after a time, he said, "Did Azizi know?"

Ambessa shook her head. "No one but me and Rudo. And now, you."

Rictus bowed his head solemnly. "Your secrets are my secrets." Then he asked her the hardest question: "Do you trust him?"

"How can I?"

"Good. I'll make sure the sailors keep a watch on him. They say he must have been a stowaway."

"How can I not?" she murmured, as if Rictus hadn't spoken at all. She trusted Rudo with the life of their child, that secret, and as far as she could tell, he hadn't betrayed it. He'd only betrayed her—and her ambitions. "He could help us find Rell."

"Is she worth the risk?" There was a challenge in his tone, in the sharp turn of his mouth. He had grown close to the girl, had spent as much time training her on this journey as Ambessa had.

Rell could be her heir. Or she could protect the heir. Either way, Ambessa had made promises to her. If Mel ever showed her powers, and if Ambessa could get Rell back—together, they might be unstoppable. The sheer strength of Rell's powers, of her fighting ability, coupled with the elegance of Rudo's magic . . . a dangerous thought. An intoxicating thought.

"She is one of my own now, Rictus. I would no more abandon her than I would you."

"I would expect you to leave me behind if it risked your objective."

It was supposed to be a simple statement. Factual. And yet, it pricked a tender spot. None of her visions could come true without defeating Ta'Fik.

"When he comes to speak to me tomorrow, let him in."

"How do you know he'll come tomorrow?"

"Trust me. He's more stubborn than he looks."

Rictus raised an eyebrow. "He looks pretty stubborn."

Ambessa smiled, remembering the laughter of a young man with luminous skin and eyes that shone like gold in the Basilich sunlight. "I know."

As predicted, Rudo knocked on the captain's door the next morning, escorted by Rictus, just as one of the sailors was bringing Ambessa her breakfast. The bigger man eyed Rudo warily.

Ambessa took the meal at the captain's table and gestured for Rudo to sit. "Rudo. You said you know where Rell is."

"You said she's your protégé?"

"Yes. Her parents entrusted her care to me." She couldn't bring herself to trust Rudo fully, but he was a smart man, if not smart enough to keep himself out of trouble.

"Not Mel?" Rudo narrowed his eyes. "Or—you have another child, don't you?"

Ambessa ignored his probing. "Where?"

"They will have taken her to a laboratory in the desert south of Tereshni. Inyene will try to . . . modify her." His jaw tightened and he looked away, fighting some inner battle.

"What do you mean 'modify'?" Ambessa's lip curled.

"I watched Inyene strip one mage boy of his magic and give it to another." His voice lowered to a whisper and he looked aside, the lines on his face deepening. "It left the child . . . *nulled*. He was alive, but it was a husk of a life."

She suspected that he had done more than simply watch. The only thing that matched Ambessa's disgust seemed to be his own. If she didn't hurry, that would be Rell's fate as well.

"To what purpose?"

"It's what the Rose wants."

"Grasping mages," Ambessa spat.

Rudo narrowed his eyes. "Is it so different from what you do?"

"At least I do it with my own bare hands, my own power—"

"So do we."

Ambessa exhaled sharply. "So you came here."

"I told you. I couldn't do it anymore. It wasn't worth it. I want out of the Black Rose, but the only way out is as a corpse. I'll never be fully free. They'll hunt me for the things I know, and I'll be in hiding for the rest of my life. I'll probably never be able to see you again, and—I don't dare see Mel. So I want to take something from them, too. I want to end something I should never have let them start."

Rudo clenched his fist tightly on the table.

Ambessa took another gull-berry from the plate. The juice popped sweet and sour on her tongue. It gave her time before she spoke.

"How can we trust you? You say you've just come from them, and that you've been responsible for creating our enemies."

Rudo looked Rictus up and down, alighting on the rookern wrapped around Rictus's forearm. "And you are afraid of what my magic can do against your steel. I understand."

"So give me something in return. After I stop in Bel'zhun, I'm going to Tereshni to face Ta'Fik—" She held a hand up over his protests. "Ta'Fik first. It has to be. These enhancements you made to Ta'Fik's soldiers. They were stronger than us; they fought without tiring. Could you do that to us? It could make the difference in—"

"No." Rudo pushed back from the table, away from Ambessa.

"If you and Inyene have done all you said, all his remaining warbands will be rune-strengthened. Help me defeat him."

"If you knew what you were asking me, you would not ask it." He closed his eyes, clenched fist trembling.

Ambessa did not reach out to comfort him.

"There is a cost," he added. "Not just to me, but to the soldiers. Side effects. It is only a temporary power, and it is not kind afterward."

She recalled the soldiers in Gintara's warband, the seizures that struck them at random on the field. Gintara's feverish pallor when she was imprisoned. *Side effects.*

"I understand," she said coldly. She stood and gestured toward the door. "When we disembark in Bel'zhun, you will remain under guard. I cannot have you jeopardizing the lives of my children."

"Ambessa. Please. Don't be like this." He stood, holding his hands open in front of him.

"Be like what, Rudo?" She tilted her chin up.

"So cruel." His words were barely audible over the working of the sailors and the snap of the wind in the sails outside the cabin.

Ambessa marched back to him until they were a breath apart. "Call me cruel and tell me that you have never known me, not once. I would do anything for the good of this family."

Rudo smiled sadly. "Oh, Ambessa. My love." This time, Rudo brushed his fingers against her face.

Ambessa expected him to kiss her, even found herself tilting her head up toward him against her will.

Then he turned and left her there.

She did not seek him out again for the rest of the journey.

Chapter Thirty-Two

Bel'zhun crested on the horizon, and Ambessa's grief broke with it, crashing against the walls of her chest. The Noxtoraa at the north of the city welcomed her back, its red flags and banners flapping beneath the sky bluer than the sea. Beyond the Noxtoraa, the spires of the old buildings twinkled, their golden tips thought to come from the Sun Discs of old.

And beyond those spires, her children.

They had better be unharmed.

"It's not safe for me to be seen here," Rudo murmured as he disembarked beside her. "There are Rose members working in the city. But I've promised you my aid. I'll wait for your decision beyond the western Noxtoraa."

Ambessa pursed her lips. "We have rooms enough at the compound. You could hide there."

"The better to keep me under guard, I know." Rudo shook his head and pulled his hood lower. "It's too risky, on all counts."

"Fine. I will *consider* your offer. But I make you no promises."

Rudo made an impatient noise through his nose. "We don't have time for you to *consider*. Not for my sake or yours."

Rudo's words were too true for comfort. Moreover, during the rest of the ship's voyage, she had come to the conclusion that she couldn't do this without Rudo, no matter how angry she was at him for creating the rune-soldiers or getting Rell stolen.

Inyene would pay alongside Ta'Fik.

"Go." Then, "Be safe."

When Ambessa and Rictus arrived at the Medarda compound, it was quiet. At first, Ambessa feared the worst. There was no one in the great courtyard, no one walking along the pathways between the different buildings or strolling the gardens. But the house guard who stopped her, demanding to see her ring, seemed untroubled. She tried to make herself easy but didn't stop scanning her surroundings.

This was the Medarda hold. She should be safe.

"Mother?"

Ambessa spun around, her heart leaping into her throat.

"Mother!"

Mel stood beneath one of the white pillared arches, a graceful simulacrum of a Noxtoraa. She was breathing heavily and held the edge of her skirt in one hand as if she'd come running. Just behind her was Kino, strolling in an attempt to hide his eagerness but failing—a wide grin spread across his face.

Mel ran to her and almost jumped into her arms until she saw the ginger way Ambessa held herself.

"Mother, you're hurt." Mel searched her mother up and down, her hands hovering just above Ambessa's shoulders.

Ambessa blinked away the mist in her eyes. Kino had come with the shadow of a beard and a haunting in the hollows of his eyes. Joy and sorrow both. Could she blame them?

"Only a little. Come here. Kino, come here."

She held each of them close to her chest and drank her fill of them.

They gathered in Ambessa's chambers. Servants made the rooms presentable as quickly as possible, airing them out and dusting the sofas. Ambessa was grateful for the refreshments. Bel'zhun's warmth surprised her. So did her exhaustion.

Despite her hunger, despite her weariness, she needed to know.

"Did you hold rites for him?" Ambessa asked softly.

Her children nodded. The grief in their faces was heavier than she could ever hope to comfort, even if comfort had been one of her skills. It was not something Menelik had prized.

"I know you both will do his memory credit. You never once disappointed him. I know it." Then, "*Was* it an accident?"

Kino and Mel shared a glance. In that way of siblings, it said much but told Ambessa little.

"We don't know," Kino said gruffly. "I haven't found anything to point to a guilty party, but..."

"Elora and I haven't found anything either," Mel said. "And Tivadar swears she had nothing to do with it."

"Tivadar." Ambessa scowled. "You were serious. You and the girl are close, then? Who is Elora?"

Mel pulled back from the table. "We're friends. Elora is a friend, and so is Tivadar. Elora helped me out of the carriage the day..." She trailed off, looking down at the table.

Ambessa softened her tone, almost an apology. "You can't trust Tivadar. She is Ta'Fik's daughter before anything else. Just like Gintara. Where is she?"

Warily, Mel asked, "Why?"

This was unlike Mel, to question her, to evade. If there was any chance that Mel would take up her mantle one day, Ambessa needed to make the necessary actions clear. She had coddled Mel too long by letting the girl learn politics but not blood.

"Because her father had your father killed. Because her father sent warbands powered by magic to our home. Even now, all my warbands are in Rokrund, defending Rokrund Citadel to what may well be their last breaths while I try to cut Ta'Fik at the root. Tivadar is that root."

Horror dawned on Mel's face. "What will you do to her?"

"She will be my hostage. Ta'Fik will relinquish his claim on me, or he will lose her, too."

"Too?" Kino interrupted, leaning forward.

"Gintara died leading Ta'Fik's warbands." It was not strictly a lie.

"Oh no." Mel covered her face with her hand. "Tivadar will be devastated."

"It is the way of war. You should know this." Ambessa crossed her arms over her chest. "If you truly care for her, make sure she cooperates. Let her help persuade Ta'Fik that he should do everything he can to keep his remaining child."

"You don't have to do this to her. Just talk to her. She would listen."

"Would she? Or has she fooled that soft heart of yours?"

Mel murmured something, but her head was still lowered, and Ambessa couldn't make it out.

"What was that?" she asked. "Speak clearly if you have something to say."

"I said, you don't know anything about her." Mel's eyes were bright and fierce. "I've spent more time with her than you. *I've* gotten to know her. Her relationship with her father is . . . complicated."

Ambessa heard what Mel didn't say: *Just like ours.*

"Complicated enough that she would betray her own father for my sake? Ha!"

"Perhaps!" Mel jumped to her feet. "But you would have to

give her a chance to make that decision for herself, without a knife to her throat. Do you even know how to do that, Mother, or is it always blood first?"

The words hit Ambessa like cold water in the face. She stared at Mel, mouth open to rebut or rebuke, but nothing came out.

She tried to make the sight before her make sense. Mel, her face flushed, her chest heaving with her anger and this new-found defiance. The gold of her tattoos stood out upon her bare shoulders. For a moment, she looked just as astonished as Ambessa. Then her expression hardened.

Kino stood, too, and put a calming arm around his sister. "Mel, Mother's right. Tivadar is a Medarda. A *real* Medarda," he added with a twist of self-deprecation. "She'll do whatever she needs to win, including put a dagger in your back."

"No, she won't. I'll prove it to you, if either of you would just give me a chance instead of treating me like a naive child." She turned back to Ambessa, and Ambessa was driven back to speechlessness by the desperation in her eyes. "Will you never listen to me? Will you never trust me?"

The words echoed something Rell had once said to Ambessa when speaking about her own parents. *They only wanted to live through me. They never let* me *live my life. I was just a toy doll that made them money.*

Was that how Mel felt? Was it the curse of every parent, to puppet their child until they turned and cut the strings them-selves? She had not meant to stifle Mel, only to make her stronger. Even as she felt herself relenting, Ambessa wondered if this was just more proof that Mel was unfit. But she would give her this chance. Once more.

Kino looked helplessly between the two of them. "Mel, Mother, please—"

"Speak to Tivadar. Tell her that I'm going to Tereshni. Tell her that her father has broken the Code and that I will have my due. If she joins me, she can take his place as steward. We will have an end of it."

Mel's wariness returned. "Truly? You'll spare her?"

Ambessa stood, too, forcing her daughter to look up to meet her gaze. Mel did, the coal of anger still burning in her hazel eyes.

"If she helps me defeat Ta'Fik."

Heart heavy, Mel knocked on Tivadar's door.

"Come in!" An energetic voice came from the other side.

Mel followed the voice all the way to Tivadar's bedroom, where the other woman was dressing for the evening. She'd gotten so far as her trousers and a sleeveless shirt. Before Mel's mother had arrived out of the blue, they had planned on going out with Kino and Elora for the evening. It had become a regular occasion as their friendship grew. Their uneasy détente had been shaken after Azizi's death, but Mel sought Tivadar out to apologize. Tivadar had joined Mel and Elora on the hunt for Mel's father's killer, and they had grown closer. Tivadar came to Kino's fetes with Mel with a minimum of grumbling, and Mel went to Tivadar's Reckoner fights. They whiled away the rest of their time on walks, discussing what they might like to do in the future, if their parents had no say—Mel showed Tivadar the art from the Rakkor painter and talked about how she might like to become a dealer of fine paintings. Tivadar confessed that she would like to join one of the sand-dancing troupes from the Great Sai.

These dreams were nothing more than cloud castles in the air, as Ambessa's arrival had reminded Mel.

"You're early." Tivadar was rummaging in her clothing chest, and her voice was muffled.

"Tivadar?"

Tivadar froze. The tone of Mel's voice was enough warning. Slowly, she straightened from her search. Without turning to face Mel, she asked, "What is it?"

"You should sit—"

"Don't tell me what to do." Tivadar's fist clenched at her side around a long over-robe. Her shoulders were tight with tension. "What happened?"

"My mother has returned. She brings news from Rok—"

"What. Happened." Still Tivadar didn't turn, but her fear was evident in her every muscle.

Your cowardice is hurting her. Speak plain.

"My mother says Gintara is dead. Tivadar, I'm sorry."

The fist holding the robe convulsed, followed by a gasp like a punch in the gut.

"How?" Tivadar whispered.

Mel edged farther into the room. "In battle. She was taken by the Wolf, like she would have wanted, I'm sure."

Tivadar rounded upon her. "You don't know what she would have wanted."

Mel raised her hands defensively in front of herself. "You're right. I don't. I'm sorry. You've just told me so much about her, that I thought . . . Forgive me."

Tivadar looked away again and said nothing for a long time. Mel waited. When Tivadar turned back to her, her eyes were red-rimmed and her cheeks were wet.

"Did your mother do it?" Tivadar growled. "Did she kill my sister?"

"I don't know. She didn't say." For their friendship, Tivadar deserved the truth. "But Gintara led a warband against Rok-rund Citadel. Our home. She and Ta'Fik broke the Code, my mother had the right to defend—"

"Fuck the Code." Tivadar's mouth twisted in grief. The coiled tension that came before one of her outbursts was building.

"The Code exists to protect us from this."

"Oh, now you want to follow the Code? I thought it was an excuse for warmongering?"

Mel closed her eyes. She might have said that once. She might even believe it still. But her mother had given her this task and she would do it.

"I do believe my mother means the best for this family. All of us," she added, "not just her children."

Tivadar snorted. She threw her robe back into the clothing chest and sat heavily on her bed. She covered her face with her hands.

"I need to write to my father."

Mel sat gingerly on the bed beside Tivadar. "That's not all I came to say."

Tivadar dragged her hands down her face and regarded Mel. "Your mother wants to take me hostage."

Was it written so plainly on her face? No. It was simply the most natural response.

"I made her let me speak to you first. She would accept your help."

"Help the woman who killed my sister?"

"Your father was just as guilty—"

"I know!" Tivadar leapt up and strode to her writing desk. "I know he's just as guilty! I know that all this is his fault." She yanked open a drawer and took out a folded letter. She waved it in Mel's face. "My father gave me these instructions weeks ago. Probably the same time he ordered Gintara's attack."

Mel held herself stiffly on the bed. "What did he say?"

"Can't you guess?" A bitter smile curled Tivadar's mouth.

"He...asked you to kill me?"

"But unlike you, I didn't *do* his bidding." Tivadar balled up the paper and threw it across the room.

"You know what it's like to have a parent who's as difficult to love as they are to disobey." Mel looked down at her hands, folded in her lap. "I fought with her—to let you live."

"How generous."

Tivadar was right to be so angry. It was a betrayal.

"If you want to run," Mel started slowly, each word heavier than the last, "I won't tell her. But you should leave tonight."

Tivadar narrowed her eyes and opened her mouth to speak, but Mel rushed over her.

"However, if you go with my mother, you can speak to your father first. That's all she wants. For you to talk him down. No more blood needs to be shed if we can get them to talk. Like us. Otherwise, they won't stop trying to kill each other. We know who will fall next."

Tivadar suddenly looked far older than her seventeen years. She knew the answer as well as Mel did.

Us.

"So I take it Kino's party is off, then," Tivadar said with weary sarcasm.

Mel laughed softly in relief. "I think so. So you'll go with her?"

Tivadar stared vaguely into the distance. "I suppose you'll know if I'm still here in the morning."

Despite the catching up Ambessa had done with her children, it felt like none of them had spoken to the heart of what they wanted to say. She could not help but wonder how Rell would have fit in with the other two—the young wolf to her foxes. Instead of leaving with Mel, however, Kino lingered.

"May I speak with you privately, Mother?" Kino's voice carried the weight of his seriousness as it hadn't during lunch.

Ambessa didn't let her apprehension show. Irrationally, her first thought was that he had learned the truth about Mel's father. But Rudo was outside the city, far from the compound.

"Of course." Ambessa led him back to her private study.

She put her hands on her hips, as she had when Kino was young and in trouble for stealing sweet buns from the kitchens. "Tell me."

"It won't be easy to hear, I'm afraid. Would you like to sit down?"

Ambessa raised an eyebrow.

Kino chuckled, but it was tinged with darkness. "Of course not. It's about Father. When I went to Valif, to get his help as you said, I also asked him about Father's death. Did you hear how he died?"

"The carriage accident," Ambessa said carefully. "Ta'Fik was behind it."

To Ambessa's horror, Kino shook his head. "I don't think so. There's something bigger. Valif had his own suspicions." Kino lowered his voice. "He says—"

"Whatever you do, Kino," Ambessa hissed, backing Kino up against the closed door, "you are not to finish that sentence. Have you been looking through my papers?"

"So you know about the Bla—"

"Hsst." Ambessa stepped closer, holding a warning finger up between them. "You will not go searching for them. You will not ask anyone else about them. Your investigations end here."

"But we *have to*—"

Ambessa slammed her hand against the door beside Kino's head. The wood reverberated with the force, and Kino flinched. "You will obey me in this. I say this not as your mother but as the head of this clan. Leave it."

"They killed Father. Don't you care?"

Ambessa looked into her son's eyes. They were full of angry, unshed tears, and for all the man he pretended to be, he was just a child to her. Her sweet little boy. She cupped her hand against his cheek.

"I swear to you, Kino. I will not rest until that debt is settled. You are not ready for this fight. Do you understand me?"

Though he was as tall as her now, he glared sullenly up at her from beneath his long lashes. When he was a baby, she'd spent countless hours admiring those eyelashes against his cheeks.

"Yes, General." He straightened and bowed. "By your leave."

She wanted to call him back. To explain that Ta'Fik was intricately woven with the Black Rose. Ta'Fik was too large a problem to be left unchecked. But she said nothing as he opened the door and left her with a sinking feeling in her gut.

Rictus came in after Kino left. "Are you all right?"

Ambessa flung herself back against the wall.

Her heart was still wrung sore from the way Mel had looked at her—not just with anger, but with hatred. Now this. It was bad enough that Azizi was dead, but for him to be a victim of the Black Rose? And why? Was Rudo wrong? *Had* they learned about Mel? Or was this just because Azizi was close to Ambessa, because he was inconveniencing their plans for Ta'Fik?

She would demand Rudo tell her the entire truth.

And she would bear Mel's anger as long as she had to, if it would keep her safe.

"I'm fine."

She always was. She had no choice.

Chapter Thirty-Three

The next morning, Ambessa called Mel to accompany her to Tivadar's rooms. A small squad of the Wolf's Reapers followed, ready to apprehend Tivadar by force if necessary.

"I hope you were able to reach her," Ambessa muttered.

"I told her what you told me, and I said that you would spare her if she helps."

"Mm."

Ambessa knocked on Tivadar's door with three firm raps. When there was no answer, she raised an eyebrow at Mel. "I don't suppose she keeps an early training regimen?"

"I don't know." Mel pursed her lips.

Another three raps. Nothing. Ambessa opened the door.

The small anteroom with its small side table and cushioned chair were empty, left almost desolate in the silence. The bedroom looked like it had been abandoned in haste: the coverlet on the bed unmade, the clothing trunk hastily emptied—some clothes still remained, as did a small sharpening stone for a blade.

Ambessa turned slowly to Mel, and the guilty, stricken look on her face told all.

"Where is she?" Ambessa asked.

"I don't know," said Mel in a small voice. She lowered her eyes and shook her head. "I don't know. I thought she would stay."

"But she did not!" Ambessa snapped. "Now she is likely on her way to Tereshni, ruining all hope of surprise that I depended on."

Her disappointment only deepened when Mel flinched at her words, hunching into her shoulders. Perhaps she had been right all along. No matter how Ambessa tried to impress upon her the importance of the decisive strike, Mel was too generous with her affection. She let it cloud her judgment when ruthlessness was needed.

Ambessa swept past Mel. She could not bear to look at her daughter right now, and she was afraid what other words would come out that she would not be able to take back.

"Rictus, prepare to leave." To the Wolf's Reapers, she said, "Your duties remain the same. Protect my children."

Ambessa hesitated at the doorway of the abandoned rooms. She could sense Mel standing behind her, holding herself together. Waiting for Ambessa to say something.

There was nothing to say.

"Mother?"

Ambessa turned at Kino's call, the sound of his loping footsteps on the paving stones. She and Rictus were on their way to the stables, their packs slung over their shoulders. It almost made her feel like a young soldier again. They would take three horses and meet Rudo down by the westernmost Noxtoraa.

Ambessa still wondered if she should go back inside, speak to Mel. She didn't want to go into what might be her last battle with this rift between them. The disappointment was so fierce, though, that it brought frustrated tears to Ambessa's eyes.

Besides, she told herself, she needed all the speed she could get to make up what advantage Tivadar had.

"Kino."

"You're leaving already?" He slowed to a walk beside her.

"Yes," she said shortly. "Your sister's actions have made speed even more of a necessity."

Kino's brown eyes were compassionate as he looked back toward the compound. "She did what she thought was right, Mother. Don't fault her for that."

"If she wants to be treated as an adult, she can bear the fault for her actions." She lengthened her stride for the stables. "Did you come to berate me?"

"No, as a matter of fact," Kino said tartly. "We received a messenger hawk." He handed Ambessa a tightly curled scroll.

Her breath caught at the Noxian imperial seal stamped into it. Darkwill? She slid her thumb beneath it and snapped it open.

Your vastaya has proven useful. A useful gift deserves return in kind. Part of my fleet is in the Channel. Send word to the admiral— tell her what you need. The bird is enchanted. It knows the way.

The weight upon Ambessa's chest lightened, just a little. She could not know how far away the admiral and this fleet were, so better not to depend overmuch on it. But she would write to her.

"Here. Quickly." Ambessa dug through her saddlebags and found the oiled leather pouch where her maps, papers, and inks were stored. She pulled out a charcoal pencil and scribbled hastily on the back of the tiny scroll before rolling it up. *Tereshni port. Sink any military ship in Ta'Fik Medarda's fleet.*

Then she had another thought, unrolled the scroll, and scribbled again. *Stop all Ta'Fik ships en route to Rokrund.*

"Seal this and send it back immediately."

Kino took the scroll and bowed. "Of course, Mother."

He hovered uncertainly before leaving, and it tore at

Ambessa's heart. She softened her tone, saying, "Come here."
She clasped him to her chest and held him close, inhaling the
smell of him: scented oils on his skin, the oils in his hair, and
the waft of fresh flatbread from his breakfast. He held her tentatively at first, but the longer she stayed, the tighter his grip.
She put her hand to the back of his head. "I will return soon."

"I know." Kino pulled away and held her by the shoulders. He
smiled crookedly. Azizi still lived in his eyes.

Ambessa and Rictus found Rudo at the western Noxtoraa. In
his hooded robes, sitting on the ground, he looked like a beg-
gar. As they approached, however, Ambessa realized that he
was crouched on the ground with his packs spilled out before
him. He had a piece of canvas and with quick strokes was painting the sun as it rose above the Noxtoraa. The morning sky was
clear and blue, and from Rudo's position on the ground, one
could see the sun just below the Noxtoraa's arch. In a few minutes, the sun would disappear briefly, illuminating the arch with
a godly glow.

Ambessa didn't know which sight was more stirring—the
sun beyond the arch, or Rudo's deft surety as he worked.

Rudo kept them waiting in silence as he worked through several more strokes before he spoke.

"Have you decided to trust me, then?" He still studied his
work, tilting his head and looking between the painting and the
subject.

"Unfortunately, we have no choice."

"You always were a flatterer." Finally, Rudo looked up at
them. He noticed the third horse. "And practical. I always loved
that about you."

Beside her, Rictus bristled, but Ambessa took no offense.

"This place where...your people...take their stolen mages. Where is it?"

Rudo stiffened, and his glance around them was less than casual, but those leaving and entering the city were too intent on their own business to hear their murmured conversation.

"South of Tereshni." He started putting his paints away. "There are ruins; they have a heightened magical presence. It made our work easier. Are we going there?" He sounded both eager and apprehensive.

"How far?"

"From Tereshni? A couple days' ride."

Ambessa shook her head sharply. "No."

But Rudo didn't relent as they rode west, through dry scrubland, hard-packed earth, and sifting dunes.

"She's in danger, your little protégé," Rudo said. "The longer we wait, the less likely she is to have her magic, let alone *herself*."

"I don't understand what you mean," Ambessa said with frustration. Though Rudo had always spoken of the Black Rose and its pale woman with both admiration and fear, it was hard for her to fathom the true nature of the danger.

"It's—" Rudo scowled as he tried to find the words. "You're a warrior. Your arms, your legs, they're not just a part of your body but they are part of your identity. Imagine someone cut off all your limbs. Not only do you have to heal from the physical damage, but the psychological toll would be immense." He stared into the distance. "I don't know how permanent it is, but it breaks something in them."

"And there's Mel," Rictus said softly on her other side.

"What about her?" Rudo said sharply.

"Nothing," Ambessa said. "Only that—I thought that Rell would make a good companion for Mel. They could balance each other. Rell has the fortitude to do things that Mel is...too soft for."

If Rell lost her magic, even if she didn't become a *null* as Rudo called them, she would not be as valuable an asset for the family.

Is that all she is to you? Another asset?

The voice in her head sounded hatefully like Ta'Fik.

"Too soft?" Rudo asked. "Or just different from you?"

Ambessa turned a cold stare on him. "You have no right to judge my raising of our child. You were not there; you have not been here."

Rudo worked his jaw as if chewing down his excuses and swallowing them. Ambessa was glad. If he'd offered them up, she might have punched him. Instead, he said, "With each iteration, Inyene makes Ta'Fik's army stronger. The last soldiers had barely any magical recoil at all. The final company may be unstoppable. We need to stop Inyene."

Ambessa sighed as the choice she would make came into sharper focus.

"She's a good kid." Rictus wasn't ready to let the subject go.

Rell *was* more than an asset. Ambessa had grown to care for the girl over their many months of travel and fighting together. She'd watched her training in the arena for over a year before that, paying attention to her growth. Even without her magic, she was promising.

But with it, they could change the structure of every battle.

They could even beat Ta'Fik.

Ambessa looked between both men. "If Inyene's rune-soldiers are getting stronger with each trial, the answer is clear. We barely stood against the ones we faced, side effects and all. If Ta'Fik remains unchecked, Rokrund will fall, and then Bel'zhun. Ta'Fik will win, and with him, your pale woman. We ride to Tereshni. With the help of Darkwill's admiral..." She faltered. Her plan was barely a sketch, but one thing was clear. Ta'Fik had to die. This had to end.

Ambessa knew how to sacrifice her heart for the sake of victory.

They rode swiftly enough and looked unassuming enough that none of the desert raiders were tempted to stop them to see their goods. There would be juicier prey in a merchant caravan.

When they stopped to make camp, though, Ambessa's heart was far from easy.

"I'll take the first watch," she said, after dismounting and relieving her horse of its burdens. She left Rictus and Rudo to the setting of the camp, and walked a wide circuit.

It wasn't long before Rudo's footsteps joined hers. He didn't speak, only walked beside her in a silence that managed to be companionable, despite everything between them. He even hummed softly to himself.

In his nearness, she realized how little she knew him now—perhaps how little she had ever known him.

"And where have you been, all these years?" She couldn't help the second question, a barb: "What other monsters have you created for your master?"

He took his time answering. "I have traveled the world. Noxus. Shurima. The Serpent Isles. Even Demacia, though that was not by choice."

"And I suppose it is all too secret to share with me?"

Rudo shook his head, but chuckled. "Oh, Ambessa. I barely know what I was doing in those places myself. The Rose is... We are each like a hand. Some of the things we do are in concert with the whole—" He mimed scooping water with both hands. "Others times, we move completely independently, at our own whim. But we must always act when called upon."

Ambessa had no answer for him. His body was warm beside hers. The desert night was cool around them. They walked in silence, with nothing but the skitter of sand as burrowing animals rose to the surface.

Finally, Rudo broke the silence, asking awkwardly, "How was Mel? And the rest of your family? Your husband and son? Kino, was it?"

At the mention of Azizi, Ambessa felt a chasm widen in her chest.

"Azizi is dead," she said, so softly that the night seemed to swallow it up. "Ta'Fik had him killed. He almost took Mel as well. Which is why I will take everything he loves before I kill him myself." She looked above, as if she could see what was to come in the lines of the stars. Some mages were said to do that. She wondered if Rudo could, with his celestial magic, but she decided it was better not to know. She had seen her destiny once before. "If I have to face him with no army at my back but Rictus, I will."

"When?"

"What?" The simple question caught Ambessa off guard.

"When did he die?"

Ambessa opened her mouth to answer, but realized she couldn't. She started to count back in her head—the battle at the mines, the ride from the Immortal Bastion, from Vindor, from Trannit. A whole lifetime seemed to have passed since she first left Bel'zhun, but she didn't know when Azizi had actually died.

"I should have been with him," she said to herself.

At the admission, her legs went limp, her knees soft as water. She sagged to the ground. Her fingers scraped against the hard-packed sand. Since she'd found out about his death, she'd kept herself focused on the next step of her vengeance. She'd avoided probing the wound that was his absence. Worse, if she didn't think about it, it felt more like it did whenever she was away from Rokrund on one campaign or another, and she would see him as soon as she returned home. As long as she didn't slow down enough to face the reality of it, she was fine.

She closed her eyes, and a shudder took her body.

"You haven't grieved him, have you?" Rudo knelt beside her. "Or your grandfather, knowing you."

Ambessa shook her head. "My grandfather died as he would have wished—a battle wound. The Wolf has taken him now. And Azizi...the Lamb. Death is necessary in the pursuit of victory. It fuels me."

It was the first thing her grandfather taught her. *To be a warrior is to know death, to welcome it when the time is right. You cannot fear it and deal it at the same time.* Even Azizi's death. What difference was his death, compared to a wound taken in a duel? Just another blow between her and Ta'Fik, and Gintara her counterstrike.

His gentle hand caressed her back, over the wound Gintara's basilisk had made.

"That's not grieving, Ambessa. That's vengeance. That's denial. I don't remember you being so angry in Basilich."

Ambessa pushed herself to her haunches to better regard him in the starlight. His eyes almost seemed to glow. She traced the outline of his face in the night, first with her eyes and then with her fingers. He closed his eyes beneath her touch. In another era, she would have taken him right then in the sand.

"Things have changed since then," she said, as much to herself as to him.

Rudo brought one hand up to her neck, tilting her face up. "Have they?"

The crunch of heavy boots approaching made them spring apart like youths. Rictus, his arms crossed over his broad chest in disapproval. "Dinner is ready."

Ambessa pushed herself to her feet, ignoring the hands both men offered to help her. She walked alone to the small campfire, and tried to pretend her heart was not racing.

Chapter Thirty-Four

They arrived in Tereshni a few days later. They didn't overtake Tivadar on the journey, though Ambessa pushed the horses as fast as they could go. She'd wished more than once for Amenesce's swifthorns.

The inn they found was a recommendation from Rictus. The Busted Knuckle was the sort of place a Reckoner might go if he were saving his coins for drink, or to pay off a debt he'd bought with drink. Any of the patrons looked like they could have been the namesake of the place, with their crooked noses and gnarled hands.

"People don't ask questions here," Rictus said to Ambessa's raised eyebrow.

Still, Ambessa went in with her hood up. So did Rudo. When the innkeeper stated the price for two rooms, Ambessa handed it over without arguing, making sure he understood she was paying for his discretion. She also ordered a hot meal and a hotter bath.

"Bathhouse is separate, ma'am. You have to go to Dormun Road." He pointed lazily in the general direction of this supposed bathhouse.

Ambessa snorted in disgust. "Fine. I'll take the food first. Have it brought upstairs."

The innkeeper started to say something sarcastic, but he closed his mouth at Rictus's deepening scowl.

The three of them gathered together in one of the rooms. It was time to take stock of their resources and plan the next stage of their attack. Losing Tivadar would make it harder, but not impossible.

"I have a friend in the city," Rictus said. "From the old days. He could stir up trouble for us. A distraction."

"That's one option. I'm also expecting Darkwill's ships. They have their instructions. If they arrive on time, they'll be distraction enough. Better yet, they'll draw away any rune-soldiers Ta'Fik has in Tereshni when his ships are targeted. But we need a way into Ta'Fik's manse." That, or they needed to lure Ta'Fik out of it. "If it gets around the city that I am here, maybe he would join the hunt for me..."

"No," Rictus and Rudo said at the same time. They looked tartly at each other, then Rictus continued.

"You'll be captured."

"I'll be brought straight to him."

"With no way to get out again," Rudo said. He was interrupted by a knock at the door.

Rictus opened the door for a servant with a tray of heavily spiced meat wrapped in a spongy fermented flatbread. He waited until the servant was gone before closing the door again.

Then Rudo continued. "Let me go, instead. If Inyene isn't there, Ta'Fik can't do anything to stop me. I can help you finish this. And if Inyene is there...well. I can help you finish this."

"You alone, against Ta'Fik's rune-soldiers?" Ambessa shook her head once, sharp. "You wouldn't survive."

"You don't know what I can do." Rudo met her eyes steadily. He ruined the picture of confidence by murmuring, "It would serve me right for what I've done. You must promise to destroy the laboratory, though."

"You're going to take me there, which means you won't be dying like a martyr to assuage your guilt. Am I understood?" Ambessa covered her sudden, jagged fear with command. "Besides. The strategy isn't sound. What if you go in and speak to Ta'Fik? Does he know you've left the—them?"

"Inyene will have told him. I could tell him I've come back, that I needed time to think, but I've recovered."

The food grew cold before them as they ran through their ideas, building upon them, discarding them, turning them about until Ambessa's mind was full of branching paths, the future a maze, and each turn but one more step toward her destiny with no way to know which was false.

Ambessa sat in the common room alone nursing a cup of beer that was, if not delicious, at least cool. This wasn't the type of place to serve the bold Noxian wine she preferred. Rictus had gone to speak to his old friend, and Rudo had hinted that she should join him in the baths, but after their journey together, she wanted to keep her distance. He clouded her mind when she needed it clearest.

The common room was rowdy at night, as a tavern called the Busted Knuckle was bound to be, so when Tivadar entered the place and looked around, Ambessa almost missed her. Tivadar was slight in comparison to many of the patrons, and looked like the child that she was. A single earring glinted from one ear, and a stud in each cheek. Ambessa bowed her head low over her drink and watched the girl scan the room before striding to the innkeeper.

A short exchange. A coin upon the bar. Ambessa slid one hand beneath the table to the knife at her belt. She waited for the innkeeper to look her way, or make some sort of signal to Tivadar, but nothing passed between them that she could recognize. Perhaps the Busted Knuckle deserved its reputation.

Tivadar's scowl as she left the inn told Ambessa that it did. She owed the man a substantial tip.

After the door shut behind Tivadar, Ambessa wove between the chairs and tables and bellowing gamblers to follow the girl outside. Ambessa spotted her swiftly. The girl might have been a great fighter in the arena, but she was so lost in her thoughts, or perhaps so arrogant, that she didn't turn at Ambessa's approach until it was too late.

Ambessa caught the girl around the neck with her forearm and dragged her backward into the dark crook between a tailor's shop with its shutters closed and a glassmaker.

Tivadar's elbow sailed backward into Ambessa's gut, but Ambessa flexed the muscles rigid. Next, Tivadar bent over, trying to throw Ambessa over her shoulder. Ambessa went, landing on her back in the hard-packed dirt with a gasp, but she took Tivadar with her, holding the girl against her chest, arms and legs wrapped around her. The alley smelled of piss and rotting food.

"Tivadar," Ambessa hissed as the girl struggled against Ambessa's strength.

Tivadar suddenly went limp. "General? General Medarda?"

Ambessa made sure not to slacken her grip, no matter how Tivadar tried to disarm her.

"We're going to get up slowly, child. And then you're going to come with me."

"I was looking for you, General." Tivadar held on to Ambessa's forearm, but she no longer struggled against her.

"I'm sure you were."

"Mel told me you wanted my help, so I'm here."

"Mel?" That did shock Ambessa's grip loose. Tivadar rolled away and bounced to her feet, spry with her youth.

"She said..." Tivadar clenched her fist tightly before releasing it slowly. "Did you kill Gintara?"

Ambessa watched the shallow rise and fall of the young woman's breath. Everything she needed hinged upon this answer.

Holes in the plans she and Rictus and Rudo had tried to make could be filled with Tivadar's help.

"No." Ambessa stood calmly, brushing her trousers off. That part, at least, was not a lie. "I did not. But if you had seen the paroxysms your father's experiments made of her, you would not begrudge her warrior's death."

Uncertainty flickered over Tivadar's face, half in shadow, half illuminated by the enchanted glow-lights on the streets outside their alley.

"What do you mean?"

Ambessa described with painful grief the agonies she had seen the rune-soldiers succumb to when the magic bolstering them gave way.

"In his ambition, he was willing to sacrifice her for his own gain. And you—let me guess." Ambessa stepped closer, one hand open. "He asked you to hurt my children in my absence, didn't he? Don't you know you would never have survived that encounter? They're surrounded by my most trusted warband."

She did not mention how, somehow, someone had killed Azizi despite the Wolf's Reapers. It could not have been this young warrior, green as a spring sapling.

Tivadar shut her eyes, her jaw clenched tight as she tried unsuccessfully to hold back her tears. Ambessa enveloped the girl in a hug. Though part of her tracked the movement of Tivadar's hands to make sure she didn't reach for a weapon, another part of her, deeper than all, longed to sink into this embrace. It pulled at the strings of her own loss, threatening to undo her.

"Come, child. Will you help me? Your father will pay for what he did to her. For what he's done to both of us."

Sniffing, Tivadar stepped back and scrubbed her face with her bare arm. "One condition, General."

"Name it."

"I will be the one to confront my father."

Ambessa raised an eyebrow. She had her own visions of vengeance for her meeting with Ta'Fik. "I cannot promise he will live—"

"I get to speak to him." Tivadar spoke not like a demanding child, but like a woman.

Ambessa nodded solemnly. "As you wish."

"This is never going to work." Rudo frowned at Ambessa. "I'm telling you, let me go in first." He sat on the floor with his back against Ambessa's bed, his legs crossed, hands gripping his knees. Not unlike Rictus, in fact, who sat opposite him, but where Rictus sat stiffly, with the patience of a boulder, there was an odd fluidity in Rudo's pose, even when still. "You need someone to see what's happening inside."

Rudo wasn't wrong in one respect: It would be easier if Ambessa knew more of Ta'Fik's habits, if she knew whether or not the other mage was present, how many rune-soldiers he had, and how many were merely human. But they had no time; she had already been too long gone from Rokrund Citadel. Who knew if it still stood?

It does. It must.

Ambessa turned back to the girl. "Tell us all the ways into and out of the mansion. If something goes wrong, I want to make sure we have an escape route."

Tivadar hesitated for a moment, as if weighing the cost of what was surely closely guarded information. Then she sighed. She put her finger on the sketch she had made on a piece of Ambessa's courier paper. Here, the front door; there, Ta'Fik's study where he usually worked in the morning; and there, the room where he entertained guests and brokered deals—with warlords from the Great Sai, dignitaries from Nazumah, even leaders of the Shakkal raiding clans, depending on who needed the most mollifying or who could offer him the rarest goods to sell north to the rest of Noxus.

"Here," she said. "There are tunnels. This one leads from my father's suite to this midden yard here. But if something goes wrong, it will be difficult for you to get into his room." Tivadar bit the inside of her cheek doubtfully. "Not to mention, he keeps the key on his person."

"I see." Ambessa stroked her chin as if she were concerned for her own safety. "Anywhere else?"

"There's also the kennel exit. From the kitchens to the drake-hound kennels. It's not really a secret, just a servant's exit, so they can take the scraps from the kitchen to the hound-keeper." Tivadar drew a square for the kitchen, and then a path and another square.

"It's aboveground?" Ambessa clarified.

"No, tunnels as well. It goes through the meat cellar."

"I see. That's probably our best option if things go wrong." Ambessa met Rictus's eyes over Tivadar's head. Her lieutenant nodded.

"All right. When do we go, then?" Tivadar sat back on her haunches.

"We're waiting on a distraction."

When they finished, Ambessa let Tivadar go get lunch downstairs, with a nod for Rudo to follow her and make sure she didn't run away. She held Rictus back.

She tapped the master bedroom on Tivadar's sketch, indicating the hidden path. "Your friends. How quickly can they barricade a door?"

"Enough coin and it'll be done tonight."

"Good. We attack tomorrow, Darkwill's ships or no."

"Yes, Kreipsha."

Chapter Thirty-Five

The night before battle called for indulgence. A moment of the softer pleasures before the jagged joy of the hunt. She took the name of the public bath that the innkeeper had mentioned and told Rictus to watch over the girl.

Before she left, though, Rictus lowered his head to whisper, "Are you sure we can trust him?"

The same question Ambessa had struggled with over the last week.

"I trust him only as far as I need to. But there are things between me and him that even you can't protect me from."

Rictus gave her a baleful look, but he nodded.

The bathhouse the innkeeper sent her to was public, but it was clearly intended only for a certain class of the public. There were several different kinds of rooms—one for scraping one's skin in the steam, one for cold, one for hot. In others, you could be massaged. The sounds that emerged from still other rooms told Ambessa that this particular bathhouse probably shared purpose as a brothel. Perhaps she would indulge a little more than she expected.

After the excoriating clean of the flat scraping stones, Ambessa went to the hot pool. It was late, and so she was alone when Rudo joined her. He was naked, his thin body still as lean as it had been in their youth but not unblemished. There were new scars here and there, though not near as many as she had picked up. He was more beautiful than she remembered.

He smiled crookedly as he noticed her admiring him. "And here I thought you had forgotten all we once were."

Ambessa didn't smile back. She tilted her head and asked, "Why are you so determined to risk yourself?"

Because she recognized this drive to throw oneself headlong into danger. She'd seen it in soldiers who had lost companions they were close to in battle—out of guilt for their own survival, despairing a life without the one they loved, they would throw themselves into battle recklessly, furiously, partly out of vengeance but more so a desire to join their loved one in death.

Rudo paused in the middle of lowering himself into the hot water.

"Forgive me," she said softly, but Rudo shook his head. He submerged himself, letting the water close over his dark locs before rising.

"You're right." He swam up to Ambessa, holding her eyes significantly, but only took his place against the wall behind her, draping his arms across the stone. "The pale woman and the others are my family, as Menelik is yours. A brutal family that measures its affection in blood spilled. You know what that's like. Inyene, the one who developed this rune magic, for the rune-soldiers and for stealing magic—they're very dear to me. We were friends—more than friends, they're a sibling to me. I'm sure I would have mentioned them back in Basilich." His weariness was plain in his voice. "I couldn't leave them. I always thought they needed me. Lately, I've realized they were propping me up as much as I thought I was helping them. It was easy to let my decisions hinge on them— wherever they went, I would follow, because they needed me."

"And now?" Ambessa could feel the heat of him near her, the flush of her own body responding to his proximity. She blamed it on the heat of the pool.

"Now...they're endangering my child. They're endangering you. They're destroying young mages. Surely I have to find my spine sometime?" He laughed self-deprecatingly.

Ambessa didn't laugh. "Will they be with Ta'Fik, or will they be at this laboratory?"

"I can't say. Their allegiance to Ta'Fik is just so that the pale woman has a hold on one of Noxus's strongest families."

"The Medardas. Is that what all of this has been about?"

Rudo stared at the water as he skimmed a hand back and forth across the surface. "Some of it."

"Some?"

Rudo circled in front of her. His expression was achingly tender. He put his hands on her waist as he had so many years ago. "I've missed you," he murmured. "Every day of every year since we parted—I've thought of you, and of her. I wished I'd never left."

Ambessa looked down at her hands on his forearms. She ran them against the ropy muscles, tracing them up to the crook of his elbows. Over the planes of his chest. Over his lips. He shivered and kissed her fingers. She felt him stir beneath the water.

"You had to," Ambessa said, just as softly. She took his hands and locked them behind her hips. "Tell me the truth. You will fight for me? For *us*?"

Rudo met her gaze, hazel eyes unblinking. The flickering torchlight of the underground room was dim, but Ambessa could see the fervor in his face. The light danced upon his golden tattoos. He was a being of shadow and light, heartbreakingly beautiful even now.

"I would do anything for you, and for her, I would do even more."

Ambessa caressed his cheek, the faint stubble rough and comforting at once. She pulled his face to hers and kissed him.

"Have you had enough, then?" Rudo asked. "I'm an old man now."

Ambessa turned to him in the bed. They had returned to the inn. In the darkness, she could make out the gleam of Rudo's smile, and the curve of his throat as he tilted his head back—in exhaustion, this time, instead of pleasure.

"I see that," Ambessa said. "Remind me to stick with the younger ones next time."

The jest rolled off her tongue carelessly, and caught her with an unseen barb—Azizi was gone. And though they had both had lovers apart from each other, there was a pain in this permanence that lying with Rudo had sharpened.

Rudo sensed the change in her mood and wrapped himself around her, curling her into his chest and pulling the blankets over them. He held her in one of those perfect silences he had always been so good at.

The problem with his silences, however, was that they always made her want to fill them, and with the things she most wanted to hide.

"I will fight Ta'Fik until I have no breath left in my body, Rudo. He killed my husband and threatened my children. He wants to take what is mine by right."

"But...?"

Ambessa closed her eyes. To her surprise, tears spilled over her cheeks.

"What if he is right?" she whispered. "I know why he hates me. And why he hates the Code. Why he hated Grandfather Menelik, no matter how he preened for the rest of the family while the man was on his deathbed. I didn't believe he'd be so bitter after all this time, and yet—look at me. I would do the same. However long it takes, I won't rest until he pays for Azizi."

"What did you do?" Rudo's voice was a warm rumble against her back. It promised forgiveness.

Was that what she wanted? Was that the key that fit in the jagged wound she'd left covered for so long?

"Zoya."

Ambessa remembered running.

She remembered the smell of the hunt: the grass where the drakehounds had passed, when she bent low to mark their traces; the earth turned by their claws; blood from their latest kill; the sour sweat of fear and adrenaline from her fellow hunters.

Those other hunters were as much her prey as the drakehounds—hopeful warriors, there to join the Medarda trial of strength. Anyone from the Medarda provinces was allowed to test themself in the exhibition. The reward was land, a title, and the favor of Menelik. It could lead to having a warband, a fleet, or, as Ambessa hoped, one day leading the entire family, as Eskender had led the Medardas from Shurima to Noxus—even adoption, if you were not born a Medarda. All they had to do was slay a mighty beast. Still shy of her nineteenth year, Ambessa was one of the youngest challengers.

The three of them took the field together. It only made sense. Though it was against the rules to kill the other competitors, it *was* permitted to disable them from the competition, one way or another. Together, the three of them were enough of a deterrent. However, they were also noisier. Ta'Fik with his bow and arrows, long daggers strapped all over his body, tromped noisily as they tracked the drakehounds through their mountains. Zoya was a good tracker, but she glanced nervously around them—the drakehounds would smell her fear long before Ambessa could sight them. Ambessa and Ta'Fik had told her she wasn't ready, told her to wait until the next year's trial, but Zoya had insisted.

As they passed through a craggy section of the mountain, thick with trees, the drakehound scent grew stronger. She held up a fist to halt the other two.

"What—" Ta'Fik started, but Ambessa flung her hand over his mouth with an angry glare.

"Stay here." She would go up to the den alone. Neither of them wanted this as badly as she did. Neither of them was *ready* like she was.

Neither of them deserved it like she did.

"You said we'd stay together—" Zoya protested, but she, too, fell silent under Ambessa's look.

"I agreed to no such thing," she murmured, barely daring to breathe the words. "Ta'Fik, stay with her. You'll be safe back here."

She didn't wait for them to accept the order, only crept forward, noting here the pile of dung and there the roughness on the bark where drakehounds had rubbed themselves repeatedly over time to mark their territory. That odd combination of reptilian and canine scent mingling.

A Medarda strikes her own path.

Then she saw it. A cavern in the rocks. The snuffling and scrabbling of beasts within. Ambessa readied the spear in her hand and crept to the entrance.

She gasped in unexpected wonder at the sight. The drakehound matriarch lay on the ground as a litter of pups gamboled around her. Their mother watched them with an almost indulgent weariness. Ambessa didn't know if it was her gasp or if the drakehound caught her scent, but the beast jumped up, the spines of her hackles raised.

A harsh growl erupted behind Ambessa and she spun, keeping the matriarch on her left. One of the sentry hounds had caught her scent; she was about to fight for her life.

But no. The hounds had found different prey.

Down the hill, a few smaller hounds closed their hunting circle around Zoya and Ta'Fik. The siblings stood back to back, Ta'Fik with his daggers out, Zoya with her two short spears.

But more movement caught Ambessa's eye—a figure streaking up to the den from the east. Headed here, for *her* prize.

"Ambessa!" Zoya cried, shrill and terrified, throwing all pretense of stealth to the wind. "Help!"

Behind her, the drakehound matriarch's rumbling belly growl was an unmistakable warning: *Go protect your family, or I will protect mine.* Her eyes glowed red; her tongue scented the air.

Ambessa glanced back toward Ta'Fik and Zoya. They fought viciously—how they were trained to. They would be fine, she told herself. They would be fine. And she would have her kill.

"Ambessa!" Ta'Fik shouted. For a moment, they locked eyes, Ta'Fik looking up as Ambessa looked down from the height of the den.

"Wait!" she called back. She didn't know if they heard her because at her shout, the matriarch pounced with an earsplitting shriek.

This is what happens, she told herself. A law of nature that everyone and everything understood, from every Noxian warrior to every drakehound—*strength is survival.*

It was not until much later that she would recall the look of confusion on Ta'Fik's face as she hesitated, then turned away. Confusion turning to hurt turning to hatred. She would replay it often in the months that followed. In the months she spent feeling more and more alone despite the accolades and admiration. The months she spent training the drakehound dam's litter and claiming the strongest pair for her own. Quench and Temper. The months she spent sailing her new ship to hide from the truth.

She dived, rolling away from the drakehound's pounce. Claws skittered on stone, and the pups whined in the back of the cave. The dam snarled and lunged for Ambessa again. Ambessa spun the blade of her spear forward, but the drakehound snapped at the wood, almost capturing it. Ambessa yanked it back before the dam could secure her hold and jabbed her in the haunch. The dam howled.

They circled each other, but as soon as Ambessa stepped toward the pups in the back, the dam screeched again and jumped between Ambessa and her young, her spines flaring even more violently.

Ambessa hesitated. Something about the limping matriarch stirred her. Her ferocity. Her beauty. Killing her would be a waste.

She threw her spear down. She no longer heard the screams coming from down the mountain. There was only this. She took the rope from her belt. It was supposed to be for tying the corpse of her conquest, but she looped a quick lasso and held it, waiting.

A cry of triumph came from behind her, and Ambessa turned, grinning, thinking it was Ta'Fik. She would not begrudge sharing this moment with him, not really. But it wasn't him—decades later, their face would be nothing but a blur in her memory. They saw Ambessa and her rope, they saw the drakehound. They raised their own spear and hiked their arm back to throw it.

"No!" Ambessa roared as she leapt. She hip checked them, and their throw went wide.

The spear clattered harmlessly to the back of the cave, but the pups yipped and cried in alarm. Their dam gave a bone-rattling screech, the only warning before she pounced. Ambessa rolled away while her competition stared in open-mouthed horror as their death came with sharp teeth.

Ambessa slipped the lasso over the drakehound's head at the last second and heaved. The dam gagged and choked on the rope, straining for her prey as they scrambled away. The rope burned her hands as the drakehound's strength pulled. She growled and Ambessa growled back, a contest of will, but the harder the drakehound pulled, the weaker she became, her air cut off. When the dam finally collapsed, Ambessa approached slowly, still clutching the rope despite her raw palms.

The matriarch looked up at her with one rolling eye, her split tongue lolling as she panted for breath.

Ambessa felt a kinship now with that matriarch, one that she couldn't understand then. The fury in a mother's eyes, the refusal to surrender. Perhaps it was that feeling that kept her from killing it, even then, before she knew what that feeling was.

At the time, however, Ambessa had been flush only with triumph as she dragged her defeated prize down the mountainside.

Even when she found Ta'Fik surrounded by the bodies of the three drakehounds and Zoya herself, the flare of triumph didn't dim. Ta'Fik knelt over Zoya, calling her name and calling for help. His own arms dripped bloody where the drakehounds had gotten him. Zoya's body, too, was marked: claws across her belly, her back, the bite at her shoulder.

The brief glance Ta'Fik gave her was already hollow-eyed with grief as Zoya whimpered with pain.

"Will you at least help me carry her to the healers?" he asked, his voice devoid of all inflection.

Ambessa held up the rope leash she'd secured to the matriarch; she couldn't keep the wild beast tethered and carry Zoya at the same time.

"Of course." Ta'Fik scoffed. "Then go fetch someone who will."

Ambessa told herself that Zoya would be fine.

"She died two days later."

"Of her wounds?"

Ambessa nodded. "Ta'Fik didn't leave her side. And I...I couldn't face him. I threw myself into the celebrations, instead. Menelik's approval was all I needed to tell me I'd done the right thing."

"You believed in Menelik."

"More than I believed in anything." She stared ahead of her, not truly seeing the wall of the inn or the blankets over their bodies. "I have wondered, though...Mel makes me question everything. Including the Code itself. Have I lived my whole life wrong, following it? The battles I've fought. The way I've loved my children." She shook her head, and Rudo squeezed her tighter to him.

"We could speak to Ta'Fik. Maybe...some kind of accord. Someone else could be chosen to lead the family."

Ambessa turned in Rudo's arms and ran her fingers through the thick strands of his locs. She'd been careful since Zoya about making attachments. Now there were only three weaknesses in that armor. Four, if you counted the new one she had made, traveling with the feisty young fighter from the Reckoner Arena. If she was so weak that she couldn't keep herself from hurting again, she would protect those faults in her armor fiercely.

Ta'Fik had already stolen one. He would not steal another.

"This ends with Ta'Fik in the ground."

"You could forgive him."

"Not for what he's done. Beyond Azizi, he's sullied my name in the family. Half of them blame me for Menelik's death. He will clear it before he dies."

Rudo inhaled deeply, then sagged. She pulled away slightly, the better to see his face. His eyes were shut, but he opened them to meet her gaze. His expression was one of resignation.

"What?" Fear made her heart beat faster, made her skin hot and sticky against Rudo's. "What's happened? What do you know?"

"I also have a confession."

Ambessa shook her head and pushed his head down against her chest. "I don't want to hear it. You don't have to confess anything to me." Not because she didn't believe it, but because she was afraid, so afraid of what he was about to say. It had been so good, so briefly. "Please, don't."

He swallowed, and the sound was loud in her ear. "I will clear your name to them, Ambessa."

"What do you mean?"

"I will turn myself in and clear your name." His voice was quieter.

"What?"

Quieter still: "It was me. I killed Menelik." The rest came out in a trembling whisper.

"At her order." Ambessa barely had the breath for words.

"I did it on my own." Rudo's voice was hoarse, but pleading. "The pale woman's spies expected him to announce Ta'Fik as his heir the next day. I killed him for you."

Her throat seemed to close. "You knew how much my grandfather meant to me."

"I knew how much taking up his mantle meant to you. Means to you. Look—look at how far you've gone to secure it."

The warmth of their skin was suddenly clammy, his touch repulsive. She pushed away from him and gathered the blankets around herself. Rudo stared at her, begging without words for permission to unburden himself. To upend her world.

Ambessa spoke around the lump in her throat. "He would never—not Ta'Fik."

"He had, Ambessa. He had. It was witnessed and signed. I destroyed the will, and I killed the notary. I don't ask you to forgive me, but I will make up for this—"

"'Make up for this'? What does that *mean*, Rudo? You killed the man I looked to as my father for—for—"

"For you."

"Get out, Rudo. This is the only mercy I will give you, and only so that I never have to look my daughter in the face and tell her that I killed her father."

Rudo was not graceful as he got up from the bed and dressed again. "You need me."

There was no vitriol in it, nor pleading. It was a statement of truth, and Ambessa could not deny it no matter how spiteful she felt. But she would not throw away everything she had fought so hard for now, at the last.

Even though it is not rightfully yours? Even though Menelik himself thought Ta'Fik would be the better head of the clan?

She wanted to go back to that night she spent with Menelik and ask him where she fell short in his eyes. What had she not done? Why was she not enough? Had she not lived the Code modeled in his own image? Had she not brought her family glory and prosperity?

Was it only that her children were unfit to follow?

Or did he finally know what had happened that day with the drakehounds? Did he think Ta'Fik had behaved more in keeping with the Code? Why did he think Ta'Fik would unite the clan against the future he feared, and not her? What did Ta'Fik have, what had he done, what did he know *that she did not*?

Thanks to Rudo, she would never know.

"Ambessa?"

"Leave me, Rudo. I need your magic, yes, but I need nothing else."

"I will keep my end of the bargain," Rudo said carefully. "You will have your opening."

"Wait," Ambessa said as he reached for the door handle.

Rudo turned back around, hope lighting his eyes.

She held the question between her teeth. The answer would be beyond bearing.

"Azizi. Did you kill him, too?"

Rudo's face fell into such sorrow that Ambessa almost believed it.

"No. I swear to you, I had nothing to do with that."

When she was alone, Ambessa did not weep but measured herself in the darkness against everything she should have been.

Chapter Thirty-Six

Ambessa stayed alone in her rooms the next morning. Rictus came, and then Tivadar, but she only told them *wait*, she would know when the time was right. She paced the small square of the room, her bare feet quiet against the rough clay floor.

In truth, she was paralyzed. She was no longer risking everything—her life, her children, *her honor*—to enact Menelik's will. To follow through with these plans, she would be going against him. She laughed bitterly at herself. Would she have had the courage to go against him when he was alive, or would she have accepted it as wisdom? She could not see it.

Perhaps he had, with his vision of the strife in the Medarda clan's future. Was this the fate he had foreseen, or was there worse to come? If Menelik thought Ta'Fik was truly the best Medarda to help them weather that future, Ambessa would doom the entire clan with her arrogance.

Medarda over all.

Her drakehound gauntlets waited on the splintery table by her bedside. Her sword belt and its long knife hung on a peg next to her cloak.

She had been made for this, not him. She could not deny her fate, not when she had seen it so clearly when she had been taken to Volrachnun by the Wolf himself and brought back. She would not have come back if not for something greater.

Still, she hesitated over the gauntlets, tracing a snarling tooth in the metal. Thanks to Rudo, she'd spent half the night tonguing the wound of Zoya's loss. Ambessa hadn't wanted her to die. Maybe Rudo was right. What if she could forgive Ta'Fik, if he could forgive her?

Rictus's firm knock at the door jerked her away from those thoughts.

"Come in." Ambessa straightened her back, slipping back into the composure of command. Like armor, it would protect her.

Rictus closed the door behind him. "The runner you hired— from the docks. He says there are ships flying Darkwill's flag. They're firing on all galleys bearing Ta'Fik's colors."

Ambessa exhaled sharply, clenching her fist in muted celebration. Not a moment too soon. Her blood thrummed in her veins.

"Should we get into position?" he asked.

"Your friends—did they finish their task?"

Rictus nodded.

Ambessa turned back to her gauntlets. Once she began, there would be no turning back.

She slid her hands into them, took comfort in their worn grips.

"Get the girl."

The four of them staked positions on a market road near Ta'Fik's home to wait for Darkwill's "aid" to have an impact. It was a main thoroughfare, so while it was busy, it was the most likely path any soldiers would take from Ta'Fik's to the docks. They were dressed in nondescript warrior's clothing, with decent armor but nothing that would mark them out as special. Ambessa's drakehounds attached to her belt were ostentatious enough. She would put on a mask to enter the palace when the time came.

As word of the fighting at the docks spread, everyone shopping and strolling turned to one another in alarm. Ambessa did, too, feigning shock. Tivadar's concern was genuine.

"What's going on?" she asked.

"Hush," Ambessa said. "We'll find out soon enough."

Tivadar frowned dubiously, but she followed Ambessa's lead, turning back to the wares of the stall in front of them. Fine bolts of light fabric, a shade of red to rival a drakehound's eyes. With a pang, Ambessa remembered the day she'd spent with Rell, picking out cloth and getting fitted for an outfit worthy of a Medarda.

"I will come for you," she whispered.

"What?" Tivadar asked.

"Nothing," Ambessa said quickly. Then she saw a runner sprint up the street and toward Ta'Fik's house.

To call it a house was an understatement. It was just short of a palace, outstripped only by the home of Tereshni's governor. A brilliant white stone wall decorated with carved latticework surrounded the place. The runner stopped at the arch where two soldiers waited, showed them some sort of credentials, and sprinted through when they let him pass.

Ambessa moved from the cloth stall to an azirite merchant, pretending to glance over the glittering blood glass while watching the arch out of the corner of her eye.

"Are you going to buy, or no?" The shopkeeper looked suspiciously down her nose at Ambessa. She wasn't impressed by Ambessa's silent glare. She shooed with her hands. "Go, then. Save room for my paying customers. No time for 'browsing.'"

Ambessa narrowed her eyes at the woman, but someone grabbed her arm roughly. It was Rudo.

"There," he hissed.

A squad of soldiers marched at double time from Ta'Fik's palace. The Medarda star was stitched onto the back of their matching red cloaks. If they glowed with unnatural strength, Ambessa couldn't tell from here. As they jogged down the market street, pedestrians scrambled to get out of their way, clutching their parcels indignantly—and yet, all of them with an air of fear. No one dared to speak ill toward Ta'Fik's soldiers. That said much for his reputation in the city.

"Wait," Ambessa whispered.

She signaled to Tivadar and Rictus, too. Just a little longer, to see if any more would leave. By her count, that squad had only been fifty strong. Tivadar said he usually had at least two hundred on the grounds at any one time, but the bulk of his forces would probably be committed to the Rokrund attack. That left over one hundred in Ta'Fik's compound if the girl could be trusted.

Over one hundred rune-soldiers. Those were not good odds, but she had faced worse and survived.

When no more soldiers seemed forthcoming, Ambessa made the call. If they waited any longer, the soldiers might return from the docks.

She strode up next to Tivadar and whispered, "Take us in."

Tivadar nodded sharply and left the fine necklace she'd been fondling and strode toward the palace. She walked with her chin tilted up, a swagger that matched the opulent walls. Rudo walked beside Tivadar. He was not in disguise. He could not move like a soldier; that would have driven suspicion faster than his own face. Ambessa and Rictus followed behind, flanking them like an honor guard. Ambessa wore her lion mask over her face. Rictus wore the beaked face of a blood eagle.

Tivadar halted in front of the same guards who had stopped the runner bearing tidings of the dock.

"Kiram, Toleus!" The girl greeted the guards with her arms wide open. "It's good to see you!"

The one on the left smiled, while the other frowned.

The frowning one spoke first. "I thought you were in Bel'zhun."

"I was." Tivadar's acting skills were admirable. Her lip curled and her voice turned surly. "The situation there has changed. I need to speak to my father. Is he in?"

The smiling one nodded, though he was no longer smiling. "He is. I'm afraid the news hasn't been good here, either. I'll save that for later. It's good to see you. Save us a spar. We'll make sure you haven't gotten soft fighting with those show ponies in the arena."

Tivadar's face fell as he spoke. Ambessa knew what they were both thinking; word of Gintara's death must have reached Tereshni.

"Thank you, yes. I should go find him, then."

Kiram and Toleus uncrossed their weapons to let them through, but Rudo stopped between them.

"And Inyene? Are they in?"

"The other mage?" asked the guard on the right. He stiffened as if noticing Rudo for the first time, but bowed slightly, suddenly more formal. "Yes, sir."

"Very good." Rudo moved on without deigning to look into the man's face.

Ambessa had never seen this man standing in Rudo's place. Drawn to his full height, with his expression cold and his voice disinterested, Ambessa saw how easily cruelty could dwell side by side with the laughing, dancing man she had once fallen in love with. Somehow, she had forgotten—she had let herself be something different, someone new in Basilich. She had taken it for granted that he might be doing the same. The real Rudo, this Rudo, was the one capable of things Ambessa couldn't imagine.

The walls of the palace itself were even more impressive than the latticework outer wall. Chips of azirite and flecks of gold were set into the stone so that the whole place looked like sunset or sunrise, even in the glaring noon. More guards threw open great wooden doors painted green and studded in gold. The wood alone was a luxury on the southern continent. Ta'Fik flaunted his wealth almost as blatantly as Darkwill.

Tivadar led them into the palace's entry hall. The floor was a mosaic of pale stone interspersed with green and more azirite. Ahead of them, a wide corridor—more like a gallery—branched off into various doors. Ambessa overlaid them onto her mental image of the map Tivadar had drawn for them in the Busted Knuckle. One of them was Ta'Fik's favorite sitting room. The formal dining room, and beyond it the kitchens. The library.

To their left and right, stone stairs ascended to the upper floor. One soldier stood at the base of each. These soldiers didn't greet Tivadar as the pair outside had. They stood at attention, staring into the middle distance. There was no indication that they were rune-soldiers.

"He's probably upstairs in his study," Tivadar said. Ambessa didn't answer; in this disguise, it was not her place. It seemed, instead, as if she were talking to Rudo.

Tivadar caressed the smooth stone railing almost absently as she walked up the stairs. Ambessa turned to meet Rictus's eyes through their masks.

They could not go upstairs—they couldn't risk getting mired so deeply in the palace that it would be impossible to get out, regardless of the escape passageways Tivadar had divulged. More importantly, Ambessa couldn't risk losing her quarry entirely.

Ambessa let herself trip on the edge of a stair as they climbed. She stumbled, reached for the back of Rudo's vest. He wore it open, his chest with its inked golden loops bare. He turned to catch her, but his expression was that of the cruel Rudo, disdainful of the lowly guard who deigned to grasp him. His grip was tight upon her arm.

"Be careful, soldier," he said. With his eyes, though, he searched her face. She nodded.

He held her gaze and her arm a moment longer. That moment drew out, and she understood what he was saying with his touch. This was goodbye. He took two more steps up before he ran back down the steps. His tattoos glowed as he stretched out his hand to grasp the neck of the soldier at the base of the stairs.

The soldier screamed, her back arching as a glow emanated from her eyes and her chest. Ambessa watched in horror as a jagged shape burned through the woman's armor until she could see it lurid against her chest. *A rune.* Then the glowing symbol seemed to *peel* itself away from her, and as it did, the screaming grew more agonized.

"Halt!" shouted the soldier at the other stairs, at the same time as Tivadar cried, "What are you doing?"

The second soldier sprinted over, eyes glowing with the burst of inhuman speed. "Alarm!"

"General, what is he doing?" Tivadar cried.

Ambessa didn't answer. She ran past the second rune-soldier. "I'll go get help," she said, disguising her voice to sound like a desperate soldier trying to flee.

A hundred fifty rune-soldiers. How many would heed the desperate calls of their fellows? When rune-soldiers streamed from the nearest rooms, their attention went immediately to Rudo, who danced through them like golden death. Every time he touched one of the rune-soldiers, he ripped their runes from them. He was the only threat that mattered.

Ambessa glanced at him only once as she ran back the way they'd come.

This would be the last time he danced. Rudo knew this. He knew it as he held Ambessa one last time. He knew it as he watched her vanish into the depths of the palace. He would do this thing for her, and for himself. He had made promises.

It was almost easy to strip the rune from the first soldier. She was not expecting Rudo, and his resolve gave him strength. He felt her pain, though, as she spasmed against his body. Though she had survived the placement of the rune, he did not think she would survive its removal.

Behind him, the young Medarda girl screamed at him, or about him. She reminded him of Mel, but only because they were of an age. The beautiful, kind young diplomat he'd met in Bel'zhun was nothing like this brash young warrior.

He had regrets, like any man about to die.

He dropped the first soldier to the ground and stepped over her body to reach the second. He spared only a moment to look for Ambessa once more, but she and her large lieutenant were already gone.

The second soldier put up more of a fight. His rune lent him a speed that forced Rudo to evade, dancing around him like a dust mote in a sunbeam. Finally, the man thrust at Rudo's belly—and Rudo was not there. He twisted to the soldier's outside and grasped the man's forearm. Rudo slammed his other hand against the man's forehead, bending him backward. The soldier's knees buckled as the rune left his body.

"What are you doing!"

The girl's cry finally broke through Rudo's focus. He pitied her her confusion. She was just another pawn in Ambessa's game, but unlike Rudo, she had not realized it. She was unwilling. She glanced at the doors on either end of the upstairs landing gallery. Boots thundered from all directions. He didn't have time to watch her weigh her safety against her father's.

Rudo passed her as the first rune-soldiers spilled onto the landing. They met him halfway up the stairs, and the dance continued. Knowing that this was the end made it easier to flow through them. There was peace in it. Maybe this was how Ambessa and other devotees of the Wolf felt. He laughed at the thought of joining those warriors in Volrachnun, and the rune-soldier before him flinched in horror. He tasted copper in his mouth. The first sign of his magic taxing his body too far.

He grabbed them by the throat and stripped their rune, too. With every rune he took, the magic within him built. Eventually, it would all be too much.

"You?"

Rudo turned at that familiar, beloved voice filled with anguish. Inyene stood at the top of the stairs on the gallery overlooking the grand entry hall. Their hands were already outstretched, ready to fight whoever had caused the guards' alarm. Upon seeing Rudo, their hands dropped slack at their sides. They looked as if Rudo had slapped them.

The soldier Rudo held sagged from his arms, collapsing on the floor as the rune on his body vanished into the air. It left a faint afterglow before disappearing completely.

"Inyene. Please. We don't have to fight. Come away with me. Let this be over."

The betrayal in their face turned to disgust. Inyene's magic swirled around them, then the blood-red coils rushed at Rudo.

Chapter Thirty-Seven

The sun was unbearably bright after the cool darkness of the palace interiors. Ambessa squinted, shading her eyes as she gathered her bearings, looking for the outbuildings from Tivadar's sketches. Far to her left rose a larger building—the barracks. Which meant the two buildings to the right—

"You there, report!" One of the guards from the palace wall, Kiram or Toleus, shouted. Both men were running toward them, weapons drawn. Even from this distance, Ambessa could see the glow emanating from their eyes.

Did the same magic that gave them strength connect them to the other rune-soldiers? How else could they have known something was wrong so quickly? And yet, they still thought Ambessa and Rictus were part of Tivadar's escort.

"Let me," Ambessa whispered to Rictus. She jogged toward the men, glancing behind her fearfully. "There's—the mage— He's gone mad— He's attacking—"

The friendly one rushed forward without even waiting for more, but the one who had scowled looked Ambessa and Rictus up and down with disgust.

"So you flee like cowards? What kind of Noxian are you?" He reached for Ambessa's arm. "Turn round and face him. At least meet the Wolf on your feet and not with your belly up."

Ambessa cursed the guard's principles. She couldn't let him drag her back inside—she had an appointment to keep.

She pushed his arm away and swiveled a hook into his kidneys. He wasn't there when the punch should have landed, though. The light in his eyes flared at his burst of unnatural speed, and the counter with his mace whistled toward her head.

Then Rictus was there, his great halberd absorbing the blow. The rookern wrapped around the haft crackled as it absorbed the strength of the rune-soldier's attack. The glow in the man's eyes flickered. Without his magic, he was no stronger than a normal soldier. Rictus chuckled.

The rune-soldier backpedaled. "Kiram!" He called for his companion. As soon as he unlocked from Rictus, his eyes burned again. His speed returned and he rushed at Rictus, all his attention on the greater threat.

It left Ambessa time to slip into her gauntlets. The leather padding inside them felt like coming home. She caught Rictus's eye, and he understood her without words. When Toleus closed with Rictus again, Rictus used his halberd to lock the man close, and the half-moon blade of Ambessa's drakehound caught him in the back.

He coughed a spray of blood into Rictus's face as he died, but Rictus was already maneuvering away from the corpse in a deft circle that put him between Ambessa and Kiram as the last rune-soldier charged, sword first, at her back. Ambessa, likewise, circled behind Rictus, shaking Toleus's body from her drakehound blade.

Despite the rune-soldier's strength and speed, they took him down like a pack of wolves takes down a deer. It was a pleasure to fight beside Rictus. They had trained so often and for so long together, it seemed they had always shared this language of steel and breath.

Ambessa could not help but remember how different it was to fight these rune-soldiers when there were hundreds of them, and you were surrounded.

"That way." Ambessa ran toward the two buildings with Rictus at her side.

They were halfway there, crossing the length of the grand outer court, about to turn around the corner of the palace, when they both heard the rushing boots behind them. Five rune-soldiers, unaffected by Rudo's magic. They must have been patrolling the perimeter of the building.

With one last look of longing toward the outbuildings, Ambessa turned to face the oncoming soldiers.

Rictus noticed her glance. "I'll take them."

"I don't intend to leave you here to die." Even Rictus, with his own strength and skill, with his rookern, couldn't fight five of them at once.

"I owe you my life many times over, Kreipsha." Like Rudo earlier, Ambessa could sense Rictus's quiet acceptance. Unlike Rudo, it seemed like Rictus had always been prepared for this moment.

Ambessa's chest tightened painfully. "Stop that."

"Don't waste this chance."

"I said, stop that."

But he stepped in front of her and bellowed as he rushed them. Ambessa followed close behind, keeping the rune-soldiers from taking advantage of the open space and circling behind Rictus as he nullified their magical strength and countered it with his own natural gifts. One fell, and then another, but it was slow— despite the rookern, the rune-soldiers were still powerful, and their speed kept Ambessa dodging, hunting for openings that closed faster than she could take advantage of them. And all the while, her window of opportunity was closing.

"Kreipsha," Rictus growled through his teeth. "Go!"

Ambessa's back was pressed against his. She felt the rapid beating of his ox-strong heart all the way in her own bones. The rune-soldier in front of her arced a cut at her head, and Ambessa punched her gauntlet up to throw it aside, but she couldn't follow the opening without exposing Rictus's side. She launched the drakehound blades from their catch and let the chains spool out. She swung wildly, forcing the rune-soldier to keep their distance.

"I have your back," Ambessa gritted back.

"It will all be for nothing!" Rictus's fervor grew with the force of his own efforts.

He was right. She *knew* he was right.

"Ambessa. Trust me," he said softly.

Yes. "I trust you, old friend."

She threw her chained blades out again, following them to leap at the surprised rune-soldier. They parried one of the half-moon blades with their sword, but the second caught them in the side and lodged there. Ambessa retrieved it. Behind her, Rictus still battled the other two. Still more were running from the palace entrance, straight for him. In the fullness of Rictus's battle rage, not a stroke of his halberd was wasted.

She ran for the kennels.

A hush smothered the world as she entered the shaded space. The fighting she had left behind sounded distant. Compared to that, this snuffling and whining and the playful yips of pups was peaceful. There were dogs and drakehounds here, though they were kept apart. Not all dogs were comfortable with drakehounds. Even the domesticated drakehounds had something wild in them that true hounds distrusted.

Their cages were spacious—drakehounds grew bad-tempered in cramped spaces—and were locked with heavy bolts. Food could easily be slipped through the thick bars, but they weren't set wide enough for a drakehound to fit its muzzle through. The hounds—drake and canine alike—looked well-fed and well taken care of.

The odor was comforting and familiar—the stink of animal waste, the smell of damp dog, and something reptilian. The lingering smell of fresh meat, coppery and heavy on the air. The hay of their bedding. It took her into her past effortlessly. She spent a lot of time in the Rokrund kennels after that fated hunt. The drakehound matriarch's pups were brought from the mountain, too. The dam was more manageable with her pups nearby. Ambessa squeezed the grips in her drakehound gauntlets. Quench and Temper, faithful even now into their deaths.

It probably transported Ta'Fik just as easily. Tivadar said he avoided the kennels whenever possible.

It would be the perfect place.

She looked for the cellar door that Tivadar mentioned and found it in the corner next to the shelves of training implements—leashes, false prey, the like. It was easy to find, clearly used often.

Ambessa settled in to wait in the shadows where he would have to pass her if he wanted to reach either of the two exits. The drakehound nearest her was a young female. She sniffed in agitation. The blood on the weapons. Ambessa clicked the command for "ease." The drakehound whined but put her chin on her claws.

While she waited in the darkness, Ambessa couldn't help it—her mind wandered backward again.

This time, to the last moment she remembered the three of them being happy. She and Zoya and Ta'Fik on the cliffs near the sea. That sound, more than anything else, was the sound of home. The waves crashing against the unyielding rock. But there was a quieter place where the water was deep but not rough, and many Rokrund youths, especially those who wanted to prove themselves brave, would leap off the edge, flying—for just a moment—like dragons.

Zoya had always had more courage than sense. Ambessa had admired that in her, though. Zoya hadn't yet been to battle, but in the training yard she fought with a ferocity that made even her comrades stare. Menelik did not try to temper her, but let her run free. So she ran free now, sprinting toward the edge of the cliff as if the sky itself would catch her. It didn't, of course; the sea did. She flipped once and arrowed down, hands first.

Ta'Fik remained above with Ambessa, waiting anxiously for her to resurface. She would, eventually; she always did, sometimes near the cliffs, sometimes farther away if she felt like testing the limits of her lungs. It never eased Ta'Fik's worry.

"What if she landed wrong?" he would ask. "What if we're in the wrong spot and she hit her head?"

"Relax," Ambessa would say. And then she would point out the dark spot that was Zoya's black braids as the youngest of them waved from the foam.

Usually, Ambessa would jump next, and Ta'Fik would jog down to the cove and meet them at the beach. This time, she caught his arm. "Stay," she said. "Jump."

Ta'Fik locked up. She had never forced him to admit his fear, and she didn't intend to now. She only wanted him close. The distance from the top of the cliff to the water seemed greater than normal.

"I'll meet you down below." He glanced uncertainly over the edge.

"I'm nervous," Ambessa blurted. She released his arm but held out her open hand. "Will you jump with me?"

Ta'Fik swallowed. She knew he loved her when he let out a shuddering breath and took her hand.

They ran together, steps in sync. She heard Zoya's laughter of delight, and as they flew, Ambessa knew nothing could break the three of them apart.

The creak of the slate cellar door broke her out of that ancient memory.

"*Away?* Are you mad?" Inyene took in the carnage of the entry hall. Those soldiers still alive were only just now realizing that they had lost their strength and speed as they got groggily to their knees. "The pale woman will have every hunter on your scent! *Why?*"

Tivadar looked between them both in horror. "Stop! Please, Inyene, where is my father? We just want to speak to him! Rudo, where did Ambessa go?"

"Ambessa?" The hurt on Inyene's face turned to bewildered anger. "You brought her here?"

"*I* did—" the girl cried, but Inyene wasn't listening.

They extended their hand in a claw, and Rudo's blood slowed in his body. His heart beat harder to keep it pumping. Inyene's magic was like a hand inside his body. Rudo turned himself into a beacon to burn the unwanted touch away, scorching Inyene like a fire.

Inyene flinched back as if they really had burned themself on an open flame. Then, raking Rudo up and down with their gaze, their mouth dropped open in sudden understanding.

"*Mel Medarda,*" they whispered in astonishment.

Rudo looked down at himself, saw the patterns of glowing lines across his body, the patterns that shaped his magic. The patterns he couldn't help modeling, in his own way, on his daughter's body the one time he had met her.

Forgive me, daughter, for I have damned you.

"You and Ambessa." Inyene shook their head incredulously. "You didn't just ally with her—you've been fucking her. For how long? Sixteen years? All our plans—have you been feeding them to her all along?"

Rudo bared his teeth. Tivadar—*Mel's friend*—still watched from her place on the stairs. She stared at Rudo in shock.

At either end of the entry hall, upstairs and below, more of the rune-soldiers appeared. They watched the mages warily, as if waiting for Inyene's command. He could feel so many of the runes; those he'd placed himself, he felt more easily than the others.

On the upper floor, Tivadar held her arms out, steadying, as if the oncoming soldiers were unruly horses.

"Stop," she said. "Wait a moment— I'm here for my father—"

Rudo reached for the runes and *pulled*. It felt like tearing paper—including the shearing sound along the cord of his own magic. That excess magic rushed in on him, making him stagger.

Inyene growled in frustration as a handful of rune-soldiers fell, screaming, but spared them only a glance.

"Run, you foolish girl!" Rudo groaned. For a wonder, the girl obeyed, taking the upstairs door opposite all the rune-soldiers.

"Does she know?" Inyene snarled.

Rudo didn't know which *she* Inyene meant. He remained silent, pulling his threads of light back into their long, pointed rays. Though they were made of light, they were as sharp as azirite blades and just as deadly. He leapt for Inyene, but they dodged, pulling blood from one of the dead rune-soldiers on the ground.

"Does the girl know her father is a mage?" Inyene cast the blood like a whip. Rudo leapt aside, but it still scored his bare ribs. "Does she know she belongs to the Black Rose?"

Fury Rudo didn't know he could feel surged up. "She *does not*. She will be free."

And for that to be true, this secret would have to die with Inyene.

"Oh, Inyene," he said, full of grief mingling with the rage. He had known this choice would come—between the Rose, his first family, and Mel, his second. Had already made it years before. He'd stayed with the Rose to protect her.

He should have stayed away.

"When the pale woman finds out, she'll bring Mel into the fold. Why didn't you just *tell* me?"

There, beyond all the rest, the hurt. Rudo had been overjoyed when Ambessa had told him he would be a father, but he had been brokenhearted, too. He couldn't share any of those feelings with Inyene then.

"She's not a mage. I want her to live free, not dancing to someone else's manipulations."

He surged at Inyene again. This time, Inyene swatted his attacks away. They had never been this strong before. The stolen magic they had runed onto their body kept their magic steady, while each attack left Rudo more and more drained.

Laughter burst from Inyene, cruel and bright. "You mean like her own mother's manipulations?"

The blood near Rudo's feet congealed and grasped his ankles, yanking him onto his back. Rudo braced himself for an impact that never came. Inyene held him in coils of blood, tightening around his wrists and ankles.

"Rudo, we were your family." Inyene stepped over to him. Tears clung to their eyelashes. "My brother."

The pain in their voice wrenched at Rudo's core but not near as much as the idea of leaving Mel alone. Leaving her to face whatever cruelties the pale woman might force on her.

"Families don't force each other to torture innocents, Inyene. Those children could have been *us*."

"But they weren't, because *she* found us and took care of us. She taught us. We *owe* her."

Rudo could hear what they were really saying, though. That Rudo owed *them*. For everything they'd gone through together. They'd been so close, and still Rudo had never once trusted them with this, his closest, most beloved secret.

"I couldn't tell you, Inyene," he whispered. "I wanted to so many times. She's so beautiful."

Then he reached for the runes again with all his strength. Inyene, who was concentrating too hard on holding Rudo in place, couldn't react quickly enough. Rudo pulled all of them, each one he could feel, and yanked them into himself.

The power hit him like a torrent, and redirecting it was harder than moving the great mountains of Targon. He was burning down to his bones, every piece of him aflame.

"Rudo, stop—" Inyene's voice cut through, shrill. "Rudo, don't, it's too much power, you can't— Rudo, it will kill you!"

Rudo didn't stop. His jaw stretched open in pain, but no scream came out. He saw nothing but white light.

"Rudo!"

Chapter Thirty-Eight

Ta'Fik emerged from the dark hole into the kennels, cursing. Ambessa watched him from the shadows. Her eyes had grown used to the half-light. He flinched when the drakehounds turned their burning eyes on him. His breathing was labored. He'd fled in haste, but not so quickly that he was unarmed. A curved sword hung at his waist, and if she knew him—and oh how she knew him—he would have daggers secreted about his person.

She could have struck him as soon as his head crested the trapdoor, but that went against the Code: *A Medarda fights with honor.* More than that, though, she wanted to test herself against him. She wanted to test *him*. To see if Menelik was right.

Ta'Fik dusted off his coat and trousers and made for the exits. Ambessa rose from the darkness, blocking his path.

Ta'Fik scrambled back, a throwing dagger flipping into his hand, just as she'd expected. He threw it and she dodged, the barest shift of her shoulders. It brought her face into the light.

"Ambessa," Ta'Fik hissed. "I should have known it was you."

"You should have."

"How did you get in?"

"We have unfinished business, Ta'Fik."

Ta'Fik straightened from his crouch to look down his nose at her. "You lost, Ambessa. I'm head of the clan now." He clicked his tongue.

The drakehounds followed the sound.

"Fight me, Ta'Fik. Single combat. We'll decide who leads the clan like Noxus decides everything."

To the victor, the spoils.

Ta'Fik laughed darkly. "How primitive. Death and destruction are not the only ways to build an empire. You should know this by now. And if Menelik didn't see that, more's the pity." Behind his words was the bitterness of a jaded young man.

Rudo hadn't lied—Ta'Fik truly didn't know that Menelik had chosen him over her.

Again, the thought threatened her resolve, but she refused to yield to the doubt.

He isn't *the right choice. The Black Rose is* using *him. He'll only be a pawn.*

"Draw your sword," Ambessa said softly. "If you're worthy, prove it."

Ta'Fik sighed. "I have nothing to prove to you, Ambessa." He drew his sword anyway. "I proved everything I needed to when I stayed with her and you didn't."

His words launched her forward. Ambessa expelled the burn of her rage into not a wild conflagration but a focused flame of an artisan. But Ta'Fik was almost as fast as the rune-soldiers, shifting one way and then the next. Beneath his elegant coat, he wore the same light Medarda armor that Ambessa preferred. When he backtracked, she followed. When he tried to get around her to the exits, she met him with her gauntlets, forcing him back again.

Around them, the drakehounds hissed and screeched while the dogs howled. They weren't expecting this—some of them probably wanted to join the fray. Ta'Fik flinched at their growls, unnerved.

After another unsuccessful attempt to escape, he hung back, breathing heavily. Ambessa's back and shoulders ached with the weight of her drakehound gauntlets.

"The Code is part of this family," Ambessa said across the wounds separating them. "All the way back to Eskender. It's what unites us, what strengthens us, and what will save us from the vision Menelik had."

"Save us?" Ta'Fik laughed, cold and bitter. "The Code will destroy us. Tell yourself the truth, Ambessa. Are you fighting for the family, or to see yourself at the top? The dream Menelik painted for you, painted for all of us? Selfishness as strength." He paced to her right, holding his blade ready. She matched him step for step. "What a surprise to learn we can't all sit at the top, wasn't it? Some of us have to be at the bottom. Some of us have to fall," he growled, baring his teeth. "You let Zoya fall, Ambessa. You didn't have to, but you did anyway."

He lunged across the space with a thrust.

"I did." Ambessa parried the thrust with one gauntlet, but the blade still scored across her shoulder. "She wasn't strong enough."

"What are we?" Ta'Fik snarled, slashing again. He was no longer fighting to escape. He was fighting for the vengeance he'd wanted for decades. "Drakehounds, to eat our young? To cull the weakest from the pack?"

His words called to mind the day more vividly than it had been in years. Zoya's cries. The snapping of the drakehounds' jaws. The crack of bone. Ambessa hadn't looked back. She couldn't look back. If she had, she wouldn't have been able to claim the matriarch. That coup had won her their grandfather's favor. It had shaped the trajectory of her life, her children's lives, and their children's lives.

It had cost Ambessa only her dearest friends. What did one life weigh against all the rest Ambessa had done?

It had given her the strength to win, over and over again. It had brought her to this moment.

She parried his cut and Ta'Fik danced out of reach again. He took her silence as it was meant.

"Why should I even bother to ask? Of course you believe that. Everything Menelik has done has been to prune us until only the deadliest remain."

Not everything. He chose you. She deflected that mental blade, too.

"Is that not what you've done? Where is Gintara now?" Ambessa flexed her hands in her gauntlets. Let him set the pace for now.

"Gintara. Don't you dare speak her name to me." His voice shuddered with pain when he said his eldest's name. "She fought for the same cause I do. Something greater than ambition—she fought because she loves her father. Tell me, Ambessa. How do your children feel about your Code? You've wasted Mel's potential." Ta'Fik scoffed. "You don't even think she's good enough to be your successor."

Ambessa thought of Mel's diplomatic heart and Kino's playful ease. How often had she wished them harder, more like her? Now, as she faced the possibility of death yet again, knowing that if she failed, they would die, too, she wished it even more. She wished they would have *someone* to protect them.

They clashed again, more desperate now. The myriad wounds on their bodies, on their hearts, finally taking their toll. The breath of Kindred was hot against their necks.

Ambessa recalled the vision she'd seen the first time she died. A gift granted by the Wolf. "Now is not my time," she whispered, half prayer, half challenge. "You showed me when it would be my time."

Kindred mocked her mortal assertions. Ta'Fik parried her next punch wide, and before Ambessa could follow through with another, he slashed upward, cutting her right forearm. Blood filled the gauntlet, and her grip on the handle inside grew limp. She jerked her hand out of it and staggered back.

"Admit it, Ambessa," Ta'Fik said. "Your love is a shallow pool beneath the cruel sun of your ambition. You would throw your own children to the flames if it would get you what you wanted."

Ambessa's heart clamored a denial that her mind refused to acknowledge. *I would not.* In all her dreams, her children were *at her side.* They ruled with her; they ruled after her.

And if they refuse this vision? What good are they to you then?

In that vital moment of distraction, Ta'Fik lunged again. Ambessa barely saw the blow incoming, but she heard Rictus yell her name. She parried with her left gauntlet at the last moment. Instead of splitting her from her shoulder to hip, he merely scored a cut down her left cheek and across her body.

But Ta'Fik had put too much strength into the killing blow, and it left him open. With the last reserves of strength in her body, Ambessa ignored the searing pain across her chest and sent an uppercut into Ta'Fik's unguarded belly. Ribs cracked as her gauntlet made contact. The drakehound blade bit deep.

"If you're so much better than me," she growled in his ear while he hung on her gauntlet, "tell me why we've met here, at the same spot?"

Ta'Fik fell. Ambessa's blade had finally bitten through the resilient armor, and thick, dark blood oozed. But his was Menelik's blood. He didn't stop fighting. Ta'Fik struggled to his feet, one hand on his ribs, the other still gripping his sword as he pushed himself up from the ground.

He lunged again, but the strike was stilted and weak; he

couldn't put the force of his body behind it. Ambessa looped one arm over both of his and smashed her forehead into his. The lion mask crushed Ta'Fik's nose bloody. He sagged in her arms, dazed, and she let him fall. The sword clattered from his limp hand, and Ambessa kicked it away.

"Father!" Tivadar cried out behind Ambessa.

The young warrior came running, and for a moment, Ambessa thought this was the end. She didn't have another fight in her, not against this fresh youth. But Tivadar didn't come with bared blades. She fell to her knees beside her father.

"Father, please. Surrender."

Ta'Fik looked up at Tivadar, his eyes full of wounded betrayal. Cold. He turned to Ambessa.

Tivadar turned to Ambessa as well. The betrayal in her eyes matched her father's. "You said you would let me speak to him!"

Ambessa saw Mel in Tivadar's face. Mel, pleading for the Binan girl's life. Tears coursed down Tivadar's face.

"Let it end here," Tivadar whispered. "We could make a new code, all of us. *We* are Medardas. This family is what we say it is. Mel taught me that."

"Step aside, child," Ta'Fik said, stealing the words Ambessa meant to say. He didn't take his eyes from Ambessa's. He reached feebly for the azirite-encased drakehound tooth that he wore on his neck. "It's time."

Tivadar's words echoed in Ambessa's mind. What Mel had taught her. Mel was still too soft, and yet, that softness had saved Ambessa's life. She clenched her one working fist. The left gauntlet creaked, reminding her of the keen blade it bore, waiting.

Waiting.

Ambessa had made this choice before. So many times in her life, it had always come to this. With Zoya. In battle, when she could have saved one soldier for the sake of the victory. Leaving Azizi and the children alone in Bel'zhun. Leaving Rell in her mage prison. Leaving Rudo to die with the rune-soldiers.

It was Menelik who had made her strong enough to bear these choices, Menelik and the generations of Medardas before her whose teachings had solidified into the code that marked her path.

"Step aside, child," Ambessa said softly. She took off her remaining gauntlet and pulled one of the slim daggers from her boot sheath.

"Please," Tivadar begged.

Ambessa knelt and plunged the blade up and into Ta'Fik's heart. The armor gave beneath the direct pressure. Ta'Fik closed his eyes and grabbed Ambessa's hand, holding it against his ribs until he went slack.

Behind her, Tivadar sobbed. Ambessa bowed her head over her friend's body. Even now, despite everything, she could close her eyes and feel his hand in hers as they leapt into the sky together.

Ambessa stood, and let Tivadar clutch her father to her chest. Ambessa could not tell, yet, if she had made a new enemy. Prudence told her to end the whole line here and now, but she was weary of prudence. Exhausted by *vision*.

And yet.

She knelt behind Tivadar, her boot knife still dripping Ta'Fik's blood. "I wish it had not come to this, child," she whispered in the girl's ear.

Tivadar looked up at her in surprised confusion, and Ambessa drew the blade across her throat.

Chapter Thirty-Nine

Daughter and father bled together on the floor of the kennels. The drakehounds and dogs snarled and whined, standing on their hind legs, snapping and clawing at the bars of their cages.

Ambessa reached over to snap the azirite-encased drakehound's tooth from Ta'Fik's neck, but stopped at the last second. She held the tooth in her hand, turning it in the light. It gleamed, the blood glass more vivid than the dark puddle beneath them. She wanted to keep it for herself, so that she would always be reminded of the costs she had paid—but it was not hers to take. She tucked it back into Ta'Fik's shirt, leaving a bloody handprint upon him.

"Kreipsha," Rictus said at her elbow. "We should go."

She allowed him to help her up and lead her into the daylight. It was like stepping into another world. The sky was blue and the sun bright. Rictus looked as bad as she did. His arms were striped with blood, and a deep puncture in his thigh leaked. They needed to get to safety and a healer.

"Rudo?" she asked hoarsely, following the trail of rune-soldiers back to the palace. A few of the bodies bore gaping red wounds from Rictus's halberd, but many more were marked only by the scorch marks of those jagged runes.

Rictus followed her gaze. "Something happened. While you were with Ta'Fik. A light. Brighter than anything I've ever seen."

Ambessa inhaled sharply. "Rudo..." She limped faster.

"Ambessa, wait!"

She ignored him. That beautiful green door to the palace hung open, inviting, but inside...At first, all looked as it should. Empty, the mosaic floor clear of bodies, no sound of fighting. But she recalled there had been a carpet on the floor, a beautiful, hand-woven thing. There had been bodies, the first two that Rudo had attacked. Had those soldiers survived and run away? Unlikely that they all had fled. She scanned the room with a new wariness, expecting an ambush. She turned to Rictus, to tell him to be ready.

He knelt on the floor by the doorway, examining the stone. He rubbed at something with his thumb and sniffed it, then looked around.

"What is it?"

Rictus didn't want to meet her eyes. He pushed himself heavily to his feet.

"Ambessa, I'm sorry."

Ambessa looked at his hand—it was gray with soot. There had been a fire.

A light.

She realized with a start that what she had taken to be an open door was actually no door at all. Her mind had glossed over the impossible, creating a narrative it understood.

"What happened to the rune-soldiers?" she asked him slowly.

"Their runes—they burned out of their skin. They dropped where they were, in spasms."

"He did this," she breathed.

Whatever Rudo had done, it had scorched the entire room clean—all that remained was the stone. But surely he had survived his own magic?

"Rudo?" she called. Her voice was reedy at first, but she cleared her throat and called again, limping from room to room.

They limped through every room, holding each other up by the end, and still they didn't find him. Only servants, peeking their heads out to see if the coast was clear and ducking back behind closed doors when they saw them. Rictus was flagging, though, his breathing becoming more laborious.

"Sit," she commanded him when they found what must have been Ta'Fik's favorite sitting room, according to Tivadar.

Rictus protested and made to follow her, but his leg chose that moment to buckle. Ambessa caught him and eased him down to bleed all over Ta'Fik's embroidered silk pillows. With the last of her strength, Ambessa banged on the door where she'd seen an older woman and two youths peeking out.

"We need healers," she demanded. "We mean no one else here any harm."

Her firm but even tone did much to persuade them not to resist, at the very least. After more coaxing, she managed to get those with decent hands for needle and thread, and some wine for the wounds and for the pain. There was no illusion that Ta'Fik's staff felt safe, but this was Noxus. Such turnovers were the way of things. Their fear was not Ambessa's problem—

But of course, it was now. She was the clan leader. She would install the next Medarda steward over Tereshni, and they could take this palace, if they wished. Ta'Fik had no heirs.

"You will have another steward here soon," she told them when they finished. "Feel free to seek other employment if you wish, but you may also stay and ready this place for its next occupant. You will be compensated."

Whether the household would stay or take this as an excuse to loot the place and be gone, Ambessa did not care.

"And us?" Rictus said when the last of the servants had left them alone.

"Rell."

She closed her eyes and sagged back into the cushions where the matronly woman had forced her to sit. The newly sewn wound across her chest pulled painfully, but it was not so painful as the aching void within her. Perhaps it was better that Rudo's body had been lost in his celestial conflagration—if she had to see him burned and broken, she feared she would lose a part of herself that she could not afford to lose, not yet.

"You know where?"

"Rudo told me."

In the morning, before they left the inn. He had spoken to her urgently, trying to explain how to find the underground laboratory in the ruins. She pretended to ignore him. Just in case, he said.

Just in case.

She opened her eyes wide, staring at the tiled ceiling, willing her eyes to dry.

She turned to action instead.

"Now. Can you ride?"

"Now?" Rictus asked in surprise. At the look on her face, however, he simply nodded. "Now."

"I promised her." Ambessa's throat thickened and her words shook, so she gritted them through clenched teeth. "The men I loved are dead. I have killed Ta'Fik and cut his branch off the tree of our lineage. I do not regret any of this, because it means victory." If she told herself this often enough, it would be true. "So I am going to ensure that victory to the fullest. I will take Rell back and make the Black Rose regret all it has done in its meddling."

"Then we ride."

Before they left, Ambessa went to Ta'Fik's study and wrote letters of surrender to his warbands in Rokrund, informing them that their leader was dead. She stamped them with his seal and sent them by messenger bird.

Then she enlisted the servants' help. They dug two pits behind the kennels and stood Ta'Fik and Tivadar within them, weapons strapped upon their bodies, with their backs to the Immortal Bastion.

Noxus, looking ever outward.

The ride that should have taken only two days under normal circumstances took four. Despite the horses they commandeered from Ta'Fik's stables, their wounds forced them to stop, even though Ambessa would have ridden through the night. She had lost too much blood and was dizzy with it.

They rode deeper and deeper into the desert south of Tereshni, and Ambessa was beginning to think that Rudo had lied when the ruins appeared out of nowhere. The sand dunes shifted, and then, like a mirage, there they were, the jagged stone walls of an ancient time, broken by something too magnificent and terrible to imagine. What remained of the ornate outer walls was worn mostly smooth by wind and sand, but there had once been fine carvings.

She dismounted gingerly and looped her reins over the crumbling remains of a pillar. She drew her sword in her left hand. Her right hand wouldn't hold a weapon for some time.

And what will you do against a cabal of mages? asked a cruel voice in the back of her mind.

Ambessa scoffed the thought away. She knew that her weapons were unlikely to be the best option, but she wouldn't wander this place defenseless. If that pale woman wanted something from her, maybe there was a bargain to be made. And then, when the time was right, Ambessa would take her vengeance.

The entrance was a dark mouth, gaping hungrily in the ground. Sand sifted over the stairs where it had fallen in thick layers. She and Rictus shared a glance.

They went down.

The rooms below had been equally ravaged by time—or by something else. Broken stone doors, cracked stone tiles in the floor. There was no furniture or decoration except that the walls were carved, very occasionally. The pearly gray stone was not the same as the sandstone above. Ambessa touched it. Smooth and cold against her palm.

The laboratory was quiet and empty.

Rell was not here.

Instead, she found a room that looked like an infirmary, with two beds. An acrid stench burned her nose. Upon closer inspection, the beds were more like litters, and each litter was fitted with leather restraints. Ambessa touched one, imagining Rell strapped into it. The leather was worn smooth with use and discolored with sweat. She placed the odor—it was the same foul smell of containment she'd found with the vastaya the Binans had kept prisoner.

There was also a desk, covered in neatly stacked books. It was all so tidy, as if the owner would come back soon to resume their work. The sorrow she'd felt at the emptiness was overwhelmed by fury.

She returned to the corridor and looked questioningly at Rictus, who emerged from a different room.

"Was there any sign of her? Any tracks to follow?"

Rictus shook his head. "No sign of struggle anywhere."

Where could they have taken her?

Ambessa roared out all the mounting fury she'd been holding

in and aimed a punch at the wall. Rictus caught her before she could make contact, but his impact sent waves of pain through her chest. She struggled against him, and he wrapped both arms around her, pinning her arms to her sides as carefully as he could without hurting her further. It slowed her down enough to realize how foolish she was being.

She was a Medarda. She would channel her anger.

She went back into the room with the litters and flipped through the books. They must have been Inyene's. They were written in a precise, small hand, and though she could read them, she didn't understand them. She did recognize some of the runes sketched upon the pages, though. They matched the ones scored on the bodies of the rune-soldiers outside Ta'Fik's palace. Beside those sketches, there were discussions of desired effects and negative side effects, as well as the effects on the mage doing the casting.

Then she saw, toward the end, the word *null* appear for the first time.

Subject B: Catatonic. Could not revive. Null.

Subject C: Catatonic. Could not revive. Null.

Subject F: Catatonic. Could not revive. Null.

Subject G: Catatonic. Could not revive. Null.

The list of *null*s filled an entire page.

Was Rell one of them?

Ambessa slammed the book shut, but she exhaled her fury slowly this time. Then she rose, taking the books with her. With Rictus's help, she combed the entire site for more of these notes; they found a study and emptied that, too. They brought them outside.

"What will you do with them?" Rictus asked, staring at the stacks dubiously.

"Burn them."

The pyre of Inyene's notes burned through the night. She watched them from the top of a dune. She stood alone. She had finally convinced Rictus that what she needed most was not friendship but solitude. Her cheeks were wet with the tears that she couldn't let even him see. She had won, and yet, she had failed. This was the closest she could get to watching the Black Rose's creations die.

She had lost Rudo. Oh, how it ached to know the last things she'd said to him were curses. And yet, she was grateful that they *had* had that last night together. She couldn't help but think of what he'd said before. How she hadn't mourned Azizi or Menelik properly. Only vengeance.

Menelik had said little on the subject of mourning. You buried those who fought with honor, and then you moved on. What else was there to say? The Wolf took them, and they rode in the great hunt of Volrachnun. The battles of the living continued.

Ambessa struggled to be so tranquil. Had her grandfather ever loved anyone? It seemed impossible to love and bear this weight—every life was so fragile, and she couldn't protect them all. She hadn't protected any of them.

And because Ambessa hadn't protected Rell, so went the future of the family's safety. She smiled, thinking of the girl chasing moon-eyed after Amenesce's bowlegged young rider. There was so much Ambessa had wanted to teach her—and Rell had wanted to learn! Ambessa had not realized how badly she longed for someone open to the knowledge that she wanted to pass on.

Rell and Mel would have made an extraordinary pair.

Ambessa took a deep, shuddering breath. The tears slowed.

She was the head of the Medarda clan. She had to harden herself to this loss and all others. The only way to do that without admitting faults into the bedrock of her heart was to never let love take root there at all. Not again.

This was the sacrifice demanded of a leader.

Vision. Might. Even guile, the slippery purview of cheats and mages.

And sacrifice.

She closed her eyes and recalled the vision of herself and the throne. The golden light. Around the periphery of her vision, she thought she saw the Wolf of Kindred. She felt his grave-breath.

"I told you, it was not my time," Ambessa whispered.

"And who are you to bargain with the masters of death?"

Ambessa turned slowly. The voice was Rell's voice, but the words were not Rell's words. Indeed, when she turned, she saw Rell, as clearly as she had the last time—at the party in Rokrund Citadel, at Katye's celebration. She was even wearing the same clothes. The girl was as fierce and angry as she ever was. The determined set of her mouth filled Ambessa with something suspiciously close to regret.

A Medarda does not regret. To live in the past is to miss the opportunities of the present.

"Who are you?" Ambessa asked warily, stepping back. Deep inside, she knew the answer. The orchestrator of her woes, even more than Ta'Fik. *The pale woman.*

"You don't know me?" The mage clicked her tongue, then grinned wickedly with Rell's face. "How disappointing."

Rudo told me about you, Ambessa almost said, but at the last second, she recalled herself. It was more important than ever for that link to remain secret.

"You were behind this," Ambessa said. "You took her. You led Ta'Fik to this."

"Don't insult your dear cousin. He took quite a lot of initiative, you know." The woman turned into Ta'Fik and circled Ambessa. "Ta'Fik knew exactly what would goad that old Menelik into one last battle. Dying without naming Ta'Fik his heir complicated things, but good riddance to the man. He was always something of a thorn in my side. Ta'Fik was much more...biddable."

Ambessa held her tongue. Beneath her cloak, she shifted her hand minutely so that she could grasp her dagger from her belt unnoticed. She didn't let the shape-shifting mage out of her sight.

The pale woman's silky voice grew hard. "You, on the other hand...You're quite the irritant. You've taken my poor little puppet. Years of work, gone, along with two of my most powerful mages." The mage-as-Ta'Fik pouted and snapped her fingers. A crackle of black thorny magic flared and vanished. Then she smiled, showing her teeth. "Did you truly think those were the only records we had? I've walked this world for more generations than your family has existed. This isn't even a setback."

"What have you done with Rell?"

Suddenly, the woman was in Ambessa's face—she was impossibly fast. "Your little urchin is going to replace the mages you took from me." She reached for Ambessa's jaw, and Ambessa struck upward with the dagger, aiming under the mage's chin.

The pale woman leapt back, laughing. Tendrils of magic like thorned vines leapt from her hands.

"Rictus!" Ambessa called. It was all she had time for before the tendrils wrapped their fingers around her.

The magic bit like a rose's thorn, too, pricking Ambessa's flesh as it constricted her chest.

Mockingly, the mage took Rictus's form, his height, his broad chest and shoulders, his deep voice. "You are so small, so pathetic, and yet, you've managed to disrupt years of effort." The mage cocked her head. Rictus's brown eyes watched Ambessa with curious condescension. "While I could end your wretched life now, I'm not going to. You intrigue me. I haven't been intrigued in a very, very long time. And then, when I tire of you, I will crush you, and the precious Medarda name will be no more."

Was this what Menelik's vision was about?

Ambessa bit back her scream against the pain as the magic twisted tighter and tighter around her. Fire, stabbing all over her. In between gasping breaths, she growled, "I will—uproot—your entire cabal—before I die."

The pale woman laughed, and it was not Rictus's laugh but a woman's—her true voice. "Be careful who you trust. These sorts of entanglements are always a risk." The words sounded familiar, but Ambessa couldn't place them. When the false Rictus vanished, along with the thorns of magic, the laughter echoed through the night.

"Ambessa!" Rictus sprinted up the dune as fast as his wounded leg would allow. His rookern glowed on the shaft of his halberd, but there was no magic for it to dissipate. The pale woman was already gone.

"I need to get back to Bel'zhun," Ambessa said breathlessly, pushing herself to her feet.

"You're in no state to ride—"

"She was here. That—*the pale woman* was here. Kino. *Mel.*"

Rictus looked around, wary. No one had passed him going down the dune, and he could see no one on the other side. He turned to her with concern and reached for her, but she stepped back, her oath to keep her heart apart from all others fresh in her mind.

Was this a dream?

Ambessa clenched her fists and started—they were wet. She held them up to the light of stars. There, pricked in both of her palms, were deep puncture wounds. A trickle of blood streamed from each hole down her wrists.

She rubbed the blood with a thumb, and it smeared. The hole was gone. The pain was not.

"Ready the horses. We ride to Bel'zhun."

They were riding through the darkness when Ambessa remembered—those were *her* words. Words she had said to Rell in Nika Fallow's shop. Only the dressmaker could have heard them.

Fear clamped a cold fist around Ambessa's stomach.

Chapter Forty

Ambessa rode into Bel'zhun as the sun set, half sliding off the saddle. A week of riding and she was glad to even be upright.

Was the Vindoran steward still alive?

There was much to learn and to tell, but first, she needed to see her children.

The pale woman's visit in the desert had harrowed Ambessa more than she let on to Rictus, but he could tell something was wrong, even now.

"What's wrong?" Rictus asked quietly as they rode into the Medarda compound. He scanned the area, alert.

Ambessa slowed her rapid breathing.

"It's quiet. Too quiet."

"Hmm."

They stood a moment longer, though, and they began to see signs of life. A servant carrying a basket of bedclothes to be laundered. The strut of a chicken escaped from the kitchens and, in the distance, laughter from those same kitchens. It wasn't that everyone was gone, or in danger.

It was simply peace.

She hadn't recognized it at first. Ambessa swallowed her

embarrassment and blinked away the stinging in her eyes. A calm before the storm.

Mel and Kino were both at the compound, and both safe, though she had to reassure them that the same could be said of her, despite the weeping cut across her collarbone and her arm. After she'd bathed and been seen by a proper healer, they shared a quiet dinner, the three of them and Rictus. Wolf's Reapers stood at attention along the walls.

The meal was simple but hearty. The true feasts would come later, when all the other business had been taken care of—notifying the stewards, dealing with those who had opposed her in favor of Ta'Fik, like Dauvin, and rewarding those who had supported her, like Amenesce.

"What news of Rokrund?" Ambessa asked.

"They hold," Kino said, grinning broadly.

"Support came in from Krexor," Mel elaborated. "After you left, I sent word by messenger hawk to Steward Lisabetya, explaining Ta'Fik's trespasses against the Code. She understood, and sent troops immediately to their aid."

"They just barely kept Ta'Fik's warbands out of the Citadel. And Grand General Darkwill's ships kept their reinforcements from reaching Rokrund. Amenesce said the Krexorian blades matched nicely against those...soldiers." Kino's jaunty tone shifted. "Did you find out what they were?"

Ambessa stared hard at Kino. Did he know that the rune-soldiers were connected to the Black Rose? Had he continued to dig after she had expressly forbidden it?

"Amenesce is alive. That is good news."

"She was a week ago," Mel said quietly. "Did you send word from Tereshni to Ta'Fik's soldiers?"

"I did. With Ta'Fik dead, they will have no choice but to surrender." Ambessa chewed a bite of grilled fish as she studied Mel. She could tell that Mel wanted to ask about Tivadar, so she quickly turned the subject. "What about the Suns?"

"They've been strong allies while you were gone." Kino awkwardly cleared his throat. "In fact, I should go. I'm speaking with Valif early tomorrow."

"Give him my thanks. He did well to keep the city out of Ta'Fik's hands."

Kino smiled crookedly. "It's going to be a very expensive favor, I'm sure."

As her children prepared to leave, though, Ambessa gripped Kino's shoulder as Mel walked away. Mel looked back, first questioning, then hurt. She left quickly.

"Yes, Mother?" Kino asked warily.

Ambessa pulled him back into the room.

"I told you to leave it alone."

She tracked his face and found the tell—ever since he was a child, his eyes darted to the side before he lied. As an adult in a Great House, used to the charm and cajoling of manipulation, he'd learned to turn the glance into a self-deprecating smile or a shrug, but it was still there.

"Don't lie to me, Kino." She pressed his shoulder against the wall.

"I did! I am!" he said. "You told me to stop, I've stopped."

"I command it, Kino. They are too big for you to take on."

His eyes shone with frustrated tears, but he bowed his head. "I understand."

Ambessa sighed. "Go, then."

When he was gone, Rictus stood beside her.

"Tomorrow, I have to speak with Mel," she said. "I can't put it off."

"You're going to do it, then." There was a hint of reservation. Rictus understood why she was doing it, but he didn't approve.

"I have no choice. Kino has already been asking questions about them, and that kind of talk travels fast, and always to the wrong ears. It can't come back to connect them to Mel."

Rictus nodded. "I'll have a ship readied to sail to Piltover tomorrow."

He turned to go, but Ambessa put a hand on his forearm. If she was supposed to dig up every root of affection, so be it, but Rictus would remain. He was less a soft spot in her heart and more a shield to it.

"Thank you, my friend," she said.

He nodded again, then left.

Ambessa took this meeting in Menelik's old study. Her study, now. There was a strategy table with a large map of the world from Ionia to Mount Targon, from the north of the Freljord to the south of Shurima, covered with the figures of warbands and supplies Menelik had used to mark the campaign that had killed him. Before Mel arrived, Ambessa paused over that map, barely brushing the pieces with her fingertips.

A knock on the door. Ambessa sat in the tall, rigid chair at Menelik's desk. Her desk. It was an old travel desk that didn't fit with the intimidation of the chair. Perhaps he had kept the desk out of sentiment.

"Enter."

Mel came in and closed the door behind her, looking around the room as she did so, making her own assessments, just like Ambessa. Too late for Ambessa to notice all the ways her daughter was like her—she'd spent so long focused on the ways she was not. Mel carried a large square object, wrapped in a protective cloth.

"Sit down."

Mel straightened her shoulders and raised her chin. "Mother, what happened to Tivadar?"

Ambessa had never felt the need to lie about her actions, as if they needed to be covered up or the consequences passed on to someone else. A leader took responsibility for everything—the right and the wrong, the brilliant and the mistaken. But faced with Mel's knowing expression and the disgust that followed, Ambessa couldn't bring herself to speak.

"She's dead, isn't she?"

Ambessa nodded slowly. "She died in the struggle against Ta'Fik."

"You killed her." Mel's voice trembled, and the parcel in her hands shook. She held it closer to her chest. "Mother, she was my friend."

Mel's pain was harder to face than any rune-soldier's blade. It almost made Ambessa second-guess herself. Had there been a way to spare Tivadar? Ambessa had not seen it, not without risking everything that was to come.

Without looking at Mel, Ambessa said, "I did only what was necessary."

"Did she go to her father? Did she betray us?" Mel groped for a justification that made sense to her.

With none to give her, Ambessa remained silent. Mel understood.

"She helped you. She helped you and you still killed her?" The cloth-wrapped parcel crinkled under Mel's anger.

"I don't expect you to understand—"

"You're right! I don't understand; I will never understand. You have no regard for anyone or anything but yourself and your own ambitions." Mel's voice rose in her anger. "I made her a deal, Mother! That you would protect her if she helped you! You promised me!"

Ambessa stood and snapped, "The situation changed, Mel! I had no choice. She was a danger to this family."

"You always have a choice, Mother!" Mel shook her head, her lip curling. "Maybe she and Ta'Fik were right about you. Maybe *you* are the danger to this family."

Ambessa gasped sharply. Mel was not the same child who had watched in speechless horror as Ambessa killed Lady Binan. Oh, how she had grown while Ambessa was away. Despite the sting, pride welled in her. Mel glared at the desk.

"Look at me."

Mel raised her gaze, and Ambessa's heart lurched. Rudo's eyes stared back at her, their softness. Their reproach. That expression was also distinctly Mel's own, an acuity that belied her tender soul. How sharply she must have seen into Tivadar's heart. Vision was hard to teach. And what potential would Mel have if she manifested her father's magical ability? What a weapon she would make, what a lieutenant at Ambessa's side! Her death-vision returned, and this time the woman in it was clearly Mel standing next to Ambessa's throne.

She let the vision dissipate. Mel's safety was more important than any dream of power.

And Ambessa wouldn't have to see Mel's revulsion every time she did her duty by the Medarda name.

"I have prepared a ship to take you to Piltover today. You will—"

"What?" Mel's face fell in panic. Suddenly, she was young again, uncertain. "What do you mean? Why—"

"You will work with instructors who will teach you how to look after our interests there."

Mel's brow knit over those clever eyes. "For how long?"

"Until I summon you back. You have much to learn before you join me at my side, and you clearly find my teaching distasteful."

"You're—you're exiling me?"

"You will go to Piltover." Where magic was rejected. Where it was impossible for the Black Rose to have even a toehold. No one would think a girl that Ambessa Medarda rejected as weak would have any power worth harnessing.

"Why? Because of Tivadar?" Mel placed the parcel flat between them and planted her hands upon the edge of the desk. She was a woman now, with so much growing still to do, but there was a rod of iron in her.

Ambessa steeled herself. She had to make it so that Mel was never tempted to seek beyond Piltover's shores, never to return to Noxus. She stood to match Mel, both of them glaring eye to eye.

"I stand by what I said after you failed your test with Lady Binan. With Tivadar, you've failed again. You are too weak to be my heir, so as your mother, as the head of this family, I will make use of you as best I can. There will be plenty for you to occupy yourself with, and maybe eventually you'll have learned enough to do something worthwhile in Noxus. Perhaps your sentimentality will be more at home with those soft-spined idealists overseas."

"Failed? But I helped you." The anguish in Mel's voice almost broke Ambessa's will. "Tivadar joined you *because of me*."

Hold to the course, Ambessa.

"She did," Ambessa acknowledged. "But you risked everything on this friendship, and she nearly betrayed us to Ta'Fik. What do you think would have happened if she had chosen her father, and you were the one who warned her?" Ambessa clicked her tongue. "Pack anything you might need, your immediate effects. You may choose someone to accompany you. Your ship leaves with the tide. Do not miss it."

Instead of taking the dismissal, Mel said, "What about Kino? Does he know? Can I at least say goodbye to him?"

"Of course. He's your brother. I will inform him while you're packing."

Mel shook her head in disbelief. Tears welled in her eyes, then fell. Without another word, she turned and left. The door snicked shut quietly, as quiet as Mel's footfall. When would Ambessa hear it again?

The package Mel brought still sat on the desk. With an unsteady hand, Ambessa pulled away the cloth that covered it. A glimmer of paint on canvas. Heart beating faster, she ripped the paper away to see a painting of a mountain wreathed in sunlight. She knew the artist without even looking at his mark in the corner.

One breath, in and out. Ambessa tried to govern herself. Four. Five. She could call Mel back. *A Medarda does not regret.* Eight. Nine. Ten.

Ambessa roared her fury and pain and slammed both clenched fists into the desk. There was a glorious simplicity in the pain that danced up her arm compared to the rupture of her heart. A hairline crack in the wood, the fracture in the stone.

Sacrifice.

This pain, too, would temper Ambessa into the weapon she needed to be.

One war was ended. Another was begun.

Epilogue

Rell woke up again in a strange yet familiar place. A dark, dank corridor that smelled like sweat and fear. A bright light at the end of it. At first, she thought she was back at the arena in Bel'zhun. Maybe she was still dreaming? But her captors still had her by the arms, and the same weird gag choking off her magic chafed.

She tried to jerk away from the grip holding her, but she was too weak from whatever they'd used to put her under.

Her captor slapped her, sending her head spinning. "Watch yourself, or you'll regret it."

Rell bared her teeth at the woman. She bit off a sharp comment. *Patience is prudence.* One of the many lessons Ambessa had tried to drill into her.

Where are you, General?

"Now. I've been told you used to be quite something in the Reckoner Arena in Bel'zhun. Rather provincial, but it's not nothing. That means this should be quite easy for you. I'm going to take you down this tunnel, and in the training yard, you're going to find another young mage. You will fight until one of you surrenders. If you win, you will be rewarded. If you lose, you will be punished. I really do suggest you win." The woman smiled, showing sharp teeth.

Rell looked the woman up and down and spat on the dirt at her feet.

The woman's smile broadened. "I should say, if you attempt to refuse..."

Crackling magic encircled her, then followed the link where her hands met Rell's body. Lightning burned through Rell's veins and she jerked wildly, her body completely out of her own control. When the woman stopped the magic, Rell collapsed.

The woman bent down to Rell where she lay groaning. "Now, your match is scheduled to begin in one minute. If you aren't on the field by then, it will be an automatic forfeit. It would be a shame to lose you already. I've been told you have such potential."

The woman said those last words so hungrily that Rell shuddered away from her.

Rell imagined what Ambessa Medarda would say when she came back. Ambessa had picked her out of the arena because she *won*.

And then—someone had taken her away.

That night still haunted her. She and Tora had gone out—they'd found an out-of-the-way place to talk, and Tora—Tora had kissed her, and it didn't seem like anything could get better than that. Rell would have a new family, she'd have a mentor who respected her, she'd have a *future*. She'd even have Tora, at least until she went back to Vindor.

Then Ambessa Medarda came. Only, it couldn't be Ambessa. Rell kept telling herself that. Somehow—it had to be someone else. Rell had had nothing but time to replay that night—Where was Rictus? Or Amenesce? And that smile. It made Rell shudder.

Ambessa wouldn't have done this *to her*.

But if it wasn't Ambessa, who was it? And if it wasn't, why hadn't Ambessa come for her? She had said she would protect Rell.

"Forty-five seconds."

The cold voice of her captor pulled Rell out of her pain and her grogginess. She pushed herself to her feet. She was hungry and stiff and stinking in the same clothing she'd been wearing when they took her, and if she hadn't been conscious for most of her journey, she sure as hell hadn't been dreaming on a feather bed.

The corridor opened up to a dirt pit surrounded on all sides by jutting rock that was so dark a gray that it was almost black, like a small valley.

Immediately in front of her was her opponent, a nervous-looking young woman about her own age with brown skin and short dark hair, her fists held out in front of her.

Tora, Rell thought immediately with a pang of sadness. Of course, Tora was who knew how many miles away now, back in Vindor. She probably didn't care a bit that Rell had been locked away. So much for that kiss.

The rest of the arena was empty except for a few obstacles: jutting boulders, a dead log—a heap of scrap metal. *Just for me.*

It was the first metal they'd let her near since she tried to choke one of her captors with the iron chains they had bound her with. Rell smiled darkly.

This is going to suck for you.

Rell closed her eyes to gather herself. She was still getting used to the feeling of this…*ferromancy*. She'd always felt an affinity for steel, though. *Sharp weapons, hard heart.*

With a quick flex and a grunt, Rell scooped up the hunk of scrap metal and hurled it right back where she'd come from, straight for the woman who'd dragged her here. The metal hit an invisible wall and crashed to the ground. The woman, who was still watching, wagged a single finger in disappointment. Rell flinched at the hint of a spark shocking her fingers.

"You think you're the first one who's tried that?" her opponent asked. She still stood across from her, wary, her fists lowered only slightly. She looked even more nervous now.

"Well, it was worth a shot." Rell faced the girl and took up her own stance. "What's your name?"

"Saida. Let's get this over with."

"You think they can take us both?" Rell asked.

Saida sighed and repositioned her feet, digging them into the ground for purchase. Her fists tightened.

"All right," Rell muttered. "Let's do this, then."

She yanked back the scrap metal and sent it flying toward Saida. Saida jumped out of the way. With the ball of metal out of the way, she punched her fist at Rell—and fire came out in a hot burst streaking straight for her.

Rell yelped and dived out of the way. She rolled to put out a burning ember in her dirty jacket, then kept rolling as ball after ball of flame chased her. She wasn't fast enough to stay ahead of it, not for long.

She called the metal scrap back to her, shaping it as she ran. She'd been imagining this all the time she'd been imprisoned with nothing else to do—what she'd do with her powers when she escaped, the possibilities—!

The metal thinned and curved, sheet after sheet, until the hollow body of a horse on metal-rod legs galloped up to her, and she jumped on just in time. She could still feel the heat of Saida's fire on her boots.

"That was close," Rell muttered. "Come on," she urged her mount, even though it wasn't real. *You really have lost it, Rell.*

The metal horse took the curve around the edge of the valley smooth as a natural horse—maybe even smoother. Rell leaned with it. She didn't even need a saddle, just dug her heels and her fingers into the metal as she rode straight for Saida. She stretched the last of the scrap into a long lance, like Tora said the Vindoran riders used at tournaments. Old-fashioned, Tora had said, but really cool.

Rell lowered the point at Saida and galloped at her. She didn't want to run the girl through, but she did want to win. She hoped Saida would jump out of the way. She hoped she wouldn't. Rell picked up her speed, and Saida stood firm, concentration furrowing her brow.

A Medarda doesn't hesitate. They strike.

But before Rell could strike, the metal in her hand glowed white-hot against her palm. She screamed and dropped the lance, but skin had already blistered. The metal lance dug a harmless furrow into the ground.

Was that how Saida wanted to play? Fine. The metal horse reared, pawing the air with its hooves. Its neigh was the screech of metal on metal. Rell leapt off its back, and each sheet of metal that made the horse's body slammed into Saida, clamping each arm down before she could get away. Sheet after sheet wrapped around her, trapping her legs next, until there was nothing left but her head.

"Trying heating that up, yeah?" Rell said, coming to stand over Saida.

The other girl didn't respond to the taunting. She looked at Rell, then looked away. A tear darkened the dirt beneath her face.

The woman who'd brought Rell clapped as she came back. "Well done, Rell. Well done. I knew you'd come around. Now, let's go get your reward."

Both of them had their magic bound again, and they were brought to a small chamber where other mages waited. Judging by the utter defeat in Saida's face, in her dragging feet, nothing good happened in this room, but Rell had no idea what it was for.

Two tables waited, both of them with leather straps to bind the occupants. Saida went to one of the tables obediently, tears streaming silently.

No, Rell thought. *No, no, no.* She shoved the woman away and swung a wild punch.

"Come on, Saida, don't let them do it!" Rell's swing connected, and she aimed another one at the next mage.

The electric crackle of the first woman's magic arced Rell into a statue of spasming pain, all through the touch of one finger.

"I will sedate you if I need to." The woman's voice was cold and deadly, and she didn't release the shock of her magic. "But you won't sleep for long, I assure you."

She pulled her finger away, and the pain left Rell twitching on the floor. Someone carried her to the other table and strapped her in. She turned her head to see Saida strapped in, too.

I'm sorry, Rell mouthed.

Saida gave her a sad smile, then turned her face to the ceiling and closed her eyes.

The next moment was excruciating for both of them. Saida screamed as the mages ripped something from her—*her magic*, Rell realized with a twist of horror—and fashioned it into the spiking red rune that hovered in the air above them both. Every callous, petty thought she'd had about the girl in the makeshift arena tasted bitter now. She wished she hadn't won. But she didn't want to be the one having her magic ripped out of her, either.

Rell had only a minute to pity Saida before the pain was given to her instead. She tried to hold it in. Tried to grit her teeth and bear it. It felt obscene to think her pain was anything like what Saida had gone through. But as the rune seared the flesh of her arm, Rell growled through her teeth, her own tears soaking her hair against her will.

When it was over, she lay panting. She turned to Saida. The other girl's eyes stared blankly upward. Was she dead? Rell panicked. Then Saida blinked, slowly. That was the only sign of life she gave. She didn't look at Rell again.

Rell closed her eyes and sobbed.

The woman yanked Rell's face to hers and patted her roughly on the cheek. "Don't look so upset. You won. Keep winning, and you could end up with more power than you ever dreamed of. The power to topple nations, to rule an empire. Welcome to the Black Rose."

Rell cracked both eyes open. Through her pain-stiffened jaw, she whispered, "Fuck...you."

After that, they threw her into another cell, this time with a clay pot of water, a sponge, and a bar of soap. A new set of clothing waited for her on the cot. No more metal. She almost didn't care, she was so excited to be clean. Almost.

Saida's lightless eyes seemed to follow her. Their pain was burned into her arm.

So she made a promise to herself as she undressed and sponged away the dirt crusted on her body. Rell would escape, and when she did, she would take as many of the others with her as she could. Then she would have vengeance. They all would. On the Black Rose. On that fucking woman with her shocking touch. On Noxus, for letting something like this happen in their empire.

Ambessa Medarda had taught her all about vengeance.

What Noxus and the Black Rose had taken from her, she would take from them a thousand times over.

She would fucking tear them apart.

Acknowledgments

Any project with as many moving pieces as this one has a lot of people to thank—a lot of brilliant minds whose work was essential to mine. A collaborative process in so many ways.

Thanks to the folks at Orbit for tapping me on the shoulder and midwifing this book from one side of done to the other: Bradley Englert, Zoe Morgan-Weinman, Vivian Kirklin, Bryn A. McDonald, and Lauren Panepinto.

Thank you to the Riot Books team, William Camacho, Avalon Irons, Siege Gary, Michelle Mauk, for welcoming me into Runeterra and giving me the freedom to play and make up my own mounts! You caught me up to speed and I'm so grateful. Thanks also to the teams who enriched or created the lore and other material I got to work from, including Kiahna Manker for the walk-through of the Ambessa music video and help with the prologue, Sean Yang for help with the setting visuals, Maxwell Perlman for help understanding Ambessa's fighting style, and all the artists and authors of *League of Legends: Realms of Runeterra* for immersing me in this rich and wild world.

Thanks to the *Arcane* teams, who not only created a show I fell in love with but also helped me find the details I needed to bring Ambessa and Mel to life on the page, too. This includes particular thanks to Ellen Thomas, the voice actress for Ambessa, and Toks Olagundoye, the voice actress for Mel, as well as the numerous visual artists and animators who brought their attitudes and mannerisms to life.

Thank you to my agent, Mary C. Moore, and to my friends in every Discord, Slack, and WhatsApp group who kept me sane and smiling while I wrote two very large books and one small book at the same time. You know who you are, and you know the promises I have made. I will probably break them. Forgive me.

Finally, thank you, readers and players. (Hopefully some of you are both!) I hope you enjoyed walking in Ambessa's boots as much as I did. Now go kick some ass.

Meet the Author

C. L. Clark is the author of the Magic of the Lost trilogy (including *The Unbroken* and *The Faithless*). When she's not writing or working, she's swinging swords or chasing trails. Her short stories and essays have appeared in *The Best American Science Fiction and Fantasy*, *Reactor* (formerly Tor.com), *Beneath Ceaseless Skies*, and more.

Find out more about C. L. Clark and other Orbit authors by registering for the free monthly newsletter at orbitbooks.net.

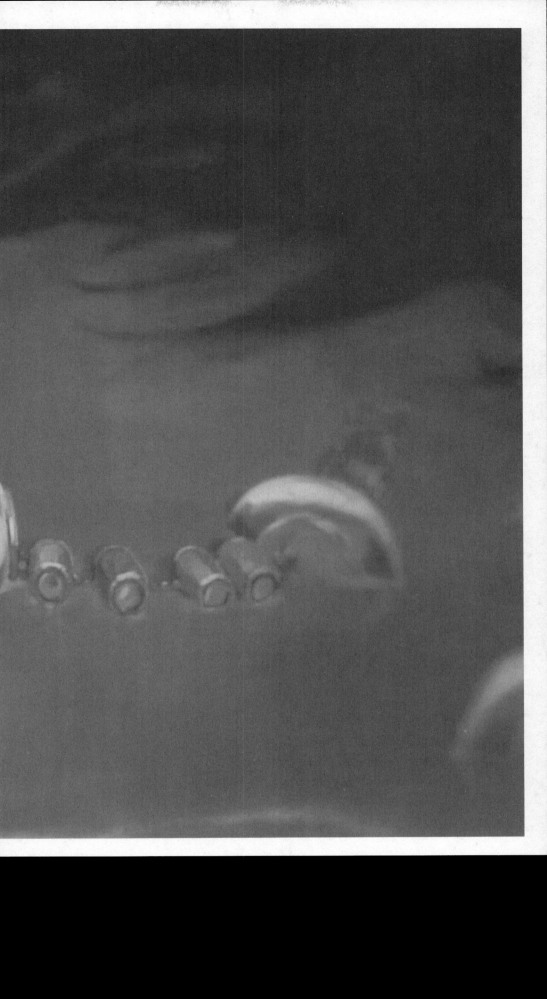